To Sue + Arthur,

Hope you enjoy — and have
a healthy + happy new year.

love
Martin + Pamela

International Match Point Scale

Difference in Points	Imps	Difference in Points	Imps
20-40	1	750-890	13
50-80	2	900-1090	14
90-120	3	1100-1290	15
130-160	4	1300-1490	16
170-210	5	1500-1740	17
220-260	6	1750-1990	18
270-310	7	2000-2240	19
320-360	8	2250-2490	20
370-420	9	2500-2990	21
430-490	10	3000-3490	22
500-590	11	3500-3990	23
600-740	12	4000 and up	24

The Bridge Team Murders

by

Matthew Granovetter

Granovetter Books
18 Village View Bluff
Ballston Lake, NY 12019
(518) 899-6670

The events in this book are fictitious.
With the exception of the famous
bridge players, who are characterized
by the author and whose words and
actions are the author's invention, the
people in this story are the author's
creation and any resemblance to real-
life persons is completely coincidental.

Printed in the United States of America

ISBN Softcover: 0-940257-13-0

ISBN Hardcover: 0-940257-14-9

Author's Foreword

The Bridge Team Murders is the third in a series of mystery/how-to-improve-your-bridge books. This one is about the fascinating strategies of imps — a scoring method used for most team tournaments and some pair events.

Though I have tried to present an accurate insider's view of the professional bridge community, the facts that make up the plot are fictitious. I certainly hope that the criminal aspects of the story never become reality. Many of the bridge hands, however, are true. The bridge lessons and advice, I hope, are absolutely true and sound — they were designed not only to entertain and enhance the plot, but to help the readers improve their games, as well.

I would like to thank all the gracious bridge stars who gave permission for me to draw their characters. Both real and unreal people intermingle in this book. In portraying the stars of the game and their idiosyncracies, I have tried, within reason, to draw flattering pictures.

I especially want to thank Martin Hoffman, who helped

enormously with many of the bridge hands, a few of which are so complex that I don't doubt some expert readers will find further analysis in them.

There are numerous other people to thank for their help: my wife, Pamela, for her editing and advice on the hands and plot; Estee Griffin and Bob Nichols for proof-reading; Tom Donnelly for his artistic cover; Rabbi Israel Rubin for his editing of the Rebbe's Torah lecture; and many experts around the world for their bridge-hand donations.

Most of all I wish to thank God for giving me whatever talents I possess to produce this work.

To my wife,
who has brought me back to Judaism

Characters (in order of appearance)

Matthew Granovetter (the author)	The Gorilla
Belsky (his detective partner)	Bobby Wolff
Pamela Granovetter (his wife)	Bob Hamman
Patty Cayne	Eric Kokish
Jimmy Cayne	Edgar Kaplan
Alan Truscott	Meckwell
Otto Marx	Seymon Deutsch
Frankenstein	Michael Rosenberg
Charlotte Stein	Ron Andersen
George Rapeé	Billy Eisenberg
The Coach	Sami Kehela
Ace Greenberg	Philip Alder
Alan Sontag	Henry Francis
Jinks Barkowsky	Brent Manley
Evelyn Barkowsky	Frank Stewart
Police Commissioner	Old Leroy
Bobby Stein	Tannah Hirsch
Catherine Stein	Giorgio Belladonna
Al Roth	Pietro Forquet
Irving Rose	Benito Garozzo
The Russian Bridge Team	Arturo Franco
Detective Kennedy	Omar Sharif
Mrs. Kennedy	Dr. O'Brien
Jacqui Mitchell	The Rebbe
Victor Mitchell	Detective Jordan
The D.A.	Tony

The action takes place in New York City, circa 1989.

The Bridge Team Murders

1

When it's 90 degrees in Saratoga, it's not what you'd call the perfect time to start traveling south. But that's what Belsky and I were doing, and the good-for-nothing air-conditioner in the broken-down Oldsmobile was blowing hot air.

Then there was Belsky's hot air.

"You know, Matt, this is the life. Getting up early in the morning, *davening* before the *yelladim* are even awake. Watching the sun rise over the Berkshires as we whimsically make our way down I-90 to the historic Taconic Parkway."

"You're happy, Belsky, 'cause you escaped your family," I whistled back at him through my hat. I was still trying to get a few minutes shut-eye. I'd been up half the night with Jimmy on the phone. There'd been a second murder and his bridge team — the very same team that was supposed to represent the United States in international competition the following day — had been reduced to four.

"Hey, c'mon, Matt. A man's got to work, support his family."

Yeah, Belsky. Sure. Seven kids and another on the way. And on top of that school's out.

"Now don't think I'm not grateful for the job, Matt. It's a lifesaver. And even if I do have to give up my week's vacation, I got to do it. For Judi and the kids."

We should have taken my car. But then I would have had to drive. What good is an air-conditioner that doesn't blow cold air?

"It's my opinion, Belsky, that the idea of man going out to support his family was a well conceived plot to get him out of the house while the dirty work was going on."

"You got a point, Matt. Would you turn that knob over there to the left?"

For crying out loud, the damn heater had been on all the while.

Belsky was a big man, husky and broad, with a hearty black beard. He used to be a cop, but ran into trouble a few years back when scapegoats were needed for the Saratoga mayor's re-election campaign. The entire force was eating free at Gurney's Deli, but Belsky was the most expendable and he got the old heave-ho. Serves him right, for eating non-kosher. That's how Belsky put it.

Yes, he was one of those born-again gurus. He tried every cockamamie cult in the book and finally came up with Judaism, which he'd been born into in the first place. Some Lubavitchers got hold of him and fed him some books about ethics, prayer and the coming of the Messiah. And now Belsky was an unemployed ex-cop, doing social work for a Chassidic religious sect, and chopping down trees at six-fifty an hour to support a family of nine. So what could I do when Pamela says to me, "You have to ask Mr. Belsky to help. He could be your partner. Besides, he knows more about detective work than you."

"What are you talking about? He doesn't even play bridge!

How's he gonna help me—"

"Do what your wife says, Matthew. That's what the Talmud teaches."

"Oh my God, not you, too?"

"Patty gave me some books."

* * * * * * * * *

I first met Patty the night she met her future husband, Jimmy Cayne. She was at a duplicate club in New York, years before they had special games for novices. Jimmy spotted her on the third round as I was trying to locate a missing queen for an overtrick in a three-spade contract. "Who is that girl? Is she a good bridge player?"

"What girl?"

"That one, the gorgeous one, sitting West at table three."

"I don't know who she is. But I'm sure she's a terrific player." I was in my shell, as they say — too busy concentrating to know what I was saying. It was one of those hands you don't know whether to take the finesse early or wait till the end, get some information and have a better shot at it. Only problem is, that always places you at risk of losing an extra trick. I hated these situations. And I always got them wrong.

Dummy (Jimmy)
♠ A J 3
♡ K 10 9
♢ J 7 3
♣ 9 8 3 2

Declarer (Matthew)
♠ K Q 10 8 7
♡ A J 5
♢ A 9 2
♣ 10 4

	Jimmy		Matthew
West	North	East	South
3 ♢	pass	pass	3 ♠
(all pass)			

Notice Jimmy's pass of my three-spade balance. It was based on a principle we had learned recently from Roth: In competitive situations, discount your first six points — partner is always playing you for that.

It made a lot of sense. How else could we play three spades when they start the bidding off at the three level?

West led the ♢K, East following. I won the ace and drew trumps in four rounds (West had a singleton), discarding a club from dummy. Then I led a diamond toward the jack. West won his queen (East throwing a high club) and continued diamonds to dummy's jack (East pounding another club on the table).

Now I was at that crossroad I was telling you about. I could try to guess the heart queen now — while it was safe to take a losing finesse — or I could play a club and try to get a little more information about the distribution of my opponents' hands.

I was young in those days. I loved to get clues and use them

14

to mathematical advantage. So I played a club. East won the ace and led the king and then the queen as West showed up with a singleton club!

This was around the time Jimmy, who was bored to tears as dummy, started asking me who the girl was at table three and whether she had talent for the game. Who cared? I mean, give me a break. I had found out that West started life with six diamonds and five hearts and was the happiest guy on earth.

Down to nothing but hearts, I cashed my ♡A, and led the jack for a finesse. East won his doubleton queen and cashed a club at the end for down one.

"Are you outa your mind?" sympathized Jimmy.

"It was five-to-two odds, Jimmy. I played it perfectly. I—"

"You think this looney-bin (referring to West) would open three diamonds with a side five-card heart suit unless they were five little?!"

The looney-bin (it was actually Otto, from the Mayfair) was laughing, and I wanted to die. Two rounds later Jimmy became charming, and the girl to my left (Patty) accepted a date with him for a home bridge match the following Tuesday. Little did I realize then that they would marry and in the course of 15 years Jimmy would go from bridge bum to investment banker. In the meantime Patty would return to school at Columbia University, become a doctor of psychology, one of the leading children's language therapists in New York, and, now (1989) become the catalyst in my life for returning to religion. Of course, it began between her and my wife. Oh, and by the way, in between there were these two murders that were still unsolved. . . .

* * * * * * * * *

We stopped for gas, coffee and relief. It must have been

about 95 degrees out there. I made a phone call to George Rapeé, who was providing space for me at his downtown office while he was on vacation. His secretary told me the keys would be waiting under the mat. Then I made a call to Harlem. When we got back in the car, Belsky started bugging me about the case, and I decided to let him in on some of the details. I didn't want him to know everything. It wasn't that I didn't trust him. I just didn't really expect him to be much help. Then again, Belsky was always underrated.

"I understand about your friend Jimmy. He's worried about his bridge team. It's only natural after two uh, whatever you call them—"

"Bridge players."

"Yeah, bridge players. So they're bumped off. But I don't understand why the police aren't handling the case themselves."

"The police have parking tickets to distribute. Wake up, Belsky! We're not in Saratoga any more. This is New York, the Big Apple, where people are plugged every other hour. You think they really have enough cops to cover every homicide? Besides, they haven't connected the case to the bridge team."

"Two people from the same bridge team are strangled three days apart and they don't connect it up?"

"They were married, so the cops think it's got some family angle. They don't understand that they were bridge partners first, husband and wife second."

"Now I'm confused, Matt. I knew they were on the same team, but what do you mean, partners?"

"Belsky," I said, tilting my head back again on the cushioned seat, and pulling down the front sun-shield, "in a bridge team you usually got six players, three partnerships. Two partnerships play each session, while the other rests. The thing that's got Jimmy worried is that he's down to four players, himself and Alan Sontag, Jacqui Mitchell and Jinks

Barkowsky. You can play two partnerships, but usually you play three — especially during a long team event like the Bermuda Bowl."

"Maybe I should have read a bridge book before I came, but who has time, Matt? You know?"

"Never mind the bridge, huh? Just concentrate on your department: the homicides. We got two people strangled to death. Isn't that enough to keep you busy?"

"First Mr. Stein, then Mrs. Stein, right?"

"Right."

"And both were found with cards stuck to their throats?"

"No, no. Charlotte had the eight of diamonds on her blouse, but he was found with a bid in his throat."

"A bid?"

"A piece of cardboard — it comes from a bidding box that the players use during the auction. It was a four-diamond card."

"The four of diamonds?"

The car suddenly swerved. I lifted my shades and let out a soft whistle. Two cows had gone astray and the farmer was chasing them across the road. We should have taken the stinking Thruway.

"Belsky, keep your eye on the road and don't worry about the four of diamonds. It was a bidding-box card that had the bid 'four diamonds' on it."

"I see. In pinochle there are no bids like that. Did I ever tell you about the time I was playing during a stake out at the racetrack? Of course I had my two oldest with me. Judi was working a day job, and the babysitter was sick. Anyway, there we were in the middle of August, eating cherry pie and lemonade . . ."

I placed my hat back over my face and closed my eyes. My wife would pay for this.

I woke up in an air-conditioned sweat. Quickly I checked

my revolver. It was still in its case under the dashboard. I noticed Belsky had some good equipment in there. There was an extra pistol, a small tape-recorder and a bugging device.

Where were we? I thought as I looked outside the window. Belsky was humming some ancient Hebrew love song that King David must have penned. I let out a yawn. The Hudson River was on our right; soon we passed the George Washington Bridge, and Yankee Stadium flashed by on our left. The Orioles were in town. Big deal. Then I remembered, and thanked my lucky stars I'd waked up in time. Of course, Belsky would say it wasn't my lucky stars. For him everything is preordained. "Everything but our choice between doing good and doing evil. That's what the Sages say. Not even a leaf falls, Matt, that doesn't affect the world." I wondered now if the murder of the Steins was preordained, or the play of a three-club contract in a home bridge game, or waking up in time to make a right turn off the Bronx River Expressway.

"Are you crazy, Matt? That's 127th Street."

"Yeah, just turn."

"But Matt, that's the center of Harlem."

"I've got an appointment on 123rd."

He was a good wheelman, that Belsky. I gotta give him credit for that. We sped across the right lane, almost hitting two police cars heading toward Manhattan. It never even occurred to me that we'd be stopped. After all, I had lived in New York for 10 years, and I knew that police were engaged in more important things than stopping motorists who jumped lanes. In fact, if you *didn't* tail-gate and cross lanes in New York, you were more likely to cause an accident than if you did.

Belsky stopped at the red light and a nice young man with an attractive soapy sponge and razor-sharp window cleaner sauntered over and began doing our windshield.

"I really hate this, Matt. I mean, this is like extortion."

I flipped him a quarter and Belsky opened the window to pay. When in Rome, you do as the Romans, kid. Or you end up eye to eye with the lions.

At 123rd I hopped out and told Belsky to take our bags down to the Caynes' apartment, where I would meet him at noon.

"What about lunch?" I heard him cry as I moved away from the beat-up Oldsmobile, and tried to cross the street against the light. There was already a firehydrant roaring away, children laughing and dripping. I loved Harlem, I thought as I stretched my arms and legs. Don a pair of sunglasses and a hat and you fit in anywhere in New York, regardless of race, creed or the color of your convention card.

2

I arrived at the Caynes' at 12:15. Belsky couldn't wait. He was in the kitchen eating a kosher pizza.

"Did you say your blessing over it?" I asked.

"Oh, you're right. I forgot. Thanks."

He mumbled something and poured himself a diet root beer.

The housekeeper told me that Dr. Cayne (Patty) was in her home office with a patient and asked if I wanted anything to eat, too. I thought of a juicy cheeseburger, but realized I'd be offending Belsky's sensibilities if I ate milk and meat in the same meal. So I settled for a tuna on rye, then retired to the den until Patty was through. There was a newspaper clipping on the coffee table. It was one of those bridge-column obituaries that appear after famous players pass away. You know the type: He was a great player, here's his greatest coup, and his opponents won't exactly miss him a lot.

Bridge by Alan Truscott
Bridge Community Loses Female Expert

Mrs. Charlotte Stein, considered by many as one of the bridge world's leading female experts, was found strangled yesterday morning in her usual chair at the Mayfair Club.

Club members were appalled when they learned she had gone down in a laydown game on the last hand of a weekly imp pairs. Later, she was found by security.

Many late-nighters thought that she had been resting up for a 2 a.m. cut-around team match.

She sat East on the diagram deal. Playing with her husband, who passed away in a similar fashion only three days previously, Mrs. Stein gained 5 imps for her team during the U.S. Team Trials last May in Memphis, with a helpful defensive play that many experts would have missed.

West dealer
East-West vulnerable

```
                    North
                    ♠ 9 7 6 2
                    ♡ 10
                    ◇ J 8 4 3
                    ♣ Q J 10 9
West                                    East
♠ 10 3                                  ♠ A 8
♡ A Q J 2                               ♡ K 9 8 7 4
◇ K 10 5 2                              ◇ A Q
♣ 4 3 2                                 ♣ 8 7 6 5
                    South
                    ♠ K Q J 5 4
                    ♡ 6 5 3
                    ◇ 9 7 6
                    ♣ A K
```

West	North	East	South
pass	pass	1 ♡	1 ♠
4 ♡	4 ♠	double	(all pass)

Opening lead: ♡A

Frank Stein's four-heart call was aggressive. However, that contract would have succeeded. North-South did best to take the sacrifice and Mr. Stein led the ace of hearts to look at dummy.

East played a discouraging four-spot, which in their style requested a shift to dummy's weaker suit. Some critics at the time said that Mrs. Stein had missed the spectacular play of the heart king under the ace. But Mr. Stein told this writer later that the unusual card of the king would, in his partnership, call for the unusual shift (a club) rather than be a simple suit-preference.

After winning the diamond shift with the ace, Mrs. Stein made the key play. She cashed the trump ace. Next came the queen of diamonds, and her partner now understood this to be her last diamond. He overtook the diamond and led a third round for her to ruff.

Down two meant plus 300 for East-West. When compared with the other room's score of 100 for East-West, the Stein team gained 5 imps.

Mrs. Stein was the second member of the U.S. international team to be murdered this week. The team, which has a bye to the semifinal (as does Great Britain), still includes James Cayne, Alan Sontag, Jacqui Mitchell and Jinks Barkowsky. They are due to start play tomorrow at the Sheraton Center in New York. Her inaction will be sorely missed.

Bermuda Bowl update: Quarterfinal matches conclude this evening at 8 p.m. The USSR vs. Canada and China vs. Italy. A VuGraph show is free for spectators.

"He should not have bid four hearts."

The voice came from behind my left shoulder. It was the coach. He was an ex-Brit; rumor had it he'd been a two-bit hustler from a Liverpool chess club who came to this country nine years ago at the age of 30, after failing to make the grade in the English bridge scene. Yet somehow, some way, he had managed to worm his way into the elite American bridge crowd and actually got hired by Jimmy Cayne to coach his team. It was against my advice, but this time I'd been wrong. He helped Jimmy's team, a mixture of old-time rubber bridge players and professionals, reach the ultimate plateau: representing the U.S.A. in the world championships.

"What do you suggest?"

"He should have walked it."

Walking a hand was not the coach's invention. It's a common coup used when vulnerable against not to try to buy a contract. The theory's been expounded before, so to make it short and sweet, I'll paraphrase. *You* bid a lot, *they'll* bid a lot. You bid a little, let them get their bids off their chests, and you come back on the next round of bidding and buy the hand.

West dealer
East-West vulnerable

```
                        North
                        ♠ 9 7 6 2
                        ♡ 10
                        ◇ J 8 4 3
                        ♣ Q J 10 9
        West                            East
        ♠ 10 3                          ♠ A 8
        ♡ A Q J 2                       ♡ K 9 8 7 4
        ◇ K 10 5 2                      ◇ A Q
        ♣ 4 3 2                         ♣ 8 7 6 5
                        South
                        ♠ K Q J 5 4
                        ♡ 6 5 3
                        ◇ 9 7 6
                        ♣ A K
```

West	North	East	South
pass	pass	1 ♡	1 ♠
4 ♡	4 ♠	double	(all pass)

Opening lead: ♡A

The coach was suggesting that West bid only three hearts. Then when North bids three spades, North-South may be finished bidding.

"But," I countered, "so may East and West. Neither one has a four-heart bid. That's why four hearts immediately is right.

Because West is unsure whether his side can make game, he should bid it immediately — putting it to North."

"Nonsense," said the coach in a pseudo-New-York accent. "You just bid your hand and you'll get the best results. The best strategy in these situations is no strategy — simply science. I suggest at the very worst a bid of two clubs, Drury."

I wanted to vomit. Two clubs! Drury! This was the type of bidding I hated. Slow, torturous, artificial bids to reach games and let the opponents have all the room in the world to explore their best contract as well. I didn't want to discuss it, but the coach continued, talking to the wall as far as I was concerned.

"After West bids two clubs, North will undoubtedly make a preemptive raise to three spades, and we won't hear from him again. East will, of course, double, not penalty, as you know. Never penalty after a fit has been found. This responsive double shows his defensive and offensive values precisely and offers West the choice of passing, converting to three notrump with the appropriate stopper, or bidding on to four hearts. Naturally, West will convert to four hearts, with four trumps and nothing in spades, i. e., he has no wastage whatsoever."

I'll "i. e." his nose, I thought to myself.

"Then you have what I call the perfect bridge result — perfect for East-West, that is. Four hearts making four, plus 620 — a huge pickup of imps. Personally, I would prefer two diamonds with the West hand, another form of Drury, showing exactly four trumps. This way East can bid four hearts himself over the anticipated three spades and the auction will be even simpler. But if you really want to know the truth — (I did not) — East should bid four diamonds over North's three spades. This lead-director will allow for precision defense, should South sacrifice in four spades. Naturally, four diamonds is a lead-director and not a slam try, as all slam tries — page 73b in the revised notes, by the way —

begin with three notrump, my modification of Meckwell Serious Three-No for competitive auctions, always applicable after third-seat openings."

"Who is this clown?" asked Belsky. And that's when I fell in love with Belsky.

"Pardon me? Who, or should I say, what, are you?"

"Listen, Buster," continued my detective partner, sticking his middle finger in the coach's shnozola. "Watch the way you talk to me. I'm hired to capture the serial killer — and I mean to find out your whereabouts last night as well as everybody else's around here."

"What is this, my man, what is this?!! Charlotte wasn't even murdered last night; it was the night before."

"Okay, okay," I said, taking Belsky's arm off the coach's fragile shoulder. "You'll ruffle his ascot. Just take a seat, big B, and I'll introduce you to the other contestants."

The coach took out a comb and corrected a curl in his wig. Okay, so he had no wig. But it looked like a wig. It smelled like a wig. Then he came over to my bad ear to whisper, "How could James possibly align himself with a persona like this?"

"Relax, coach. He's my right-hand man, so don't fret. He's a religious man and likes to get to the point. Isn't that right, Belsk?"

"Check," said Belsky, as he sat down on the couch. Then he opened up his jacket a little, just enough to let the coach see the black leather strap of his holster down the left side of his shirt. A little *tzitzis* showed as well.

About ten minutes later Patty entered the den, with a cheery smile and kind words on her lips. "Hi, boys. Don't we look nice."

Belsky and I rose to greet her. The coach nodded from his seat, where he was busy scribbling bridge notes in tricolor jet-ink pens. Belsky and Patty hit it off immediately and promised each other that they would sit down soon to discuss a little Torah (i.e., Bible). She asked me how Pamela was, and then turned on the coach. "Are you still here?"

The coach didn't look up.

"He's been here since seven a.m. The living room is filled with papers."

The coach spoke but still did not look up. "I have got to get these notes ready for James when he comes home. And the new pages must be typed."

"Okay, but clean up the living room. I've got a Hebrew lesson at three."

"Hebrew lesson?" said Belsky, his eyes aglow. "Would you mind if I sit in?"

"Belsky, for crying out loud," I said, "we're here on a case."

Patty corrected me. "All men are supposed to set aside a few hours in the day for study."

She was out to convert me along with everyone else. I asked her where Jimmy was.

"Where do you think he is? He works for a living, unlike most of you."

"I beg your pardon," countered the coach.

"But I thought we had a meeting scheduled for 12:30," I complained.

"Not as far as I know," said Patty. "Maybe you should call his secretary, Suzette, at the office. In fact, maybe your meeting is at the office."

She was right. I'd forgotten. I grabbed Belsky's arm and off we went . . . into a world I thought I'd never step foot in again . . . a land not quite flowing with milk and honey . . . no, no, this land was flowing with green stuff — Wall Street.

3

It was about 101 degrees outside, or so the doorman claimed. Belsky had parked on a side street off Fifth Avenue. There was a nice $25 parking ticket on the windshield. "What's the difference?" said my partner. "Could've parked in a lot for twenty-nine."

We took the East Drive to the Wall Street exit and then turned over to Water, where Jimmy had his office. On the top floor, overlooking the river with Brooklyn, New Jersey and the Statue of Liberty all in view, was an investment company. The place was electric with ticker tape. You could hear it, smell it, taste it.

Ace Greenberg, chairman of the board, an ex-bridge partner of mine, waved hello from his seat in the middle of the brokers' floor. Belsky asked if this is where I used to trade. "No," I said. This is where the accounts are kept and where people can phone in to make their personal stock bids. From here the brokers call the Stock Exchange.

We were told that Cayne's office was the floor below, but first we walked over to Ace.

We shook hands, and amid static and flashing stock prices he posed an important question, which had been on his mind since the previous night.

"You hold king-queen-third," said Ace. "You can follow a bridge hand, can't you?" he snapped at my partner. Belsky nodded. He was much too in awe of the whole show to say no. "King-queen third, four to the nine, ace-king-queen-sixth and void. Got it?" We both nodded our heads. I noticed up on the green ticker, Texaco had risen three points in the last minute. I hated Texaco; it's the stock that drove me out of the Exchange during my days there as a trader. On second thought, I liked Texaco. It's the stock that got me out of that madhouse.

"You're playing with Frankenstein—"

"Wait a second," I said. "Frankenstein is dead, he was strangled four days ago at the Mayfair."

"This was five days ago," said Ace. "At the Cavendish."

"You mean you were playing bridge with the deceased the day before he was strangled?" asked Belsky.

"Well, it wasn't the day after," said Ace. Then he pointed to my partner. "Say, who is this guy? Anyway, Frankenstein opens three clubs and it goes pass, so I pass with my void, right?"

From what I could understand, Ace's hand looked like this: ♠ K Q x ♡ 9 x x x ◇ A K Q x x x ♣ — and the bidding had gone three clubs by Frank Stein, his partner, pass to him. I nodded that pass was okay. After all, over a preempt, what could a guy do? Three diamonds is probably forcing and may lead to worse trouble than three clubs.

There was a pause. "So what happened?" I said, a little loudly, in order to hear myself over the noise of some computer printers that had suddenly started in the back of the room. Ace was on the phone. "Sell," he said. Then he came back to us.

"It went three diamonds, pass, pass."

♠ K Q x ♡ 9 x x x ◇ A K Q x x x ♣ —

"You mean you passed three clubs and fourth seat balanced with three diamonds?"

"Yeah, so what do you do when it comes back to you?"

I looked at Belsky. Belsky looked at Ace. Ace looked at me.

"I guess I double," I said.

"I passed," he said, "and Frankenstein gave me hell. But don't you think it's wrong to double — that they'll run to some major? I think you should take the money. Good-bye."

Suddenly Ace was back on the phone, this time buying. Belsky and I moved across the room and I contemplated the last hand. Could it really be right to pass three diamonds? I agree they may run, but then again, what a bonanza if they don't.

Jimmy's secretary, Suzette, was on the phone. She pointed to his door, and we went right in. It was a corner room that overlooked the water, with two sides of glass wall. Alan Sontag was sitting in an easy chair smoking a Havana. He looked nervous. Perhaps he was thinking it was his last Havana. Jimmy Cayne was behind his desk, talking on the phone. Facing the desk was a man I barely recognized. His name was Jinks Barkowsky, a man I had met approximately 10 years earlier, when his daughter had flipped out — she had delusions that she was a detective on a murder case (see "Murder at the Bridge Table" for details). Then I saw her: Evelyn Barkowsky, the very same girl, now a stunning woman, in her late 20s, I guessed. She gave me the once-over and smiled demurely. She was somebody to avoid and I was sorry she was here. There was one more person in the room. He was an older, distinguished man, smoking a cigarette in the far corner.

There was one chair left and Belsky soon filled it. He

looked tired, and I didn't mind. From where I was standing the vantage point was just fine. Besides, the chair was smack next to Evelyn. She opened the second button of her blouse. I have to hand it to Belsky. He tried to avert his eyes. But then he did something that was hard to believe. He reached over and buttoned it. She just sat there in a state of shock. Then again, maybe I had imagined the whole thing.

Cayne hung up the phone.

"That was the coach. I told him to completely eliminate section D of the notes. I can't take it anymore."

"*You* can't take it? What about me?" said Sontag, leaping halfway 'cross the room.

The older gent in the corner let out an aggressive throat clearing and Jimmy looked at Belsky and asked who *he* was. The two shook hands, Jimmy waved at me and said, "Matthew, this is Commissioner McKenna of the New York police force." The Commissioner! I shook the man's hand. Jimmy continued, "He just wants to say a few words and then we'll get down to team business."

The Commissioner had a raspy, tired voice. He sounded like he was ready to call it quits and move to Miami.

"I just want you people to know that the police are on the job, looking for the murderer of your friends, the Steins. It's out opinion that the murderer is a very sick individual. However, certain information has led us to believe that the murders have no relation to your bridge team, so I don't want you to go around worrying about it."

"You mean we're not gonna have police protection?!" squawked Sontag. "Jimmy, this is ridiculous. I'm not playing without protection."

"Now, now, Sonty," said Jimmy, "let him finish."

"Thank you. As I was saying, don't panic. Go about your bridge business as usual and we'll take care of the rest. Mr. Cayne here has informed me about the hiring of Granovetter to work closely with the bridge players, and I think the idea's

31

okay. He'll keep a lookout at the championships this week, and if there's anything suspicious going on, he'll inform Detective Kennedy, who's in charge of the case, and is presently staked out at the Mayfair Club. Ahem. That's not public knowledge, you understand."

"What?!" cried Sontag. "Granovetter? He's no detective. He's an amateur mystery writer. This is crazy!"

"Relax, Sonty," said Jimmy, "he's got this nice man Belsky helping him as well."

Belsky and I both nodded to the room, as if the room cared. I couldn't help but wonder why, if the murder had nothing to do with bridge, the detective in charge was staked out at the bridge club.

The Commissioner looked at his watch, gave me another quick handshake and left, mumbling something about a golf date with the mayor. I caught him down the hall and asked him for some I.D.s. He wrote me out two "special-agent" cards but warned me to lay off as much as possible.

"Don't you think the killer might be just plain evil, rather than sick?" I asked.

"That's an old-fashioned notion, m'boy. These days we tag 'em sick. Makes the killer's family feel better."

What about the victim's family? I thought, as I walked back to Jimmy's office.

"Close the door," commanded Jimmy. I put my back to it and heard it click.

"Listen to me," he continued. "The Commissioner's right. I think we'd better start concentrating on the game. If we're going to play a four-man team, we've got to start thinking about the stamina problem."

It wasn't quite a shriek that Evelyn let out. It was more like a turkey's last gobble at the Thanksgiving factory. Sontag thought it was the tires of a swerving car 49 floors below. He made a mad dash to the windows. Maybe he was just trying to get out of her range. Meanwhile, daddy patted her knee and Mr. B adjusted his tie, trying to show off his nonchalance in the face of emergency. Jimmy looked at me and I knew he knew that it was coming. That's why the door was shut tight.

"No, no, no!" she said, swirling her pretty wrist into the air. "My dad cannot play on a four-man team. You can't do this to him."

Translation: You can't do this to *me*.

It wasn't hard to figure out. She wanted on the team — badly.

"I agree," said Sonty, cigar dangling. "I mean, I'm in no condition to play four, myself." He motioned to his paunch. It's too bad I wasn't closer to him or I could have given it a nice pat.

Jimmy: "This is not open for discussion, boys. Four-man teams are always the best anyway. There'll be no worry as to who's playing and who's sitting out."

Sonty: "But I thought you wanted to add Chuck."

Chuck Burger was Jimmy Cayne's regular partner.

Jimmy: "I decided it was safer for him to stay in Detroit."

Sonty: "Great! Suddenly it's safer in Detroit. Let's call the newspapers."

Jinks finally speaks up.

"Ex-excuse me. But I think Mr. Cayne is right."

"DADDY!"

"Now, now, Evy, papa knows best. After all, to add to the team at this date will only create problems. There'll be hurt feelings, there'll be politics, there'll be all sorts of nuisances. With only a day before we start we should be concentrating on our team strategy, practice, you know. . . ."

Evy jumped up. "What team strategy!? What practice?! When's the last time you practiced with Jacqui? You haven't even seen her since you won the trials, Dad! If it wasn't for me going up there every night, you'd never know what system she plays. And the dogs, those dogs, those horrible dogs!! All on your account, Dad! And that loud television on all the time to Met baseball, listening to Victor stories until 3 a.m., and what about my figure? Seven pounds I gained for you!"

"Have you had her banana cream pie?" I asked.

"She served it last night," she retorted.

Belsky: "Banana cream pie!"

"Now, now, Evy, I know you've been a big help," said Jinks, standing up, his hands on her shoulders — it looked like he was trying to force her back into her seat.

"You're all mad, you know that?" She brushed him off and was up on her hind legs now. In a moment she'd be frothing at the mouth. "To play four in the world championships is like committing suicide. What chance do we have? All my work down the tubes!! All my typing!! They'll be coming at you from all sides, with systems, conventions, unknown splinters, unknown weak-twos, unknown preempts. And you'll be too tired to handle it all — "

"Look," said Jimmy, "this is not accomplishing anything. Matthew and I discussed it all night. We went over every option and I took his advice."

She suddenly turned her twisted (but well-proportioned) body around at me. For an instant I thought her arm was a machete. She didn't need a machete. Her eyes were red hot firesticks. I let out a soft hiss, hoping it would call her off. Then I mentally wrote a poison-pen note in my diary against my good friend Jimmy Cayne.

"Matthew has had experience in these matters," he continued. "Many times he and I have played four and it's usually been successful. You just have to know how to pace yourself. In fact, I'm going running this afternoon. If you want to, you can join me, Sonty."

Sonty's face lit up, eyes sparkling. "Great, Jimmy, and we can bid a thousand hands as we run. Shall it be Central Park or the Brooklyn Bridge?"

"C'mon, Sonty," said Jimmy. "It'll be at my place. We'll run on a treadmill in the exercise room, then take a steam bath."

Suzette's voice came over the intercom. There was a phone call for him.

"Look, I have real business to attend to. You're all dismissed, children. I'll see you at the practice session tonight. Jacqui will meet you at my place at seven, Jinks. Matthew, better give everyone your number, just in case anybody hears anything suspicious."

Those who were still seated got up to leave. Sonty passed me by with a look of despair. I gave him my card with Rapee's number on it and he gave me a cigar. Evelyn took my card, crumpled it and tossed it down her blouse. It would be safe there, I thought. Jinks smiled down at me, shook my hand and thanked me for my help. He was a tall guy with huge sweaty fingers. Then Jimmy motioned for Belsky and me to return. He waited until the rest were gone, then asked if we had come up with anything yet.

"Not much," said Belsky. "You know we just got into town."

"I'm depending on you guys," he said.

"What about her?" I asked.

"Forget it. She's a bit mad but no killer. No, he's got to be someone who wants to destroy our team — and she's our biggest supporter. For the last six months she's done nothing but take hand records, type system sheets, rewrite Jacqui's bridge notes. No, children, you'd better look elsewhere. But do us all a favor. Find him quickly. Find him by starting time tomorrow and there'll be a bonus. In the meantime I'll keep Sonty calm."

"That Detective Jordan is still holding," came Suzette's voice over the intercom.

"I'll take it in a second," said Jimmy. He turned to us. "Like I was saying, don't worry about our boy Sonty."

I wasn't worried about our boy Sonty. I was worried about just about everybody else.

35

4

It was nice outside, a pleasant 104 in the shade. Belsky and I strolled down to Battery Park. Half of Wall Street was eating ice cream cones. Belsky suggested a ride on the Staten Island Ferry and I told him it was a good idea, maybe it would help clear our minds so we could sort out the suspects. And then again maybe it was an even better idea because a little lady named Evelyn Barkowsky and a little English gent known as The Coach were about to board the dock, their hot paws in each other's arms.

We followed them through the turnstiles and on to the boat, keeping our distance. I'd have given anything to have planted a communication device on that sweet little blouse of hers. Now it would be almost impossible to get close enough to hear. Of course they might have been innocent, discussing team strategy, two-way Drury or defense to the Russian Pass. However, I had a feeling it was more than a loveboat excursion 'cross the Hudson. I looked Eastward toward the ocean and decided I was getting off this thing before I got seasick.

Belsky had a camera with him and suggested he don his shades, pretending to be a tourist. It was impossible. He'd be recognized — he was too big — and the last thing I wanted was for them to think we had seen them together. The situation seemed hopeless. "Belsky," I said despondently, "we'll never get close enough to hear them sing. I'm getting off." Then Belsky surprised me.

"But Matt, if I could just get close enough with this." And he wasn't referring to the camera. No, much better, it was the small tape recorder, useless in this instance except for one pleasing fact: "You know I stuck her with a bugging device, don't you?"

"Belsky," I said, jumping off the gangplank and waving good-bye, "You're underrated."

Across the park, I found number 24 Washington Street. The brownstone had a tag on the door that read, "George Rapeé." I slipped my card in its place, opened up the door with the key that was resting snugly under the rug, and walked up one flight to room 201. There was a speck of carbon paper on the floor, and I wondered if George had planted it there for my benefit.

Rapee's office was cozy. There were two small rooms, one for a secretary and one for George. The secretary's had a formal fireplace behind the copy machine and a fan next to the sink. I switched it on and summer dust blew in my face. George's room was filled mostly with a large mahogany desk, and had the old-fashioned advantage of no desk-top computer filling up the top. A note with my name on it was peeking out of his inkpad. "Good luck, Matt. The case sounds interesting. If you need any advice, you'll have to wait until I get back from my vacation — in two weeks. Best, George. P.S. Water the plants, first thing."

The only thing I hated worse than the smell of indoor plants was watering them, but I was glad I watered these, because sticking out from the soil was a beige envelope. I got my mitts dirty pulling it out. It was torn on top and I was sure some Joe had gotten to it first. Not good, Matthew. I went over to the desk and pulled out three sheets of stationery.

"Matt,
"If the carbon is on the floor when you entered, then someone has been snooping. Hopefully, he did not attempt to water the plants.
"Thought you might be interested in the following story, which is true.
"I am playing in the game last Monday at the Cavendish, when, after the last rubber, I am invited to dine with Frankenstein, his wife, and Otto Marx. Of course, as you well know, it is against my religion to dine with Frankenstein — as who would want to? — but I go along this time because Marx (that mad Hungarian) has done the inviting and has his own table at the Red Tulip, and I am a patsy for goulash or cabbage anytime. Anyway, we go to the Tulip and Marx is complaining about his Options people the whole time — as you know, the Market has not been good to anybody lately. Well, Frank and Charlotte are arguing over the following hand, played during the Trials (see full diagram, next page):"

I turned to the next page:

"At dinner, Marx and I are given the East-West hands on two slips of paper."

Hold on here. Where was the diagram? Had George forgotten to write the hand? No, obviously whoever had broken in before me had swiped it. I returned to what remained of the letter:

"At dinner, Marx and I are given the East-West hands on

two slips of paper. I insist on waiting until my cold cherry soup arrives, then I reluctantly agree to bid the hand with him. Frankenstein tells us that it's not a bidding problem, it's a defensive problem and I am furious, because bidding a hand is difficult enough over dinner, defending is impossible. But okay, I agree, mainly because Frankenstein announces that I am the best defender he's ever defended with and he wants my opinion. Okay, so I'm slightly flattered. But when the big oaf says, George, you should be my next regular partner — I say, Frank, I wouldn't sit down across you for all the rice in China. I don't blame you, says Charlotte, who has been sitting there all the while attacking her chopped liver like it was his liver. Anyway, we are given the auction (see diagram) and Otto starts to think about his opening lead.

"Meanwhile, by the time the waiter brings the raisin bread, I am very sorry I said yes to dinner. Charlotte, poor thing, is in tears and Frank is tormenting her, telling her that she missed the simplest play in the history of the game.

"Then, between tear drops, she says that he should never have cashed his ace, whereupon he starts screaming about the eight of diamonds — and has surely ruined the problem for us by now.

"Meanwhile, my digestion is being ruined, also, and my stuffed cabbage is ruined, too, because some of Frankenstein's hideous iced-tea spills into my dish. When the waiter comes with the main course, Frankenstein waves his knife and fork in the air at his wife, hits the waiter's arm, and the cabbage goes flying.

"Unfortunately it lands in Otto's lap. And this is where the case comes in. Otto, who you might know, has had a history of run-ins with Frankenstein going way back to when the Mayfair was on 57th Street, is not happy about what has landed on his nice blue suit — especially because he was planning to share the cabbage and his goulash with me. He gets up from the table and puts his hands around

Frankenstein's neck. Charlotte, who is very upset, gets up and tries to help her husband — though it is more likely (from my perspective) that she is squeezing tighter rather than trying to pry apart Otto's hands. In fact, I believe — though I am not the world's best observer of these things — that she is almost caressing Otto's hands as they squeeze her husband's neck. I, of course, am delighted either way, as it would not be a great loss to the world if Frankenstein exits a little early — and in fact, as events have unfolded, most people now agree with this assessment.

"Anyway, after a few seconds of wondering which way to go, I decide to save the man by splashing a little of my apple brandy into Marx's face. His temper is abated and Frankenstein comes out of it not looking much worse for wear. He, of course, is furious with Otto and tells him that a law suit will be filed by his attorneys in the morning. As you know, morning never comes for Frankenstein.

"The next day, after he is found strangled, I relate much of this to the police, though out of good friendship to Charlotte I leave out the small detail that she appeared to be helping Otto rather than stopping him. I also leave out what happened after Otto and I finish our dinner in peace (after Charlotte leaves with her husband to soothe his wounds — a difficult chore because now he starts arguing about an eight-of-diamonds play that nobody seems to have any clue to).

"Otto confides in me that things are going so-so for him on the Street (which means, he must be losing his shirt — knowing how traders tend to brag about their accounts). Apparently he has a lot of capital now tied up with Texaco, which on Tuesday took a plunge that only a Rockefeller could survive.

"As I leave this afternoon (Friday) for the safe beaches of Martha's Vineyard, I am informed by the police that Charlotte has been strangled, too. And so I warn you to be careful and advise wholeheartedly that you watch out for a certain financially-wounded animal.

"Best to Pam and the boys,
"*George*"

I looked around for the diagram, again, but it was nowhere. Then I recalled that it was the eight of diamonds that had been attached to Charlotte Stein's blouse yesterday morning — when she was found strangled.

5

I thought I heard someone at the door, but it was only an old cat that lived in the building, trying to find some cool corner in the hallway.

Back inside, the clock read 2:30. I could use a drink. The phone rang and I decided not to pick up. The answering machine came on and the caller's voice: "Hello? Matt? Matt? Are you there?"

The voice was unmistakable. It was my old friend Victor. I've known him and his wife Jacqui since I was a 14-year-old punk. Jacqui was the fourth on Jimmy's team; she was Jinks' partner.

I picked up.

"Here I am."

"Matt! What are ya doing? Ya gonna be at Jimmy's to-night?"

"Yeah, I'll be there. How are you?"

"Nuttin to complain about. Better off than Frankenstein and his wife."

"True," I said. "So what's up?"

"Well, I just called to warn ya to be on your toes."

"Sure, Victor. I'm okay. In fact, I've got a lot of clues already."

"Well, be careful. Because I got a feeling."

"You do?"

"Yeah, I got a feeling that whoever this killer is, it's someone who doesn't take kindly to ya."

"Why do you say that?"

"Well, you're out to find out who he is, ain't ya?"

"True."

There was a long pause. This conversation was going like a strong-club auction with one hand holding all the points.

"Well, then, I'll see ya later. Oh, by the way, did ya take care of George's plants?"

"Yeah, how come you ask that?"

"Just checking."

Click.

I guess what Victor meant was that he was still the Godfather — still checking to see that things were going smoothly with his clan. Luckily I was one of his clan. So was George Rapeé. So was Jimmy Cayne. But so were Frankenstein and Charlotte, too. Things, therefore, were not in the complete control that Victor was supposed to have them in.

* * * * * * * * *

The first time I met Victor was on a Sunday afternoon at the New York Hilton. It was a Swiss Teams, the first ever in New York City. Victor was wearing his sunglasses in a room with very little light. At first I thought he was using them to intimidate his opponents. Later I learned from his partners that he wore them to sleep while he was dummy. This is probably the most important tip I ever learned about how to survive a long team match on a four-person team: Don't watch declarer play the hand when you're the dummy.

It's probably a good tip for any form of the game but is especially important at imps, where the psychological trauma of watching partner go down in a contract can completely ruin your mental attitude on the very next deal — and it could be a deal that swings the entire match.

Disasters at imps come in twos and threes. After a bad board, some players try to make up for the bad score with a gambling bid or play — it may work, it may not. But much worse is when you lose your focus, lose count on a hand, lose your ability to play because you are upset. The best way to avoid such a state of mind is to not watch partner play the hand.

Then there's the arguing that goes on after the hand — arguing that would never happen if you hadn't watched and had enough facts to argue with.

Most players are stubborn, however. They want to watch because it's too interesting to see what happens. Winning is secondary to being in on the action — even as a spectator. I would guess that not watching partner play the hand must be worth 25-to-35 imps per 64 boards. That's a lot of imps, and if the whole team vowed to keep its eyes off partner's business, winning would be 100 imps easier.

Go ahead, try to refute me. You can't. And you know why not? Because you're not able to do it! Or, I should say, won't do it. Only the top of the top professionals can overcome this losing trait — it's just too difficult to take a nap in the middle of a war.

Victor Mitchell adopted me. He became my teacher but he never taught. He was like a jigsaw puzzle in the flesh. He said things that had to be pieced together; anything I learned had to come from listening, watching and figuring out for myself.

Yet Victor was everybody's favorite teacher, not just

mine. He was there the night Jimmy and Patty went on their first date to a home bridge game at Al Rand's place. That's because Victor ran these weekly imp games for the benefit of all his students. Eight boards, coffee, cake and discussion. Eight more boards, and so on. That night I got there late and had to kibitz the first set. Jimmy was playing with Patty against Amalya Kearse and Al Rand. Maybe you've seen the hand before (it was published in the book, "Tops and Bottoms") but I'll describe it briefly again, just to set the record straight . . . and because there was a lesson in it for me that I would utilize one day.

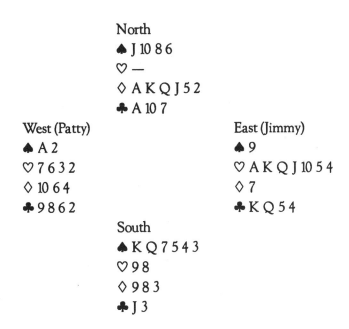

North
♠ J 10 8 6
♡ —
◊ A K Q J 5 2
♣ A 10 7

West (Patty)
♠ A 2
♡ 7 6 3 2
◊ 10 6 4
♣ 9 8 6 2

East (Jimmy)
♠ 9
♡ A K Q J 10 5 4
◊ 7
♣ K Q 5 4

South
♠ K Q 7 5 4 3
♡ 9 8
◊ 9 8 3
♣ J 3

If you take a moment to review the hand, you will see that the only opening lead to defeat a spade slam North-South is a club.

When I arrived at the 17th-floor duplex, I took a seat behind Jimmy. Out to impress his date, he made a great bid. South was dealer and opened with a weak two-bid in spades. Al Rand, sitting North, thought for a long time before bidding two notrump (asking for a feature). Jimmy realized that Rand was probably thinking of big things. So rather than bid his hearts, a suit that figured to be short in the North hand, he bid his *clubs*. Over his three-club bid, South and West passed and North bid six spades. Patty duly led a club and declarer was doomed. However . . .

North
♠ J 10 8 6
♡ —
◇ A K Q J 5 2
♣ A 10 7

West (Patty)
♠ A 2
♡ 7 6 3 2
◇ 10 6 4
♣ 9 8 6 2

East (Jimmy)
♠ 9
♡ A K Q J 10 5 4
◇ 7
♣ K Q 5 4

South
♠ K Q 7 5 4 3
♡ 9 8
◇ 9 8 3
♣ J 3

	Patty		*Jimmy*
South	West	North	East
2 ♠	pass	2 NT	3 ♣
pass	pass	6 ♠	(all pass)

After declarer won dummy's ♣A and led a trump to West, Patty thought the hand through and decided that a player as strong (and handsome) as Jimmy would never overcall at the three-level in fewer than a five-card suit. So she switched to a diamond — her only hope it seemed was to give East a ruff, if declarer had opened a five-card-suit weak two-bid along with four diamonds on the side.

Five-card-suit weak two-bids had not really come into fashion in 1969 and, needless to say, Jimmy was less than flattered by her diamond shift. The post mortem went something like this.

He: That's the worst play I have ever seen.

She: What do you want me to do? Jump out the window?

He: How could you make a play like that?

She: Okay. If it will make you happy, I'll jump out the window.

He: Nothing will make me happy.

She: Okay. I won't jump.

One can only imagine the conversation had they not been on their first date, where terrible bridge plays tend to get lost in a sea of romantic expectations.

In the postmortem Victor pointed out how East and West had been on the opposite paths in psychology. Patty, interested in psychology, was enamored with Victor's analysis.

"Well, you gotta pay the piper," said Victor in his Brooklyn accent.

Nobody knew exactly what he meant, but we all nodded. Victor poured himself a cup of coffee and continued along the same line of explanation.

"Sometimes we play the game too well. Sometimes we'd be better off playing with a dummy!"

"You mean," said Patty, the only one in the room who could come close to interpreting the grandmaster, "that if I hadn't stopped to count the hand, but blindly followed suit, I would have returned a club."

"Now that's the way to go about it," said Victor.

"That's brilliant," said Patty.

"Yeah, well, watch out. Next time the bastard will want ya to think!"

At first I thought the lesson should have been not to make

wiseacre bids like Jimmy's three-club overcall. But then, if he hadn't, what was the chance of getting a club lead? No, no, it was a great bid — the question was: How could his partner read it? The answer was difficult to take. It was a bid that *required* a weak partner. It was a "captain bid," which works only opposite a first mate, ready to follow orders.

Great players frown on captain bids — yet they make for easy bidding. Your partner opens one notrump and you are suddenly in position to make captain bids. You can sign off in a suit, bid Stayman to ask partner to tell you his major, or transfer if you're playing transfers and force partner to play the hand from his side. It's easy to bid when you are the director and even easier when you're the guy taking orders. That's why in my early 20s I became interested in relay systems. The idea of such a system is that one player (usually the player with the stronger hand) keeps asking coded questions to his partner, who responds in bids that say specific things about his hand. Relays are well-known at a basic level. Stayman is such a bid. Blackwood is another. But a whole system based on questions and answers requires two players who are willing to study notes and practice their bidding for maybe six months to a year before effectively getting it right at the table.

* * * * * * * * *

I was thinking about these things and dreaming about auctions that could never be when I heard the cat again. Only this time it wasn't a cat and I was the patsy. There's nothing worse than getting doubled in a voluntarily bid game, and the same goes for being held at gunpoint in your own office.

"Keep 'em up, higher."

I tried to judge the height of the guy behind me. My hands were reaching for the ceiling as he went through my pockets.

Then he gave himself away. A ten-spot dropped to the floor between my shoes and he didn't bother to reach for it. He wasn't after money. He was after information, a commodity I could well afford to negotiate.

"Just tell me what you're looking for, punk."

"Shut up. I'm no punk. I'm twenty-one."

This was too easy. This was almost a laugher. If I led a spade up to the king, he would hesitate with the ace.

"I've got a feeling — punk — that you're looking for a bridge hand. And that bridge hand is already on the open market. Like about two hundred thousand people will be reading it in next month's ACBL Bulletin."

"What are you talking about? Only four people know the hand, and two of them are dead — do you hear me? Dead! So don't you start telling me any lies. I've had enough of you bridge experts—"

Ah, a wounded colt. I decided to get soft.

"You're tickling me, kid. Look over there in the flower garden."

As he moved his right hand I came down on the wrist — gently. He was a kitten, after all. The gun slipped out like a fresh deck of powdered Kem cards. It was across the floor before we could properly say hello to each other. And before we could exchange greeting cards, it was in the hands of the girl in mauve polka dots.

6

I don't like polkadots. And I hate mauve. But I would have excused her had she not been sweating so profusely, and it wasn't Chanel number five that blew by my nose. This one had better be quick. First things first — I had to get her away from the fan.

"Watch the spider web," I said. She moved nicely.

Then I couldn't help one more jab at the boy. "When you told me you wanted to see me, you didn't mention bringing your kindergarten class along."

"Shut up," the boy without his gun commanded.

Polkadots was panting. One lousy staircase and she was panting. She must have been around 27 by my account, but she looked at least 10 years older. She had her father's face. I hoped the personality didn't come along with it.

"I told you not to bring this," she said to him.

"Yeah, well, give it to me. Don't you understand we'll never find out anything if we don't use a little muscle?"

"I'm sick of violence," she continued. "I'm so sick of it I think I'm going to be sick." She covered her face. I stepped back a good 10 feet. If she did it here in the office, I vowed I would jump out the window.

"Put your head between your legs," I ordered. Then I realized it wouldn't fit.

I opened the window and the hot air did wonders. There was a trumpet player outside blowing a tune from old Broadway. I couldn't place it, and I didn't feel like dancing either.

The music stopped, and after a few minutes of nerve-racking silence, we all sat down nicely and spilled the beans.

They were brother and sister, of sorts. That is, each had a parent who married the other. Her name was Catherine Stein. The last time I had seen her was at the Mayfair Club 20 years ago, when she was sitting by the windowsill playing with her crayons. Maybe you remember the case. I documented it in "I Shot My Bridge Partner." I was a punk myself in those days. Her father was the very same lately deceased Frank Stein, and her step mother was the late Charlotte.

And him? His name was Bobby and he was Charlotte's son from another source.

You've heard of how a child of two stage actors is born in a trunk. These kids lived in a duplicate-board case. Traveling from tournament to tournament, with summer vacations on cruise ships, they probably spent half their childhood working as bridge caddies. I heard once though the grapevine that the girl had a nice set of lungs and was now singing torch songs in the West Village. I'm sure it was an act to miss.

Who his real father was is a mystery that will never be solved. But never mind from whence he came; more important was where he was heading.

"You're gonna end up in the clink or worse," I warned. "Just leave the job of detection to the professional detectors."

"I don't care what you say, I'm gonna get the guy that killed my mother."

"And what about your father?"

"He can go to the hell, for all I care," he said. And he may have been close to the mark there. Anyway, rather than bore you with the dribs and drabs, I'll summarize the conversation in one line. He hated pop; she hated mom; I hated them all.

Meanwhile they had given evidence to the police, and on their own they were playing Mr. and Ms. Detective. At one point she shook with rage at him and I wondered if George was up to date on his furniture insurance.

"Mr. Granovetter, please!! I just want it to end. I just want the police to find whoever did it and then I can concentrate on my theatrical career. Isn't there anything you can do to help us capture this monster?" Then she started to sob.

I looked at her as sincerely as I was able. I would have patted her on the head if she'd been a puppy. Luckily for me, she wasn't. I offered her my handkerchief and she made mincemeat of it. There's nothing worse than an orphan's tears.

"Listen to me, kids," I said softly. "Give me twenty-four hours to come up with the culprit. If I don't have him by the time the semifinals of the bridge championships start, you can have my badge."

"BRIDGE CHAMPIONSHIPS!" she screamed, spitting on me at the same time. "WHEN WILL YOU PEOPLE GROW UP?! THAT'S WHAT RUINED MY FATHER. THAT'S WHAT MADE HIM MARRY HER!"

I quickly shut the window, afraid someone would hear her and call the fire department. I wondered if she reached those notes in her crooning.

The boy just sat there and listened politely. His sister went to the water cooler and broke it.

"She hates the game," he confided. I nodded.

"That explains her tone of voice."

"Me," he said, "I could care less — know what I mean? I mean, bridge, chess, checkers — they're all the same to me: games, ways of escaping reality. My mother loved to play bridge and I don't blame her. What other relationship could she possibly have with that man? At least with bridge, she didn't have to actually . . . touch him."

"Do you play the game?" I asked, why, I don't know. Maybe I was unable to deal with Polkadots and the conversation was turning sour.

"I play a little," he admitted. "I know what Stayman is and I know a transfer or two. Maybe I'll pursue it, maybe I won't. Maybe I'll show the whole world what kind of bridge player my mother really was."

"Excuse me," I said. "I hear that the world is still spinning, so there are things to be done. It was really nice meeting both of you." I kept the gun.

The sky was overcast. The temperature must have dropped a good three or four degrees. The street was starting to empty as the rich and famous and their underlings took off early, some for the Racquet Club, some for the Yale Club, and some for the bridge club — there were some of those, too.

And where was Belsky?

Had I been a smoker, it would have been a good moment to light up. But I wasn't, so I just stood there watching the world pass by. Eventually I decided to call it quits and headed by foot past the shady lanes of Downtown, New York. The air smelled of fish, and I didn't mind. The case stunk, too. The suspects were all there, each of them with a better motive than the next. Perhaps it would have been a good idea to visit the morgue, but I was out of steam, and besides, they would wait for me.

I passed Belsky's car, hoping he was alive in the back seat or some such thing. But there was no Belsky. I considered using the spare set of keys, but how could I do that to a partner? He was bound to return to the car someday, and would be very unhappy to see it not there.

So I walked, and walked, and pondered. Take them one by

one, I thought. Eliminate if you can, Matthew. Play it like a tough bidding problem. Okay. Let's start with Jimmy. Why not? Just 'cause he's a success and a friend of mine doesn't mean he didn't do it. He's friends with the police Commissioner, too. And his motive? He wanted to play four all along. He was sick of sitting out, of losing imps while his teammates played without him. He wants to win and maybe he saw this as the only way. But if he ordered the killings, who did it?

Neah. C'mon Matthew. Not Jimmy. He's lost plenty of tournaments. He'll lose again. No, it has to be someone with more passionate hate. Someone like Otto Marx. I mean, the guy was seen strangling Frankenstein only hours before the real murder occurred. Then again, who would do that? Who would be stupid enough to strangle someone in full view of 50 people and then risk doing it again later? And even Otto would be smart enough to use a gun, a knife, something, anything but his hands, after he had already been seen with his hands around the victim's neck.

Then there's the girl, Evelyn. Completely mad? Mad about bridge. If she were the team's biggest supporter, as Jimmy said, why would she knock off one third of the team? I remembered when she first entered the bridge scene, a groupie at the age of 17. She was considered a "10" by most of the pros. And they thought well of her bridge game, besides. But she would need a helper. Motive? Yeah, she's got one — she wants on the team so much that she would knock off anybody, including her old man. Now, c'mon Matthew, don't even think that way. And what in the world would make her believe that Jimmy would replace any departed team members with her? Granted, she's a good player, but Jimmy is not going to add a lunatic to his team.

Then, of course, there were the Stein kids. But the police were on that track, and from what I could tell from first impressions, it was a track leading into a void dummy. No, it had to be a bridge thing. There's where the passions were.

It had to be someone, perhaps, like the coach, a guy who hated the Steins for their archaic four-card-major system. But not the coach, because if the coach were passionate about the game, he was more passionate about winning; and you don't win by strangling your own teammates — especially the strongest pair on the team.

As I continued to sort out the clues, I looked up and found myself at the graveyard of Alexander Hamilton, who was shot to death in a duel about two centuries ago. Probably an overtrick was involved. Maybe a whist game, maybe something bigger. The subway was too close to avoid, so I journeyed down into the cool stale air and covered my ears as the train screeched its way into the station. As I got on board, some fingers wrapped around my elbow. Jinks Barkowsky did not look good. No, I would say he looked like he'd seen a ghost, but then that's what he confided to me as we sat down quickly on the cold aluminum seats.

"I've been following you for the last nine blocks," he added.

"Calm down," I advised. "Why have you been following me?"

"I was afraid someone would see us together."

"Who would see us together?"

"You know, like I told you: Frankenstein."

7

The train doors shut and we headed uptown. I tried my best to calm him down. I used reason, then I tried logic, and finally I had to hit him.

"You're a Rhodes Scholar, Jinks, a math professor, a distinguished scientist. Is it reasonable that you should see a man who was strangled to death five days ago?"

"Not at all, not at all. Only you know nothing ever kept Frankenstein down. Even after the opponents made a game or slam, he would fight like crazy for the next partscore. I tell you, if there's a guy who could come back from the dead, it's he."

"Okay, Jinks, try this on for size. Is it not possible you dreamt him? Maybe you fell asleep for a minute while walking up Broadway. You know how you absentminded professors drift off, start thinking numbers and stars and things. Maybe you were dreaming about a double squeeze and he entered your mind to break it up."

"No, not at all. I was awake the whole time. I was walking past Chemical Bank and there he was, coming down the street, stopping for a hot-dog like he always did. And when we passed each other he gave me a look I'll never forget. My whole body turned to hot jelly. I almost collapsed on top of a teller machine."

With that he began to shake again, but most of the passengers did not pay heed. The way the train was winding its way forward, half-crashing into walls and slipping along the edge of the tracks, there were a lot of people shaking. Unfortunately there was only one way to stop him, so I gave him a slap across the kisser and his eyes turned green again. There being not many good Samaritans hanging out in the subways, I think I could've given Jinks a bloody nose and still been ignored.

We got out at 23rd Street and headed over a block toward Metropolitan Life. Across the street was an innocent looking apartment building, where the Mayfair Club was carefully clothed. We buzzed our way in and I uttered a little prayer to nobody in particular (or so I thought), when suddenly I felt the icy air-conditioning against my sweat-stained face. Jinks went straight into the back room where some of the internationalists were playing for stakes they couldn't afford. Little did I realize that this was the last time I'd see Jinks, at least in this world.

"Can I get you a cup of fresh coffee? A sandwich? Whatever you want."

Al Roth was our host, and as he walked around the club's dining room in his poised but swift gait, I couldn't help but wonder what keeps motivating the now 72-year-old bridge legend. He gave up playing the game seriously about 10 years ago. Now he still runs the club, which deals mostly in poker and backgammon. Every once in a while, though, he reinstates the late-night imp cut-around game, the original training ground for many New York experts.

I remember the first time I played in it. It was like entering
a den of lions. Coming from the duplicate bridge world, I felt
the sensation of excitement on every hand, every bid and
play. The stake in those days was $2 an imp, and $100 could
easily be won or lost in an evening. Because I had about $20
to my name, I *had* to win to survive my debut and keep my
account above water.

I was 19 years old and I remember the moment I first asked
Al if I could join the game. "You want to play imps, kid? Take
my advice and stick to the penny rubber bridge for a while."
So I kibitzed, and even that was nerve-racking. The next
night I stayed late, hung around the back room and made like
I belonged. When the count of players was 11, Al said he
would make up the 12th. But then a man named Otto Marx,
a recent Hungarian immigrant who worked part-time as the
building's janitor while studying to be a chemist, pointed to
me and asked if the kid with the acne had been counted. I
tried to look nonchalant, but my insides were buzzing. Yeah,
yeah, someone said, let him in. "What's your name, kid?"
someone asked. "Uh, Granovetter — with an 'e-r'." "We don't
have enough letters for that."

On a rectangle magnetic board, posted on the wall, were
names of players on individual 3-by-5-inch tags. Next to each
name, Roth wrote a number from 1 to 6. Somebody stuck
together a tag that read "GRANO" and, after consulting
Roth, added a 5 to it. A man named Dr. B., who I knew from
the penny game, instantly complained. How the hell could
this new kid's handicap be less than his? (Dr. B. had a 6-imp
handicap, and it never improved for as long as I knew him.)
Word suddenly seeped into the back room from the front
office that Roth said I wasn't as bad as I looked. (This little
bit of praise from the great master left me in a state of
euphoria for days.) Soon all the tags were taken down from

the scoreboard, turned upside-down on a card table and shuffled by Roth himself. Then piles of four were turned over in three stacks, indicating the three teams for round one. Almost everyone groaned about his team. I looked sheepishly at my squad. I knew two of the players from the rubber games, and I innocently placed myself in their general vicinity, just to let them know I was ready and able to be matched up with a partner. My team was Frankenstein (handicap of 1), Jimmy Cayne (handicap of 2), and Gussie Addles (handicap of 5). I knew Gussie and Frankenstein, but had yet to meet Cayne.

Eventually the three of them looked up at me, and Frankenstein quickly complained to Roth how could he possibly give a newcomer anything lower than a 6. Gussie, who had been playing bridge and whist for give or take 70 years, was also a bit peeved for having the same number. I overheard Cayne suggest to Frank that I partner Gussie. Actually the way he put it was: Let the two goofballs play and we'll hope they cancel each other out.

I knew Gussie was an underbidder and set my mind to the task of bidding a little of her hand as well as my own. I went to get coffee, spilled it immediately across my pants, and sat down at table one, East.

The three tables were spread out, two in each corner of the back room and one in the front. Gussie and I would play East-West at tables 1 and 2, four boards against each team, while Cayne and Frankenstein fought it out at table 3, North-South. And when I say fought it out, I mean with each other. Later that season, I learned from Victor the importance at the Mayfair of beating your partner to the correct post-mortem analysis. You see, it wasn't enough to play well if you wanted the respect of the other players — no, you had to analyze well, and fast. It was all part of the action, part of the "fun."

I can't remember all of the hands that first round, but we won both matches, as fate would have it — and I say that because had fate dealt me losses on the first round that night, I would have had to quit, go to work for a living, and maybe have an entirely different life! But having won the first matches, I was comfortably ahead and could allow my name tag to be shuffled into countless more imp games.

The way the scoring worked was this: First we compared each board with our teammates' score and then *imped* it against the imp scale. The imp scale can be found inside most duplicate convention cards. It looks like this:

International Match Point Scale

Difference in Points	Imps	Difference in Points	Imps
20-40	1	750-890	13
50-80	2	900-1090	14
90-120	3	1100-1290	15
130-160	4	1300-1490	16
170-210	5	1500-1740	17
220-260	6	1750-1990	18
270-310	7	2000-2240	19
320-360	8	2250-2490	20
370-420	9	2500-2990	21
430-490	10	3000-3490	22
500-590	11	3500-3990	23
600-740	12	4000 and up	24

The scale works by adding the scores of both pairs on your team and finding the total on the Difference-in-Points column. Say that you score plus 200 for defeating a three-spade contract two tricks, vulnerable, and your teammates go down only one trick in the same contract at the other table. The scores add to 100 (+200 and -100). You look for 100 in the Difference-in-Points column and see that 100 falls between 90-120 and is converted to 3 imps. Your team wins 3 imps. The other team loses 3. It's as simple as that.

Notice that the higher the Difference-in-Points on a board, the more difficult it is to win imps. The imp scale was well calculated to reduce the chance of one deal making or breaking a match. Three 5-imp part-score victories can offset one 15-imp slam disaster. Without the conversion to imps, however, it would be much more difficult for a team that lost a slam swing to fight back. The slam disaster would be about minus 1500 total points, while the three partscores would add to about 500 points.

Besides *imping* each deal's result in the late-night cut-around game, we also had to total the four imp scores of each match, add or subtract our team's handicap difference from the other team's handicap, and then add or subtract 3 more imps per match, depending on whether we won or lost. Finally, after screaming, yelling, or gloating for an appropriate period of time, we totaled the whole thing up and multiplied by $2 to see how we made out financially.

I won about $76 the first match I played, and was called a moron only once by my teammates, which was pretty good. In fact, I continued to be lucky (I thought, skillful) and finished the night with a money score of $166. This was more money than I had ever heard of and I even paid for my own share of dinner that night (morning, really — I am speaking of 3 a.m.) in Chinatown, where the players often went following the imp game.

It was not all high finance and glory, however — it was also a learning experience that very few bridge players obtain in their lifetime. It was not only a learning ground, but a killing field of the imp variety, where your mistakes were highlighted by the loud and unrelenting, unsympathetic partners, teammates and opponents. You were mentally rated on every move, and you could not help but improve if you had any talent whatsoever. Some of you readers may want to contrast this with your own early experiences at the bridge table, which were probably far more gentlemanly or ladylike. Good manners were not part of this game, and if a wealthy bridge student (who perhaps was used to being coddled by his professional teacher/partner in the duplicate arena) happened by one evening and entered the fray, he quickly learned that he had joined the great equalizer, that his worldly money and powers would serve him no good as he was stripped naked, cut and swallowed by the likes of Frankenstein, Cayne and the other pleasant fellowship of the Mayfair.

My first lesson on imps came that first night during round two. I was partnered with Cayne, who had the choice of playing with Dr. B., Otto Marx or me, and was thus forced into a corner.

The lesson centered around the risk/reward ratio of the imp scale. I was feeling a little loose from my success in round one, so I made a typical matchpoint overcall that put me in the hot seat later in the auction. See if you can tell exactly where I went wrong. I held:

♠ A Q 10 2   ♡ 5 2   ◇ A 9 8 7 6   ♣ 9 8

We were at favorable vulnerability, and the dealer to my right (Frankenstein, for the record) opened one club. I overcalled one spade (not one diamond), and Otto Marx, to my left, bid two hearts. Cayne, my partner, jumped to four spades and Frankenstein, on my right, bid five hearts. I passed, pleased with my side's excellent defensive bidding — after all, we had pushed them up to the five-level, where we had a chance to beat them — when the bidding continued pass on my left and five spades by Cayne. Frankenstein doubled, ending the auction. Here was the whole deal:

Cayne
♠ K 9 7 6 5
♡ 6
♢ 2
♣ Q J 10 4 3 2

Marx
♠ 8 3
♡ K Q 10 9 8 4
♢ K J 5 4 3
♣ —

Stein
♠ J 4
♡ A J 7 3
♢ Q 10
♣ A K 7 6 5

Young Granovetter
♠ A Q 10 2
♡ 5 2
♢ A 9 8 7 6
♣ 9 8

Marx led the ♡K. Frankenstein overtook, cashed two high clubs and played a third one. I ruffed with the ♠Q, cashed the ♠A and finessed dummy's ♠9, losing my fourth trick. I was down two, minus 300 points. Meanwhile, we could have defeated five hearts two tricks! After a diamond or spade lead from Cayne, we would score the ♢A, a diamond ruff in his hand, plus two spade tricks. Well, reader, where had I gone wrong?

Cayne was gentle on me. He put it this way: "Don't show up here again."

After the red around my eyes subsided to an embarrassing shade of pink, he gave it to me straight: "You should've doubled five hearts — to stop me."

Needless to say, being the punk I was, I was in no position (psychologically) to double a player like Frank Stein at the five-level with only two sure tricks. And, tactically speaking, it was something I would never dream of doing at matchpoints, my weaning ground during my teenage years. The lesson of matchpoints was to push them to the five-level and try to beat them. But at imps, there was more to it, because the sacrifice might be worth 4 or 8 imps. For example, had they been cold for five hearts (650), and our teammates been in it, we would have scored 650 minus 300, or 350 net, for a gain of 8 imps. Had we gone down three tricks, minus 500 against a vulnerable 650, we would still score a net (as a team) of 150 points, which is 4 imps on the imp scale.

East dealer
East-West vulnerable

North (Cayne)
♠ K 9 7 6 5
♡ 6
♢ 2
♣ Q J 10 4 3 2

West (Marx)
♠ 8 3
♡ K Q 10 9 8 4
♢ K J 5 4 3
♣ —

East (Frankenstein)
♠ J 4
♡ A J 7 3
♢ Q 10
♣ A K 7 6 5

South (Young Granovetter)
♠ A Q 10 2
♡ 5 2
♢ A 9 8 7 6
♣ 9 8

Marx	Cayne	Stein	Granovetter
West	North	East	South
—	—	1 ♣	1 ♠
2 ♡	4 ♠	5 ♡	pass
pass	5 ♠	double	(all pass)

Meanwhile, I had committed a cardinal sin of the Mayfair Imp Game: I had made my partner go wrong — I had made *him* look like the fool. The lesson was not: Be conservative and overcall one diamond on these hands. No, far from it. The lesson was that once you make a bid that deceives partner about the length of your suit (in this case, the spade suit), you must do something to warn him, if there is a chance that he is still involved. Not only was there the possibility of us cashing two spade tricks, but, as Cayne put it, "When I jumped to four spades, didn't it occur to you that I rated to have a singleton, and that that singleton was likely to be in your long suit?"

It had not occurred to me. I had been bidding by rote: Get in quickly at the one-level, and let them have it at the five-level.

Later that night, over Chinese, I mentioned the notion that had I held a fifth spade and gone down only one trick in five spades, they would still be down at five hearts, and yet I would not have doubled them, and Cayne's five-spade bid would still have been a loser. It was perhaps a mistake to mention this to some hard-nosed veterans in the middle of a 3 a.m. chop-suey feast; and indeed, got me egg foo young in my face, as Cayne commented that a player who lost a trump trick with our combined holdings was not of mental capabilities to determine the chance of a 6-5 yarborough producing setting tricks.

And, the final lesson of the hand, which did not occur to me until I was home in bed dreaming, was never to underestimate your opponents. While I had been mentally gloating in the bidding (at the five-level) at having pushed them up with my so-called daring favorable-vulnerability one-spade over-call, it had really been my opponent (Frankenstein) who had pushed *us* up, at *un*favorable vulnerability!

I had a lot to learn.

8

"Cream or milk?" asked Roth a second time.

"Sorry," I said, "I was just thinking about the old days. I'll take it black."

We sat down and I asked him if he minded if I took notes as we talked. He handed me a pad and pencil.

"I've got lots of good bridge hands," he said, eagerly.

"No, I meant notes about the murders."

"The police already took notes," he said. "Let's discuss my new bidding methods."

I was desperate for more clues, not bidding methods. "How do you think the murders will affect the U.S. team's chances in the Bermuda Bowl?"

"Chances?" said Roth. "What chances? They'd be lucky to beat my two-cent players."

I nodded, though I didn't think the situation was that bad.

"They lost their two best players," continued Roth, "the only two players who ever left my club with plus accounts."

That was interesting, I thought. I wondered if Roth would

let me see the books. But he did me one better.

"He was plus $400. And she was plus $2,500."

"Really," I said.

"Yeah, that's why I let her son play on the account."

Hmm, so the kid wasn't so nonchalant about the game as he made out.

Roth continued: "On the other hand, it's tough for any of those foreign teams to win, so maybe Jimmy's team will win by default. If they would only listen to me, they would have an easy time of it."

"They have a coach, you know," I said, stirring up trouble.

"Coach? That wimp? He's got them all crazy. When I had Sontag listening to me, he could at least detect an opening bid. Now he's lost it — completely lost it." Al moved his big wide palm across my face. It was like the whole world had changed color in front of him. Either that, or he was swatting flies.

"Everything is a problem, where there used to be no problem. Every bid on the second and third round of an auction is suddenly a frightening proposition. He's gotta keep back-tracking, whispering, watching every step, every move, 'cause he's afraid, scared, completely intimidated."

"True," I said. "But you can't blame him after two of his teammates are strangled to death."

"What are ya talking about?" asked Roth, suddenly. "I'm talking about afraid of his opening bid."

For 40 years, Roth has advocated the sound opening bid as the base for building secure bidding sequences. His critics have attacked him for losing on hands that don't meet his solid requirements, hands that never get a chance to get in the bidding after the first-round pass. Roth has countered that the critics don't appreciate the vast number of plus scores that his style achieves, because they haven't tried it themselves. His critics concede that Roth's system may be okay for team games, for imps, but at matchpoints you can't survive without getting into the auction with light hands. Roth counters that nobody has won more matchpoint events than he and that the secret to winning at matchpoints is to play a style a little different from the other players. Also, by passing a hand others would open, you have a chance to listen to the bidding and learn clues for the play of the hand, should you eventually declare.

I asked Roth what he'd been working on. He took me into the office and handed me a copy of his next article for Bridge Today Magazine. His new series, Ask Doctor Roth, was becoming quite controversial, because readers liked his conservative stance in a world overflowing with liberalism.

Yet Roth is still the inventor. When I asked him if he had any other clues on the case that he could help me with, he motioned me to his filing cabinet. "Come here," he said, his finger waving. "I've got some new gadgets you might want to try."

The first was a new way to bid over our one-notrump openings.

"Look at this," he said.

I looked. It was just another bridge hand.

♠ x
♡ A x x x x
◊ K x x x x
♣ x x

"Partner opens one notrump. What do you do?"

"Well, I could transfer to hearts and . . . "

"See any other ideas?"

"Well, I could start with non-forcing Stayman and rebid two hearts."

"Forget non-forcing Stayman. Besides, if partner has four spades, he's gonna bid two spades, and even if he bids two diamonds, and you bid two hearts, he's gonna pass if you play it not forcing."

"So what's wrong with that?" I asked, getting very tired of this.

"You're still a child. You're cold for seven diamonds!"
The other hand was:

♠ A x x
♡ K Q
◇ A x x x x
♣ A x x

He was right. But how do you bid these two hands to seven diamonds?

"You don't have to get to seven to do well. If I get to six diamonds, I'll get a great score. If I get to five diamonds, I'll probably do well at imps or matchpoints!"

Then he wrote down the auction:

1 NT   2 ◇ (transfer to hearts)
2 ♡   3 ◇ (not forcing)
6 ◇

Yes, if you played the rebid of three diamonds as not forcing, you could succeed. I then demanded to know what I would do if I had a hand that wanted to force. Al pointed to the next auction in his notes.

1 NT   2 ◇ (transfer)
2 ♡   2 ♠ (artificial, game force)

Not your everyday sequence, I thought. Still, you're not losing much. Then Al demonstrated another spectacular hand:

♠ A J x	♠ x x
♡ K x	♡ A x x x x x
◊ K x x	◊ A x
♣ A Q 10 x x	♣ K J x

1 NT	2 ◊
2 ♡	2 ♠
3 ♣	4 ♣
4 NT	5 ♡
7 ♣	

Al was certainly conjuring up a lot of grand slams these days. But he made his point again. "Even if you reach a small slam, you will win 10 or 13 imps against an expert team that stops in four hearts."

"Not bad," I said. "Any other goodies?"

"Ah, suddenly you're interested, huh? Here. How do you bid this hand after partner opens two clubs?"

♠ x x
♡ Q J x x
◊ x x
♣ K J 10 x x

"I bid two diamonds, waiting for now."

"You'll wait, don't worry. Partner comes back with two spades."

"Well, I can't bid three clubs — that's double negative — so I bid two notrump for now."

"Partner bids three spades."

"I bid four clubs . . . maybe."

"Whatever that means! Now look how I bid the two hands."

♠ A K x x x x	♠ x x
♡ K x	♡ Q J x x
◊ A K	♣ x x
♣ A Q x	♣ K J 10 x x

2 ♣	3 ♣ (less than a positive)
4 NT	5 ♣
6 ♣	

"And what do you do with a positive response?" I challenged.

"I bid two diamonds. That shows all positive hands, at least an ace and a king or an ace and two queens. Two hearts is a negative and the other bids are natural suits, but less than a positive. These are the types of hands that responder usually picks up opposite a two-club opener, so these are the types of definitions I use."

"Fine," I said, "but give me something in the cardplay." I knew Roth preferred to discuss bidding, but I was tired of his new gadgets that always had perfect examples to go along with them.

"Cardplay? Cardplay? There's nothing new in cardplay. In fact, everyone is playing worse and worse. It's a myth that today's stars are great cardplayers. In my day, Stone and the rest of them outshone everyone today. Here — here's a play you could use someday. It was a favorite of Phil Feldesman in the old days."

Al scribbled on the pad:

♠ Q x x x
♡ x x
◊ J 10 x x x
♣ x x

♠ K x
♡ A Q
◊ A K Q x x
♣ Q J 10

"You reach three notrump and lefty leads a heart. How do you play?"

I studied the diagram. I don't know, dammit. I have only seven tricks, and if I go after clubs, that's all I'll make. I can make one more in spades. "Okay, I go to dummy in diamonds and lead a spade to the king; if East has the ace, maybe he'll jump up to win the trick and return a heart. Otherwise, maybe it's a doubleton and I can duck one on the way back, setting up two spade tricks. How'd I do?"

Roth shook his head.

"You were right at least about needing two spade tricks. But the easiest way to get them is if the ♠A is on your *left*. You win the lead, cash the king of diamonds and if West has a singleton diamond, or better yet, a void, you're halfway home."

"What? What do the diamonds have to do with it?"

"West thinks you want to finesse his partner for the queen. You lead the ♠K, in a so-called attempt to get to dummy. West ducks his ace and waits for the second round. There's your two spade tricks."

Suddenly there was a loud cry from the back room. We went to check on the proceedings. "Must be the cutthroat game," said Roth. "Some of the foreigners are having fun."

9

Some of the furnishings were new. Some of the people were new. But the place still smelled of delicious stale sweat, which clung to the wallpaper from the long late hours of cardplay. I wondered which chair Frank and Charlotte had choked to death in.

A throng of standing kibitzers was arguing around the corner bridge table, while the poker crowd in the other part of the room ignored them, splashing chips on a table. I could tell you what the argument was about if I understood Chinese, because half of them were from the Chinese bridge team. A cloud of smoke covered the table itself, and half hid the heads of the players. I couldn't make out Jinks in there — perhaps he had gone outside for a walk. One pair was obviously Russian, one Joe calling the other Vladichek, while Vladichek kept referring to Pladichek. Their opponents were made up of one guy I didn't recognize — a middle-aged man with a mustache and dark glasses — and a toothless bum with a young face but gray hair. It soon occurred to me that the bum was no bum, but was Irving Rose, of London, an old bridge acquaintance of mine. I moved in to say hello.

"Bloody well done, bloody well done!"

Suddenly emerging from the Chinese was Otto Marx. "It's a clazy ting," said Otto. "I can't understand what they say, and they can't understand what I say!"

Two kibitzers were also Russian. I could tell because each one was carrying a bag of caviar and at first I thought the excitement was over the sale price of fish eggs rather than the final contract.

"Granovetter!" said Irving. "Ever see a hand like this?"

I looked down at the table where the players had spread their cards. Obviously a claim had been made at trick two.

North
♠ 6 2
♡ —
◇ 7 4 3 2
♣ A K Q J 8 6 4

West
♠ Q J 9 8 5 4 3
♡ 5 4 3 2
◇ K 9
♣ —

East
♠ —
♡ A Q J 9 7
◇ J 10 8 6 5
♣ 5 3 2

South (Irving)
♠ A K 10 7
♡ K 10 8 6
◇ A Q
♣ 10 9 7

Vladichek	Mustache	Pladichek	Irving
West	North	East	South
2 NT	3 NT	4 NT	5 NT
(all pass)			

The auction was quickly explained to us. East-West, a

Soviet pair, were playing a system based on the Slavic Club, in which the opening bid of two notrump showed a preempt in an unknown suit with a four-card suit on the side. North bid three notrump in an attempt to prevent East from locating either of West's suits. East bid four notrump to ask his partner to bid his lower suit and Irving, unsure whether his partner was showing the minors or a solid suit, and under the influence of a "wee bit of jet lag" besides, concluded the fascinating auction with a five-notrump call. Everyone passed, demonstrating the top-level discipline of describing one's hand and then shutting up for the rest of the auction. It's discipline like this that wins imp matches, said one of the English-speaking Chinese in the crowd.

Roth took me aside to offer his view. "Not one of them has his bid," said Al. "Irving comes closest. In my day, we never had auctions like this, and if we did, we would finish them off with a double."

By the way, the play of the hand was over at the end of trick one. Vladichek (West) had led the ♠Q out of turn — he didn't realize that North had bid the notrump first — and Irving, who had 10 top tricks (two spades, one diamond and seven clubs), ducked the trick. West was endplayed, forced to give declarer his 11th.

The dummy was looking very pale, despite the triumph on the last hand, and when he took off his sunglasses, I barely recognized him. It was Detective Kennedy of the NYPD. I asked him to step outside with me, and he started to argue about the merits of his bid.

"Don't you see? Don't you see? I hoisted them by their own petard. It's the only way to deal with these foreign doodads. You've got to fight fire with fire—"

"Detective Kennedy! Please," I said. "It's me, Granovetter. I need information on the case. Didn't the Commissioner tell you I was coming?"

"Granovetter? Granovetter? Ohh, Granovetter. But come, come, into the street, where nobody can hear."

Outside nobody *could* hear. Traffic was bumper to bumper on Park, and horns were honking. The detective looked like he hadn't slept in days. He smelled worse. But then, if you'd been staked out at the Mayfair Club for three days and nights, you would not smell like roses either.

"I've learned a lot," said Kennedy.

"I'm glad to hear it," I said. "To tell you the truth, this case is impossible."

"The case?" said Kennedy. "I'm talking about the differences between imps, duplicate and rubber."

I first met Detective Kennedy when I was an 18-year-old college punk. It was his first case, and it involved the Stein girl, who had been only seven at the time, her falling out the window at the old Mayfair Club, and later the murder of my own partner during a rubber bridge game. Kennedy had been assigned to the case because of his knowledge of bridge (he was an amateur duplicate player). But now, 20 years later, he was still a homicide detective, assigned to cases that nobody else wanted, and apparently still a bridge hack.

"Did you know that the partscore at imps was worth double the partscore at rubber?"

"Listen, you crazy cop," I answered roughly, trying to shake him up. "We've got to do something about finding the killer. We can't stand around 23rd Street all day and discuss imp strategies."

"That's the trouble!" he said, his stubbled mouth contorted in anger. "You guys don't care about the partscores! You lose a million matches by one, two, three imps and then you think, 'games and slams, games and slams, that's all that counts.' Do you realize, Granovetter, that in the last two nights I've lost nine — NINE — consecutive imp matches by less than a single partscore swing!"

He was delirious now. I looked at my watch. Five-thirty. And I still had a date with the city morgue. It could wait, I thought.

"Where do you live?" I asked.

"Live?" he asked, rubbing his red eyes.

"Yeah, live, reside, abode, the wife and kids, apple pie, Nintendo. . . ."

The cab drove to the Long Island address that I found in his wallet. On the way there, Kennedy told me that Charlotte entered the Mayfair Club a few minutes past midnight Monday morning, after an evening of imp pairs at the Cavendish Club uptown. She sat down in her favorite seat, put her head down on the table and fell asleep.

Meanwhile he joined in the cut-around imp game (they used the poker table rather than disturb Charlotte) and lost all six matches. Then he went to Chinatown with the rest of the players. When he got back, Charlotte was still asleep and he went to sleep, also. Later in the morning, the janitor tried to wake her and it was discovered that she had been strangled.

Traffic was slow, and the Detective, after asking if I had seen Jordan (his junior partner), rested his head in my lap and fell asleep. I found the autopsy report in his inside jacket pocket.

Charlotte Stein had been strangled in the same manner as her husband, with a material of soft leather or cloth, not with human hands. Both Steins had also been drugged. The only difference in deaths had been the cards found on their bodies. Frank had actually choked partially on the 4◊ bidding-box card that had been placed inside his mouth. Charlotte had the ◊8 playing card pinned to the top button of her blouse. She had been a modest dresser, but I knew her background — she certainly had not been a modest dame. Okay, I thought, that was 20 years ago when she tried to seduce you — people change. In fact, her bridge game had changed, so anything was possible. She had been raised a fanatical Roth-Stoner, inflexible, stubborn and ungiving in even the simplest two-suited auctions. I remembered one now. She had been my partner in a Swiss Teams. We were both pros, on a team with Frank and his sponsor.

Matthew	Charlotte
♠ A K J x x	♠ Q 10
♡ x x	♡ x x x x
◊ A K 10 x x	◊ Q J
♣ x	♣ x x x x x
1 ♠	1 NT
2 ◊	2 ♠
3 ◊	3 ♠
pass	

I had rebid diamonds, giving it one more shot to get to game — if her hand matched. She bid three spades. I passed. Diamonds were 4-2 and we still made 10 tricks. She was furious with me for not having bid the game myself over her three-spade preference. We lost the match on this deal, and when I suggested she bid four spades over three diamonds, she told Frank never to hire me again.

Suddenly, as the cab stopped, I started to sweat. It dawned on me that *I* had had the five-point hand, not Charlotte. And that *I* was the one who hadn't evaluated properly. What was wrong with me? The usual bridge player's ego, I supposed. I had been so bad on the hand that as the years passed my mind had twisted the scenario so that I could sleep at night without the dreaded little voice in my ear telling me what a bad bid I had made.

No, Charlotte's game was not the one that changed. Mine was. She had continued to improve with age, both in her bidding and her cardplay, which is why it didn't make sense what happened the night she was strangled. The hand she had gone down on was in the News obit section, and just as I was about to peruse it, the cab driver said, "That'll be $48, bub." I told him to wait. He told me he doesn't wait. I told him we were cops. He told me to prove it. I flipped him my I.D. He told me he'd wait. I gave Kennedy a small shot of whiskey that the driver had in his front seat, and he revived.

The house was not a house, it was a mansion. I was afraid I was at the wrong place, but his key worked fine. I dropped Kennedy off on his couch, where he went back to sleep in a hurry. Then I moseyed on out to the pool, where four teenagers, two girls and two boys, were half-innocently splashing around in the deep end. They didn't notice me or care as I ventured further. Behind the pool was a cozy beach and a private dock to the Long Island Sound. A houseboat was anchored with the name, "The Finesse," written across the starboard. I walked back to the pool and almost stepped on someone. Lying face down on a towel with only the bottom of the bikini showing must have been the good detective's wife.

"Don't get up," I said, as I passed by her sunglasses.

She didn't.

"Pretty little place you have on a cop's salary," I continued, trying to make friends.

"I'm not a cop," she answered. "Are you a cop?"

"I'm working on the case with your husband, who, by the way, I brought home and just laid to rest on the couch."

"So, you're a babysitter."

"You're good," I said, "you're really good."

"I'm better than you think." She leaned on her elbows, placed her palm up across her eyes to shield the early evening sun, and gently whistled. Two Dobermans, who hadn't had their dinner, emerged from underneath some lounge chairs. I smiled sweetly and tiptoed back from whence I came, without even waving goodbye.

Back in the city, the taxi was speeding along again, weaving in and out of the dusk traffic. The paper's account of Charlotte's last hand was short and, I hoped, accurate. For there was the name Otto Marx, once again.

West dealer
North-South vulnerable

```
                    North
                    ♠ J 9 8
                    ♡ J 9 2
                    ◇ A 9 4
                    ♣ K Q 10 5
West                                East
♠ 3                                 ♠ A Q 10 7 6 5 4
♡ Q 7 6 5 4 3                       ♡ 10
◇ 8 5                               ◇ 3
♣ A 9 8 2                           ♣ J 7 6 4
                    South
                    ♠ K 2
                    ♡ A K 8
                    ◇ K Q J 10 7 6 2
                    ♣ 3
```

West	North	East	South
pass	pass	3 ♠	4 ◇
pass	5 ◇	(all pass)	

West led the ♠3 and when East won the ace, Mrs. Stein (South) dropped the king. This was a normal play for the U.S. champion, considered by many to have been this country's best female player. East, thinking that West had started with the ♠3-2 doubleton, switched to the ♡10. Mrs. Stein won in hand, cashed two high trumps and led the ♣3. West, Otto Marx, found the only play to defeat the contract. He ducked his ace. When dummy's queen held, declarer was in trouble.

Desperately, she led a club and ruffed it. Then she returned to dummy with a trump and led the ♣Q, hoping that East had started with three clubs to the jack. In that case the ♣J would fall and she could discard a major-suit loser on the trick. West would win his ace, but another club winner would be established in dummy. East, however, had four clubs, and no loser-on-loser play materialized.

Critics pointed out that Mrs. Stein had not been up to her usual snuff. "There was," said the kibitzer, who is the coach of the U.S. international team that Mrs. Stein was due to play on, "a simple alternative after the ♣Q held. She had only to lead out the heart suit. On the third round West wins but is endplayed."

It was a good point, I thought. Another line of play was to play out all the trumps and then lead the club up. West would be forced to come down to two clubs and two hearts. Dummy would hold three clubs and one heart. She leads a club, and even if West ducks, she can lead another club to endplay him.

There was something bothering me about the hand, but before I could put my mind to it, we were in front of the Caynes' apartment building. The fare was $97 . . . plus tip.

Upstairs, in the Cayne living room, there was a commotion. They were fighting about the very same hand.

Sonty: "That's not the hand, I keep telling you. It must have been fouled. East had the heart queen and the ten and the three. I held the hand at my table. You think I can't remember it? My shape was 7-3-1-2. I opened three spades in third seat, the hand on my left bid three notrump, my partner, Mrs. Mendelsohn, bid four spades—"

"On a singleton?"

"Yes, Mrs. Mendelsohn loves it when I play the hand, loves

it! Then the guy to my right doubled. So there I was in four spades doubled."

"What happened?"

"What do you think happened? Mrs. Mendelson put her dummy down and I claimed down six. You don't think I was going to play it out, do you?"

"This is all nonsense," said Jimmy, who was sitting in his boxer shorts, knee-high golf socks, and white shirt. Jimmy was never one to be overly dressed for the occasion, and, in fact, enjoyed the freedom of casual dress after a hard day's work at the office. "The whole point of the hand is West's failure to double. If he doubles, then leads a spade, it's a guaranteed singleton."

"C'mon, Jimmy," said Sonty, "you don't expect anybody to think declarer is dropping the king with king and one."

"Why not? It's a baby play. It's automatic. AU-TO-MA-TIC. What has declarer to lose?"

I couldn't help but remember that it was Jimmy who taught me the trick of doubling the final contract to alert partner that you're leading a singleton. It's a good concept — but rarely used because of the danger of their making a lot of doubled contracts. After all, there is no guarantee that partner has the ace of the suit he bid.

It is also a rarely used concept because most players are still caught up with matchpoint philosophy during team events. They just can't shake it, and the coach keyed in on this.

"I dare say, you don't expect a player like the West fellow to have the guts to double, do you? He's probably played duplicate his whole life, with a few imp games here or there sprinkled in. He would abhor the idea of doubling as a gamble; he would be too afraid of their making it for a bottom. He doesn't realize that there are no bottoms at imps, just amounts of points to be won or lost. For that matter, he cannot imagine the ratio of imps lost to imps gained by making a percentage double."

"I thought the paper said that Otto was West."

The coach turned to me. "No, he was North. The paper botched everything. They didn't even print my name, for God's sake!"

"Where are the Mitchells?" asked Patty, who had just breezed in with a tray of pink lemonade. "Well, don't we look dapper this evening," she said to the coach. He had on a flowery sort of shirt, with a fresh, yellow ascot under a navy blue blazer, with one of those stupid captain signs on the lapel.

"Anybody hear from Belsky?" I asked. I was getting worried.

"Yeah, where's Belsky? asked Jimmy. "For that matter, who's Belsky? Oh yeah, he's your partner."

"Jinks is missing as well," said Patty. "But I think I heard from Belsky."

"There are the Mitchells at the door," said Sonty.

"You've got to calculate it," continued the coach, talking to no one now but perhaps the piano stand. "If they don't redouble — and they so rarely do — your downside is about minus 750, a loss of 150 from the expected 600 at the other table, or 4 imps. On the other hand, if you defeat a game that you would otherwise have let make, you receive 200 instead of minus 600, for a win of 13 imps. Why, it's more than three to one to double in these situations — three to one."

"You've got to put on pants," said Patty.

"You've got to call the Mitchells and tell them they're late," said Jimmy.

"We're here," said Jacqui.

We all looked up. Yes, there were Jacqui and Victor, and with them were three others, two Siberian huskies and one Barkowsky — but not Jinks. No, his daughter Evelyn was standing next to Victor, her long hair touching Victor's ear, her long fingers playing music around one of the leashes.

10

Before I could get my hellos in, Jacqui had me in the corner for a private word.

"Listen to me, Matthew," she said, in a strong, harsh whisper. "I don't mind your playing detective and all that — although I don't understand why your wife has allowed it — but that's your business. Meanwhile, you have to do me one favor if you want me to cooperate."

"What's that, Jacqui?"

"Keep that girl away from Victor. If I see her hanging around my house or dogs again, you're gonna have another murder to investigate."

Victor went to light a Camel, and when he couldn't find his matches, Evelyn was there lighting it for him. In the meantime Jacqui had unpacked a chocolate cream pie she had whipped up for the affair and sent it into the kitchen with the housekeeper. The dogs were under the card table, panting, and the coach moved over to Evelyn and whispered something in her ear. It was not a sweet nothing — I can tell you that. She took the leash that had been in her hand, folded it over and made like she was going to brand him for life. He stepped briskly away, more agile than I would have given him credit for.

I greeted Victor with a nod and he stared back through his dark glasses and puffed away. Finally he moved the Camel to the side of his mouth and said, "You look like a truck ran over you."

"Thanks, Vic," I said. "It's been a long day."

"I heard about it."

How he heard about it, I don't know, but it was generally assumed that whatever was going on that affected life in the circles of New York bridge was known by the bridge Godfather.

"You made Al very happy," said Victor, "listening to some of his new gadgets."

"Yeah, well, he's still pretty clever."

"Yeah, you go ahead and use 'em."

There was a phone call for me. Maybe it was Belsky. Then I remembered what Patty had said, about him calling earlier. "Why do you think it was Belsky on the phone before?" I asked her as I crossed the room toward the hallway.

"Because it was somebody talking Yiddish."

I picked up the phone in the kitchen. It was my wife.

"Well, have you solved the case?"

"How could I solve the case? It hasn't even been 24 hours."

"Well, c'mon, you can't take forever. Besides, we're invited to Shabbos next weekend at Rabbi Rubin's."

"Shabbos?! For crying out loud, suddenly we're celebrating the Sabbath? Jimmy's tournament begins tomorrow and goes through the weekend. I've got to be there for as long as it takes to catch the killer."

"The Sabbath is in the Ten Commandments, isn't it? Along with murder and stealing."

"Oy *vey*. I don't think Sherlock Holmes could solve this case before *Shabbos*. You'd better come down. This thing is liable to blow sky-high any minute and Jimmy may need all the help he can get."

"I'll sky-high your nose. I'm not bringing the children into the middle of Manhattan while you're involved in one of your murder cases. (Pause.) Look, I'll check the train schedule. If I can, I'll make it down there tomorrow."

"Okay. I'll tell Patty you're coming."

"Wait. Before I go, Mrs. Belsky wants to talk with Mr. Belsky."

"No can do. Mr. Belsky isn't here."

"What did you do with Mr. Belsky?" (Stifled cry in the background.)

"I didn't do anything with Mr. Belsky. He was on the Staten Island Ferry the last I saw him. By the way, does he speak Yiddish?" (Footsteps in the kitchen. I turned around. Evelyn was next to me — too close.)

"Now you listen to me, Matthew. Mr. Belsky is your responsibility." (Aside: "There, there, Mrs. B., he's okay, he's on the ferry.")

"No problem. I'll see you tomorrow." (Evelyn holds a Perrier in her left hand, while her right hand starts singing tunes down my back, with an ice cube dripping along the way.)

"Bye."

"Bye." (I turn to Evelyn, swatting her hand.) "You got a problem?"

"No, you do." She dropped the ice into my pants. I stood there and let the water seep through. I considered briefly taking her over my lap, then thought better of it. She was an impossible suspect. How could I avoid her and keep tabs on her at the same time? I wanted to take a close peek at her blouse to see if Belsky's bug was still there, but if I did I'd only egg her on.

86

"You're an eavesdropper," I said, without much wit.

"Cut the crap," she said. "Your wife is coming to town, and if you don't help me look good in front of the team, I'll make her believe things even you've never dreamed of."

I wished her father were here to give her that spanking. But Jinks Barkowsky never showed up, not that night, not the next morning, not ever again. That part of the story, however, will have to wait.

We were there for a practice match. The Bermuda Bowl quarterfinals were concluding tonight and the semifinals would start the following afternoon. Without Jinks Barkowsky, Jacqui had no one to practice with. Evelyn coyly suggested that she sit in for her old man. "After all, I know the system they play better than anyone."

Jacqui admitted that even she (Jacqui) didn't know all of her and Jinks' notes by heart, but suggested that Victor fill in instead. Evelyn countered by pointing to me and saying she would play with me on the other team. I was less than thrilled about this, not only because of our friendly encounter in the kitchen but because Evelyn was looking like she was out to prove something — and that something was that she had the talent and the know-how to play with the best, and if her old man was missing, she was the obvious replacement.

Our teammates would be the coach and Patty. Evelyn and I sat down East-West against Jimmy and Sonty. We would play eight hands and then compare.

Although it sounds ridiculous, this so-called practice match had more tension than a national championship. Here were peers versus peers. All eyes were watching for the slightest error, the minutest blunder. Granovetter, you've lost it. Cayne, you stink. Sonty, keep your hand back. Evelyn . . . well, dammit, where *was* her old man?!

Board One: Three notrump down after the defense takes the first five club tricks.

Board Two: Four hearts down after the defense takes the first four diamond tricks.

Board Three—

All right, I'll run that last one by you again. *Almost* the first four diamond tricks. The deal looked like this:

North
♠ A 8 6 4
♡ K 3 2
◊ Q 10 3
♣ K 7 5

West
♠ J 10 9
♡ Q 9 4
◊ A 9 6
♣ J 10 9 4

East
♠ 7 5 3 2
♡ 6
◊ K J 8 7
♣ 8 6 3 2

South
♠ K Q
♡ A J 10 8 6 5
◊ 5 4 2
♣ A Q

Sonty	Matthew	Jimmy	Evy
South	West	North	East
1 ♡	pass	1 NT	pass
2 ◊	pass	3 ♡	pass
3 ♠	pass	4 ♣	pass
4 ♡	(all pass)		

It was a beautiful auction, but sometimes when you reveal too much, some of the flowers begin to wilt. South rebid two diamonds, temporizing over the forcing-notrump response, and North showed a limit raise with three trumps. South cuebid his spade control, North cuebid his club control and South bid four hearts, denying a diamond control.

I listened carefully to the auction as if it were a concerto and led a low diamond in appreciation. Evelyn won, led a diamond back to me and a third round went to her. Then came the fourth diamond, and they could probably hear it snap out of Evy's hand as far away as Brooklyn.

Sonty had no recourse. He tried ruffing with the ♡10. I discarded, showed my Q-9-x, and claimed down one.

From the conversation afterward, I gathered North-South were playing "Serious 3NT," which means that if either player had bid three notrump, he would be saying that he had a serious slam try — whereas the cuebids were now well-defined as *non*-serious.

I had to admit that without the aid of listening to these non-serious cuebids back and forth in clubs and spades, I might have led one of those two black suits from my J-10-9 combinations.

That only got Jimmy's goat, and he criticized Sonty. "You don't have enough for a non-serious cuebid."

"What do you mean I don't have a non-serious cuebid? It was absolutely non-serious."

"What hand could I have for you to make a slam?"

"How about the ace of diamonds, ace of spades, king of clubs? Is that too much to ask for?"

"You're looking for perfect cards."

"That's what a non-serious cuebid asks for. Had you bid four hearts instead of four clubs on your terrible hand, he would've led a club.

"I can't do that. I have to show you my control."

"Why can't you bid three notrump?" I asked.

"Because they play that as Serious," cried Evelyn, perhaps more in defense of the system than in Jimmy's defense. "He *had* to bid four clubs. It's in the team notes." Or did she have another reason for taking Jimmy's side?

"Yeah," said Jimmy. "It's in the notes. He could have a hand with short diamonds, needing the club king for a slam."

"Maybe we should chuck the notes," said Sonty.

"Maybe we should not worry about an obscure hand like this."

Meanwhile in the other room, the coach was in the South seat. Playing with Patty, he opened one heart and a similar auction developed, that is, up until three hearts, when — not playing any part of the notes — the coach bid three notrump, a natural attempt at an alternative contract. Patty passed. The defense took the first four diamond tricks and then got out with a black suit. Patty cashed the ♡A and ran the jack, successfully.

```
                      North
                      ♠ A 8 6 4
                      ♡ K 3 2
                      ◊ Q 10 3
                      ♣ K 7 5
      West                              East
      ♠ J 10 9                          ♠ 7 5 3 2
      ♡ Q 9 4                           ♡ 6
      ◊ A 9 6                           ◊ K J 8 7
      ♣ J 10 9 4                        ♣ 8 6 3 2
                      South
                      ♠ K Q
                      ♡ A J 10 8 6 5
                      ◊ 5 4 2
                      ♣ A Q
```

Coach	Jacqui	Patty	Victor
South	West	North	East
1 ♡	pass	1 NT	pass
2 ◊	pass	3 ♡	pass
3 NT	(all pass)		

"It may appear to you experts that I played a simple queen-over-jack rule," she said later during the scoring break, "but that wasn't it. I knew we were the weaker team, so I tried for a swing by taking a slightly anti-percentage play. Besides, if the hearts were 2-2, four hearts, the contract likely to be played at the other table, would be cold. As the King Solomon ruling suggested, split the baby in two and what good is it? So I played for the suit to split 3-1. And it did."

"But it didn't have to."

"Ask and you shall receive."

Board 3 was a passed-out hand and Jimmy insisted we not shuffle. He was right. His team won 14 imps on it!

North
♠ A J 8 2
♡ K 7 4 3
♢ 9 8 2
♣ A 4

West
♠ K 4 3
♡ Q 9 8
♢ A 7
♣ J 10 6 5 2

East
♠ Q 9 6
♡ A 10 6 5 2
♢ Q 10 4 3
♣ Q

South
♠ 10 7 5
♡ J
♢ K J 6 5
♣ K 9 8 7 3

Jacqui	Patty	Victor	Coach
West	North	East	South
pass	1 ♢	1 ♡	2 ♢
3 ♡	pass	pass	4 ♣
double	pass	pass	pass

At our table, Jimmy passed the North hand, and everyone else passed as well. At the other table, Patty opened one diamond, Victor overcalled one heart, the coach raised to two diamonds and Jacqui bid three hearts, inviting game. This went around to the coach, who decided the vulnerability was right to push his opponents up one. He bid four clubs. Jacqui doubled, and Patty went to refill the lemonade, forcing the coach to play his own dummy.

Jacqui made the fine lead of the ♡Q. She had supported hearts, and therefore would not be fooling her partner as to the number of hearts she held. It was also likely that declarer, who had both minors, would be short in hearts.

As I was informed later, the coach was appalled at dummy,

but played on anyway, the rules requiring that. He ruffed the second heart and led the ♣7, passing it smoothly to Victor's queen, as Jacqui ducked with only two honors, not three. Victor led a low diamond and the coach smiled as he flew king into Jacqui's waiting ace. Jacqui continued hearts, and declarer ended up with four trump tricks and the ♠A. It wasn't the best-played hand of his career, but then again, as the coach said later, he had very little to work with. He was also a good sport about it and did not blame Patty in the least for opening the bidding. "Mandatory opening, good hand for the weak notrump, too bad. Don't know how James decided to pass the hand, but I hope he sticks to the notes when the championships commence."

"As long as you had to play it," added Patty, with a slightly murderous smile on her lips.

I knew why Jimmy had passed the North hand. It was Mayfair Standard, where 12-point openers are optional, not mandatory. When you have to open on three small, and have to start hiding under the table when partner raises you or bids clubs, maybe you should have second thoughts about opening the bidding in the first place. Sometimes Jimmy remembered the old Mayfair days — good training will always take precedence over "the notes."

"I didn't even consider opening," related Jimmy at the table. "You would have opened, Sonty."

"With that hand?" protested Sonty, fingering through the cards. "Well, maybe I'd put a diamond in with my hearts and open one heart."

"That's *good*, Sonty. It would keep them out of hearts. Then your partner could bid his three-card spade suit and play two spades, the perfect contract."

We all laughed. Except for Evelyn, of course. She had a habit of rubbing her forefinger against her back molars and making squeaking sounds with them. She was doing it now and the pups under the table were not happy about it.

Board four was a great hand for Roth's system, had we been playing it.

North
♠ A
♡ J 8 2
◊ 7 6 5
♣ 8 7 6 5 3 2

West
♠ J 9 8 7 5
♡ Q
◊ K Q 3
♣ A K Q 4

East
♠ Q 6 4 2
♡ A K 10 9
◊ A J 8 4
♣ 9

South
♠ K 10 3
♡ 7 6 5 4 3
◊ 10 9 2
♣ J 10

Matthew	Jimmy	Evy	Sonty
West	North	East	South
1 ♠	pass	4 ♣	pass
4 ◊	pass	4 ♡	pass
4 ♠	pass	5 ◊	pass
5 ♡	pass	5 ♠	(all pass)

Four clubs by Evelyn was a splinter (short clubs) and a game force in spades. I gave it a squeak with four diamonds, because she could easily have had five spades to the ace-king and an ace. She cuebid hearts and diamonds and I showed my second-round heart control. With nothing else up her sleeve — at least bridgewise — she steadied the ship at five spades, and I passed, lacking anything in the trump department.

Jimmy led a club. I won and took a breath. We had stopped

on a dime, but were still in trouble. If the trumps were 2-2, I was okay, but if they were 3-1, I'd better lead through the hand with the singleton if I were going to lead a low one to an honor. Trouble was, I had no clue as to who was likely to be shorter in trumps, Jimmy or Sonty.

Funny how my partner chose this occasion to refill her drink. I could feel the heat of her glare as she passed my shoulder. Finally I led the ♡Q to the ace. Nothing significant happened. Then I decided that if Jimmy had short spades, he might have had a long suit to preempt over one spade, so I led a spade from dummy and when South played low I put up the jack. As you can see, it was not the best play. Sonty still had two more trump tricks, and I was down one.

Before sweetie-pie came back to the table, I pleaded with my opponents to fake the score on the pad. They argued about it for a while, Sonty saying that if I were a real detective, what did I have to fear from an irate dummy? Jimmy knew better and wrote minus 650 on the pad. "But notice," he said, "I did not preempt with my six-card club suit."

Meanwhile at the other table, the Mitchells had bid their way to slam! The coach was not happy about their simple bidding method (1 ♠ - 3 ♠ - 4 ♣ - 6 ♠) — an advocate of Roman Keycard Blackwood since its inception, the coach would have liked to have heard somebody ask for aces and at least stop at the five-level. Unfortunately, the coach's scolding was not heeded as much as it might have been had the slam been defeated. Patty led a club and Jacqui, who was simultaneously needle-pointing and reading a Sue Grafton novel, took time out to saunter over to dummy and lead the ♠Q. The coach covered with the king and Jacqui knew how to handle the suit on the next round.

"Honor your mother and your father," Patty chastised the coach, "not your opponents."

"It's very rare that the opponents are missing the ace and

king of trumps in a slam," said the coach, defensively.

"True," said Patty, "but if you had a little humility, you might have thought about playing low."

In the post mortem, it added up to about 17 imps for the Cayne team. Evy, of course, insisted it was only a swing of 750, 13 imps, and I finally admitted to having gone down in five — it being only a 4-imp mistake now. Evy was a better sport about it than we all gave her credit for. She did not say a bad word to me, but I did not fail to notice that she removed the switchblade that she carried in her left stocking for self-defense, and placed it calmly in her blouse pocket.

Board five was a push board. Both tables stopped in two clubs (a rare feat these days, two clubs usually being some kind of checkback or forcing call).

Board six was one of those hands that comes up every other lifetime. You know, where both sides can make three notrump, depending on the lead. . . .

North
♠ A Q 10 5
♡ 9 7 3
◊ K J 3
♣ 6 3 2

West
♠ K 3
♡ 10 8
◊ 6 5
♣ A Q J 9 7 5 4

East
♠ 9 4 2
♡ K 4 2
◊ A Q 10 9 8 7
♣ 8

South
♠ J 8 7 6
♡ A Q J 6 5
◊ 4 2
♣ K 10

Nobody had a clear opening bid, which made matters worse. In any case, the scenario was this:

1. If West declared three notrump, North's best lead was a heart.

2. If North declared three notrump, East's best lead was a club.

3. If East declared three notrump, South's best lead was a spade.

4. And if South declared three notrump, West's best lead was a diamond.

What did it all mean? I guess that whoever got his suit into the bidding protected his side from disaster.

The best auction might have been:

West	North	East	South
1 ♣	1 ♠	2 ◇	2 ♡

After this, nobody can make anything!

However, our auction was:

Matthew	Jimmy	Evy	Sonty
3 ♣	pass	pass	3 ♡
pass	4 ♡	double	(all pass)

I understood the double as short clubs and led the ace and another club for my partner to ruff. She did. Because I was careful to lead the ♣Q on the second round, she was careful to get out a spade, and sit back and wait for her two diamond tricks. Phew! Got by that one, I thought.

At the other table, Jacqui opened my hand one club, Patty passed, and Victor bid one diamond. The coach overcalled one heart and Jacqui rebid two clubs. Patty bid two hearts and Victor tried two notrump. Jacqui raised to three notrump and the spotlight fell on the coach. Would he, could he, find a spade lead? He thought and thought and finally led . . . the ♣10.

It was an attempt at brilliance, for in all his time spent in America, the coach had never been able to impress Victor Mitchell, and this probably was a good example why. Victor said thank you when dummy came down (nobody was quite sure if he was thanking Jacqui or the coach), and slipped the ♣J over the 10. After some difficult discards by North-South, he took the rest of the tricks and made Patty feel good about the possibility that they had missed a slam.

"Not a grand slam" said Patty. "I've got the ♠A."

North (Patty)
♠ A Q 10 5
♡ 9 7 3
◊ K J 3
♣ 6 3 2

West (Jacqui)
♠ K 3
♡ 10 8
◊ 6 5
♣ A Q J 9 7 5 4

East (Victor)
♠ 9 4 2
♡ K 4 2
◊ A Q 10 9 8 7
♣ 8

South (the coach)
♠ J 8 7 6
♡ A Q J 6 5
◊ 4 2
♣ K 10

The coach's cards were in the duplicate board before Patty could see them.

"And your partner has the ♡A," said Jacqui, who spotted everything despite having read a full chapter of her book.

"Good," said Patty. "Because I'm really rooting for *you* guys. You don't think it will do me any good if *the coach and I* win, do you?"

Board seven never made it to either table. Detective Kennedy was in the doorway, trenchcoat dripping wet from the storm outside.

He was looking better, even with all the water. Patty offered him a drink. He hedged. "I never say no when I'm not on a case."

Nobody knew what that meant exactly, so we tossed him a bottle of Glenlivit and a fresh glass with ice.

Then he announced that he had bad news, very bad.

The coach, however, insisted on comparing boards one through six first. I have to give the coach this much credit: Despite his poor results, he was insistent on analyzing the hands — for the team's benefit.

11

Detective Kennedy was patient. He even went so far as to offer his own views on some of the hands, which led to an argument on board six as to whether the West hand (♠ K 3 ♡ 10 8 ◊ 6 5 ♣ A Q J 9 7 5 4) was a one-club opening bid, a three-club opening bid or a first-seat pass. The coach was insistent that the only way to come close to describing both the preemptive value and medium strength was to employ two-way two-bids.

Some readers may be familiar with the concept. An opening two-bid (two clubs through two spades) shows at least two types of hands: 1) a strong two-bid in the suit opened; or 2) a weak two-bid in the next higher suit. In this case, a bid of two spades would be made, showing a strong two-bid in spades or a weak two-bid in clubs. Partner bids on the assumption (and likelihood) that you hold the weaker type, and signs off in your suit or bids two notrump to ask how good the weak two-bid is.

"This is too good for a weak two-bid," argued Kennedy. We all nodded our heads and the detective's eyes gleamed.

I could see that the man was someone who took his bridge seriously, so seriously that lost in the general ambiance of a practice-match post mortem he had forgotten why he had come — which was, in my recollection, to impart some tragic news.

"You must find a bid that comes closest to representing the hand," said the coach. "Certainly a weak two-bid is better than a pass."

"I disagree," said Jimmy. "If you pass and later back in with clubs, partner will know you were in between a weak two-bid and a one-bid."

"He might think you have a four-card major on the side," argued the coach, "and it might lead to all sorts of implications. Suppose the opponents start bidding and raising hearts, while you overcall in clubs. Now partner thinks you have four spades and bids on that assumption."

"So if he bids four spades, I bid five clubs. Is that so bad? I have a seventh club."

"But the king of spades," said Evelyn, insistently. "Suppose they bid spades and partner plays you for hearts. Now the spade king has defensive potential only."

"Naw, naw," said Jimmy. "They might lead the ace. It may be worth a trick in play and nothing on defense. Isn't that right, Sonty?"

"These theoretical conversations are over my head," said Sonty, his hands up in the air in dismay. "I don't even know what the other hand is and nobody knows what the bidding is."

Victor turned to me.

"Now you see why I won't allow myself to be on this team."

"Victor," said Jacqui, who had been working on her needlepoint more feverishly than Madam deFarge. "Don't you think we should call the Mayfair and at least try to find out where Jinks is?"

"Jinks!" exclaimed Kennedy. "I forgot all about him."

The detective stood up and waved his arm. "Please, ladies and gentlemen and bridge players, please be seated, I have some bad news."

"Bad news," cried Evelyn, her hand to her mouth.

"Yes, yes," said Kennedy. And he walked over to Evelyn and put his hand on her shoulder. "Your father, dear . . . "

"What?" cried Evelyn.

"Stop torturing everyone," said Patty. "Just tell us."

"Ahem. Jinks Barkowsky was found strangled—"

"Oh no!" cried Evelyn.

"Yes, yes, an hour, well, let's see (looks at his watch), no, now maybe an hour-and-a-half ago. He was found in the IRT subway entrance at 23rd Street."

Evelyn began to sob. I watched her closely. I'd been a drama major in college, so I tried to make out whether those tears were true. On the other hand, she could have been using the Stanislovsky method. In fact, I made it my business to observe the rest of the faces in the crowd as well. All expressed deep concern. But that concern could have been as much for the fact that the team had lost another member as that the world had lost a particularly nice guy.

"I hate to say it," said Jimmy, "but we're down to three."

"Jimmy!" chastised Patty.

"I agree with Patty," said Jacqui.

"Tis a pity," said the coach, without defining whether the pity was the loss of Jinks or the fact that the team was down to three players.

Suddenly the doorbell rang. It was loud in the gloomy quiet of the moment. In walked Belsky, his arms around two big brown grocery bags.

"There's more in the elevator," he said to the housekeeper. "I forgot — Where's the kitchen?"

"Belsky," I called out. "Where have you been?"

"Matt!" he said, coming into the library. "I've been to Brooklyn! And, boy, do I have news. You know our two friends who I was following on the Fer—"

"Shh!!!" I motioned to the girl and the coach.

"Ah, yes, . . . but what's the matter?"

Detective Kennedy came forward. "Another member of the team is no longer with us," he explained, as tactfully as he could, for there was no use in pouring fresh salt into Evelyn's wound.

"That's okay," said Mr. Belsky, not fully comprehending the detective's drift, "'cause there'll be enough now for seconds for everyone." Whereupon he began to unpack baloney, salami, corned beef and other delicacies from his bags. "And it's all *glatt* kosher!" he bragged.

I had to hand it to Mr. B. He had come back with the goods that night, albeit edible ones. I had my fill of cream soda and in the middle of a corned beef on rye, when no one was looking, I grabbed my partner's shirt sleeve, edging him into the library.

"You got the car downstairs?" I asked.

"The car? Yeah, of course, that was my old man's car; I would never lose that car."

"Let's go, then."

"Just one second," he said, grabbing a box with a string around it.

"I hope that's the tapes."

"It's the *ruggaluch*."

Outside the rain had let up. A warm breeze was blowing and the raindrops made the cracks on the concrete pavement sparkle in the streetlights. I was exhausted, Belsky was exhausted, but another bridge player had bit the dust and somebody had to pay for it. That somebody was not going to be Jimmy Cayne, if I could help it. The way things were going, if the newsboys ever got a hold of this story, he was gonna be *numero uno* in the frame-up department. Who else was a close friend of the Commissioner of police? Why else would the police put a man like Kennedy in charge — an obviously bumbleheaded bridge-aholic with a badge and a house in the country he couldn't naturally afford? What other suspect had as good an alibi as "Why would I want to bump off my own team?"

"Why would he?" asked Belsky.

"Because, Mr. B.," I said, "his team stinks. You don't know Jimmy. He loves to win. He'd rather lose the first match of a team event than go to the final and lose. In short, he hates pain. And pain is losing in the big one — the final of the world championships.

"When it comes time to lay an indictment, the D.A. will cut him to smithereens. One: He puts together some cockamamie New York team to play in the Grand National Team Event, because the rules require all the members of the team to reside in New York, and there aren't enough top experts to go around. So who does he pick? Three *schlemiels* from the Mayfair Club. Granted, they are highly-rated rubber bridge *schlemiels*, but knock-out teams is another ballgame.

"Two: The team manages to win — mainly because the other teams are worse and nobody, absolutely nobody, knows nothing about team strategy; and then the six of them go on to win the U. S. Team Trials. How? I don't know. Probably part luck, probably part skill, probably their opponents are so busy bidding spades when they have hearts and clubs when they got diamonds, that they lose count at trick three on half the hands.

"Three: With the world championships a week away, he perceives his chances of winning dwindling — maybe the coach is putting poison in his ear about the quality of some of the players or maybe the girl, Evelyn, is barking about the difficulty of playing against the international systems and conventions. Either way, he's been seduced into believing his best chances to win would be to knock off a few weak links.

"Four: He makes a plan — one by one, he's going to eliminate the bad elements of the team — he's gonna trim fat — he's gonna skim the team down to size, to two perfect partnerships. And who's he gonna get to do the dirty work? I don't know. Maybe the girl, maybe the coach, maybe both.

"Five: Frankenstein gets the ax. Perhaps the best player on the team, Jimmy will argue in his defense, but a reputation for being the worst team member, the one who causes rifts, fights, and otherwise general unpleasantness among the other players. Ask any late-night Mayfairite to take the stand and see if he wouldn't openly be proud to have been the killer himself!

"Six: Charlotte gets it next. After all, who needs Charlotte when her partner is out of commission? Some say she was a great player. Others say she could only play *his* system. In either case, she had to go or the team would be stuck with a hanging limb.

"Seven: He's happy to play four till he gets the low-down this very day on Barkowsky — his failure to practice with Jacqui for the last two months.

"Eight: Barkowsky goes. Jimmy makes like he's upset. His team is down to three players. Only, says the prosecutor, which three? Jimmy, Sontag, and Jacqui, that's which three — the three professionals. And what will Jimmy do about it?

"Nine: I'll tell you before it happens, Belsky. He's gonna get the ACBL committee for the U.S. international team to agree to let him add three more pros. Or maybe he'll throw in one bum, to try to avoid suspicion. Who knows? The point is that —

"Ten: Cayne's got a new team, a team that has a chance to win the world championship, and a perfect motive for the D.A.'s office to send him up the river for life."

Speaking of the river, we had walked all the way down to the East River, when I suddenly turned to Belsky to ask: "Where's the car?"

"Up at Third Avenue, Matt. I was following you."

We retraced our steps in stormy silence. When we finally got to the Oldsmobile, Belsky started searching for his keys while he asked, "So you think he really did it? Like hired these henchmen to do the strangling and that sort of thing?"

"It doesn't matter what I think, Belsk; it matters what the D.A. thinks, and I think the D.A.'s gonna think he did it."

"Well, then, who do *you* think did it?"

"Belsky, I got no idea who did it. If I did, you think I'd be standing here on 59th and Third in the rain while waiting for some *shmiggeggie* to find the keys to a deadbeat car?!"

He found the keys and I got in on the passenger side. My gun was damp, so I replaced it with a Colt .22 from under the dashboard. Belsky took the recorder from his breast pocket and put it on rewind.

"What's that?" I asked.

"That's the tape of the English fellow and the girl. You know, on the Ferry."

"Well, why did you let me go on ranting all night about Cayne when you were sitting on incriminating evidence all this time?"

He turned to me and with all the sincerity he could muster, which was quite a lot, he said, "Matt, I'm not what you like to call a kibitzer. I always let a guy play out his hand. So I didn't interrupt you. In last week's *Pirkos Avos*—"

"What?"

"*Pirkos Avos* — Ethics of the Fathers. We study it during the long hot Sabbaths of the summer. Anyway, one of them was this sage's suggestion that you should always be careful before you interrupt somebody who is ranting or raving or generally upset, you know?"

I gritted my teeth. I guess it wasn't any different in crime detection than it was in bridge. You tend to think your partner's an idiot. It's just a natural reaction.

"Your wife says hello, Belsky. Now play the damn tape."

106

12

The voice on the tape player was discussing the Ten Commandments. "Now let's see who can name them all. I'll bet there's one that you won't come up with. Nobody ever does. . . . "

"Why are we listening to this, Mr. B?" I asked as kindly as I could under the circumstances. The rain had let up almost completely now, and though it might have been cozy sitting in that parked Oldsmobile on a warm summer night with the sweetheart of my choice, it was not cozy with Belsky.

"This must be one of the tapes I got in Brooklyn, you know, at the Judaic Book Store," he answered.

I spoke slowly, trying not to hiss like the snake in the garden of Eden. "Where . . . is . . . the . . . tape . . . of . . . the . . . suspects . . . you . . . were . . . tailing . . . on . . . the . . . Staten . . . Island . . . Ferry?"

(Pause.)

"Matt, I left it in Brooklyn. But not to worry. I can arrange for the owner of the book store, where I left it, to send it over to Manhattan today with his brother-in-law, who I happen to know works at a store on 47th Street. And this is the best part: I am positive that I recorded them, because I played it back and heard their voices distinctly."

"Do you remember any of what they said?"

(Pause.)

"Matt, I can't honestly say I do. I just played back a little to make sure my batteries were working. It was at the store."

"And were your batteries working, Mr. B?"

"Matt, they were, indeed."

It was another one of those times in life that I wanted desperately to light up, and I gave the Surgeon General a silent curse as I looked outside the car window. A Woody Allen movie was playing down the street, and a line of uptown yups licking on Häagen-Daz ice-cream were starting to queue up. I didn't feel like going to the morgue tonight — not tonight. But then I thought of Jimmy, the team, the trouble, and the wife who wanted me home. And I knew we had to hit the morgue sooner or later. . . .

When we arrived downtown, the joint was jumping. There were cops, doctors, nurses, scientists, lawyers, and a lot of ordinary ladies and gents as well, hanging around — I supposed to see whether the latest victim was the wife who ran off with the boss or the pop whom nobody'd seen for 13 years. Then there was my contingent: the ones relating to the case of Jinks Barkowsky.

I checked my revolver at the front desk, though I didn't really see what difference it made in a morgue.

"Some guys aren't always dead," the young clerk with bifocals explained. "There's a difference, you know, between legally dead and really dead. We had a case a few years back where a body was brought in filled with five bullet holes. His wife came to identify him. When she did, she claimed his pinky was still moving, took out a gun and shot him five more times."

I noticed Evelyn's name on the guest register. She had signed in at 11 and signed out at 11:20 — quick visit. We took an elevator two floors below basement level. When we got out I saw Detective Kennedy down the hall talking to two other men, not big men, not small men, but mean men.

The three of them spotted Belsky and me and made a bees' path to our noses.

"You Granovetter?" said the clever-looking one in a three-piece suit.

"Yeah, that's right," said Kennedy before I could answer.

"Murphy, assistant district attorney." He held out his hand. I shook, hesitantly.

"This is Lieutenant Koslov; he's taking over from Kennedy."

"What's the matter with Kennedy?" I asked, though it was a stupid question.

Murphy hesitated; he was about to tell a lie. "He's on leave this week."

"I already had this week planned as vacation," explained Kennedy. "You know, so that I could kibitz the world championships."

"Kennedy's filled us in, but we want to know what you know about the strangulations."

Then the one that looked like a gorilla spoke up. "And after you tell us what you know, shamus, you can go take a walk."

"I'm a private dick, Mr. Murphy," I said, trying to look him straight in the kisser, but not succeeding, his kisser being one of the ugliest kissers I'd ever seen. "As for your friend here, since I don't talk to monkeys in suits, you tell him my client has hired Belsky (I nodded toward my partner) and me to find the killer, and I'm not laying off until we do."

"Let's run 'em in," said the Gorilla. He went for my collar with his big hairy claw, but Belsky met him halfway. The sharp clap of Belsky's palm on the Lieutenant's wrist echoed in the underground chambers, and a few people down the hall glanced up at the noise. I recognized someone down there. Maybe two people.

"Tell the Lieutenant to lay off, Murphy, and I'll cooperate. But if he's gonna start swinging from the start, you can go do all the dirty work yourself. By the way, do you know anything about bridge?"

The assistant D.A. shook his head. That was good, I thought, he'll be working in the dark for at least a few days, and it will give me time to investigate unimpeded.

"It's no secret you're working for Cayne," said Murphy. "Let's hope for your sake that you're not working for the guilty party."

"Let's book these guys, Mr. Murphy. They stink."

"Lay off," said Murphy. "Look, Granovetter, I'll keep Koslov at bay, but you have to translate what these guys are saying down there." He pointed down the hall. Now I saw clearly who they were: Bobby Wolff and Bob Hamman of the Dallas Aces. What the hell were these two doing at the New York City morgue?

"Why can't Kennedy translate for you?" I asked.

Murphy hesitated again, then he took me by the arm and whispered in my ear. "Forget Kennedy. He's a front for the department. He would have been retired years ago if it hadn't been for his family."

"Well, how the heck did he get that wife and house of his?"

"She hit the lottery big a couple years back. Didn't you see it in the papers? C'mon, let's go look at the body."

Down the hall the eight-foot-deep cubicles were stacked five up and 30 across, like a filing cabinet of neatly packed sardines. Only they weren't sardines. Everything was white, the cubicles were white, the walls were white, the uniforms of the attendants were white; then there were the ghosts I was imagining, hovering around the drawers. Two were sipping white coffee, and one said to the other how he

110

wished he could hang around here forever, there being so many interesting stories going on, but alas, he knew he would end up slipping his way out of a grave or, worse, jumping out of some fiery ashes.

The real-life Wolff and Hamman were hovering over cubicle 14 B. I gave them a hearty handshake and a friendly hello, nice to bump into you, isn't it a small world and all that jazz.

A thin, oriental woman, dressed in white, with a mask around her nose and mouth, was in charge of the corpses. She was having trouble opening one of the cubicles. Finally she checked a number on a slip of paper and moved to another cubicle. She began fiddling around with some keys. Now she was having trouble finding the key to 14B. "Is there some reason you had to lock him in there?" I asked.

"This is worse than a safe deposit vault, Mister. You steal one of these, it's big money."

Finally she opened 14B. It was the wrong one. It was a woman who'd been run over on the Triborough Bridge the night before, and no one had been in to identify her — not that anyone could.

"This is the bridge one," she insisted.

"No, no," said Wolff, "We meant the one who *played* bridge. You know, the card game."

"You're joking me, huh? What happened? He got killed at the bridge table, ha, ha."

As the attendant made merry and went back to look at her records, I slowly eased my feet over to a wide table in the corner, where certain interesting items lay, tagged with labels of formerly healthy people. Here were things that the corpses were carrying on them at the time of their check in: pocket combs, wallets, cyanide pills, and other fancy stuff. As I studied the items, my eyes could not help but fall upon a little rubber bridge scorepad with the words Mayfair Club written on top. Indeed, the tag on it read: Barkowsky. I looked closer and saw that the top sheet had been ripped one-third of the way down. Silently I cursed myself. You're *putzing* around too much, Matthew. You let her get here before you. I checked to see that no one was looking, then ripped out what was left of the top sheet and quickly put the pad back on the table. Then I stuck the torn paper inside a handkerchief in my shirt pocket.

Luckily, everyone else was too busy to notice me. They were all hungry to see Jinks' corpse. The attendant finally had the right cubicle opened, and a thin sheet lay over the man. She unfolded it and we all took a polite peek.

His gray face now matched his gray hair, poor guy. Other than that, he didn't look so bad, considering his current situation.

"Looks like the time Frankenstein dropped him in a five-club cuebid." said Hamman.

"That was in the '69 pair trials, wasn't it?" remarked Wolff.

"I thought Frankenstein was going to put him out to pasture right then and there," said Hamman, before breaking into a respectful chuckle. It was good to see everyone enjoying themselves. Then the D.A. pointed to the body's neck. It had two reddish marks on it that the D.A. claimed could only have come from a tight squeeze, and while the Gorilla took out a ruler to measure them, Hamman continued to reminisce as friends of lately departed will do: "I remember when I squeezed him in that six-notrump contract in the third segment of the trials. His partner could have broken it up at trick one."

You'd think that the Gorilla was fitting him for his wedding suit, the length of time he took with his ruler. Meanwhile Belsky was holding his nose, and Wolff was shaking his head in dismay.

"You can't blame Jacqui. How could she find a spade lead after our auction?" He turned to me. "That's why I leapt to slam rather than cuebid. You'd be surprised how many times that keeps them from the best opening lead."

I had to admit to not knowing the hand, and Hamman was gracious enough to write it out for me. He couldn't find a pencil, but Belsky noticed one sticking out of Barkowsky's pants that must have been overlooked when he was checked in. I leaned over the Gorilla and lifted the pencil from the corpse, who didn't seem to mind. Then Bob wrote the hand on the inside of a fresh convention card he had in his back pocket.

```
                    Wolff
                    ♠ x x
                    ♡ K J x
                    ◊ x x x x
                    ♣ A Q J 10
   Jacqui                              Barkowsky
   ♠ K x x x x                         ♠ A x x
   ♡ x                                 ♡ Q 10 9 x x x
   ◊ J 10 9                            ◊ x
   ♣ x x x x                           ♣ x x x
                    Hamman
                    ♠ Q J 10
                    ♡ A x x
                    ◊ A K Q x x
                    ♣ K x
```

Hamman	Jacqui	Wolff	Barkowsky
1 ♣	pass	1 ♠	2 ♡
3 ◊	pass	4 ◊	pass
4 ♡	pass	6 ◊	(all pass)

Hamman's opening bid had been a strong club and Wolff's one-spade response was artificial, showing three controls (an ace counting as two and a king as one). This was a bid taken from the Blue Team Club system, the system that was used

113

successfully by Garozzo and Forquet of the Italian Blue Team during their reign as world champions in the 1960s.

Wolff leaned over the diagram and added his two cents. "Over four hearts, if I bid five clubs, I would be pinpointing the spade lead. So I bid an inelegant six diamonds and Jacqui led a heart."

Wolff
♠ x x
♡ K J x
♢ x x x x
♣ A Q J 10

Jacqui
♠ K x x x x
♡ x
♢ J 10 9
♣ x x x x

Barkowsky
♠ A x x
♡ Q 10 9 x x x
♢ x
♣ x x x

Hamman
♠ Q J 10
♡ A x x
♢ A K Q x x
♣ K x

Hamman	Jacqui	Wolff	Barkowsky
1 ♣	pass	1 ♠	2 ♡
3 ♢	pass	4 ♢	pass
4 ♡	pass	6 ♢	(all pass)

I couldn't really imagine Jacqui not leading her partner's bid suit anyway, I thought. Then I looked at the hand again. Hamman had said he squeezed Barkowsky, but how? Jacqui could obviously guard the spade suit, but maybe Barkowsky had more difficulties than it appeared. If declarer wins the ♢A and rattles off nine minor-suit winners, the position is:

114

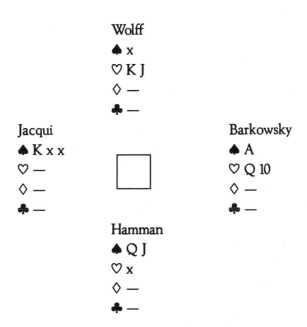

Wolff
♠ x
♡ K J
♢ —
♣ —

Jacqui
♠ K x x
♡ —
♢ —
♣ —

Barkowsky
♠ A
♡ Q 10
♢ —
♣ —

Hamman
♠ Q J
♡ x
♢ —
♣ —

Now if declarer leads a spade, Barkowsky is endplayed.

"On the actual deal," said Wolff, "Barkowsky threw the ♠A, a nice play, in case his partner had the king-jack of spades. But she didn't, and Bob made a spade trick at the end."

"Another slam off a cashing ace-king," roared Hamman. "The cookie crumbled."

Meanwhile, back at the morgue, our friend Barkowsky had been thoroughly poked and pinched by the Lieutenant and the D.A. and was now safely back in the cooler, awaiting his next caller.

"By the way," I asked Wolff, "why in the world are you here?"

"I just had to see for myself," said Wolff. "I couldn't believe a third murder had taken place."

"You mean the World Bridge Federation sent you," I said.

"Well, not exactly," he said. "It was the ACBL. After all, without Jinks now, the League can't provide a team."

"So they're down to three players," I said. "What of it? Can't they just add someone?"

"Not so easy," said Wolff. "You know there are laws and by-laws that cover these types of situations."

The D.A. stepped in. "There are ACBL bylaws that cover strangulations of bridge team members?"

"No, don't be silly," said Wolff. "I mean rules that state if the winning Trials Team cannot field at least four players at the time of the World Championships, then the team that lost to them in the Trials will take its place."

"Wait a second," I said. "That's *your* team!"

"Listen, I don't make the rules. I was just sent down here to check on things."

"Well," I objected, "did you check on the other two corpses as well?"

"Excellent point," said Wolff. "But until now there was no problem. The first two victims were expendable — it was when the team was cut down to three that the officials got concerned."

"Well, how can you be sure the others are dead?" I asked, trying to lead him into a trap — that is, if he knew something that could be trapped.

"I assume they are. After all, they were written up in the obituaries."

"Yeah, but you're here checking on Jinks. What makes *him* different."

"I can't wait for tomorrow's obits. Tomorrow the semifinals begin and the ACBL needs to field a team."

"True," I said, "but how did you two know to fly in tonight? There was no reason for you to be here, unless . . . wait a second, is it possible to see Mrs. Stein?"

"Mrs. Stein?" said the attendant. "She's not here. She left yesterday."

Wonderful. I had missed her by a full day.

"Did she leave a forwarding address?" I asked.

"You're a funny man," said the attendant. "You go look in the check-out book. But I think she went to a place in the Bronx."

"We flew in," said Wolff, "because I'm head of the ACBL committee for international events. And Bob is here at Jimmy's request."

Perhaps, I thought. Then I turned to the attendant and asked if she were here when they brought in Charlotte Stein's husband.

"What's his name?" she asked.

"Frank Stein. He would have come in about five days ago."

"Frankenstein," corrected Hamman, letting out a short cackle. "Let's call him by his proper title."

"No Dr. Frankenstein here," she answered. "You're joking me again, huh?"

13

When we set our feet upon the dark wet pavement, I took a deep breath. The night smell of city garbage collection and restaurant leftovers was strong against the cooling dampness. Still, better up here than down there, I thought.

It was impossible to check the coroner's report on Frankenstein until the morning, because the records were filed away for the night. So I decided to call it a day. "I hope it hasn't been too rough on you," I said to Belsky.

"Rough? No, no. Why, the Talmud says every day should be spent as if it were your last."

I wondered if Jinks Barkowsky had known that.

Back at the Caynes' apartment, dark shadows covered the path down the hallway. I bumped into myself three times before reaching the back den, where the light was on. Jimmy was sitting on the sofa, studying his bridge notes. I sat down across from him, wondering why he was still bothering with his notes when half his team had evaporated. The semifinal was to start tomorrow afternoon and my guess was the United States team was not going to be Cayne and Company. More than likely, somewhere in the city at this late hour, ACBL officials were meeting to determine the substitute team, the one including Hamman and Wolff.

But how I had lost faith in the powers of Cayne.

"We've added three players," said Jimmy.

"You've doubled your team?" I answered back. "Why couldn't you just add one player?"

"There'll be a meeting tomorrow morning with the ACBL and WBF. They're going to allow us to play on the condition we add three. They're worried that at the rate the team is dropping if we add only one or two, we won't last through the final."

The World Bridge Federation was not the easiest organization to manipulate and the ACBL had by-laws set in stone. To add any players to the team would require quite a lot of politicking, especially when the rules specifically stated that if the winning Trials team could not field four players, the losing finalists would replace them. I mentioned this to Jimmy.

"Don't worry about it, Chewy," he said.

He called me Chew or Chewy, short for Matchew, whenever he was feeling fond of me. He gave everyone he liked pet names, but used them only when things were going particularly well. Suddenly I was in Jimmy's good books — I didn't know why.

"For starters," he continued, "there's probably no such rule. Who has a rule for a six-man team dropping to three? Then, even if there is a rule, it won't hold up under these unusual circumstances.

"They pity us, Chew. After all, we've lost three people in less than a week."

True, they would have pity. But then Wolff and Hamman

were pretty smart cookies. I told Jimmy about my morgue visit, not all of it, not the part about a certain body that the attendant had no recollection of, but he scoffed.

"Why do you worry about these things? Trust me when I tell you it's under control. Better yet, let me put it this way: If we're kicked out of the world championships, I'm quitting bridge for life."

"Who are you proposing to add?" I asked, suddenly getting excited.

His answer was on a piece of paper that he passed to me across the coffee table:

Submission for approval by WBF as additions to the North American team:
Original Surviving Members:
James Cayne
Jacqui Mitchell
Alan Sontag

Additions:
Matt Granovetter
Otto Marx
Victor Mitchell

The first thing that struck me, of course, was my name on the list of additions. Flattery will get you everywhere in bridge and I'm no exception. My heart was pounding, my blood pressure was up. Still, I was sober enough to notice the incredible addition of Otto Marx, sandwiched between me and Vic Mitchell.

I tried to act nonchalant. I made as if it were no big deal that my name was on the list. But he had me on a string. I knew it, and I couldn't cut it off. Did he think I was getting too close to solving the case? Was he really involved in the murders? I risked a mild objection. . . .

"Okay," I said, "I understand Victor — he can play with his wife. As for me, I don't fully get it. Certainly my time would be better spent investigating the case away from the bridge table."

"Or perhaps you'd be better off *at* the table," he answered.

"Maybe you're right. Maybe you think I'd make a good decoy. But what have you given me for a partner? I thought you wanted to win a world championship. Nobody's going to approve of Otto Marx, anyway. Come to think of it, why not take Hamman and Wolff as your third pair?"

"You're making an assumption that they want to play."

He was right. Why would anyone in his right mind want to play on this team? Can it be worth risking your life to win a Bermuda Bowl?

On the other hand, it didn't make sense. I had no partnership with Otto Marx — nobody did. He was a rubber bridge player; I doubted he had ever played a long knock-out match in his life. Yes, he was a veteran of the Mayfair imp game, but he was a wild man. His favorite bridge theory was that there were two of them (the opponents) and only one of you (his partner), "so why not go to town, eh?" By going to town, Otto meant making preempts on five little, doubling for penalties on singletons, and other offbeat maneuvers designed to wreak havoc on the opposition. When I thought of the idea of sitting across from him against world-class competition, I was no longer thrilled to death by the prospect of playing.

But what a lie that is! What a lie I told myself! Had Jimmy given me Ghengis Khan as a partner, I would have been thrilled. Here was a chance to win the Bermuda Bowl. And I didn't have to go through the year-long process of winning a major championship, then winning the Trials. Tomorrow, yes, tomorrow, I could sit down in the semifinals of the Bermuda Bowl and if I were lucky, smart, able, I could capture the event that all experts long to win.

Suddenly it occurred to me that I'd better get some sleep.

It was bad enough that I hadn't played bridge in months. But to play tired, with a partner who required constant alertness, was very bad.

Belsky appeared in the doorway. He was finishing what looked like a corned beef on rye.

"So how's the case coming?"

"Belsky!" said Jimmy. "Sit down, Belsky, the case is coming along fine; we've got our suspects down to a half dozen people — but don't sit on my cigar."

"Listen, Jimmy," I said, "it's past midnight. Don't you think we should get some rest?"

"Don't worry, Chew. Rest is for matchpoints. Once the adrenalin starts to flow, you won't need anything but a basket to catch the imps they'll be dropping in your lap."

He was right in a strange sort of way. Thinking back, many of my successes at teams have come when I was exhausted. The reason is weird, but significant. At imps, your object is to win the big points, the games, the slams, the doubled undertricks. Like rubber bridge, imps is for the most part a game of baseball — a game that requires clutch hitting. You can drop overtricks and misdefend occasional partscores, but you have to be there on the big hands. And even on those hands, the objective — to make or break a contract — is simpler than at matchpoints.

At matchpoints, you usually have to do things to earn points. You have to be aggressive and carefree. You have to earn your points against 13 different types of partnerships — some strong, some weak. You must score heavily against the weak ones, because if you don't, you'll lose to a pair that has scored heavily against them.

At teams, you win by not doing bad things! You can afford to sit in your rocking chair and relax; you'll pass many hands you would have bid with at matchpoints. The reason is: You don't have to outdo the 40 or so other contenders in the field. No, you have only one set of opponents and you have a good

122

pair — your teammates — protecting you at the other table.

I learned this the hard way. It was about 15 years ago and I was a punk kid, thinking I was a hot-shot player, and it was round seven of a Swiss Teams. We were leading and now up against one of the better teams in the field. I picked up ♠ Q 3 ♡ 9 5 4 ◊ A K 8 5 3 ♣ K 9 8. Nobody was vulnerable, so it all seemed innocent, safe and *normal* when my right-hand opponent opened the bidding one heart and I over-called two diamonds. When the smoke cleared, I had taken two tricks.

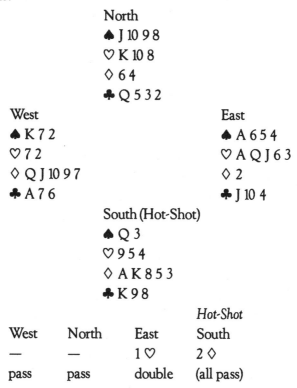

North
♠ J 10 9 8
♡ K 10 8
◊ 6 4
♣ Q 5 3 2

West
♠ K 7 2
♡ 7 2
◊ Q J 10 9 7
♣ A 7 6

East
♠ A 6 5 4
♡ A Q J 6 3
◊ 2
♣ J 10 4

South (Hot-Shot)
♠ Q 3
♡ 9 5 4
◊ A K 8 5 3
♣ K 9 8

West	North	East	Hot-Shot South
—	—	1 ♡	2 ◊
pass	pass	double	(all pass)

West led a heart. East won the jack and switched to a trump. I ducked and West continued trumps. I won my ◊ K and looked around. I remember we were playing in a ball-room at the Hilton Hotel, and mostly what I was looking for was a place to exit.

```
                    North
                    ♠ J 10 9 8
                    ♡ K 10 8
                    ◊ 6 4
                    ♣ Q 5 3 2
West                                        East
♠ K 7 2                                     ♠ A 6 5 4
♡ 7 2                                       ♡ A Q J 6 3
◊ Q J 10 9 7                                ◊ 2
♣ A 7 6                                     ♣ J 10 4
                    South (Hot-Shot)
                    ♠ Q 3
                    ♡ 9 5 4
                    ◊ A K 8 5 3
                    ♣ K 9 8
```

Forced to play a card, I eventually tried the ♠Q, thinking that I'd set up some spade tricks while I still had the ♣Q in dummy for a possible entry. West won the ♠K and persevered in trumps. I won the ◊A and persevered with a second spade. This spade attack by me did nothing to lessen the joy of the defense. East won the trick and shifted to a club. West won the ace and then drew my last trumps. East by now had discarded his two other clubs and two spades, so when West played his second heart through dummy's king, East tabled his cards. Down six. Had I attacked clubs immediately, I could have held it to down five.

At that time the score was only 1100. Since then, nonvulnerable, doubled undertricks are worth an extra 100 points starting with the fourth undertrick. So in today's scoring, I would have been minus 1400. It hardly mattered. My teammates played in two notrump with the East-West cards after South had passed the one-heart opening bid by East. They scored plus 120. It didn't match well with my minus 1100.

You might say I was unlucky. Why hadn't I caught partner with the West hand rather than the North hand? Okay, let's switch them and see what would have happened.

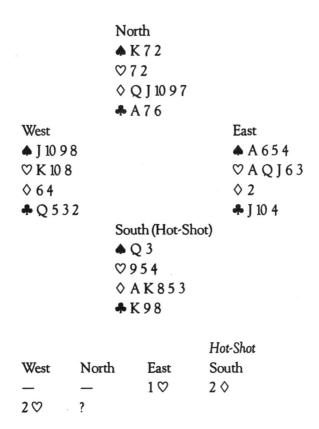

North
♠ K 7 2
♡ 7 2
♢ Q J 10 9 7
♣ A 7 6

West
♠ J 10 9 8
♡ K 10 8
♢ 6 4
♣ Q 5 3 2

East
♠ A 6 5 4
♡ A Q J 6 3
♢ 2
♣ J 10 4

South (Hot-Shot)
♠ Q 3
♡ 9 5 4
♢ A K 8 5 3
♣ K 9 8

West	North	East	*Hot-Shot* South
—	—	1 ♡	2 ♢
2 ♡	?		

Now let's say the auction began the same way. North would certainly raise diamonds, maybe three, maybe four, maybe a cuebid of three hearts along the way. But no matter what he does, we will probably go minus.

If we buy the contract in four diamonds, we will be minus 50 (losing a spade, two hearts and a club). If we allow them to play three hearts, we will be minus 140 (they lose a spade, a diamond and two clubs), assuming declarer is wise enough to attack clubs before drawing trumps, so that he cannot be tapped out before setting up his ninth trick. However, it is more than likely that North will compete to four diamonds, so the play in three hearts is irrelevant.

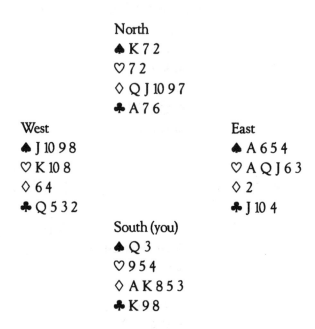

North
♠ K 7 2
♡ 7 2
◊ Q J 10 9 7
♣ A 7 6

West
♠ J 10 9 8
♡ K 10 8
◊ 6 4
♣ Q 5 3 2

East
♠ A 6 5 4
♡ A Q J 6 3
◊ 2
♣ J 10 4

South (you)
♠ Q 3
♡ 9 5 4
◊ A K 8 5 3
♣ K 9 8

The point is: Had you passed one heart, you could balance with three-diamonds when two hearts comes around to you — you've really lost nothing by passing on the first round. With three little hearts in your hand, after learning about their heart fit, the balance of three diamonds becomes a safe bet.

At matchpoints, against a weak pair, you might risk the direct overcall, simply because the sound of your direct overcall intimidates weaker players. Also, if you catch the hand with two little diamonds as your partner, you are in far less trouble at matchpoints, where you will have lots of company — other players in your seat will have made the same dubious overcall.

Against strong opposition, however, in either pairs or teams, it is better to pass over one heart. At teams you do not have a lot of other players matching your overcall — just one guy (in your seat at the other table). So at teams, you have to watch your step.

Now what has all this to do with the idea that when you are exhausted it can work to your advantage?

When you are very tired, you are less likely to bid on shaky values! You are also less likely to make waves — do things that create action and, often, confuse partner. If I am playing imps with an active player, I prefer that he be exhausted — so exhausted that he just sits there and does his best to make the book bid. And speaking of active partners, there was Otto Marx.

* * * * * * * * *

". . . and he's been added to the team," said Jimmy, talking to Belsky. Apparently I had gotten lost in my own thoughts.

"Ah," said Belsky. "So he's in the catbird seat, as they say in the trade, huh? We lure the murderer to go after Matt, and I go in and nab him just in the nick of time. Sounds good to me."

I let out an ungrateful yawn.

"Chew," said Jimmy. "I'm sending you to bed. Otto will be here at seven this morning and I want you two and the coach to go over your system."

On our way back to the library, where a cot and a convertible were set up, Belsky had to bring in religion once again.

"You know what the Talmud says about murder, don't you?" he said. "If someone's out to murder you, you should get up earlier and kill him first."

"I thought the commandment says 'thou shall not kill.'"

"No, no. It's commonly mistranslated. It's 'thou shall not murder.' You can kill in self-defense."

So, just to play it safe, I set the alarm for six.

14

Otto Marx stood over my bed, crumbs from his morning croissant raining on my pillow. The alarm hadn't gone off.

"Eets not my style to play all these checkbacks, check forwards, check returns. . . ."

He was reading from some coffee-stained notes, shuffling papers back and forth between bites.

"And these tlansfer bids, they are all clazy. I prefer two-under tlansfers. That way, if partner ees tired, you can tlansfer back."

"Let me see those notes."

I got up and stood on the bed to peer over his shoulder. The notes were typewritten and on the top of each sheet was a page number with the heading: "Modified Cayne-Sontag System for Granovetter-Marx." There was also an index page, which listed more than 200 exceptions.

I quickly slipped into my robe. Belsky was in the corner, saying his morning prayers. I took Otto's arm and led him through the hallway to the kitchen.

"Where'd you get this stuff?" I asked.

"I don't know. It's a clazy ting, but this morning, when I come up the elevator, the doorman, he gives me a package with these notes inside."

"Well," I said, pouring a cup of coffee, "they must be from the coach. But I'll tell you the truth. We have one morning to fill out a card — and I have no intention of playing all those damn conventions."

"This is what I say, too! Hey, Glanovetter, we are a partnership made up in heaven!"

Otto put his arm around my shoulder and started to shake me up and down.

We sat down and had breakfast. The crazy Hungarian had not changed much in the 20 years since I last saw him. True, he was older, grayer, but his wry smile was still plastered on his thin and stubbled kisser. Occasionally he would twitch, and I wondered how that had come about.

Over cornflakes, he slipped some photographs out of his wallet. "These are my wife and little ones," he said.

"Very nice," I nodded, not really looking too closely.

"Thees is why I go into the Stock Market. To make everyting for them."

I took out a napkin and began to list our conventions based on a Standard American card.

"Okay, to begin with, notrump openings."

"I play them," said Otto.

"Yes, but the range."

There was a moment's silence.

"Well, I use good judgment," said Otto.

"Yes, but what about the point count?"

"Well, the point count ees depending on vulnerability."

"Then we play strong vulnerable, weak not vulnerable?"

"Well, eet depends also on the hand we hold."

I could see we were getting nowhere, so I marked "variable." Then I moved on to Stayman.

"Forcing or not?"
"Correct."

"What about transfers?" I asked.
"Tlansfers are my favorite. I like to play the Mayfair style. You don't have to accept if you don't want to."
"Then perhaps we should not play transfers."
"If you like, but I prefer them like I said before — two under, giving the option."
"Fine, two under transfers, nobody's ever heard of this before, but we'll do it, it'll confuse everyone."
"Now that's the way I like to play."

"What about Texas?" I asked.
"Texas ees also—"
"I know, I know, two under."
"Ahh, you know my style."

"What about two notrump? Twenty to 22?"
"Ees good."
"Transfers?"
He nodded.
"Two under."

I didn't bother asking about gambling three notrump. I knew he played everything gambling.
"How about major-suit raises? Forcing, limit or weak. I prefer forcing."
"Ees good."
"Forcing in the minors, too?"
"Ees good."
"Forcing in competition?"
"Ees good."
"And if we have a limit raise or preemptive hand, what do we do?"

"Ees perfect. We pretend we have the forcing, and everyone passes."

"All right, let's move on down to two-bids. Weak, strong, or two-way?"

"Why not thlee way?" suggested Otto.

"How does that work?"

"Well, we open a stlong-two bid in the suit we tink we have. We open a weak two-bid in the suit below the suit we tink we have. And we open a medium two-bid in the suit two below the one we tink we have."

"Sounds a bit confusing," I said.

"Ees very good. I use it all the time at the Mayfair for many years. And no one, not even my partner, knows how to handle it."

"Fine. And two notrump in response asks for clarification."

"Well, we can say if we tink we have the medium hand, but better to leave the other two extlemes ambiguous. This way, they don't know until the third round, and by then eet's too late for everyone."

"Anything else before I turn the napkin over?" I asked.

"Not much," he answered.

"Weak jumps in competition?"

"No."

"Checkback Stayman?"

"No."

"Drury?"

"Only by an unpassed hand."

"Otto, Drury is to find out if third-hand is light, not first hand."

"Why not? First hand is better light than third hand."

"Good point, but the rest of the world is playing it differently."

"Which is why we will make such a good partnership!"

I turned my napkin over.

"How about defensive bidding. Negative doubles?"

"Ees good, but not as good as penalty."

"With a penalty, you just pass and wait for partner to reopen with a double."

"Ees nice, but partner never does. But okay, okay, if you want to be the boss on thees one, we play negative doubles."

"Responsive, too?"

"Just negative."

"Notrump overcalls."

"Same as if we open," said Otto.

"But we haven't quite defined those," I protested.

"Even better."

"Just say check if you like it," I suggested. "Overcalls, seven and up."

"Check."

"Jordan."

"Check."

"Michaels in the minors, color in the majors."

"Check. But wait a second."

"Yes?"

"Which color?"

"If they open one heart, two hearts shows the black suits," I explained.

"Ahh, no. I plefer to beed natural over their opening."

"But that's ridiculous! You don't overcall one heart with two hearts to show hearts!!"

"You don't, but I do. Ees much simpler and direct than tlapping."

"But I like to tlap — I mean trap."

"Everybody, he likes to tlap. I think it's clappy."

"Opening leads. Fourth-"

"You forgot psyches," interrupted Otto.

"This is a new partnership. Let's not psyche."

"Ees no good. The best theeng for a new partnership ees the psyche."

"How can we build any trust in each other if we psyche?"

"Tlust? I haven't tlusted my partner in 20 years at the rubber bridge table. Why should I tlust you after one morning? Better we tlust nobody, and better still, nobody tlust us."

"Psyches, frequent."

"Ees good."

"Fourth best leads or third and fifth?"

"Ees difficult. I plefer fourth, but third when we must cash all our tlicks at once."

"Okay. So at slams and five levels or against preempts, we'll lead third and fifth, otherwise fourth."

"Second best against slams," he said. "Ees clearer."

Just then Jimmy walked into the kitchen. He was still in his boxer shorts. On the one hand I hoped he hadn't heard any of our conversation or we'd be thrown off the team. On the other hand, maybe that was for the best.

"Did you see the paper?" asked Jimmy. "The Italians won their last match and play the English in the semifinal."

It was exciting news, because the Italians weren't just any Italians. They were the famous Blue Team, regrouped for the purpose of recapturing the world title they had lost 20 years ago. But on the other hand, they were, you might say, the over-the-hill Blue Team. Yet, to have played for six days straight required tremendous stamina — at least I thought it did.

More important, however, were *our* opponents. Did the Russians win or the Canadian team?

"Who won in our bracket?" I asked.

"Who do you think?" he said. "Canada won 4 imps on the last board of the night to win by 2."

We all cheered — it was not that we loved the Canadian

team. No, we cheered because Canada clearly had an easier team than the Soviet Union. In fact, any team was easier than the Soviet Union, not because the Russians were great card players, but because they had three partnerships playing big-pass systems with countless artificial gadgets. Contrast to the Canadians, who had two pairs playing natural and one pair playing Precision. Everybody was shaking everybody else's hand as if the match were in the bag. I thought they were going to break open the champagne.

"No convention headaches," cried Jimmy. "No defense notes, no overcalls of opening passes!"

Yes, it was easier to play when you had to worry only about your own bids. Then it dawned on me that we were no great shakes ourselves (as the reader by now is well aware).

I now noticed that behind Jimmy stood a robe-clad Bob Hamman. Apparently Bob had come in late last night and slept in the den. And I now remembered what Wolff had said about Jimmy asking Bob to come to New York. I soon learned that he was here to help with Otto's team-bridge training. I was finished with Otto, anyway, so I got up to leave the room, but Bob suggested I sit down and listen, too.

"It won't hurt you to be in on the conversation," said Bob. "Where's the coffee?" He went to pour himself a cup, then noticed the time on the coffee clock. "For crying out loud, I didn't know it was still dawn!"

We spread out along the kitchen counter, Hamman, Jimmy, Otto and I. Hamman made a few grunts, cleared his throat and spoke to his students.

"First of all, this is Jimmy's idea, not mine. There's probably nothing I can tell you that will help unless you go in with a high degree of confidence. The most important thing in any bridge game, imps, pairs or rubber, is your ability to take it on the chin, get up from the mat and continue fighting on the next hand. You've got to be able to shake off a bad result — 'cause you're gonna have plenty of them. I've seen many

134

teams in my day lose only because a pair gets four or five bad results in a row. You've got to avoid that pitfall. One of the big differences between the forms of the game is that at teams you play a lot of deals in a row against the same pair. You've got to be the pair that owns the table — not your opponents. You've got to take a bad result and completely wipe it out of your mind. Don't even think about the last board. If you do, you're liable to make another blunder on the next board, and the next board, and so forth."

"I know what you mean," said Otto. "Like the times I lose beeg in rubber."

"That's why at rubber, you quit when you're behind — not when you're ahead," said Jimmy, though as far as I knew, few rubber players stuck to that strategy. "Psychology is half the battle."

Hamman bit into a bagel and took half of it off — then he cleared his throat again and swallowed, not necessarily in that order. "Right, you both made good points. Now let's look at the technical side. Second point: The differences between pairs, rubber bridge and teams are easy to understand. Consider a boxing ring. A pair game is 400 drunks wrestling with each other and the one who is standing at the end is the winner. A rubber bridge session reduces the number of drunks to five or six. A team game, however, is two great boxers going at it for 15 rounds.

"Then there's the way you fight. Take baseball as a comparison. Matchpoints is a game of singles and stealing bases. Rubber bridge is a game of longball, homeruns and strikeouts. Team games are somewhere in the middle, and require tremendous patience at the plate.

"Most people recognize that the overtrick situation at imps is relatively meaningless. On the other extreme, the 10-to-13-imp swings are where the money is at teams — the game and slam swings, the doubled undertrick swings — just like at rubber bridge. Some players are very concerned about the partscores and nonvulnerable games, the 6- and 7-imp swings. And maybe they're right, but for the most part, I don't concern myself with those. The partscore is crucial in rubber bridge, where you can put two of them together to score a game, but at imps it's too tiresome to worry about every partscore. What you should be doing is wearing out your *opponents*, by bidding games and making *them* work hard to beat you.

"So Otto here isn't far off the beat with his Mayfair training. Better that he is an experienced money player than a matchpoint maven. His instincts will be correct, most of the time. Bid games, even if you occasionally overbid to them. Make your opponents sweat on every possible hand, and by the time you get to board 12 or 13 of a 16-board set, you may see the fruits of your pressure."

By the fruits of your pressure, Hamman meant the mistakes your opponents would now commit on the last hands of the set due to their weariness from defending close game contracts earlier on. It was a subtle lesson, I thought, and I didn't expect it from Hamman. But he'd been through countless bridge matches and knew what he was saying. I was relieved to hear my own opinion confirmed that rubber bridge is very close to team bridge in philosophy. My partner was a madman — true, enough — but at least his basic instincts would be to aim at the big scores.

Hamman went on to discuss the stamina problem and how easily it could be solved by taking periods of rest — something most players never dream of doing. He jotted out a list of times we could reserve our energy for the all-important big hands:

1) When you are dummy.

This was a biggy. Most players watch their partners play the hand, ready to launch into a tirade when declarer goes down, or nod in approval when declarer makes his contract.

Let's face it. The whole thing is a waste. Unless you're there to teach, what's the point? Only to waste your own energy for the next deal. What a winner does when he is dummy is relax. How you do that is up to the individual, but the key is not to follow the play of the hand. Be a robot as you pull the cards from dummy, and *think about something else.*

"I like to hum music when I'm dummy," said Otto.

"I used to know a guy who did that," replied Hamman, "but he was a fake. I knew it because whenever I made a questionable play, he went into a death eulogy."

2) When the contract is made.

Overtricks are imps, but not a lot. At the point a contract is secure everyone at the table who wants to play his best on the next deal should heave a sigh of relief and relax. Some of us play too hard for overtricks and too hard to stop them. Worse, when the hand is over, some defenders are still busy trying to find a line that would have defeated the contract, usually a play their partner should have made. They are getting ready for the explosive post mortem, another waste of precious energy.

"At the Mayfair," I said, "you've got to be ready for the post mortem, or you'll get eaten alive by the other players."

"In a tournament, you have your choice," said Hamman. "Get eaten alive by your teammates or by your opponents — I prefer my teammates. Besides, I don't discuss the hands with my teammates!"

3) When the contract is down.

Assuming it's not doubled, the contract goes down, and the hand is essentially over. Yes, it may go down more, but the intensity of the players goes down with the contract, and rightfully so.

"Thees is why overbidding ees not so bad," said Otto. "I never go down as much as I deserve."

That was reassuring, I thought, but strangely enough, he had a point.

4) When the contract is a partscore.

This went along with Hamman's treatise on going after the bonus scores and putting pressure on the defense. At matchpoints, of course, this was not true at all. Making or beating a partscore was just as important as making or beating a slam, because the comparison of scores against the other tables was the determining factor in your score. At imps, partscores were not to be sneered at, but they were no great shakes either. They were usually a third of the value of games, and therefore provided times to relax a little, if you could afford it.

"The determining factor in all these cases is the individual, what hands he's just played and how many boards are left. If you're feeling good or you were just dummy, then by all means work your hardest on the deal, partscore or not. If there are only a few boards to go. . . ."

5) When there are only a few boards to go, never relax!

When time's running out, you become a basketball player and go into full court press. Soon the game will be over and you can relax all you want. The whole business of pacing yourself refers to the early hands. The worst thing you can do in a bridge match is to make a mistake on the last board, and the second-worst is the next-to-last board. And yet this is where the most serious errors are made!

"What you want," said Hamman, "is for the opponents to make these last-minute errors. When you enter the last stages of a match, you have to mentally pick yourself up and force every ounce of energy into your decisions."

"I know what you mean," I said. "Sometimes I say to myself, 'Pretend that these are the last four hands of your life, and that the world is watching.'"

Patty Cayne entered the kitchen. "You boys will have to leave now. I've got the Rabbi coming at 10:30."

We all nodded and got up to leave.

"Oh, I forgot to tell you," I said. "Pamela is coming in this morning to help with the case."

"Good. She'll get to learn with the Rabbi as well. I was just speaking to Belsky. He says the investigation is coming along nicely."

The investigation?

What investigation?

I had forgotten all about the three murders. All I could think about was the impending championship and the strategies for imps.

15

L ife in the fast lane.
Four years ago I had given it up for the publishing life
in the country. Now I was back on the New York track and
the track was wet, hot and slippery. Worse, it was heading in
two directions at once. How could I investigate a triple
murder and prepare for a world championship bridge match
at the same time? And who did I have to help me? My partner
at the bridge table was Otto Marx, a mad Hungarian rubber
bridge player. My partner in the investigation was Barry
Belsky, a religious zealot, who spent more time searching out
kosher food from delicatessens than trailing the suspects.

I went back to my living room, introduced Belsky to Otto
and put the beds into the couch. Some Rabbi was coming
today. That meant talk of rules and laws, restrictions and
boundaries. I made it my business to be out of here before he
arrived.

After leaving Otto with instructions to fix up the convention card, I took Belsky's arm and led him to the elevator and down to the street.

"A nice man," said Belsky as we entered the rush-hour commotion along Fifth Avenue. "Showed me pictures of his wife and kids. Very nice. Once thing though, Matt."

"What's that?"

"He's a lefty. When we shook hands his left arm came out."

"So?" I asked.

"So, it may be nothing, but the mark on the late Barkowsky's neck last night was on the right side. Which means that whatever was used to strangle him was pulled from the left — or at least pulled more tightly from the left."

"Good point," I admitted. "Are any of our other suspects left-handed?"

"I don't know. I guess you don't notice until they actually go out of their way to do something with the left hand."

"Yeah, but like you said, Otto seems so innocent. At first I thought, why not the mad Hungarian? He actually tried to strangle Frankenstein only hours before his death in full view of an entire restaurant. And he has training as a chemist, so he would know how to drug his victims before strangling them. And he was Charlotte's partner the night of her murder. Maybe he lost big a few weeks ago in the Wall Street nosedive. Maybe Frank, Charlotte and Jinks were all financially involved in Otto's stock fund, and maybe that causes him to murder half a bridge team. But that's a lot of maybes. I think we should check out Otto's financial records — maybe you can do that today while I'm playing bridge — go down to his office when he's not in."

"I'd hate to snoop behind his back," said Belsky.

"Belsky, that's what we are paid to do."

We didn't use the car that morning because of the bad traffic. Instead we walked down to 47th Street and Seventh, where the video, computer, and tape industry was making headway into the storefronts of the diamond and jewelry district. At one of the stores, which was run by black-hat *Chasidim*, we tracked down the brother-in-law of the Brooklyn book-store owner and learned that the tape of the coach and Evelyn had been ripped by his two-year-old son, but that he could fix it if we would give him until the afternoon. Terrific, I said. We'd be back.

Then we took a taxi back to the morgue.

We went to a hall of records and asked to see the book of check-ins for corpses on the night of the 15th, the night that Frank Stein was strangled. The book had his name there, all right. He checked in at 3 a.m. Yet I wondered why the caretaker down on level B had not recalled him. It wasn't like you could miss a corpse like Frank Stein. His nickname was not only a joke on his real name and a clue to his personality, but the guy looked like the monster that the name is associated with. Unfortunately, she was off duty now and wouldn't be back till the evening shift.

While we were there, I also went over the record of Charlotte Stein. She checked in on the morning of the 17th and was taken for burial that very afternoon! The signature of her son was on the release column. Flipping back a couple of pages, I searched for her husband's release. But my fingers were soon cold and stiff in a lost cause. According to this record book, Frankenstein checked in, but never checked out. Could it mean that he was still at the morgue? Of course not. He would have had to have been picked up by somebody, presumably his daughter. She was overdue for a visit, I thought.

Belsky and I walked out of the morgue in thoughtful silence. At the corner I used a pay phone to ring her Soho apartment. There was an answering machine, and I left my number. There was also a message that she would be singing that evening at a nightclub on 10th and Hudson.

Things were not exactly rolling, but at least the weather

had improved. The temperature was down to a cool 90, and Belsky and I stopped in a luncheonette for a cup of coffee. I told him the truth, that I was finding it difficult to concentrate on the case with the bridge match on my mind.

"Who could blame you?" he said. "The semifinal of the world championships is no small matter. Why don't you let me take over the investigation for a while and you get some rest for the match?"

It was a tempting idea, but how could I leave it in his hands? It was as if he wanted to declare the next three game contracts, and I should sit as dummy and not even watch. Too dangerous, I thought. When you feel you have to hog the hand, you hog it, and, with Belsky as my partner, I planned to do just that.

"You know," he said, "in the Torah, when Moses' father-in-law Jethro saw that Moses wasn't able to handle the task of solving the daily problems of 600,000 families, he suggested that Moses appoint judges, and junior judges, to apportion the tasks."

"Must you always quote the Torah?" I said, sipping the last of the coffee.

"Well, maybe I should at least take over the stakeouts. After all, you're going to be playing bridge, and you can't be in two places at once."

"Okay, you have a point."

I took a New York Times that was left on a seat and opened it to the obituaries. There was Barkowsky. And there was the address of his burial. I tore it out and passed it to Belsk. He wanted a job, let him have this one. The funeral parlor was on the way uptown, so we taxied up and I dropped him. Then I continued to Harlem, where I had my own appointment. The time was 9 a.m. and when I reached 123rd Street the place was steaming.

* * * * * * * * *

The meeting for team-replacements on the North American squad came to order promptly at 11 a.m. in a meeting room at the New York Sheraton. Belsky wasn't there, so I presumed he was still at the gravesite, or wherever the body of Jinks Barkowsky was taken after his funeral.

Outside the meeting were a number of players speaking Russian, and also the Canadian player Eric Kokish, a writer for my magazine, Bridge Today. He came up to me and, his nose straight in my face, said: "Have you heard the news?"

I shook my head no.

"It's unbelievable. The Russians are protesting a scoring error."

I moved past him into the room. I had my own troubles. Around the large meeting table were members of the WBF executive committee and some select members of the ACBL board of directors. Bobby Wolff was there, as was Hamman. There were also the other four members of their team, which had lost to Jimmy's team in the Trials a few months back. The famous Meckwell — considered by many the best partnership in the world. (Jeff Meckstroth and Eric Rodwell had been coined Meckwell by the international bridge press.) Then there was a Texan, Seymon Deutsch, who had just returned to the game a few years ago after a 20-year hiatus, and in the space of one short year had earned a World Team title. Even our friend, Michael Rosenberg, was there as Seymon's partner.

It occurred to me that they were there for a reason, and that reason was to be ready to take the place of our team in the semifinal, should the committees rule Jimmy's team ineligible.

I *knew* it wasn't as easy as Jimmy said. And I felt a big chunk of disappointment making its way into my veins. Dammit, I wanted to play!

Sonty came and sat next to me. "Did you hear the news?" he said.

"The Russians?"

"Yeah, and if they win the protest, they're in and the Canadians are out."

Jimmy arrived; he gave me a nod, as if to say: don't worry. He obviously had not heard *the news*. The gravel came down and Wolff addressed his audience.

"Okay, folks, let's get this started. We're all very tired, and we still have another matter to deal with. I think, as both an ACBL director and a WBF executive member, I can speak for everybody when I say that what has happened here in New York the last week is tragic. Probably the only good from it all is the tremendous press we've received."

We all nodded. There was Wolff's optimism again. He was obviously the kind of guy who could find a good point in even the worst of scenarios. I made a point of remembering to invite him to my next wake.

"Point of order," a voice said from the other side of the table. It was Victor Mitchell, raising his hand. I had missed him before and was very glad to see him now. Victor had a lot of influence in the bridge world, and was, of course, in our camp. "Do you think it's fair that the chairman of this committee is a member of the team that may be appointed our replacement?"

There was quiet in the room. I felt a nudge from Jimmy's elbow.

"Well," said Wolff, "as you know, Victor, nothing in life is exactly fair. And I'm certainly not going to vote on the final decision."

"I'll see to that, Victor," said Edgar Kaplan, who was sitting between Wolff and the WBF president, Jimmy Ortiz Patino.

"Now," continued Wolff, "why don't we go straight to the rule book. Edgar?"

Kaplan took out a piece of paper, and read, "Bylaws of the ACBL world championship team selection. Point 247c. The winning team of the trials will represent North America in the semifinal of the Bermuda Bowl. In such a case that the winning team cannot be represented by at least four of its members, the runners-up in the trials will replace the winners."

I could see Meckwell sit up tall in their chairs as the words were read. Rosenberg looked over at me in sympathy and whispered, "Sorry, but rules are rules."

"And the next line," said Victor to Edgar.

"Ah, the next line. Yes, I'll be happy to read that, Victor. Here it is, now, the fine print, item d: If the ACBL sees fit, it may augment to any international team that is lacking in a fifth or sixth member."

Eric Rodwell spoke up. "But not a fourth member."

Suddenly the door opened. It was the coach, and he wasn't looking his best. His ascot was in in his hand, and his shirt was ruffled at the edges. He was carrying his jacket. Then there was the red stuff dripping beneath his right ear.

"Are you all right?" asked Jimmy.

"Fine, fine," he said. "But I was apprehended from behind and this note was pinned to my ear."

The members of the committees were standing now, and some of them gathered around our side of the table. The coach had his ascot against his ear, soaking up the remaining stain.

I averted my eyes. I didn't mind dried blood, but I hated the dripping kind.

We all tried to get a look at the note, but the coach folded it into his pocket and took out a batch of papers from under his jacket. "Here, I stopped and made copies on the way uptown."

Everybody grabbed a copy. The note read:

"If you continue to play, you do so at your own risk. I will not allow the North American team to win the Bermuda Bowl."

16

The Cayne mutiny was about to commence.

"Speaking for myself," said Sonty, "I think we have to stick to the rules. You guys can play — I'm going on a cruise."

"That's very sporting of you," said Wolff, "and we'll take your offer to withdraw under consideration. Due to the circumstances, I think we should take a vote. Gentlemen."

The players rose and left the room, everyone showing great camaraderie. There were a lot of, "Oh, what the heck, you play"s and a few "Some things are more important than a world title"s. All in all, it appeared that Meckwell were still interested in playing, but the rest of us were content to call it a day. It was only a few minutes before everyone was called back to the room. The verdict was unanimous.

"Both committees have agreed," said Wolff, "to allow the original team leeway, and permit them to add the names on this addendum, Granovetter, Marx and Mitchell. The ACBL feels that the best chance for an American victory would come from the team that has already been toughened by the events to date. The WBF has also agreed to reduce the number of boards in the semifinal and final to 64 each, with the proviso that should the U.S. team be reduced to three again during the course of either match, it will be forced to forfeit."

Bang. The gavel came down.

"Next," said Wolff. "Send in the members of the Russian and Canadian teams, please."

* * * * * * * * *

The team regrouped at Jimmy's apartment. In the library a rabbi was giving a lesson to four women and one man. I half-recognized one of the women as I made my way to the back of the apartment.

Belsky excused himself from the class and met me in the hallway. "What happened at the funeral?" I asked.

"Just a minute," he whispered. "The rabbi is talking about *Loshen Hora.*"

"*Loshen* what?"

"Shh. It's a law. In Judaism you're not allowed to say anything bad about another person. It's the power of words, and the harm they can do. Did you know that life and death rests on the tongue?"

"I thought it was: Sticks and stones will break your bones but names will never hurt you."

"Just the opposite, Matt. The world's got it backwards. You can fix a broken bone but you can never repair a reputation once it's been slandered."

It was interesting stuff, I suppose, but with the latest developments, I was dying to know who was at the Barkowsky burial party and what was said.

"Detective snooping is not *Loshen Hora,*" I told him. "This is clearly in the line of duty."

We moved into the spare bedroom and sat down. Belsky told me his story.

148

"Well, first, Matt, I went to the parlor. It was a closed coffin; as you know, Jews don't have open coffins, so there was no way to get another look at Jinks."

"It doesn't matter, Belsk. Just tell me who was there." And, I thought, who wasn't.

"When you go into these places, you become quite introspective, you know? There I was, and I signed in the book, then went over to the line where people were paying respects to the daughter. I didn't know it, but the mother was long since gone."

"She died three years ago," I said. "Go on."

"Well, the line was no line, if you get my drift. It was a shame. There couldn't have been more than a dozen people there. And Jinks was a nice guy, right?"

"Bridge players don't really like funerals," I said, excusing the group in one quick sentence.

"It was all right, though. Because, luckily a whole group of young college kids showed up — must have been his students at the University. I say luckily because they made up the *minyan*."

He paused.

"I know what a minyan is. Ten men."

"Yeah, very good. Anyway, there she was — Evelyn — all decked out in black, and looking like a million dollars, in a way, 'cause between you, me and the lamppost, there was an insurance agent there, and I found out through a little small talk that the late Mr. Barkowsky had a life insurance policy in his daughter's name that would leave her enough money to play *mah jongg*, if not bridge, the rest of her life."

"Good work, Belsky. What else?"

"Well, when she saw me, she seemed to put on the tears a little spritzier than usual, and I noticed the D.A. there also, and he was noticing the tears as well with a suspicious eye or two.

"Then the Rabbi came out and gave a speech that wasn't

really the best I ever heard. He talked about how Moses had not gotten into the promised land before he died, and compared it to Jinks not making it to the world bridge championships this week. A little weak, but I think the card-players in the crowd enjoyed it."

"Anyone we know there?"

"Well, let me see, there was that guy Marx, the Hungarian. He came in late, though. Then there was the fellow from the Mayfair club — I think his name is Roth. And there was a tall guy, who I didn't know, and he stood in the back and didn't talk to anyone."

"Did you get a look at him?"

"Kind of."

"Did he look . . . like a monster?"

"A monster? Hmm, come to think of it, he wasn't what you would call debonair. He had a ghoulish sort of face, if that's what you mean."

I took a deep breath. No, it couldn't be, I thought.

Sonty stuck his head in. "Are you coming? Jimmy wants the whole team for a strategy meeting."

"Okay, I'll be right there," I said.

Sonty came closer and confided "Don't you think this is a little crazy? I mean, we're risking our necks just for a bridge title."

"Well, you've won it once, Sonts. The rest of us would like to win one, too. Besides, Belsky is on the job. If it makes you feel any better, he can personally stake out near your table."

"Happy to oblige," said Belsky.

"It doesn't make me feel any better," said Sonty.

As we rose to switch rooms, I remembered to ask Belsky if he had gone to the cemetery.

"Yes, Matt, and I brought flowers, too."

"Did you see anybody new there, anything different, any clues?"

"There was only Evelyn and the rabbi — and he was

Reformed, it turned out. It was very sad, Matt. I even helped her with the shovel and we said a couple of psalms. There was one thing, though. Right after we lowered him in, on our way out, my foot felt something funny underneath it. It was sticking out of the dirt and I pulled it out. Here, wait a second, here it is."

Belsky pulled out a convention card, a dirty, old convention card, that must have been dropped by somebody visiting the cemetery — either that or left by one of the residents who no longer had a use for it. On the top of the card where the names of the players are printed were the words: "Charlotte and Frank Stein." It was their card all right. From strong notrumps to four-card majors to forcing jump raises.

I folded it carefully, put it inside my back pocket, and left the bedroom in a state of dizziness. I didn't like spooky things. And this had Stephen King written all over it!

"Belsky," I said, taking a deep breath, "would you mind going down to police headquarters? I want you to check where Charlotte and Frank Stein were buried."

* * * * * * * * *

In the den, the coach was holding court. Sonty, Jimmy and Otto were lined up on the couch, each with a xerox copy of yet another set of notes. I noticed that the Mitchells were absent from the meeting and figured they had a low estimate of its worth. The coach, who was looking remarkably chipper for a guy who had recently been attacked and had had a note pinned to his ear, passed me a copy, and I took a seat next to him. I heard the bathroom flush, and out came Evelyn. She took a seat on my other side. Still in black from the funeral, she was now wearing glasses and was looking very business-like.

The heading on the first page of the notes was: "Defense to the Russian Pass."

"Wait a second," I said. "Have the Russians won the protest?"

If they hadn't, this was surely a waste of time.

"They're meeting now," said the coach, "but it's a sure thing."

"What was the protest?"

"A scoring error by the Canadians on the next-to-last board. It was accepted by the Russians, and even on VuGraph no one noticed it but me."

"Hold on now," I insisted. "Are you saying that if it weren't for you, we'd be on our way to playing the Canadians this afternoon?"

"Of course not. If you must know, it was really Evy here who caught the error. Now it doesn't matter who caught the error. That's history. The point is the error was made and is being corrected by committee. I am sure we will be playing the Russians, and we'd better get on with our preparation if we are to put up a decent battle.

"As I was saying before Granovetter came in, it's important to distinguish the difference of defending against the Russian complex-meanings and the defense I set up for you with the more common artificial sequences, such as Stayman or Transfers."

"Could you say that in English?" said Jimmy.

"Ahem. The secret to success against the Russians is to always treat their artificial bid for what it means, not what it says. Against two clubs, Stayman, for example, double is generally used as a lead-director for clubs. But against a bid that may be much weaker, the double is a takeout of whatever suit the bidder is showing by his bid, not the suit he actually bid."

"Ah," said Otto looking at me, "like our system — where any bid can mean something difflent, if we choose."

Everyone looked up at me, now, perhaps wondering what kind of system Otto and I were planning to play.

"You are playing what I outlined?" asked the coach.

"Of course," I said. "Continue with your defense."

"Here, turn to page 2."

We all turned to page 2.

Said the coach to Evelyn: "I thought we put the summary on page 2."

Evelyn to the coach: "I put it on page 7."

The coach to the team: "Turn to page 7."

We turned to page 7.

Page 7 had a bridge hand on it with the following bidding diagram:

West	North	East	South
Pass	Double	Redouble	Jump Shift

I wondered how you could double the opening pass, but before I could get my one cent in, there was a small argument from my right to my left.

The coach: "The summary, Evy, where's the summary?"

Evelyn: "The trouble is your page 7 is not my page 7. I told you a hundred times not to count the cover page as a page."

The coach: "The cover page is a page, though. Why do you deny that?"

Evelyn: "Nobody in America counts the cover page."

The coach to the team: "Would somebody please tell my assistant here that the cover page is real and not existential."

"C'mon, already!" screamed Jimmy. "Let's go to page 8."

"No," said Evelyn, "jerko put it on page 6."

We all turned to page 6.

"There," said Jerko (a name for the coach that I found endearing), "Basic rules for artificial defenses. Rule number one: Treat artificial bids according to their strength.

a) Against strong artificial bids (strong being where the opponents have made at least one bid at the 16-point level or higher), play lead-directional doubles and lead-directional bids.

"b) Against medium-strength bids — bids that appear to be in the 12-15 point category — play strength-showing doubles, which refer to the suit or suits implied, not necessarily the suit bid.

"c) Against weak artificial bids — less than opening-bid strengths — we play complete offensive strategy, using double as our strongest bid. It might be takeout of whatever their bid implied, but a cuebid serves that purpose better."

"Fine," said Jimmy. "You got that, Sonty?"
Sonty: "I got it, but what do I do with it?"

"All right," said the coach. "Let's go to some examples. Turn to page 3."
"Two," said Evelyn.
We all turned to page 2.
"Here we have a perfect example of three types of defenses to the same auction:

West	North	East	South
1 NT	pass	2 ◊*	?

*2 ◊ is a transfer to hearts.
What does double mean?

a) If one notrump was a strong notrump, double = lead directional;

b) If one notrump was a 12-14 notrump, double = a takeout double of hearts;

c) If one notrump was a 10-12 notrump, double = a strong hand, not necessarily takeout of hearts.

"Wait a second," said Jimmy, choking on his cigar. He started to laugh, suddenly he was giddy. "What's this? What is this?"

He was pointing to something on page 53.

"That's not for you, James," said the coach. "I don't plan to play you against that pair."

We all turned to page 53. There at the top was: "Defense to Plotsky and Schlotsky's '35-Pass System.'"

Underneath was the following:

"As the opening pass by Plotsky and Schlotsky suggests any of 30 hand patterns and 5 strengths, I suggest that we defend in the same manner that they offend. That is, we hoist them by their own petard, by passing in second seat with the same patterns and strengths. This would then, in turn, force third seat to defend against our second-seat pass and place fourth seat (we) into the perfect position of being able to double third-seat's defensive opening."

We all started laughing now. This had gone too far.

"This is not a laughing matter," complained the coach. "If you don't fight fire with fire, you will be at a tremendous disadvantage. Even on the simplest terms, you must make them pay the consequences of their actions. If your opponent opens a natural one club, you double for takeout of clubs. If your opponent opens one club meaning diamonds and hearts or spades and clubs, your double must also be either takeout of diamonds and hearts or takeout of spades and clubs. If their opening bid shows seven types, so must your double. It's perfectly logical."

"It's looney," said Jimmy. "And besides, I can't take it any more. We're going back to level-one defense, Sonty."

"Well, at least level two," said the coach. "You just can't survive in today's world on level one."

As I was leaving the apartment, I bumped into the woman I had half-recognized earlier at the rabbi's lesson — she was my wife.

"Well? Have you solved the case?" Pamela asked.

"How can I have solved the case? The case is almost as complicated as Jimmy's defense to the Russian Pass."

"Look at yourself," she said. "You're all dishevelled. Here, take my comb. Listen," she continued, "Patty and I are just saying goodbye to the class and then we're going to help you."

"Great," I said, not really meaning it. "But right now I have an appointment at the office."

"But don't you have to play bridge at one o'clock? Forget your office, come have some lunch and rest a bit. Patty said that Jimmy has his heart set on winning this championship. It's going to be his last tournament, and your first concern has to be playing your best.

"And what about the three corpses and the serial killer who's still loose out there? You think you and Patty can handle that?"

"And do you think the killer can handle me and Patty? Anyway, let's do one thing at a time. Eat some lunch and take a nap."

So I did. And it was a great lunch and it was a deep sleep. But by the time I awoke, the first 16 boards of the semifinal were almost over.

* * * * * * * *

At the Sheraton, I headed straight to the ballroom. There a VuGraph show was just finishing. Concurrent presentations of both semifinal matches were on the big screen. Any passerby who didn't know it was bridge might have thought that it was a film festival. But instead of a film, it was a computer printout of a bridge hand flashing on the screen in front of 50 rows of "kibitzers." Up on the podium to the right of the screen were the commentators — Billy Eisenberg, Edgar Kaplan, Sami Kehela and Ron Andersen — analyzing the fine points and entertaining the crowd between bids and plays.

Standing near the back was Al Roth. I was surprised to see him there, although on occasion he would venture out of his Mayfair shell into the bridge community.

"Granovetter, your team needs you," he said, not unsarcastically. "I've never seen such bridge. That's why they won't put me up there on the microphone. I'd tell the people the truth: how bad the bridge has become."

"What's the score? Are they finished, Al?" I asked.

"What's the difference what the score is? Do you think the way your team bids, they really deserve to win anything? Did you see the hand they bid to four hearts and the Russian team bid to six clubs? If Cayne and Sontag were using my methods, they'd have been in six clubs in three bids."

Al told me the two hands. They were:

West	East
♠ A K x	♠ 10 x x
♡ A K J 10 x x x	♡ x
◊ K	◊ Q x x
♣ A Q	♣ K J x x x x

The Russians had bid:

pass	2 ♣
2 ♡	3 ♣
6 ♣	

Cayne and Sontag bid:

2 ♣	2 ◊
2 ♡	3 ♣
3 ♡	4 ♣
4 ♡	

Four hearts made of course, but six clubs also made. The Russians had started with a strong pass and East "responded" two clubs to show a long club suit and a limited hand. West showed hearts and East rebid his clubs. By now West had a reasonable picture of things and leaped to the six-club slam, which had the advantage of his being able to ruff out the heart suit to discard losers from the East hand.

West	East
♠ A K x	♠ 10 x x
♡ A K J 10 x x x	♡ x
◊ K	◊ Q x x
♣ A Q	♣ K J x x x x

Cayne and Sontag bid:

2 ♣	2 ◊
2 ♡	3 ♣
3 ♡	4 ♣
4 ♡	

Cayne and Sontag, however, were using Step Responses, and the two-diamond response showed a king or less. Unfortunately, Sontag could never really show his decent club suit. His three clubs was a second negative and though four clubs was natural, it didn't have to be headed by two honors.

"In my methods," said Roth, "East simply bids three clubs over two clubs, like the crazy Russian auction. It shows a semi-positive, a good, long suit and, presto, you're in six clubs."

Well, that must have been a 13-imp loss, I thought.

I moved quickly into the throng and tried to get a glimpse of the scoreboard. I first spotted the score of the other match. Great Britain: +35, Italy +27. A few lines below was our score with one board to go. Russia +33, USA +6.

Good grief, it was a rout!

The last board was now up on the screen:

Board 16   VUGRAPH
West dealer
East-West vulnerable

                        North
                        ♠ A J 8 7 6 3
                        ♡ 10 9 3
                        ◊ K
                        ♣ Q 10 6
West   East
♠ 10 9 5 4   ♠ Q 2
♡ J 8 6 5 4   ♡ —
◊ 4 2   ◊ A J 9 8 7 6 5
♣ K J   ♣ 9 8 7 3
                        South
                        ♠ K
                        ♡ A K Q 7 2
                        ◊ Q 10 3
                        ♣ A 5 4 2

Closed Room
V. Mitchell Plotsky   J. Mitchell Schlotsky
West   North   East   South
pass   pass   3 ◊   3 NT
pass   ?

It was a great hand for the Mitchells. After a three-
diamond preempt by Jacqui, the South player for Russia
overcalled three notrump.

"Understandable," said Eisenberg on the VuGraph microphone. "The overcall of three hearts may look normal, but it
doesn't show the strength of the hand. Three notrump should
work out, though."

"Yes," said Kaplan, "but somehow bidding your long suit
usually works out better."

"There you go again, Edgar," kidded Kehela, "with your radical views."

```
                       North
                       ♠ A J 8 7 6 3
                       ♡ 10 9 3
                       ◊ K
                       ♣ Q 10 6
West                                        East
♠ 10 9 5 4                                  ♠ Q 2
♡ J 8 6 5 4                                 ♡ —
◊ 4 2                                       ◊ A J 9 8 7 6 5
♣ K J                                       ♣ 9 8 7 3
                       South
                       ♠ K
                       ♡ A K Q 7 2
                       ◊ Q 10 3
                       ♣ A 5 4 2
```

Closed Room

V. Mitchell	Plotsky	J. Mitchell	Schlotsky
West	North	East	South
pass	pass	3 ◊	3 NT
pass	4 ◊	pass	4 ♡
pass	4 ♠	pass	5 ♣
pass	5 ♠	(all pass)	

Indeed, the sage was right. Over three notrump, North tried for slam with an advance cuebid of four diamonds, followed by four spades. South misunderstood and thought the cuebid was a two-suiter, otherwise why not bid four spades directly? The five-club continuation led to a precarious contract of five spades.

Jacqui (East) led the ◊ A, then switched to a club. Declarer ducked and Victor (West) won the king and gave his partner a heart ruff. That was down one, and though the panel all said Victor would score a trump trick as well, they were wrong. Declarer proceeded to ruff himself down and trump coup Victor for a brilliantly played minus 50.

At the other table the Russians did themselves in with a convention that many Americans also play.

Open Room

Pladichek	Cayne	Vladichek	Sontag
West	North	East	South
pass	pass	2 NT	?

"I'm surprised Cayne did not open a weak two-bid," said Eisenberg.

"Perhaps he is disciplined," retorted Kaplan.

"Maybe he is playing the strong two," said Kehela.

"Meanwhile," said Andersen, "the Russians have unveiled their secret weapon, the opening two notrump: a preempt in an unknown suit. I wonder if this will give North-South the same headache that the simple three-diamond preempt did in the Closed Room."

I recalled the same opening bid the day before at the Mayfair. Apparently the panel was unaware that the bid showed a side suit as well — not that it would help the Russians. . . .

Open Room

Pladichek	Cayne	Vladichek	Sontag
West	North	East	South
pass	pass	2 NT	double
pass	pass	3 ◊	?

Kehela: "The auction is heading in the same direction, but Sontag has gotten in his double a round earlier."

Kaplan: "Ah, yes, it may prove that the direct three diamonds took away valuable bidding space."

Eisenberg: "I don't think the auction *will* go the same way now."

It didn't. In fact, by the time the auction had been completed, Jimmy and Sonty had taken six natural calls and accurately described both hands!

North
♠ A J 8 7 6 3
♡ 10 9 3
◇ K
♣ Q 10 6

West
♠ 10 9 5 4
♡ J 8 6 5 4
◇ 4 2
♣ K J

East
♠ Q 2
♡ —
◇ A J 9 8 7 6 5
♣ 9 8 7 3

South
♠ K
♡ A K Q 7 2
◇ Q 10 3
♣ A 5 4 2

Open Room:

Pladichek	Cayne	Vladichek	Sontag
West	North	East	South
pass	pass	2 NT	double
pass	pass	3 ◇	3 ♡
pass	3 ♠	pass	3 NT
pass	4 ♡	(all pass)	

First was the double to two notrump, showing strength. Then the pass of the double by Jimmy (North), also to show strength. Then the three-heart bid, natural, the natural three spades, three notrump and four hearts. Both partners had described their suits and values nicely, all thanks to the fact that the opening bid had been an artificial two notrump instead of a natural three diamonds.

"Well done by the Americans," said Andersen.

"Very interesting," said Edgar.

"Illuminating," said Kehela.

"I agree," said Eisenberg.

It didn't take long for Sonty to play the hand. West led a diamond to East, who returned a club. Sonty went up with his ♣A, cashed the ♠K and ◊Q, discarding a club, then ruffed a diamond in dummy, West discarding a spade. Sonty cashed the ♠A and ruffed a spade, then led a club. He leaned over and claimed, because he could ruff a club in dummy, ensuring 10 tricks.

The screen flashed and the score changed. It read: Russia +33, USA +16.

Well, that was better. We had picked up 10 imps on the last board.

In a few minutes, Jimmy and Sonty appeared in the back of the VuGraph room, and I rushed over to congratulate them for their last hand. Unfortunately, they were arguing over some of the earlier losses, which is the way of champion bridge players — they remember the disasters better than the successes.

17

"It doesn't matter," said Jimmy, in not his kindest tone. "When you have a singleton in my suit, you've got to say *shpritz*."

"*Shpritz*? Did you see this hand?" cried Sonty. I shook my head. "Tell me the truth — would you double? The bidding goes two hearts on your left, showing an opening bid with five hearts and a five-card minor, four spades by partner, five hearts to you. And you have singleton, ace-third, king-jack fourth and queen-ten fifth. Now tell the truth."

The truth is I could hardly follow the hand. And there was Sonty looking for a sympathetic post mortem. On the other hand, there was Jimmy, ready to lower his esteem of my bridge game if I answered that I *wouldn't* double. It also occurred to me that it wasn't in the best of team spirit to be arguing over this hand when we had to go back and play 16 more deals in a few minutes, so I hedged with "Look, I've already been through this with Jimmy years ago. He likes to risk a double when you can alert your partner that you're short in his bid suit. What was the hand?"

Sonty
♠ 5
♡ A 5 3
♢ K J 6 5
♣ Q 10 9 7 6

West	North	East	South
2 ♡	4 ♣	5 ♡	?

As Sonty flashed a copy of the the bidding in front of me, Jimmy said, "The double is not only to alert me, but what if I'm two suited? — I might bid my other suit and hit a big fit."

"You can't bid your other suit," said Sonty. "It might be their second suit!"

"I think he's right about that," said the coach, who was standing next to Sonty now. Jimmy let out a scowl. "But on the other side of the coin," continued the coach, "Jimmy's right about alerting him to the singleton spade. It's not matchpoints, you know, so you've got to make risk-ratio calls."

"Of course," said Jimmy. "He's been playing too much matchpoints."

Sonty shook his head and stormed away, muttering something about not being able to stand lessons from the coach. In the meantime, I took a gander at the full deal:

West dealer
Neither side vulnerable

North
♠ A Q J 9 8 7 2
♡ —
◇ 10 9 2
♣ 8 3 2

West
♠ 6 4
♡ K J 10 9 4
◇ A Q 8 7 4
♣ A

East
♠ K 10 3
♡ Q 8 7 6 2
◇ 3
♣ K J 5 4

South
♠ 5
♡ A 5 3
◇ K J 6 5
♣ Q 10 9 7 6

The bidding was underneath, and I detected Evelyn's handwriting:

Pladichek	*Cayne*	*Vladichek*	*Sontag*
West	North	East	South
2 ♡	4 ♠	5 ♡	pass
pass	pass		

2 ♡ = opening bid with hearts and a minor

Opening lead: ♠A

First trick: ♠A, 3, 5, 6.
Second trick: ♣2

It was a good move by the Russian declarer to drop the ♠6

on the first trick — of course, it's standard high-level false-carding, but necessary. If he had played the ♠4, Jimmy would have known that Sonty's ♠5 was a singleton, because Sonty would always play the higher one from a doubleton. It was a shame, I thought, that declarer did not hold the 7-6, instead of the 6-4. Then Sonty's ♠5 would be the lowest, and known to be a singleton.

"What could I do?" said Jimmy, peering over my shoulder at the diagram. "I knew from the bidding that declarer held diamonds, and if he was 1-5-5-2, I had to shift to clubs when Sonty held the ace-queen."

It was true. The club would disappear on the ♠K if Jimmy did not shift. "My choice," continued Jimmy, "was to play Sonty for the ace-queen of clubs or play him for a singleton spade and an ace. Well, if he had a singleton spade and a side trick, he might have doubled to alert me to the short spades. Isn't that standard?"

Standard is not exactly the word I'd use. "But hasn't this come up before?" I asked. "Didn't we have this conversation only yesterday?" I said, foolishly throwing a piece of Sonty's fat into the fire.

"Yes, yes. I remember now, too."

"But Alan doesn't pay attention at my team meetings," complained the coach.

"What's the difference?" said Jimmy. "He should know this. It's too much matchpoints with Mrs. Mendelsohn That's all. No more Mrs. Mendelsohn. He's barred from playing matchpoints for two months," vowed Jimmy as he walked away in disgust.

Before I knew it, Sonty was back.

"C'mon, this is crazy. I've got one sure trick and my partner preempts. They might make six hearts, for all I know."

"It would be rare for them to make an overtrick," said the coach. "And if they make it doubled, it's only a few imps you've lost, but here we've lost 13."

I had never seen Sonty lose his cool before, but he was fuming.

"You can take your imp strategies and stick 'em. . . ."

When I saw Victor, I asked him what happened at his table. He and Jacqui were sitting East-West on the deal and reached five hearts, also. West had also led the ♠A.

"Aaaah, it was my fault," said Victor, who is always one to take the blame. "I dropped the six of spades on the first trick without remembering that they play upside-down signals. So when West saw the five of spades from his partner and the four was missing, he knew that it was a singleton."

"Run that by me again," I said.

"What am I talking to, an ignoramus? They signal upside-down! From the 5-4, they drop the 4. So when West saw the 5 and the 4 was missing, he knew I had it. I had to drop the 4, but I forgot they were playing upside-down. Got it now or do you want me to write you a book?"

Upstairs on the 49th floor, where the ACBL had taken a suite for the U.S. team to meet between sessions, the coach was pacing. When he saw me enter, he waved and I went over for a one-on-one.

"You see what happens when the players don't attend the meetings?" he said. "The Mitchells don't come and now look what happens. Upside-down signals are here in the notes, page 17b, line 6 — 'opponent's signaling system, and proper defenses.' I know Victor is considered your best American player, but can't you use your influence to get him to come to the team meetings, or at least read my defense-notes? All I ever see him reading is his stupid copy of Jaws. What kind of bridge expert is fascinated by a cheap novel about sharks?"

"Maybe he's learning how to defend against sharks," I said. Frankly, I sounded to myself like an idiot, and the coach looked at me as if I were one.

"He never gives me my proper respect," complained the coach. "And if it weren't for me, this team would disintegrate."

"I'll see what I can do," I said, not really sure that I would have the nerve to even hint that Victor look at the coach's dreaded notes.

The team was finished licking its wounds, and the coach and Jimmy conferred on the line-up for the second quarter. The Mitchells were out. Jimmy and Sonty would play in the Closed Room, East-West, against the Estonians. And Otto and I would be on VuGraph against the infamous Plotsky and Schlotsky from the Ukraine.

* * * * * * * * *

Though we were on VuGraph, and every bid and play would be seen in the theatre on the first floor, we would actually be playing in a little suite on the seventh floor. There a group of rooms had been booked by the WBF, and in each room was a table, chairs and bidding screen. In the room were also two video cameras and a microphone.

We shook hands with the Ukrainians and sat down North-South. The bidding screen was a huge, black metal unit, which was positioned about six inches above the table. It was attached to the corners of the table diagonally, so when I sat down, South, I could see my East opponent but not West or my partner. About a foot in from each corner of the screen was an extra rectangle of metal that could slide up and down the bigger unit. This would be moved up about a foot when the bidding was over so that three players could see the dummy and the defenders' cards.

There are many variations of screens, which are designed not only to eliminate eye contact between the players, but to stop any rumors, talk, or even suspicion of cheating. This screen, however, with its metal slide and black color reminded me of a guillotine. I couldn't help but wonder what would happen to someone's arm if it were too close to the sliding unit when it dropped.

On the table, under the screen, was the bidding tray. It was made of wood and had a square in the middle, with four rectangle units around the square. Attached to the four corners of the table were bidding boxes, each with multicolored cards, with bids from one club to seven notrump. Then there were lots of green pass cards, red double cards and blue redouble cards to go with it. When it was a player's turn to bid, he would pull the card from the bidding box and place it in his rectangle on the bidding tray. After two players from the same side of the screen made their bids, one of them would push the tray under the metal screen to the other side of the table. This was designed to eliminate voice inflection in the bidding.

In short, the formerly social game of bridge had been updated with a huge collection of cumbersome equipment. Nobody would hear or see his partner for the two hours we were expected to play 16 deals, that is, except for the occasional remarks made between hands.

A man with a microphone sat to my left at the corner of the table. He was going to announce the bids and plays to the VuGraph audience downstairs. With all this going on, it was no wonder that I had forgotten to discuss with Otto which defense we were going to use against the big-pass system of our opponents. So before the first board was placed on the table — the boards had been dealt in advance by computer — I rushed out of the room to find Victor. He was sitting down the hall smoking a Lucky.

"What are you doing in the hallway?" I asked.

"Waitin' for you ta ask me your questions," he answered.

"Which is our best defense to the big-pass, Victor? The

two-way double system or transfer overcalls or what?"

"Nuttin," he said.

"Nuttin?"

"You heard me. Let them get confused by their own system. Just don't let them get you confused. Play nuttin."

"You mean if they open a diamond to show hearts, we overcall a heart to show hearts?"

"Whatsamatta wit ya, huh? Don't you know what nuttin is? If ya overcall, ya got the suit you overcalled. If you double, it's a takeout double of whateva suit they bid — not the suit they say they got — the suit they actually bid. And if ya pass, you got nuttin!"

I thanked Victor and ran back to the room, where they were ready to start. When I got to my seat, I lifted up the visor on the screen and stuck my nose through. "Listen, Otto. Victor says we should play nuttin — I mean nothing — over their artificial bids. That means that we treat everything they bid as real and bid naturally. That okay with you?"

"Is okay by me. But it's a clazy ting. All morning I study the coach's defense, and now you say we don't play it."

"Look, Otto," I said, "I'm too nervous right now. Besides, I really didn't get a chance to read those notes. So, please, let's just play nothing."

"Okay by me," he muttered, "but I don't theenk it's okay by the coach."

I slid my nose back and we all took out the cards to board 17. I held:

♠ A Q J ♡ K 7 6 2 ◇ Q 7 3 ♣ A K Q

Twenty-one points. Nice hand. Otto started the auction with a one-heart opening bid. East passed. I decided to bid two notrump, natural and forcing. It was nice to be playing this jump as natural, because it would allow a natural rebid by Otto. I placed the 2NT card on the tray and slid it across to the other side. When the tray came back, it had a pass on my left and a 3◇ bid by Otto. East passed and I bid three hearts, waiting to hear what else he had to say.

♠ A Q J ♡ K 7 6 2 ◇ Q 7 3 ♣ A K Q

The tray came back with a bid of three spades from Otto. I bid four notrump. He showed one ace, and now I had a decision to make. Should I play the hand in six hearts or six notrump? There could be a ruff outstanding — if one opponent held a singleton diamond. So I bid five notrump to check on kings.

It occurred to me that most experts play the bid of four notrump followed by five notrump as not only asking for kings, but guaranteeing that all the aces are held by the partnership. I had no such agreement with Otto, luckily. He showed two kings, so I bid six notrump, the safer slam.

The opening lead was the ♣J and this was what I saw:

North
♠ K 10 9 2
♡ A J 5 4 3
◇ K 9 4 2
♣ —

South
♠ A Q J
♡ K 7 6 2
◇ Q 7 3
♣ A K Q

As much as I love to be declarer, I never enjoy it on the first hand of a match. I never seem to be entirely "there" for the first board. At one time, I had the idea that, like tennis or baseball, we should volley, take batting practice, play a

172

few warm-up deals before a match begins. But I've never followed-up on this idea, and I've often paid for it. That the brain also needs to get into third gear is an idea that is ignored by the bridge experts. And once again I was to pay dearly. If you, the reader, wish to test yourself, decide how you would play this hand before reading on.

All I could think of was: This hand boils down to the heart position. Play for the 2-2 split or take a finesse against West. So I discarded a diamond from dummy and won the first trick in my hand, then led four rounds of spades to see how many spades West held. If he were short in spades, singleton or doubleton, I was going to play him for length in hearts and finesse.

As I played the spades, however, I suddenly went into a sweat. And it was not a nice, healthy sweat. No, it was the sort of sweat that happens when you've done something terrible and your subconscious starts sending signals to the conscious, and you wish like hell it didn't receive them. Nor was it a nice message it was sending: "Trick one, you dummy; trick one, you stupidicus; trick one, trick one, trick one, you ignoramus!"

I had discarded a diamond at trick one, but I should have discarded a heart!!

Yes, of course, the hearts were my long suit, but I didn't need five heart tricks for my contract. Had I counted my tricks before playing to the first trick, I would have counted four spades, three clubs and one diamond, for eight. That meant I only needed four heart tricks for 12. Then I should have said to myself: What do I do if I misguess hearts — are there any other chances?

Oh, how utterly stupid of me. If I play the ace and king of hearts and the queen is third, I still have quite a lot of tricks — 10 to be exact (four spades, two hearts, one diamond and three clubs). I could make the other two tricks in diamonds if I could score three diamond tricks in total. There are two positions that would allow me to make three diamond tricks. If East started with the A-J or A-10 doubleton, I could lead a diamond from dummy toward my queen and then a low one back, ducking in dummy. On the third round, West's honor doubleton would be finessable. Sure, it was obscure. Sure, East would have had to have been dealt one heart and two diamonds specifically. But it was possible, and it was now impossible because I had discarded a diamond from dummy at trick one!

Meanwhile, in the middle of my a-little-too-late analysis, I had not even watched the spades carefully. When I played the fourth spade, however, everyone pitched. So they must have been 3-3. What could I do? I prayed silently, led a heart to my king, cashed my other two club tricks, and led a heart up. West followed and I went up with the ace. East discarded and I wanted to die. That was the last trick I took — I didn't even get a diamond trick — down three. All I wanted out of life was one thing: that East did not start with the A-J or A-10 of diamonds.

I asked him if I could see his hand. This was the full deal:

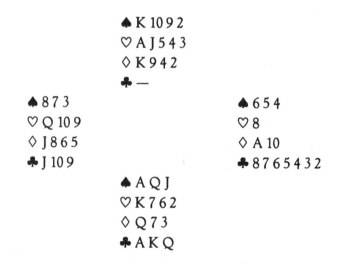

$$
\begin{array}{l}
\spadesuit \text{ K 10 9 2} \\
\heartsuit \text{ A J 5 4 3} \\
\diamond \text{ K 9 4 2} \\
\clubsuit \text{ —}
\end{array}
$$

♠ 8 7 3 　　　　　　　　　　♠ 6 5 4
♡ Q 10 9 　　　　　　　　　 ♡ 8
◊ J 8 6 5 　　　　　　　　　 ◊ A 10
♣ J 10 9 　　　　　　　　　 ♣ 8 7 6 5 4 3 2

$$
\begin{array}{l}
\spadesuit \text{ A Q J} \\
\heartsuit \text{ K 7 6 2} \\
\diamond \text{ Q 7 3} \\
\clubsuit \text{ A K Q}
\end{array}
$$

I couldn't bear it. My head was swimming. The director, Maury Braunstein, was in the room, chastising the players for slow play. Slow play? It was only the first board. And I had gone down in a laydown six notrump! In front of the entire VuGraph audience!!

I quickly pulled the cards to the next deal.

♠ 8 7 6 3 2 ♡ A K 2 ◇ 4 ♣ A 8 7 2

Pass on my right. Should I open this hand, vulnerable, in second seat? The spades are terrible, but somewhere in the back of my murky mind — and believe me, after going down in a slam you realize you should have made, your mind is far from clear — I remember an old theory . . . something about opening light with weak suits. Yes, I remember. If you have a very weak suit, you actually are better off opening light than with a good suit, for two reasons: 1) it is difficult to reenter with a two-level overcall on a bad suit; and 2) your hand will fit partner well whether he has a fit or not — that is to say, on this hand, if he has a fit in spades, the length will be valuable, while if he has short spades, the lack of wasted highcards in spades will be an asset.

So I opened one spade and then I noticed that the Russian on my right was pointing his finger to the ALERT card. A little too late, Matthew. When are you gonna get with it, Matthew? As we push the tray across, Schlotsky writes me a note in broken English: pass = 17+ points.

Lovely, I thought. And now he wants to know about my one-spade bid. We play that it is a lead-director over a big club. So therefore, over a big pass it should also be a lead-director. Wait a second. We just decided to play Victor's nuttin system over the big pass. Thus my one-spade opening was still a one-spade opening. And so I scribble on the pad: one spade = nuttin, just an opening bid in spades.

By this time the tray is back to us. Lefty has passed and

Otto has bid two clubs. Sholsk ALERTS the pass. Pass = 0-3 points. I wouldn't doubt it, 'cause Otto has made a 10-point two-over-one, I have 10 points and Shlosk has shown at least 17. Shlosk now thinks and thinks, asks about two clubs, and then finally passes. I raise to three clubs and suddenly realize that Otto's two clubs might be Drury by an unpassed hand. It was a crazy convention, and I was sorry I had agreed to it now. Meanwhile, the tray has returned to my side and Otto has bid three diamonds. Shlosk passes and I bid three notrump. I don't really know what I'm doing bidding three notrump, with a 17-point hand on my right, but there is no real alternative at this point.

My three notrump is passed around to East, who hems and haws some more and finally doubles. I would like to run to the safety of four clubs, but then I'm not sure if Otto-bird over there really has clubs. So I pass.

Oh, well, I think, how bad can it be?

Everyone passes, and after an interminable amount of time, West leads the ◊J This is the full deal:

North (Otto)
♠ 9 4
♡ 8 7 4
◊ A 2
♣ K Q J 10 9 3

West (Plotsky)
♠ 5
♡ 10 9 5
◊ J 10 8 7 5 3
♣ 6 5 4

East (Schlosky)
♠ A K Q J 10
♡ Q J 6 3
◊ K Q 9 6
♣ —

South (Matthew)
♠ 8 7 6 3 2
♡ A K 2
◊ 4
♣ A 8 7 2

Otto did have clubs, after all. But who cares? This was the sort of hand I could handle in my state. I laid down my cards, claiming nine tricks. Whereupon I was expecting a behind-the-screen screaming match between the two Russians. But it did not happen. They controlled their emotions and kept quiet. In fact, Plotksy said softly to Schlotsky, "I'm sorry," in Russian. At least that's what I was told later by the interpreter sitting on the other side of the screen.

Though the Ukranians exhibited perfect decorum, kept their cool, and retained their ability to think clearly on the next board, they were unable to overcome certain flaws in their system. Hand after hand they were passing with strong hands and Otto and I would preempt before they had a chance to find a fit. Then, when they opened the bidding without an opening bid, we would double with our good hands and they were unlucky enough not to have a good fit. By the time we got to board 32, I would have guessed we were ahead at least 50 or 60 imps. On this board, Plotsky opened two diamonds, multi, meaning a weak two-bid in either major or a strong hand in the minors. Otto doubled for takeout of diamonds, and Schlotsky passed, showing diamonds and shortness in both majors. I held:

♠ A 5 ♡ K 4 ◇ K Q J 9 8 ♣ J 9 8 3

I passed and Plotsky passed. This was down 1400, and though we might have been able to make a slam in spades on some layouts, we had no chance on this one. The full deal was:

North (Otto)

♠ K Q J 8 7 3

♡ Q 10 9 8

◇ —

♣ A K 10

West (Plotsky)

♠ 10 9 2

♡ A J 7 6 5 2

◇ 7 6

♣ Q 7

East (Schlotsky)

♠ 6 4

♡ 3

◇ A 10 5 4 3 2

♣ 6 5 4 2

South (Matthew)

♠ A 5

♡ K 4

◇ K Q J 9 8

♣ J 9 8 3

Otto led the ♣K and shifted to the ♠K. I won the ace and shifted to the ◇K. East won the ace and played a club to Otto's ace. Otto continued spades and there was nothing declarer could do but ruff the third spade, watch me overruff, draw a round of trumps and shift back to clubs. We ended up with 10 tricks on defense, for down five.

At the other table, West did not open a weak two-heart bid. "I can't open a weak two-bid vulnerable with such weak trump spots," said Jimmy later. He *was* disciplined. The opponents bid to six spades and Sonty, East, led the ◇A. This was ruffed by North, who next led a heart to the king, planning to ruff a heart and take two pitches on diamonds. But this plan failed when Sonty was able to ruff the second round of hearts.

Readers should note that even after a weak two-heart bid, the North-South players cannot punish East-West, because if North doubles, South cannot possibly leave it in. It was a great lesson in bidding conventions. When you open in a bid that is not your real suit, you give the opponents an extra round of bidding, and this may result in their ability to penalize you. Even if Plotsky had run to two hearts, in our auction, Otto would have been able to double for penalties, and that contract would have gone down four.

We got up from the table and headed to the elevator. Otto and I were both very excited about our game, so excited that I had left the scorecard back at the table. So I told Otto I'd meet him up at the suite and returned to fetch the card. It took me longer than I expected. The room had emptied out, and the score was not on the table. I looked under the bidding tray, around the corners of the bidding boxes, everywhere! Finally I found it on the floor, under my chair. Quickly I put it in my jacket pocket and ran back out and down the hall to the elevator. It was a long time in coming, but finally it arrived and I pushed floor 49. As it went up, a little voice inside my head started whistling a warning — it was a sixth sense, as they say. There was no one in the elevator with me, so there was no real reason to be nervous, but just as a precaution I moved to the corner and crouched down. If anybody had seen me, he would have thought I was out of my mind. But that's the way of the detective business. The elevator stopped at floor 48, but no one got on. I made the error, though, of not getting off. The elevator moved up another few feet and stopped cold.

Suddenly the middle of the elevator ceiling collapsed, splinters of glass and metal flying in all directions. A few hit me in face and arms, and when I touched my cheek, blood was on my fingers. I rose, pushed the red emergency button, and the elevator rang out like a fire engine. It started to move up again, and opened on the 49th floor. I skipped over the mess inside, and walked down to the suite, where I heard joyous laughter and mirth.

"Nice game," said Jacqui, the first person I saw.

"Wha'd I tell ya," said Victor. "I could see it the first

session, but the hands just didn't come up."

He was right, as usual. And the idea of using no special defenses to their bids was brilliant. We never had a problem understanding each other's calls.

Jimmy and Sonty had come out with a very good set as well, and we picked up an amazing 73 imps. We only lost 3 imps on the first board, where I had gone down three in six notrump.

Board 17

North
♠ K 10 9 2
♡ A J 5 4 3
◊ K 9 4 2
♣ —

West (Jimmy)
♠ 8 7 3
♡ Q 10 9
◊ J 8 6 5
♣ J 10 9

East (Sonty)
♠ 6 5 4
♡ 8
◊ A 10
♣ 8 7 6 5 4 3 2

South
♠ A Q J
♡ K 7 6 2
◊ Q 7 3
♣ A K Q

The Estonians reached six hearts, and after a club lead, won in hand, declarer led a spade to dummy and tried to sneak a diamond to the queen. If Sonty had ducked his ace, declarer would have been able to discard the other diamonds on his clubs. But Sonty rose to the occasion with the ace and Jimmy scored his trump queen when declarer later played for trumps 2-2.

After a few more post mortems, someone finally noticed that I was bleeding. It was the coach. "You know, you have a rather nasty cut," he said.

18

"Jimmy thinks I'm nuts."

It was Patty and the statement was one I'd heard before.

"But I told him, you concentrate on your bridge game — let Pammy and me handle the investigation."

"What exactly do you mean?" I asked, a bit distraught upon hearing that my wife was now on the killer's trail.

"We're flying to Alabama."

Jimmy was right.

"Why?" I asked.

"Why? Because we have to get the hand-records. I have to meet Pammy at the airport in an hour, so I'll make it fast. Try to process what I'm saying.

"We know that the killer left deliberate clues on the first two victims. One was the four-diamond bid and the other the eight of diamonds. The clues obviously refer hands from the Team Trials last spring, because the Steins were arguing over the eight-of-diamonds play from the Trials at the Red Tulip restaurant."

"How did you know that?"

"Otto told me. Besides, if the clues refer to some private bridge game, what would be the point of the killer leaving them? Whoever he is, he's probably demented — especially if he's leaving clues. Yet even a demented killer who is upset over a four-diamond bid or the play of the diamond eight would be logical enough to leave clues that have a chance to be understood. Trust me on this."

I wasn't sure she was right. Yes, she did recently get a doctorate in psychology, but the mental states of serial killers is a special field unto itself.

"Are you listening to me or dreaming about a bridge hand?"

"Yes, yes, I'm listening," I said.

"So we went to Henry Francis, who's doing the Bulletin for the Bermuda Bowl here in the hotel, and he claimed the hand-records from the Trials were sent to the coach. You know how the coach loves to analyze every board and keep Jimmy awake till the wee hours with his bidding improvements. Anyway, the coach told Pammy and me that he was through with those records a long time ago and had tossed them away. So we called the ACBL in Memphis, spoke to Brent Manley of the Bulletin and he said that all the records were missing from their file — very strange. Finally, I got it out of him that one set had been sent to Frank Stewart, who recently retired from the Bulletin staff. Pamela called Frank, and he has the records in his desk, but he can't fax them to us because they're partially burnt."

"What?" I said, in a daze now.

"Burnt — you know — like matches to paper burns the paper. Think about it. There was a fire down there — not a serious one, and though he saved them, they're not in great condition, especially after he dumped a bucket of water on them.

"Anyway, to make a story that was supposed to be short a little shorter, I'll get to the point. If we wait for the hand-records to be flown up here via overnight mail, we won't get them for another day, and by that time who knows who the killer's next victim will be? So we phoned the airlines, found flights, and we're heading down to Fayette, Alabama, to retrieve them. Gotta go now, wish me *bon voyage* — you'll see your wife later tonight."

"Wait a second! When will you be back? When will I see my wife again?"

"Probably midnight," she said, walking out the door. "We'll meet back at the apartment," she added.

"No," I said, scribbling a note on the back of a convention card. "Give her this — tell her to meet me there after you land."

What was the point in this wild trip? Even if they could learn what the play was or what the bid was that the murderer had identified with his victims, how would we be able to trace the clue to the murderer?

Perhaps, if I were not in the middle of a bridge match, my head would have been clearer and I would have asked Patty this before she embarked with my wife on the mad journey. But, then again, maybe the two of them knew something I didn't, and besides, to tell you the truth, the bridge match was such an emotional high that I didn't really care as much as I should have. It was only when I went to the bathroom and saw the dried blood smeared across my cheek that I suddenly realized I'd forgotten about Belsky as well.

A private eye is supposed to be responsible for his partner, whether he likes him or not. In bridge, partners are not so dear. I've known many a player who actually rooted against his partner while pulling the cards from dummy. In the criminal investigation racket, however, you not only got a bad reputation when your partner got hurt, but it was bad for business as well. On top of it all, I was rather fond of Belsky and had a responsibility to him and his family. So while the other members of my team ate their dinner, I ventured outside, hailed a cab, and took it to police headquarters. There I learned that the Steins had been buried at the Bronx Jewish Cemetery.

* * * * * * * * *

The joint wasn't exactly hopping. The late afternoon summer sun was still high in the sky and the heat was strong. I tiptoed through the entrance. There was a little guy at the desk inside the front office, and he tried to sell me a plot or two. Maybe I should have struck up a bargain, but I wasn't in the mood. He gave me a map of the place and led me to the back of the building.

"Out there," he pointed. "That's where the freshest spots are. Beautiful cherry blossoms in season now. Just head past the garden area and make a right."

It didn't take long to find him. He was sprawled out next to a headstone. I had a flask with me and gave him a drink as I lifted his head. His eyes slowly came to focus.

"Matt? Is that you?"

"It's okay Belsky. Just have another sip."

There was a bump on his head the size of a bidding box.

"What happened?" I asked.

"I'm not really sure," he admitted. "I was walking back from the Steins' grave sites when I think I tripped. Or was I hit before I fell?"

He felt the bump now. I could see the pain of it was just hitting him.

When he was feeling better, we walked back toward the gravesites. Before we arrived we saw the boy. He was standing by his mother's grave, a fresh-cut deck of cards at his feet. He didn't say a word, just stood there. Then he bent down and arranged the cards into the earth in a fashionable bouquet. On the stone he was facing were the words: Charlotte Stein — 1957-1989. Next to her was her husband: Frank Stein — 1941-1989. The boy looked up at us.

"She was the best, you know."

I wasn't sure if he was referring to her maternal care or her bridge game.

"How long have you been here, Bobby?" I asked bluntly.

"I got here a few minutes ago. I was here this morning, too. I want to make sure the grave is looked after. . . ." His words drifted off into space.

The three of us walked back together, and I made a careful note of where the graves were located. I didn't like doing it, but I had to ask a delicate question.

"Bobby, did you ever suspect your mother of having an affair?"

The kid didn't answer, so I pressed.

"Did you ever come home and catch her alone with a certain party known as Otto Marx?"

The kid started to laugh. "Otto Marx? Who would have an affair with Otto Marx? Ha, ha! Mr. Granovetter, my mom only had one love affair her whole life and that was with the game of bridge."

Back in Belsky's Oldsmobile we headed straight to a pharmacy for something to put on his bruise and my cuts as well. Then we stopped at a hardware store, bought a pick, a shovel and a flashlight, dumped them into the trunk and headed back to the hotel. Belsky told me that he had stopped by the Stock Exchange and met with some of the traders who worked for Otto. They all swore that business was booming.

When we arrived at the Sheraton, the third quarter of the match was in session and the VuGraph room was jam-packed.

19

We were still 60 imps ahead, and there were seven boards left in the session. The score was posted on the top right corner of the VuGraph screen. The featured match on VuGraph was the other semifinal: England vs. Italy. The score there was much closer, with Italy leading by 13.

I sat down in one of the few empty seats, next to Alan Truscott, bridge editor of the New York Times. He was scribbling down the hand on the screen, so I examined it to see what was so interesting. The contract was four spades.

[Board 41 on facing page.]

The auction was a little unusual, but I found out later that it was part of Benito's new club system. One club had been strong and two hearts meant a positive with spades! This effectively transferred the declarership to the South hand. North then bid four clubs as a splinter, South asked about controls and North showed three. Then South signed off in four spades.

Board 41
North dealer
East-West vulnerable

England 88, Italy 101

North
♠ K J 9 8 6 4
♡ 9 8 3
◇ A 3 2
♣ 2

West
♠ 7 5
♡ K J 10 7
◇ J 8 7
♣ K Q 10 9

East
♠ 10
♡ 6 5 2
◇ K Q 10 6
♣ 8 7 6 4 3

South
♠ A Q 3 2
♡ A Q 4
◇ 9 5 4
♣ A J 5

Rose	Franco	Sheehan	Garozzo
West	North	East	South
—	pass	pass	1 ♣
1 ♡	2 ♡	pass	2 ♠
pass	4 ♣	pass	4 ◇
pass	4 ♡	pass	4 ♠
(all pass)			

Benito Garozzo was declarer and Irving Rose already had the lead on the table: the ♣Q. We could see Benito examining the dummy in the camera shot to the right. He was deeply intense, leaning forward, even spreading out the cards with his hand, perhaps looking for an extra highcard or two. The commentators were quick to analyze the hand — maybe too quick.

187

North
♠ K J 9 8 6 4
♡ 9 8 3
♢ A 3 2
♣ 2

West (Rose)
♠ 7 5
♡ K J 10 7
♢ J 8 7
♣ K Q 10 9

East
♠ 10
♡ 6 5 2
♢ K Q 10 6
♣ 8 7 6 4 3

South (Garozzo)
♠ A Q 3 2
♡ A Q 4
♢ 9 5 4
♣ A J 5

"Rose does not play Rusinow leads, does he?"

"No, he's just trying to fool Garozzo."

"Looks like the contract depends on the heart finesse — and it's offside."

"Yes, but there is a chance for an endplay. If South can eliminate the minor suits, then play the nine of hearts, he can float it around to West, and force a heart return or ruff and sluff."

"True, but while declarer is trying to eliminate the minors, East will get in with a diamond honor and see the necessity of switching to a heart, and that will destroy any chance of an endplay."

Suddenly I felt a hand in the vicinity of my lap. I turned to the right — it was Evelyn. She started banging her fist on my leg in her enthusiasm. "Look, look at that jack of clubs," she whispered, as if she were conspiring with me on some life-threatening issue.

Benito sat back in his seat and called for dummy's ♣2. East followed low and Benito followed low also.

The hum of the audience turned into silence. It wasn't normal to duck the first trick in a suit contract when you had the ace opposite a singleton. Irving thought for a few seconds, longer than usual for him, and then switched to a diamond. Benito called for the ◊A. He wasn't going to give East a chance to play a heart through. No, the great master had his plan. He pulled two rounds of trumps, ending in his hand, then led the ♣A, discarding a diamond, and the ♣J, won by West's queen, as he discarded dummy's last diamond.

Irving played a diamond. Benito ruffed in dummy, led a trump to his hand, and played his last diamond, ruffing in dummy. Now the board looked like this:

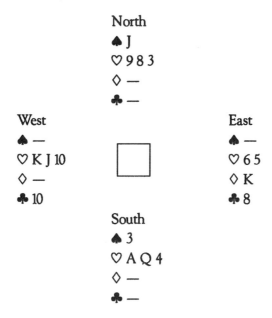

North
♠ J
♡ 9 8 3
◊ —
♣ —

West
♠ —
♡ K J 10
◊ —
♣ 10

East
♠ —
♡ 6 5
◊ K
♣ 8

South
♠ 3
♡ A Q 4
◊ —
♣ —

Benito led the ♡9 and let it ride. When West won, he was endplayed and the audience applauded, though it was impossible for Benito to hear the applause.

"I think," said Ron Andersen from the podium, "it is sometimes easier to analyze the deal when you see only two hands."

"Good point," said Edgar Kaplan. "Four hands can confuse the expert, who is used to only two."

"In any case, Edgar," said Ron, "it was another brilliantly played hand by the ten-time world champion. Most of my students like to win their aces. Here Garozzo demonstrated how not winning the first trick can be the winner."

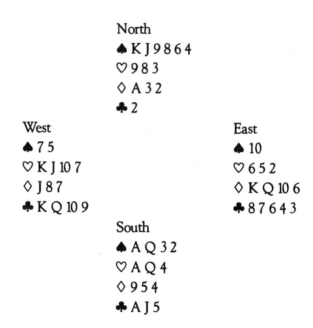

North
♠ K J 9 8 6 4
♡ 9 8 3
♢ A 3 2
♣ 2

West
♠ 7 5
♡ K J 10 7
♢ J 8 7
♣ K Q 10 9

East
♠ 10
♡ 6 5 2
♢ K Q 10 6
♣ 8 7 6 4 3

South
♠ A Q 3 2
♡ A Q 4
♢ 9 5 4
♣ A J 5

The VuGraph revealed that, at the other table, the contract of four spades was played by the North seat and after the ♢K lead was ducked, East, Giorgio Belladonna, made the correct switch to a heart. After this, the contract had to go down one.

In our match, where the same boards were being played, Karpos and Stavinsky for the Russians and the Mitchells for our team both played from the South side. Stavinsky won the opening club lead and eventually our East player, Jimmy, shifted to hearts when in with his ♢K, for down one. But Jacqui, declarer at the other table, also made the key duck at trick one and made her game. I guess because she was in the other match, none of the VuGraph commentators noticed.

I turned to Evelyn, gave her a thumbs up and asked her why she wasn't recording hands at the table.

"I just had to get away from him for a while."

By "him" I took it she meant the coach. I took out the slip of paper that I had picked up at the morgue — the one that had "Mayfair Club" on top — and passed it to her.

"You have anything to go with this?"

She grabbed it and put it in her blouse. "That was my daddy's, you louse. If you really must know, he carried it around with him in his wallet all the time. It was the score pad of his greatest rubber. He won fifty-seven hundred and thirty points in four deals. Here:"

She passed me the torn slip. Yes, it had four scores on it: +980, +1430, +1100 and +2220. Maybe this girl was on the level after all.

"Excellent hand for tomorrow's column," commented Alan Truscott on my left. "Save my seat, while I phone it in."

I nodded, then he said as he rose: "Wait a second — I forgot to tell you. Your wife and Patty Cayne were speaking with me this morning about the trial deals and their relation to the clues left by the murderer."

"What? Do you know something about it?"

"Yes, well, I mean, no, I don't. But since then I've spoken to Philip Alder, who happened to analyze all the deals at the time. He told me that he wrote every hand of interest onto his computer, and last night he happened to review them for his own edification. There wasn't one that contained the eight of diamonds as an interesting play. Nor was there a single bid of four diamonds that made any difference to the auction. In fact, he found only two four-diamond bids in the 50 or so hands he had recorded.

"Just thought that would be of some interest to you — though it doesn't really help you, I suppose, does it? Save my seat for me."

Great, I thought. The women have gone on a wild goose chase to Alabama. What a waste!

The next six hands were very slow and very boring. That was good for our side, obviously, because when you are far ahead in a match, you don't want swingy hands. I can remember two nightmarish occasions when my team, up more than 50 imps going into the final set of hands, lost the match. Only once did I actually pick up 50 after being down that much — that was with my wife in a Vanderbilt quarterfinal.

I took the time to glance around the room. There were a lot of people I knew from the old days, but there was one face that was new. It was Mrs. Kennedy, the detective's wife. I wondered what she was doing here and I wondered if she had her Dobermans with her.

When the last hand of the set flashed up on the board, the score was USA 125, Russia 65. In the featured match the score was England 98, Italy 117.

[Board 48 on facing page.]

The bidding again required explanation. One diamond was almost natural, but two clubs was an artificial game force. Two notrump showed a 6-4 shape and three clubs asked for clarification. Three diamonds, an ingenious bid, showed hearts, allowing the concealed hand to grab the heart suit as declarer. Four clubs showed exactly five controls (an ace = 2, a king = 1) and a singleton spade. Four diamonds by South asked for a cuebid of an ace or king, and North bid four hearts. Four spades now asked for further cuebidding, and North bid five clubs, denying the ♠A or ♠K (with which he would have bid four notrump) but showing the ♣A. With all that information, Benito was able to picture a slam and he bid it.

Irving Rose, in the West seat, also had the information. He

192

Board 48　　　　　　　　　　　　　| VUGRAPH |
West dealer
East-West vulnerable

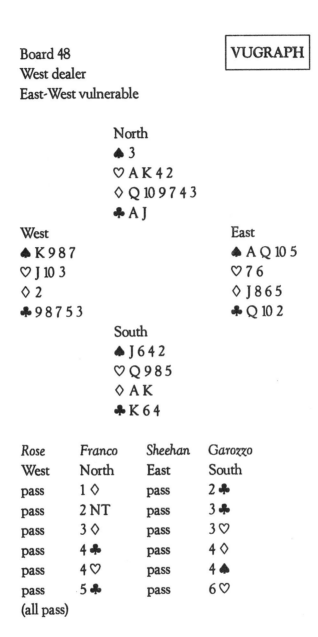

North
♠ 3
♡ A K 4 2
♢ Q 10 9 7 4 3
♣ A J

West
♠ K 9 8 7
♡ J 10 3
♢ 2
♣ 9 8 7 5 3

East
♠ A Q 10 5
♡ 7 6
♢ J 8 6 5
♣ Q 10 2

South
♠ J 6 4 2
♡ Q 9 8 5
♢ A K
♣ K 6 4

Rose	Franco	Sheehan	Garozzo
West	North	East	South
pass	1 ♢	pass	2 ♣
pass	2 NT	pass	3 ♣
pass	3 ♢	pass	3 ♡
pass	4 ♣	pass	4 ♢
pass	4 ♡	pass	4 ♠
pass	5 ♣	pass	6 ♡
(all pass)			

decided against leading his singleton because it was North's
long suit. He was also reasonably certain that his partner held
a spade honor, probably the ace. So he decided to lead the
♠K, and when it held the first trick, he continued with
another spade, tapping the dummy.

193

North
♠ 3
♡ A K 4 2
♢ Q 10 9 7 4 3
♣ A J

West (Rose)
♠ K 9 8 7
♡ J 10 3
♢ 2
♣ 9 8 7 5 3

East
♠ A Q 10 5
♡ 7 6
♢ J 8 6 5
♣ Q 10 2

South (Garozzo)
♠ J 6 4 2
♡ Q 9 8 5
♢ A K
♣ K 6 4

This was really an excellent lead, even better than a low spade, pointed out Edgar on the panel. Because if Garozzo held the ♠Q-J, a low spade and a spade return would set up a spade trick, but the lead of the ♠K followed by a spade from West would not set up a spade trick for declarer. In any case, it didn't seem to matter which spade Irving led, as long as he led one of them and the suit was continued. After ruffing the second trick in dummy, Benito drew three rounds of trumps and cashed the ♢A-K.

When West showed out, the great Italian Blue Team star led a club to the jack for a finesse against the ♣Q. His only hope lay in reaching dummy twice, once to ruff out the diamond suit, and once more to cash the diamond winners. But when East won the ♣Q, he cashed a spade trick, for down two.

At the other table, the English had stopped in four hearts and won 13 imps, making the score at the end of the three-quarter mark: England 114, Italy 117 — very close!

Before I could see what happened in our match, I heard

194

Jimmy and Alan arguing in the back of the VuGraph room. I got up and tried to see what the problem was. They were arguing about this very hand. Six hearts was reached against them and Alan had led the ♠7. When Jimmy won the ♠A, he shifted to a diamond, in an attempt to give Alan a ruff. So *there* was the reason for leading the ♠K!

Jimmy: "If you wanted a spade continuation, why didn't you lead your honor?"

Alan: "How was I supposed to know you had the ace? Besides, I led my lowest spade."

Jimmy: "The seven was not exactly a low spade."

Alan: "It was to me."

I interrupted them. "Look, it's all right." I pointed up to the screen. Jacqui and Victor had reached six hearts and West also led a spade. Jacqui, however, made doubly certain that East could not read the ♠7 as a low one by following to the first trick with the jack! East returned a diamond and the board was a push. We were still 60 imps on the plus side, so stop arguing, boys.

Up in the suite, the coach was missing, as was Otto. I was sure both of them would appear soon. Jimmy wrote the line-up card with Sonty and him in the Open Room and Otto and me in the Closed Room. Jimmy's parting advice was: Shuffle the boards well. We reminded him that, unfortunately, we play preduplicated, computer-dealt hands. "In that case," he said, "just play hard and be careful."

I asked Victor if he had any advice how to play bridge when you are up by 60 imps with only 16 hands to play.

"How should you play? Ehhhh, why don't ya go back to kindergarten."

"But Victor, you know what I mean. They'll be shooting fireworks at us on every board. Should we fight fire with fire or should we play it close to the chest?"

"C'mon. Don't get rattled if you get a bad result or two.

Remember they're the ones under pressure. Just play the game the way ya been doing and forget the score."

I found Otto at the playing area. "You're feeling okay?" I asked him.

"Ees fine by me, and I have had a glate discussion with the coach. He tell me just how to play plevent-defense."

"All right, all right," I said. Prevent defense, hmm. I wondered exactly how that applied to bridge. In football, it means that you concede to the opponents a little yardage but prevent a big touchdown pass. It was too late to discuss it with him, and we sat down to play. Before I picked up my cards to the first board, however, a loud scream came from down the hall. We all left our seats to see what had happened.

Sonty was standing in the hallway holding his arm, blood on his wrist. "It's only a drop of blood," Jimmy kept saying.

"I'm not playing!" Sonty kept saying.

We soon learned that Sonty had reached under the bidding screen for a pencil, when a knife, wedged into the portable part of the screen, had fallen onto his wrist. Luckily it had only grazed him, but it had cut right through his cards, and the board had to be reduplicated. Meanwhile, one could hardly blame the guy for wanting to call it quits, and finally Jacqui showed up and volunteered to take Sonty's place. The coach was a little distraught at the idea of fielding a new partnership at this stage, but Victor could not be found, and Jacqui and Jimmy had played before, albeit many years earlier when they were runners-up in the World Mixed Pairs and World Mixed Teams in Las Palmas. Add to that the fact we were plus 60 imps, and it didn't seem like much of a risk at all. I shook Sonty's hand goodbye by accident and walked briskly back into the Closed Room.

The Russians from the Ukraine were waiting patiently at the table, waiting patiently for the kill.

20

When I picked up the South hand to the first board of the set, I noticed a spot of Sonty's blood on my sleeve. I felt the faint, dizzy feeling that comes with its sight. So I tried my best to shake it by staring at the duplicate board. Thank God, it was everyone not vulnerable.

♠ A Q 10 8 7 ♡ A Q 2 ◇ — ♣ A K J 4 2

I opened the bidding one club, planning to jump-shift in spades. Before I knew it the bidding tray was under the screen across the table and the director was hovering over me. North was dealer. I had opened out of turn.

I suggested we throw the board out and reshuffle, but the coach, who was sitting behind Otto, and whom I could see underneath the bidding screen when it was lifted, quickly referred the director to the rule book. I stuck my forehead under the screen and gave him a "Whose-side-are-you-on?" look, but he shrugged and said, "We're 60 imps ahead. We can afford to be good sports and play by the rules."

The director explained to the Russians their options as the Russian coach translated. Schlotsky (West) or Plotsky (East) could accept my call. Neither agreed to this, mostly I think because neither understood the options. I was not feeling great at this point and took a long swig of coffee. Finally, the director informed me that my partner was barred from the auction, but I could make any call I wanted.

♠ A Q 10 8 7 ♡ A Q 2 ◇ — ♣ A K J 4 2

Terrific. What should I do? I tried to be scientific. I assumed my partner had about a third of the missing highcards and suit length. I gave him about six or seven points with about six black cards. What could we make? After a while, I decided it was too damn hard to figure out, so I just decided to bid a slam. I picked spades, because if he had only two clubs and two spades, I could at least try to get to dummy by playing two rounds of clubs and ruffing one.

My bid of six spades ended the auction. Schlotsky, a methodical player, went into his Russian tank and came out with a trump lead. I was not unhappy . . . until dummy came down:

North
♠ J 9
♡ J 10 7
◇ K Q J 9 7 6
♣ 10 3

South
♠ A Q 10 8 7
♡ A Q 2
◇ —
♣ A K J 4 2

I called for the ♠9 and Plotsky thought for a longer time

than his partner had. Finally, he played low, the 9 winning in dummy. Now what?

There were three finesses to be taken, or perhaps a club ruff in dummy instead of the club finesse. Then there was that long huddle by East at trick one. It smelled like the king doubleton — or else why such a problem?

Let's face it — my mind wasn't working fluently. I couldn't sort out all my options. Finally I decided to take a heart finesse, by leading to the queen. This had the advantage that if it lost, I could get back to dummy in hearts for a club finesse. Really it was a terrible play — I saw that when it won the trick.

Now there were three ways back to dummy: (1) ace-king and ruff a club — okay if East held three or more clubs; (2) lead a club toward the 10 — okay if the ♣Q were on my left; (3) lead the ♣J — whoever has the queen will win and the 10 will be my reentry for both finesses in the majors.

I chose number three. When the ♣J hit the table, however, both Russians ducked. Dammit! I couldn't lose a trick — and now I was really in trouble. What could I do but hope that East held more than two clubs? I led the ♣A and a low club, ruffing in dummy. Plotsky (on my side of the screen) overruffed with a big grin on his furry face! He returned a diamond and I had to lose a heart in the end, the full hand being:

```
                    ♠ J 9
                    ♡ J 10 7
                    ◊ K Q J 9 7 6
                    ♣ 10 3
    ♠ 6 5 4 3                        ♠ K 2
    ♡ 9 8 6                          ♡ K 5 4 3
    ◊ A 2                            ◊ 10 8 5 4 3
    ♣ Q 9 8 5                        ♣ 7 6
                    ♠ A Q 10 8 7
                    ♡ A Q 2
                    ◊ —
                    ♣ A K J 4 2
```

I should have taken two heart finesses from dummy at
trick two — that was my first mistake. I should have led a
club toward the 10 once I had made my first mistake — that
was my second mistake.

My head was starting to throb. Suddenly I felt a pat on my
back. I turned around. It was Evelyn. She gave me a "Don't-
worry-you're-60-imps-ahead" smile.

After this catastrophe, things went better. Well — not
exactly better — but not so badly. We didn't win any imps,
but we weren't in much jeopardy of losing imps either.
However, I did notice a tendency in my partner to preempt
on the lighter side. He opened one preempt with a jack-sixth
suit and, luckily, I held the king-queen-third, so all was well.
I wondered if this was the prevent-defense strategy he had
mentioned earlier.

Then he tried it again on the sixth board of the set, only
this time he opened on six to the 10. I held a singleton and
Plotsky doubled for takeout, while the other Ukrainian
converted for penalties. When the smoke cleared he had
gone for 1100 and all they could make was a game.

I was annoyed and I said something before the screen

came down. Otto blabbered something back about "duplicating the same tactics as the other room." But I didn't like it.

On the next board, I committed the cardinal sin that Hamman had coached us against: I let my emotions from the previous board affect my thinking.

North
♠ A 2
♡ 10 3
♢ K 7 5 4 2
♣ A K 6 4

South
♠ K J 3
♡ Q 9 4 2
♢ A Q 5
♣ 7 5 3

We reached three notrump, with the Russians silent. West led a spade. I played low from dummy and East put in the 10, my jack winning. The hand seemed easy enough. If all went well, I had three spades, five diamonds and two clubs: 10 tricks. Now what if the diamonds divided 4-1?

I still had nine tricks . . . if I didn't screw up my entries. I had to give up a diamond trick and I'd have three spades, four diamonds and two clubs. The spades were now stiff ace in dummy opposite king-doubleton in my hand. I had to unblock the ace of spades, but I couldn't cash the king before giving up a diamond. Nor could I cash the ♢A-Q without losing an entry to the ♠K.

The solution was a "perfect" safety play: I would duck a diamond. Then I could win any return, unblock the spades, reach my hand in diamonds to cash the ♠K and reach dummy in clubs to cash my diamonds.

Just to make sure I didn't screw this up, I first unblocked dummy's ♠A. Then I called the ◇2 from dummy and when East followed with the ◇6, I played the ◇3 from my hand. West showed out!! This was the whole hand:

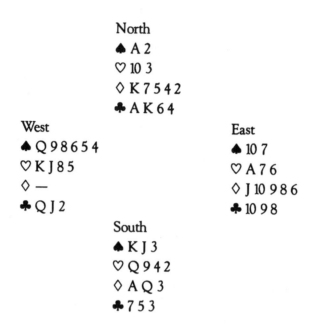

North
♠ A 2
♡ 10 3
◇ K 7 5 4 2
♣ A K 6 4

West
♠ Q 9 8 6 5 4
♡ K J 8 5
◇ —
♣ Q J 2

East
♠ 10 7
♡ A 7 6
◇ J 10 9 8 6
♣ 10 9 8

South
♠ K J 3
♡ Q 9 4 2
◇ A Q 3
♣ 7 5 3

East led back a club. There was no way for me to make nine tricks without giving up a club — and then the defense had five (three hearts, one diamond and one club).

The real safety play in diamonds was to protect against 4-1 *and* 5-0. Win the ♠J, unblock the ♠A, cash one high diamond in hand, and then, if everyone follows, lead a low one and duck it. When West shows out in diamonds on the first round, there is still time to duck a club and take advantage of a 3-3 club break. Damn, if I had just started with a low diamond from my hand, West would have shown out and I would have survived. Why did I travel to dummy's ♠A first?

I knew it had been my anger from the previous board that prevented me from fully analyzing the hand. You've got to stop it, Matthew! I screamed at myself. You've got to get in your shell and forget the bad boards.

Meanwhile, the Ukrainians were sitting up straighter and straighter in their seats, while I was slumping. The bidding on the next board was straightforward, until Otto threw in a surprise call.

Dummy
♠ 10 8 7 6
♡ A 7
◇ A 8 6 3
♣ 10 7 2

Matthew
♠ 4 3 2
♡ K 5 4
◇ K 7 5
♣ Q 5 4 3

Schlotsky	Otto	Plotsky	Matthew
1 NT	pass	2 ♣	pass
2 ◇	pass	2 NT	pass
3 NT	double	(all pass)	

What was that double? What was Otto doing to me now? Was he just trying to win back points after watching me go down in my cold game?

Otto led the ♡J and declarer played low from dummy. I was about to win my king when I thought better. . . .

I had once seen a hand like this in a Martin Hoffman book. It was likely that Otto did not hold six hearts, because with six he probably would have overcalled. That gave declarer queen-third or fourth. If I win the ♡K and return a heart, declarer can win in dummy and may knock out my partner's entry in spades or clubs. Then, after the third round of hearts is played, my ◇K will be a trick but I will have no more hearts.

If, however, I duck the ♡J and declarer wins the queen, no matter who wins the first defensive trick, I can unblock the ♡K under the ♡A and partner will score two or three more heart tricks upon either of us gaining the lead.

So I ducked the trick and declarer won the ♡Q. At the second trick he led the ◊Q, low, low, and I won my king. I triumphantly played my ♡K to dummy's stiff ace and declarer shrugged his shoulders. He called for the ♣10, which won the trick. The full deal:

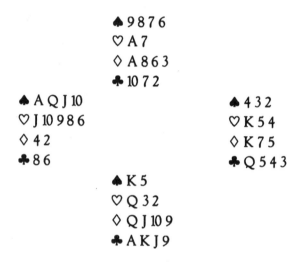

```
              ♠ 9 8 7 6
              ♡ A 7
              ◊ A 8 6 3
              ♣ 10 7 2
  ♠ A Q J 10                    ♠ 4 3 2
  ♡ J 10 9 8 6                  ♡ K 5 4
  ◊ 4 2                         ◊ K 7 5
  ♣ 8 6                         ♣ Q 5 4 3
              ♠ K 5
              ♡ Q 3 2
              ◊ Q J 10 9
              ♣ A K J 9
```

"Now I am sorry I double," said Otto, as we looked at declarer's spread hand. He had scored four club tricks, three diamonds and two hearts: nine tricks.

"Why did you double?!!" I found myself screaming at Otto.

"I don't know why, now. Perhaps, before, I thought you would understand it as lead dilecting."

"Lead directing?!!" I screamed again. "*You* were on lead."

"But you could have been on lead twice — and you were on lead at least once."

"Why didn't you just lead your spa— " I started to say, but then realized that if he had led his spade suit, declarer would have lost three spades and a diamond and still made nine tricks. Meanwhile the new board was on the table, the screen had come down, and I was in a state of panic. I turned around to Evelyn for support but she looked at me in a way I wish nobody to ever look at me again. Her face was contorted and wide-eyed. She was sick — and my series of plays had made her sick. "Well, we do have that 60-imp cushion," I said, with a forced smile. And she nearly hit me.

On the eighth board of the 16-board set, I found myself declaring a shaky four spades.

North
♠ K 5 3 2
♡ 3 2
♢ J 10 3 2
♣ A 7 6

South
♠ A 10 9 8
♡ A Q 5
♢ Q 8
♣ K 8 5 2

West led the ♣Q. I could see I needed trumps to behave, the heart finesse to work, or perhaps a couple of diamond discards for my clubs or hearts. It was all murky in my now less-than-lucid mind.

I won the ♣A in dummy and played a diamond toward my Q-8. When East played low, I put in the 8. It was a finesse and, if it worked, I would have two diamond tricks for discards. The 8 lost to the 9, however, and back came the ♣J.

At least the heart finesse worked, but there was no miracle in the trump suit, and I ended up losing a club, two diamonds and a trump.

The full deal was:

```
             ♠ K 5 3 2
             ♡ 3 2
             ◊ J 10 3 2
             ♣ A 7 6
♠ J 6                          ♠ Q 7 4
♡ 10 9 8                       ♡ K J 7 6 4
◊ A 9 7 6                      ◊ K 5 4
♣ Q J 10 9                     ♣ 4 3
             ♠ A 10 9 8
             ♡ A Q 5
             ◊ Q 8
             ♣ K 8 5 2
```

Had I put the ◊ Q up, I would have forced the ace, and the club return would not hurt because East had no more. Could I have made the hand?

I started thinking about it as the boards were exchanged with the Open Room. Was it possible to lose two diamonds and a club, but avoid a trump loser? The coach came around and put his long arm around my neck. Then he bent down and whispered: "Too bad. Yes, you could have made the hand. Diamond to the queen and ace, club return to your king, diamond to the ten and king. Now East returns a diamond, say. You win in dummy, discarding a club, take the heart finesse, cash the ace and ruff a heart. Next you ruff the last diamond in your hand. You are down to three trumps and a club in each hand. You exit a club, and they must break the trump suit for you. Trump honors are split so no matter how they play the trumps you can score the last three tricks. Standard Devil's Coup, I must say. But don't worry about it. There's still eight boards to go and you must take a chipper outlook."

All I could do was pray at this point and I was not a praying man. I prayed for partscore hands. I prayed for one-notrump contacts. I prayed that we could still hold on to win. Then the new boards came and I picked up:

♠ 8 7 5 ♡ K J 4 3 2 ◊ A K J 9 7 ♣ —

Otto opened three diamonds, which for a moment made me crazy. Then I remembered we were playing his cockamamie two-under preempts. He had spades. I alerted my Ukranian friend and he passed. I had no idea what to do. Was there a slam? How could I find out if his spades were six to the ten or seven to the ace-king?

I tried four clubs, which, if memory served me right, was the new Roth asking bid. By steps, Otto was supposed to tell me his spade strength. When the tray came back I saw the one bid I didn't want to see: four notrump. What was that? According to the notes, he was supposed to be showing solid spades. Would he really open three spades with solid spades at favorable vulnerability? Wouldn't he have opened four spades? No, he must have forgotten the four-club asking bid, I thought. The pressure is too much on him. He must think my four clubs was a cuebid and is now bidding Blackwood. So I jumped to six clubs, showing a club void and one ace. It was the correct response to Blackwood, but perhaps a foolish one — I thought, as the tray was pushed by Plotsky rather quickly under the screen. After all, a grand slam was impossible — he couldn't have solid spades *and* the ace of hearts. So why not just bid six spades with my hand?

Too late. Too, too late. Oh, was it late.

When the tray came back there were nothing but green pass cards on it, and Plotsky, a very handsome smile on his lips, reached for the final — nail-in-the-coffin — pass.

Dummy was:
♠ A K J 9 4 3 2 ♡ 5 ◊ 5 ♣ 10 9 8 6

I did not say thank you, I must admit.

And I will not bore you with the play, but one good thing did occur. The ♠Q was third offside, which meant that if our counterparts reached a slam, it was doomed. Of course, down eight was nothing to write home about, though it was nonvulnerable. I think at this point I would rather have died than come out of the room to compare scores.

"Do you need a doctor?" asked Otto at the end of the hand.

"I need a normal partner," I muttered. Then I cleared my mind and instructed him to clear his. "Don't think about the last board, Otto. That's the only way to remain sane."

"Which board do you want me to theenk about?"

I got up from the table and went to the bathroom. I had to calm myself. Putting water on my eyes would not hurt, either. I had to do something to change the course of action, but I was helpless. I hated my partner and I hated my opponents and I hated myself. In the bathroom I saw some handwriting on the wall: God is dead. I shook my head, then I prayed.

When I got back, I apologized to my opponents and said one brief sentence to Otto: "If you preempt one more time this set, I'm going to kill you." It was a mild threat, but I think effective.

Then, my prayers were answered, and, I believe, my belief in the Almighty took hold. He sent four partscores in a row, including a one-club contract that bored everyone to tears.

In return, I promised to obey many of the commandments I had not obeyed up to this point in my life, when, with three boards to go, I found myself defending a game. I even promised to obey my wife. . . .

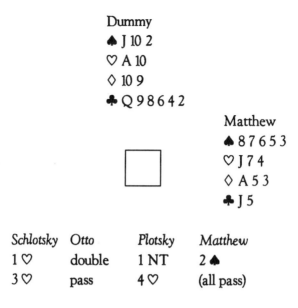

Dummy
♠ J 10 2
♡ A 10
♢ 10 9
♣ Q 9 8 6 4 2

Matthew
♠ 8 7 6 5 3
♡ J 7 4
♢ A 5 3
♣ J 5

Schlotsky	Otto	Plotsky	Matthew
1 ♡	double	1 NT	2 ♠
3 ♡	pass	4 ♡	(all pass)

Lots of bidding without much in highcards, I thought, as I gazed at dummy and back at my hand. Otto led the ♠K, which went around to declarer's ace. Declarer led a spade back and I followed with the 8 under partner's queen, to let him know that my highcard was in the higher-ranking side suit, diamonds. Otto dutifully switched to the ♢4 and I won the ace. I hoped that partner held the king, but should I return one? I stopped to consider.

Declarer had two spade tricks, probably six hearts, one club (assuming he had the ace) and probably needed either a club trick in dummy or a diamond ruff in dummy to score 10 tricks. Perhaps he had one of these two hands:

(1) ♠ A x ♡ K Q x x x x ♢ Q x x ♣ A x.
(2) ♠ A x ♡ K Q x x x x ♢ Q x ♣ A x x.

If he held hand number one, I had to return a trump or a club. Either way, he could not ruff a diamond *and* discard a club.

If he held hand number two, I had to return a diamond to my partner, before a diamond was discarded on dummy's high spade.

209

Partner's takeout double was unlikely to contain six diamonds, especially after his ◊ 4, fourth-best return. So I played declarer for hand number one and returned a club. This was the full deal:

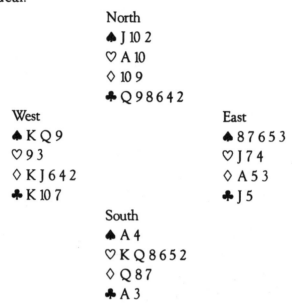

North
♠ J 10 2
♡ A 10
◊ 10 9
♣ Q 9 8 6 4 2

West
♠ K Q 9
♡ 9 3
◊ K J 6 4 2
♣ K 10 7

East
♠ 8 7 6 5 3
♡ J 7 4
◊ A 5 3
♣ J 5

South
♠ A 4
♡ K Q 8 6 5 2
◊ Q 8 7
♣ A 3

Declarer went up in clubs and played a heart to the ace. Then he discarded his club on the spade honor. Next he led a diamond, but Otto won and returned a trump to stop the diamond ruff.

Suddenly I loved Otto, and I wanted to kiss him. I felt a fantastic relief of tension as the screen came down for the next-to-last board. I turned to Evelyn, but she was long gone. So, I noted, was the coach. Our teammates on VuGraph were finishing, and they probably left to check the scores.

On the penultimate board I picked up:

♠ A K 10 6 ♡ K Q J 10 9 7 ♢ K 10 7 ♣ —

I opened the bidding one heart and sent the tray across the table. When it came back I saw three clubs from Schlotsky and three diamonds from Otto. Plotsky bid five clubs. They were vulnerable and we weren't, so I hedged with five diamonds. There was no reason to panic myself into six — there could be a ruff out, and, as Jacqui once advised me, never play partner for the perfect hand. When the tray came back, there were two passes and Plotsky thought a long time. He finally bid six clubs. Now I had a problem.

Six clubs was not likely to be a successful slam, but on the other hand, should I risk it? I can bid six diamonds, which shouldn't go for more than a trick set and may even make! But on the other hand, what if partner has a club honor or two and a weak diamond suit? Is it fair to my team to bid six diamonds without consulting partner?

Here the differences among the three forms of bridge were apparent. At rubber bridge I could bid six diamonds, or even six hearts, without worrying about criticism — I was on my own. At duplicate, I could take a shot and double my vulnerable opponents or, again, risk a slam. The result was between my partner and me. But at teams, I owed it to four other people to bid as intelligently as I could. So I passed, leaving it to partner to decide — only he knew how good his diamonds were.

It went all pass and Otto led a heart.

This was the full deal:

Dummy

♠ Q J 9 7 2
♡ A 3 2
◇ —
♣ A 5 4 3 2

Otto

♠ 8 5 4 3
♡ 4
◇ A Q J 9 8 7 6 5
♣ —

M. G.

♠ A K 10 6
♡ K Q J 10 9 7
◇ K 10 2
♣ —

Schlotsky

♠ —
♡ 8 6 5
◇ 4 3
♣ K Q J 10 9 8 7 6

Declarer won the ♡A in dummy and led the ♠Q. I covered with my king, ruffed by declarer. He ruffed a diamond and led the ♠J. I covered with my ace, ruffed by declarer. He ruffed a second diamond in dummy and led the ♠7. I played low — what could I do? — and he discarded a heart, partner winning the ♠8. Partner was endplayed and had to return a spade, setting up the fifth spade in dummy, or give a ruff and sluff.

It was a shocking slap in the face. I went into a stupor. What kind of hand was this? Who had dealt such cards? What kind of fantastic play did Schlotsky make?

I had no time to think further. The director came in and said we had five minutes to finish the last board or there would be penalties. Penalties? What penalties? What could be more penalizing than the last hand?

I picked up:

♠ 5 4 ♡ K 2 ◇ A K 10 7 5 ♣ Q 8 4 2

It went pass on my left and one notrump by my partner.

Pass on my right. I was desperate, I thought. I needed to do something, anything — some sort of swing. I bid three diamonds, which we play as the minors and a game force.

Otto raised to four diamonds and I went crazy, cuebidding four hearts. He bid four spades and I bid five diamonds, leaving it to him. When the tray came back for the last time in the match, I saw six diamonds, and I held my breath. The lead was the ♡6. This was the deal:

North
♠ A Q 7 6
♡ 7 5 4
◊ Q J 9
♣ A K 9

South
♠ 5 4
♡ K 2
◊ A K 10 7 5
♣ Q 8 4 2

East won the ♡A and returned a heart to my king. Good start, I thought. Now all I needed was the spade finesse and a good position in clubs . . . no, wait a second, maybe I could do better than hope for clubs 3-3. I could pull two rounds of trumps and try to ruff a club — if clubs were 4-2 and the player with two trumps held two clubs, I could do it. But wait . . . maybe I could do even better.

I led the ◊A and a trump to the jack. Everyone followed. Good. Now if the spade finesse was onside, I had it. I led a heart off dummy and ruffed it. Next a spade to the queen and it held! I cashed the ♠A and ruffed a spade; a club to the ace and dummy's last spade ruffed. Finally a club to the king. I pulled the last trump with dummy's remaining diamond and my ♣Q took the last trick. The dummy reversal worked!

```
              ♠ A Q 7 6
              ♡ 7 5 4
              ◊ Q J 9
              ♣ A K 9
♠ K J 8                        ♠ 10 9 3 2
♡ Q 9 8 6                      ♡ A J 10 3
◊ 4 2                          ◊ 8 6 3
♣ J 7 6 5                      ♣ 10 3
              ♠ 5 4
              ♡ K 2
              ◊ A K 10 7 5
              ♣ Q 8 4 2
```

I think there was only one way I could have left this room had I gone down in six diamonds. And that was out the window.

Luckily (or thank God — take your pick, my friends), I was able to hobble out through the door. Not that we were in great shape, mind you. We could easily lose 60 imps. But at least we had one or two pick-ups to offset the terrible boards.

I moved into the hall slowly, but then speeded up. The Ukranians were joyously running down the hall with their coach and I didn't like it. Otto was not far behind, and we made it to the elevator in time for all of us to get in.

"NICE MATCH," said Plotsky (Schlotsky nodded in agreement). I gave him my warmest smile, which at that moment was similar to Ivan the Terrible.

The elevator doors opened and we all fell out. The Russians were first to the VuGraph room. When I got there, deal 64, the final deal (the board that we had played eighth in our room) of the semifinal, was on the screen. More important, the scoreboard read:

England 126, Italy 120   Russia 135, USA 144

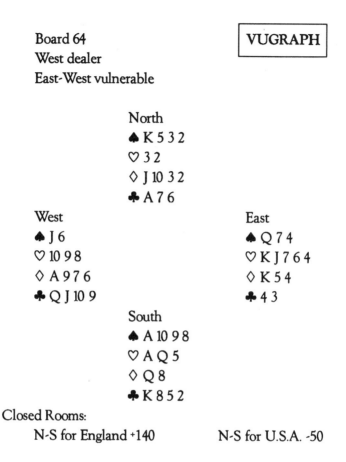

Board 64
West dealer
East-West vulnerable

North
♠ K 5 3 2
♡ 3 2
◊ J 10 3 2
♣ A 7 6

West
♠ J 6
♡ 10 9 8
◊ A 9 7 6
♣ Q J 10 9

East
♠ Q 7 4
♡ K J 7 6 4
◊ K 5 4
♣ 4 3

South
♠ A 10 9 8
♡ A Q 5
◊ Q 8
♣ K 8 5 2

Closed Rooms:

N-S for England +140   N-S for U.S.A. -50

We were 9 imps ahead, but this was the deal where I had gone down in four spades — the one that the coach had pointed out could have been made on some remarkable "Devil's Coup."

The excitement in the VuGraph room was high. At the beginning of the session, they were broadcasting only the England-Italy match, because our match looked as if it were a runaway. Now they were attempting to relate the results in both matches. The bidding was flashing in the England-Italy semifinal on the left side of the screen and in our semifinal on the right. Our result was up there, minus 50 in four spades. In the other match, the English North-South had stopped in three spades, making three for plus 140.

"The scores are so close, ladies and gentlemen," said Ron Andersen on the microphone, "that if either the Italians or the Russians bid and make four spades, they will win the match — that's what it has come down to after 63 grueling deals."

North
♠ K 5 3 2
♡ 3 2
◇ J 10 3 2
♣ A 7 6

West
♠ J 6
♡ 10 9 8
◇ A 9 7 6
♣ Q J 10 9

East
♠ Q 7 4
♡ K J 7 6 4
◇ K 5 4
♣ 4 3

South
♠ A 10 9 8
♡ A Q 5
◇ Q 8
♣ K 8 5 2

Open Rooms:

Sheehan	Franco	Rose	Garozzo	J. Mitchell	Vladichek	Cayne	Pladichek
West	North	East	South	West	North	East	South
pass	pass	pass	1 NT	pass	pass	pass	1 NT
pass	2 ♣	pass	2 ♠	pass	2 ♣	pass	2 ♠
pass	3 ♠	pass	4 ♠	pass	4 ♠	pass	pass
pass	pass	pass		pass			

I noted that Garozzo had opened the South hand one notrump, and his partner bid Stayman. They were soon up to three spades, and Garozzo, probably sensing the closeness of the match, took the push to four. Meanwhile, on the right, I was hoping the Russians would stop in a partscore, but no, they blasted into four spades without even inviting.

At both tables the ♣Q was led.

Garozzo was first to play. He rose with the ace and led a diamond to the queen. He was on target. West won and played the ♣J to the king. Garozzo led a diamond to the jack and king. East returned a heart, but Garozzo finessed, cashed the ace and ruffed a heart in dummy. Next came the ◊10 and a diamond (East discarding the ♡K), ruffed in hand. Yes, the master had reduced himself to four cards:

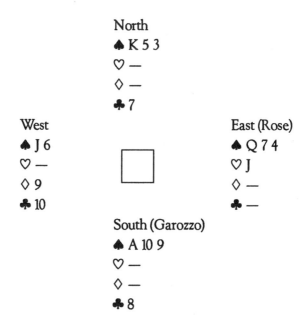

North
♠ K 5 3
♡ —
◊ —
♣ 7

West
♠ J 6
♡ —
◊ 9
♣ 10

East (Rose)
♠ Q 7 4
♡ J
◊ —
♣ —

South (Garozzo)
♠ A 10 9
♡ —
◊ —
♣ 8

He exited with a club, and Rose, who was sitting on his right, in the East position, quick as a flash ruffed with the ♠4! He then played the ♠Q. It was a fantastic attempt to fool the master. He was pretending that he was down to four trumps to the Q-J, had been forced to ruff his partner's trick, and now was leading the ♠Q from Q-J-7.

Garozzo, whose face was on the TV monitor, looked startled. Was he going to fall for this? Yet who would ruff his partner's trick with three trumps to the queen?

Garozzo played the ♠9, West the 6, and dummy the king. Now came a spade from dummy, 7 . . .

The Italian grandmaster thought and thought, while I was dying to know what was happening in my match. Finally he said something in Italian and went up with his ace — the audience cheered! The amazing, over-the-hill Blue Team had reached the final of the Bermuda Bowl 20 years after going into retirement.

North (Vladichek)
♠ K 5 3 2
♡ 3 2
♢ J 10 3 2
♣ A 7 6

West (J. Mitchell)
♠ J 6
♡ 10 9 8
♢ A 9 7 6
♣ Q J 10 9

East (Cayne)
♠ Q 7 4
♡ K J 7 6 4
♢ K 5 4
♣ 4 3

South (Pladichek)
♠ A 10 9 8
♡ A Q 5
♢ Q 8
♣ K 8 5 2

Meanwhile, however, the cards flashed back to the beginning of the hand. "Ladies and gentlemen, don't leave your seats. We have asked Maury Braunstein, chief tournament director, to hold up play in the other match until after this hand was completed. We now go to the Open Room in the Russia/USA match, where the Russian declarer, Ziggy Pladichek, also needs to score ten tricks to upset the strong USA team. There the opening lead was also the queen of clubs, and declarer, who is no Garozzo, nevertheless has had a much longer time to think about the play. What do you think, Edgar? Will the extra time help Pladichek see the Devil's Coup?"

"Well, Ron, even if he does, you have to remember that the defense also has had extra time to think."

"Wait, Edgar, they're playing.'

Declarer won the club in dummy and led a low diamond. What's this? Jimmy, in the East seat, played the ◊ K. What a play! When it held, he played a second club and Jacqui's club trick was set up while she still had the ◊ A as an entry.

"You see what I mean," said Edgar Kaplan of the VuGraph panel. "Here is a play that we see usually in notrump but almost never in a suit contract: the rising of an honor by East to clear partner's led suit before his entry has been removed."

"Edgar, I think James Cayne deserves a hand from the crowd — a remarkable play."

Applause was scattered. They just didn't appreciate the beauty of it. But when Jacqui won the next diamond, she cashed the club and played a fourth round of clubs, ruffed in dummy and overruffed by Jimmy. Down one meant an American victory, and we were still alive to play the Blue Team for the championship of the world.

21

Back in the ACBL suite, the scores were being tallied a second time. It was the coach who suggested we add them up again just to be certain. When we again realized that we had won by only a few imps, a victory cheer went up. Thank God the coach, whose victory whoop was always a decibel higher than the rest, remained silent and simply gave everyone a proper English handshake.

Everyone was there except Victor, who had gone home to walk his dogs. Even Jacqui was celebrating, unusual for her, by having a glass of Perrier and lime. Sonty was all excited about the final and had forgotten for now about his little wound. The coach and Evelyn went immediately to the desk to begin typing notes for defense to the new Italian system. Otto was looking a bit sad, however — too sad if you ask me. He was thumbing through his wallet. I walked over and gave him a pat on the back. He quickly put the wallet back in his jacket.

"It's a clazy ting," he said. "Your tliumphs come in life when you least expect them—." And least care, I could almost hear him say. He took his hat and headed out of the room. The coach eyed him and caught him at the door.

"Otto, be here tomorrow by 11 a.m. The notes, you know!"

Otto shrugged. "I don't tink your notes do very good."

"What are you talking about?!" cried the coach. "If it weren't for my prevent-defense, you would have lost all 60 points!"

Otto shrugged again. "Excuse me, I've got an appointment."

What appointment he could have at midnight I tried to imagine, when Belsky stuck his puss through the door.

"Matt, did you win?"

"Not completely, Belsky. We still have the final to play, but we won the semifinal. What have you got for me?"

"I got a chopped liver on rye in the car if you like. I discovered a great kosher deli on Madison. In the meantime I've been chauffeuring the girls from the airport back to the apartment. They just got back from Alabama."

I pulled Belsky aside.

"Good work, Belsk, but what about the tape? Did your friends from 47th Street fix it?"

He bent down and whispered to me. "The tape is still there. The guy who fixes the tapes had to leave early today — he sidelines as a *Mohel* and he had to get his equipment in order — the *bris* is tomorrow, by the way, and I can get you an invitation."

"Belsky! I'm in the middle of the world championships with a maniac serial bridge killer on the loose and you want me to go to a *bris*?!"

"But a great Rebbe will be there — maybe he can offer some advice. You know the Torah Sages were terrific detectives, because they spent 20 hours a day studying. . . ."

He continued his drivel while I said goodbye to Jimmy.

In the car, I gave Belsky the downtown address. The

nightclub was in the West Village on Hudson Street.

"The Copa Hopa?" he asked. "What kind of place is that?"

"Just drive, Belsky. Where's the chopped liver?"

"In the glove compartment. You know, Matt, that doesn't sound like a kosher place."

I took the sandwich out. "Belsky, I'm not going there to eat."

"Well, if you do, be sure to order a salad only. You can eat only cold salad and fruit in non-kosher restaurants."

"Belsky, I am not ready for all this. Why are you telling me what to eat? Only a fanatic would worry about the type of food you can eat in a New York City nightclub at 12:30 in the morning. Only a crazy person. Do you really think God cares what food I eat?"

"Matt, if your father gave you a present, wouldn't you want to please him — give him something in return? Well, you were given a bridge victory, so in return, I'm just suggesting that you keep the *kashrut* laws one night."

We were stopped at a red light in the middle of Broadway and 42nd Street. You wouldn't know it was after midnight with the number of people crossing the street, lights flashing and radios blasting.

"Look here, Belsk, you're assuming that God had a hand in the semifinal. Do you really think he spends his time worrying about the location of the queen of trumps?"

"Matt, the Sages say: Not a leaf falls that—"

"—doesn't have a purpose. I know, I know. Here, I'm eating your sandwich — okay? Pleased?"

I had it unwrapped and was ready to bite in when his huge hand came over to the bread and stopped me cold.

"The blessing," he said.

"What blessing?"

"*Hamotzi*, the blessing for bread."

"All right, Belsky, what's the blessing?"

"It won't help."

"Why won't it help?"

"You gotta wash your hands before you can say the blessing."

I took the sandwich, rewrapped it and put it into my jacket pocket for later — when I got away from this nut.

It was 12:30 on a Thursday morning and the West Village was also buzzing. It was the one thing I always enjoyed about the city — any time of day or night, there were people out on the streets. How could you be lonely in a place like this?

I asked Belsky to wait in the car and he agreed to take a short nap. I tried to straighten my tie and jacket, but I had been sweating at the bridge table and now that I was dry, I was a sticky sight.

Outside, the Copa Hopa was unimpressive, and looked like the front of a 1920s' speakeasy. There was an antique shop, which led to a door in the back that opened up to a spectacular array of lights. Cole Porter music was being piped in at the entrance, where a young lady — no, it was a man! — met me at the checkroom. The whole joint was sparkling, and I think they used mirrors to make it seem bigger than it really was. There was a stage up front — nobody was on it at the moment — and couples were drinking and eating at various tables scattered around a small dance floor.

"I'm here to meet a beautiful stranger," I said, trying to blend in.

"And what is his name?" she/he asked.

"Not he — she." I looked again at the tables. "I think I see her over there in the second row."

"Ah, yes, the one with the red chiffon. She's ordered for you, already. Follow me, not too closely, if you know what I mean."

"I don't."

She was sitting alone, sipping on a Vodka martini. I took her hand and kissed it. Then I sat down. A candle was burning. There were two roses in a glass of water in the table's center. A delicious-looking scotch-sour sat in front of my place and I raised it in her honor.

"*L'chaim*," she said.

"*L'chaim*."

She was dark and rosy herself, glowing in the soft candlelight, the vision of a biblical princess.

"We shouldn't be meeting like this," I whispered.

"That's right. You should be in bed, resting for tomorrow."

"So you heard we won."

"Not without a struggle."

"I don't think Otto was really trying his hardest."

"I wouldn't blame your partner, from what I heard."

"And how did your day go?"

"I got the goods — if that's what you mean."

She handed me a set of hand-records from her purse. They were a bit torn and black at the edges. On the top was a cover note from the ACBL Bulletin. "1989 Trials Hands. Final Between Deutsch and Cayne."

The waitress — no, waiter — came by and asked if everything was all right. We nodded and ordered another round. A young Sinatra was singing "Night and Day" in the background now. I leaned over for a kiss on the lips but caught a puff of cheek instead. There was a look in her eye that said something was not all that right.

"Okay, out with it," I said.

"You've been going to Harlem again."

"Belsky, dammit! He can't keep his trap shut. I thought that was Loshen Horror—"

"Loshen Hora."

"Whatever you call it, I thought observant Jews weren't supposed to gossip about other people — even if it's the truth."

"Except for their own good," she corrected. "Besides, it's just too stupid for you to go there anymore."

"I've got one more appointment," I admitted, taking a gulp of my second drink. "I need it for tomorrow's final."

"Do what you like, but don't let me hear about it!"

Thank God the waiter/waitress moved in on us. He set a heaping green salad on each of our plates, with some olive oil and vinegar on the side.

"You ordered for us?" I asked.

"Yes, I wasn't going to wait till morning."

I put some dressing on, and dug in. Before the lettuce hit my lips I heard her mumble a prayer. So we were saying little prayers before we ate now. This Belsky thing was spreading. Or was it Patty Cayne's influence? Or both.

I ate quickly and then asked what else we were having.

"That's it," she said.

"That's it?!"

"Yes, that's it. That's all we can eat here. Unless you want to risk a little fish — but it's got to have fins and scales."

I called the waiter over.

"Got any fish with fins and scales?"

"We have a special tonight on shark."

"No good," said Pamela.

"No fins or no scales?"

"Don't know, but it's missing one of them."

"Forget it," I said, dismissing him.

"Now I feel terrible," she said. "You've got to eat something."

"It's okay," I said, taking the sandwich from my jacket.

"You've got to say *Hamotzi* on that," she said.

"I know, I know, and wash first, too. I'll be right back."

When I returned the lights had dimmed and the stage lights came on. Then on center stage appeared Frankenstein's daughter. She looked a lot better up there than she had in the office the day before. It must have been the lack of polkadots. One thing was reassuring — she was a she.

She began with a song called "Little Cupid," but every time she said the word Cupid, I thought she was singing cuebid. She wasn't exactly a canary, but she wasn't what you would call ordinary either. It was a raspy voice, unique but too low for my taste. Strange, but she sounded almost like the coach when she sang!

Her second number was her own creation. She claimed she was recording it this week. I didn't want to bet on it. It was called, "You Trumped My Ace!"

You were my little baby
And maybe just maybe
You'd wrap those arms in a loving embrace.
But when I found out
All night you'd been out
Well baby . . . you trumped my ace!

I thought you were my boy
A box, a bid, a toy
A gift of chiffon and lace.
But then you came home
With red on your comb.
I knew . . . you trumped my ace!

"So tell me what happened at Frank Stewart's," I said between songs.

"You'd like Fayette — it's the heart of the Bible Belt."

"Yup, sounds like my kinda place."

"Patty and I had a long conversation with the local minister, who had stopped at the Stewart's for tea. He said the Baptists believe in faith as the number one way to get to heaven. Patty explained that we go for good deeds. You can't just sit around and pray and expect to be rewarded."

"Something like an argument in bridge theory — when do you go out and earn points and when do you just sit there and collect them?"

"Must you compare everything to bridge? Mrs. Stewart had a better comparison. She had just seen the old film, 'The Little Foxes,' where Bette Davis wants to kill off her husband. He takes a special drug for his bad heart. In one scene he's having an attack and can't move. So he asks Bette to fetch his drug. She just stands there — that's all — doesn't move an inch. Well, there it was: an example of doing nothing but at the same time commiting evil.

Or, I couldn't help thinking, when in bridge a defender does not help his partner with a clear signal.

"Anyway, the big connection between religions seems to be that God is watching us always. Once you know that, you know you have to be careful what you say and do."

Like when kibitzers watch on VuGraph, I thought. If you always played bridge with the idea that someone important was watching your every bid and play, just think how much more disciplined you would be. Now suppose God were watching! And He knew the rules for good and bad bridge tactics.

"That's it," I blurted out. "You just have to pretend that God is watching on VuGraph, and you'll never make a mistake!"

"You've had too much to drink," she said, pushing my drink aside.

The Stein girl was finished, and I waved the *maitre d'* over and asked him to deliver my calling card. I wrote, "Please come have a drink with us," on the back and thought about wrapping a C-note around it, but didn't.

Meanwhile, some fresh fruit arrived for desert.

"I ran into Truscott," I said. "He informed me that Philip Alder had gone through the hand-records and found no deal of interest that included a four-diamond bid or an eight-of-diamonds play."

"Patty and I figured out why. Here. On top of the records is the hand that the killer was referring to when he attached the eight of diamonds to Charlotte Stein's blouse."

I took the top sheet out and looked at it.

Board 23
South dealer
Both sides vulnerable

```
                         North
                         ♠ K 9 8 3
                         ♡ A K 7
                         ◇ 10 5 2
                         ♣ 10 7 6
West                                          East
♠ J 6 5 2                                     ♠ Q 10 7
♡ J 3 2                                       ♡ 9 6 4
◇ A J 3                                       ◇ Q 8 7 4
♣ Q 5 3                                       ♣ 9 8 4
                         South
                         ♠ A 4
                         ♡ Q 10 8 5
                         ◇ K 9 6
                         ♣ A K J 2
```

Closed Room

Cayne	Rodwell	Sontag	Meckstroth
South	West	North	East
1 NT	pass	3 NT	(all pass)

Opening lead: ♠2

"Alder was right," she continued. "There were no eight-of-diamond plays that were of any interest in the Trials, certainly not interesting enough to cause anyone to contemplate strangulation and leave a calling card about it afterwards. But on the airplane back, Patty had the idea that the eight of diamonds didn't have to be a card that *was* played. It could have been a card that *wasn't* played — and sent the killer into a frenzy. I hate to say it, but it's sort of like an analogy to the religious issue. Sometimes in bridge it's not what you do that counts, but what you don't do. The bid or play you fail to find is more often the cause of a disaster than the bid or play you find."

There was a complete description of the play, but it was in small print and I was getting tired. "Can you just tell me what happened?"

"In the Closed Room, Jimmy got to three notrump, not revealing his heart suit."

"That's because Sontag didn't use Stayman on his square hand."

"Yes, and Jimmy made three after the ♠2 lead. He played low from dummy and Meckstroth made the excellent play of the ♠7, forcing Jimmy's ace. Jimmy entered dummy with a heart and led a club to his jack and West's queen. West continued spades and Jimmy ducked. East won and continued, setting up West's fourth spade. Jimmy won in dummy and cashed the hearts, the jack dropping. Well, that was nine tricks, two spades, four hearts and three clubs. I think that Jimmy was planning to play West for the ♢A if West showed out on the third round of hearts. Jimmy could then cash two clubs, ending in dummy, and, if West was out of clubs, Jimmy would lead the last spade, endplaying West to lead a diamond."

"I think from the lead," I said, "he assumed West was 4-3-3-3, otherwise why make a lead from four to the jack?"

"Not everyone shares your contempt for four-to-the-jack leads. But you may be right this time. Rodwell was unlikely to have a better four-card suit and not lead it."

"So what happened in the Open Room?"

North
♠ K 9 8 3
♡ A K 7
◇ 10 5 2
♣ 10 7 6

West
♠ J 6 5 2
♡ J 3 2
◇ A J 3
♣ Q 5 3

East
♠ Q 10 7
♡ 9 6 4
◇ Q 8 7 4
♣ 9 8 4

South
♠ A 4
♡ Q 10 8 5
◇ K 9 6
♣ A K J 2

Open Room

Rosenberg	Frank Stein	Deutsch	Mrs. Stein
South	West	North	East
1 NT	pass	2 ♣	pass
2 ♡	pass	3 NT	(all pass)

Opening lead ♠6

"More interesting there. Michael Rosenberg showed hearts and Seymon Deutsch implied spades, so Frankenstein was in trouble on opening lead, and decided on a middle spade — in a way asking partner to shift if she got in.

"Declarer ducked in dummy and East put up her queen. Rosenberg won the ace and, like Jimmy, traveled to dummy with a heart to take a club finesse. West won and continued spades. Declarer ducked and Mrs. Stein won her ten, but was forced to shift suits because dummy had a spade tenace over her partner.

"Now here's the crucial point. Charlotte Stein shifted to the *four* of diamonds. Rosenberg played low and Frank won with the jack. He now cashed the ace of diamonds and played a third round, apparently hoping that his wife held the king, but Rosenberg won and claimed nine tricks.

"Knowing Frankenstein, you could imagine the uproar at the table."

"Wait a second," I said, "it's Frank who usually did the screaming."

"Patty was there. And it *was* Frank who did the screaming. He was screaming about his wife not shifting to the *eight* of diamonds instead of the four."

Suddenly we were interrupted by Frank Stein's daughter. I got up and pulled over a chair from an empty neighboring table. But when she sat down, her voice went into one of her famous shrieks.

"Not that hand again!!"

"Calm down," Pamela suggested. "Here, have this drink."

"I thought you didn't play bridge," I said.

"Oh, you bridge players are all alike! I don't know why I'm even talking to you."

"We're here to help find your father's killer, so please take a deep breath and relax."

She let out a hoot of some sort, then gained her composure. "I don't play, but I don't have to play to know *that* hand. All they did was talk about it, day and night for weeks. *That's* why I had to move out of the house. I couldn't stand the fighting anymore."

"Your father and your mother?"

"She was *not my mother!!*"

"Okay, okay."

"Yes," she said throwing her long hair across her shoulder. It almost touched the floor. "And all the others."

"THE OTHERS?!" said my wife and I in unison.

I flipped out my pad, but it was soggy from the sandwich.

"Who exactly was there — discussing this hand?" asked Pamela, gently.

"Everyone," she said. "Let me think. Everyone on their stupid bridge team, at least. I can't remember their names."

"Can you remember anyone specifically? Any tall people? Anyone with a Hungarian accent?"

"I don't know, I think there were people with accents — you could never tell with all the shouting. All I remember is one thing, they kept repeating over and over again."

"What's that?"

"They ate the diamonds. It made me sick."

"The eight of diamonds," whispered my wife.

I looked back at the diagram and reviewed the play in my mind.

```
                 North
                 ♠ K 9 8 3
                 ♡ A K 7
                 ◇ 10 5 2
                 ♣ 10 7 6
West                              East
♠ J 6 5 2                         ♠ Q 10 7
♡ J 3 2                           ♡ 9 6 4
◇ A J 3                           ◇ Q 8 7 4
♣ Q 5 3                           ♣ 9 8 4
                 South
                 ♠ A 4
                 ♡ Q 10 8 5
                 ◇ K 9 6
                 ♣ A K J 2
```

The ♠6 lead to the queen and ace. Heart to the ace, club to the jack and queen. Spade to the 8 and 10. Now if East shifts to the ◊8, declarer plays low and West's jack wins. West knows that East does not have the king, so shifts back to a club. Declarer will probably cash his clubs, lead a heart to the king, cash the ♠K, pitching a diamond. Then he'll lead a heart toward his Q-10 with every player holding three cards:

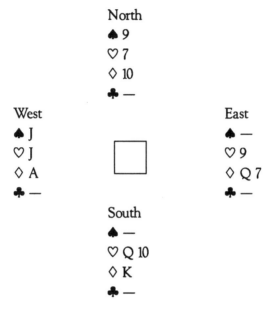

North
♠ 9
♡ 7
◊ 10
♣ —

West
♠ J
♡ J
◊ A
♣ —

East
♠ —
♡ 9
◊ Q 7
♣ —

South
♠ —
♡ Q 10
◊ K
♣ —

When East follows with the ♡9, declarer may assume that East started with four hearts to the jack and the ◊8-7-4. He may think the position is:

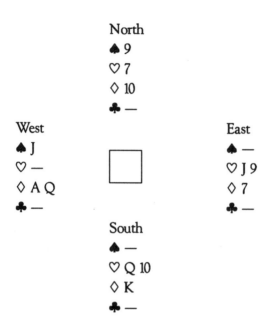

North
♠ 9
♡ 7
◇ 10
♣ —

West
♠ J
♡ —
◇ A Q
♣ —

East
♠ —
♡ J 9
◇ 7
♣ —

South
♠ —
♡ Q 10
◇ K
♣ —

In which case, he will finesse in hearts.

"More evidence you're holding out on us?" said the D.A., who was suddenly looming over my shoulder, looking down at the hand. Then, more suddenly, his Gorilla assistant swooped down and grabbed the hand-record. "File it under cards," said the D.A.

"That's my property," I protested.

"Nothing is your property in a murder case," said the D.A. "Well, you've had 24 hours. Before we go pick up your friend, Cayne, you got anything to exonerate him?"

"For crying out loud, what's wrong with you people? Can't you see this is the work of a lunatic? Jimmy Cayne is not a killer — at least away from the bridge table he's not. Besides, he's currently in the middle of winning the world champion-ship as a representative of the United States. You arrest him before the match is over and you'll have the U.S. state department all over you — I promise."

"Fair warning, my phony shamus friend, but not enough substance. Detective Kennedy said he was not the least disturbed when the third member of his team was strangled. He just went right ahead and filled out his bridge team with more slobs."

"And one of those slobs — I mean players — is a certain Hungarian refugee who I am currently tailing and will have something on very shortly. Just give me one more day."

"You've run out of steam, Granovetter. Cayne is the man behind the strings, and no matter how high up he's flying, we aim to bring him down. Bridge medals or no bridge medals, White House flags or no White House flags, we aim to get our man. We got nothing but motives on this case and all the motives point to Cayne."

"I don't understand you guys," I complained. "You're always trying to pin it on someone instead of looking objectively at the evidence."

"To tell you the truth, kid, it's not us. It's Detective Kennedy."

"Detective Kennedy? I thought he was discharged from the case."

"Well, he's been reinstated," said the D.A.

"Who put him back on? Don't they know he's incompetent?"

"The Commissioner put him back on. Ever since his wife came into millions, she's had more influence with the Commissioner than my entire staff has."

"Excuse me, officers," said Pamela. "I can't believe gentlemen as clever and charming as yourselves don't carry a lot of weight in your department."

"Well, yes, er, you're right, Mrs. Granovetter."

"Now I am a personal friend of both Mr. and Mrs. Cayne. And I know that Mr. Cayne's one desire at the moment is to win his championship. Yet this killer of yours seems to be at large and he's trying to stop the U.S. team from winning. This does not jibe with the idea that Mr. Cayne is the man behind the strings."

"Agreed, Ma'am, perhaps. But Kennedy has a theory that Cayne originally hired the killer to knock off the weaker elements of his team so he could rebuild it. Now that he's done that, something, er, perhaps an agreement or contract with the murderer, has gone astray — and the hired gun is out for revenge."

"I used to work in a law office, sir, and that is certainly a shaky premise upon which to arrest a suspect."

"Well, er, no, perhaps, but, uh, what else can we do, sister? I have the Commissioner to deal with, and he has Mrs. Kennedy and the newspapers. I've got to make a show of something, dammit."

"Well, look, why not be sensible and compromise. I suggest that you make an in-house arrest. That will be a step toward showing the Commissioner you are closing in. It will allow my husband more time, and I'm sure something dramatic will happen soon, because they're playing the final this very day and the murderer is obviously going to make another attempt at *someone's* life. Meanwhile you can stake out your fellow here (referring to the Gorilla) and once you capture the actual killer, it will be easy for you to get the whole confession out of him."

"Excuse me," I said. "but the tournament is over at the Sheraton, not in Jimmy's apartment."

"Don't interrupt me, Matthew. As I was saying, the in-house arrest will please everyone — (aside to me) *the tournament will have to be moved to his apartment, ok?* — and you'll have a great chance to capture your killer, and even Mr. Cayne, if he is really behind the murders."

The D.A. took out a handkerchief and wiped his balding forehead.

"Sister, you got a deal."

During this encounter, the Stein girl had left the table and gone to the stage for her second show. We got up to leave when I remembered that I had another question for her. I ran up to her between numbers and a few fellows in the audience started whistling. It was embarrassing, believe me.

"Excuse," I whispered to her.

"I'm in the middle of my act."

"I just want to confirm one thing with you. Was your father buried in the Bronx Cemetery next to your — uh, step-mother? — I mean before her demise — you know, she came later — What I'm getting at is, were you actually at the funeral and did see him — excuse the bluntness — set in the ground?"

"Yes, yes, yes!!! Now get off my stage, you evil, evil . . . *bridge player*!!!"

(Whistles and catcalls.)

"Okay, okay," I muttered. "I'm just trying to help, that's all. Just trying to get to the bottom of this. . . ."

22

Outside on the street, our wheelman was waiting patiently. I went around to his window and knocked. He was busy reading by flashlight. "Just catching up on this week's *parsha*," he said, some religious propaganda in hand.

"Spare me, Belsky, it's very late. Listen carefully. I want you to meet me at the Empire State Building in five minutes, on the South side."

Pamela and I hailed a cab. I told the driver to wait a second, in case we were being followed. "You mean, speed up."

"No, I mean slow down. We *want* to be followed."

We drove up to 32nd Street and Eighth Avenue, and I was correct. Behind us were the D.A. and the Gorilla.

"I don't see how you're going to convince the World Bridge Federation to transfer the Bermuda Bowl final to the apartment," I complained in the car.

"That's not your problem," said Pamela. "At least Jimmy won't be spending the night in jail."

I kissed her goodbye and told her not to wait up for me. She shook her head.

"This is the last tournament for you — and your last detective case as well. Look at you — you're exhausted — it's too strenuous. From now on you'll stay home nights and read to the children, like a good Jewish father."

The cab slowed down and I jumped out, rolling across the pavement. I moved quickly to the Empire building and watched as the D.A. continued uptown. One minute later, Belsky swooped me up and we were back on track. "The Bronx Cemetery," I commanded, closing my weary eyes.

* * * * * * * * *

Cemeteries are not as cheery at night as in the daytime. And I had half a mind to trust the Stein girl implicitly. But Belsky seemed chipper and ready for action. It must have been his religiosity that kept him in such high spirits. Frankly, I had had enough of his fanatic, good nature. We parked the Oldsmobile near the West side of the plots, took the shovel and pick out of the trunk and crept forward, flashlight in hand.

Don't let anyone tell you that there aren't a lot of spider webs on tombstones. And when it's summertime and the damp of the dark morning clouds the horizon, you get an itchy feeling. (I used the pick to scratch my back.) Finding the route to the Steins was easy. We just followed the fresh footprints that were in the muddy earth. My guess was that everybody was visiting the Steins these days — more people than when they were breathing.

Before we reached the plots, we accidentally interrupted two summer lovers. Belsky and I looked at each other and laughed. It relieved the tension and made us feel that we hadn't really descended into another world — at least not yet.

There were shadows everywhere, because the moon was three-quarters and the clouds were scattered. I heard owls and Belsky claimed he stepped on a live rabbit's tail. We kept to the footprints, however, and came upon the graves we were looking for.

"You want the pick or the shovel?" I asked.

"I'll take the shovel," he said.

"Hold it; let's just make sure we got the right one."

I put the flashlight on the tombstones. The one on the right read "Charlotte Stein," so we went to work on the left.

After 25 minutes, I took my jacket off and sat down. This was not easy work. Belsky, bless him, had more strength and continued to hack away. In an hour's time we had reached the coffin, but the dirt was piled too close around the edges and we had to keep digging. Another ten minutes gave us the corners and finally we had air around all four sides.

"One problem, Matt," said Belsky.

"What?"

"How are we going to lift it out?"

"Is it really necessary? We just want to open it, take a peek and close it again. In fact, I was thinking you would do the peeking — my stomach being queasy and all."

"I don't mind, Matt, but we need some rope and a hook."

After some brief consideration, we undid our belts, hooked them together and let them down. They just touched, thanks in no small part to both of us having put on weight last year.

"You see," said Belsky. "All those Sabbath dinners came in handy after all."

"I knew you'd get Judaism into this somehow."

"It's in everything," said Belsky.

"We still need a hook, Rabbi."

We sat down and considered the situation. Perhaps, I thought, Belsky could go down head first and I could hold his legs. No, he was too big and I would drop him. Well, then, maybe I could go down head first. No, I didn't want to be the one to look into the thing. As I was thinking, I overheard Belsky mumbling. Don't tell me he was praying! This was a fine time! Suddenly I was very uncomfortable. Something sharp and cold was sticking into my rear. I moved a bit and saw silver shining in the dirt. I dug the dirt away quickly with my fingers. Unbelievable! It was an empty aluminum duplicate board. Either the corpses had a duplicate club around here or someone had dropped it on a visit. But why would someone bring a duplicate board to a gravesite? It was Board 18. North-South vulnerable. Hmm.

"Well, I guess that didn't work," said Belsky.

"What are you talking about?"

"Sometimes when I need help, I pray directly to God — even with small things like a misplaced checkbook or a video that the kids want to watch. You know we believe in a personal God — you just have to ask and often, like a father, He'll come to your aid. So I was asking for Him to help us find a hook."

"Here it is," I said, brandishing Board 18. It glittered in the moonlight.

We used the pick to break it open and hammered it with the shovel into a U-shape. Then we tied it with shoelaces to the end of the belts.

"One more prayer needed," I said. "That the coffin isn't locked."

"It wouldn't make much sense to lock a coffin, would it?"

"No, I guess not."

We dropped the belt again and fished around for the handle. When Board 18 hooked around, we pulled and felt the tug.

"Here," said Belsky, "we have to pull from this side."

"Are you a fisherman, Mr. B?"

"Sometimes," he said, huffing and puffing a little, "I take

the kids to the pond to catch old rubber boots."

We pulled some more and felt it coming. We pulled some more . . . and more . . . and finally . . . clang!

It was off. I stepped back and tossed the flashlight to Belsk. He bent down and looked. I shut my eyes and prayed.

"It's okay," he said. "You can look."

"How can I look? I can't stand to go fishing either. I can't stand the sight of worms."

"You can look. Trust me. There's nothing much to see."

I opened my eyes, bent down next to him and gazed into the coffin.

There were no crawling things. There were no skeleton bones. There was no Frank Stein, either!

There was, however, a manila envelope, and we scooped it up with the hook. Then we closed the lid as best we could and shoveled the dirt back on top. It was a much easier job on the way out.

Back in the car I opened the envelope. There was handwritten letter inside. It appeared to be signed by Frank Stein and Otto Marx's name was in it. My eyes were very tired, so I decided to wait until I got back to read it. I closed my lids and when I opened them again, good old Belsky was tapping me on the shoulder. "We're here."

I shook my face and got out. The ocean was close by, and the smell of the cool salty air refreshed me. "You want to come up?" I asked.

"No, I'm going back to the apartment and sleep on the pull-out. I'll see you tomorrow. By the way, what do you think happened to Mr. Stein's body?"

"Let me put it this way. There were very few people who wanted him for company when he was alive. There are probably fewer now that he's dead."

Belsky nodded, though even I didn't even understand what I had said. Then I continued:

"Three possibilities, Mr. B. 1) His body was stolen; 2) He

was never buried there to begin with and his daughter is lying; and 3) He never died."

"I hope it's not three," he said.

"Me, too."

I gave my partner a pat on the back and, various papers in hand, made my way up the stairs to George Rapee's office. Inside, all was as I had left it. I poured the coffee into the automatic and took a seat at his desk.

First I examined the contents of the envelope. It was in legal lingo, but the gist of it was decipherable. Frankenstein was asking his lawyers to file suit against Otto Marx for trying to strangle him at the Red Tulip restaurant.

The only conclusion I could make was the obvious: Otto had finished the job he left undone at the Tulip. He murdered Frank in order to stop the lawsuit — and buried the document in Frank's grave. As against that, I had to consider the fact that Otto's business was doing fine, and money was not a chief concern of his. As against that, why the missing body? Could it be — and this was clearly conjecture — that Frankenstein was indeed still alive, enraged with anger and out to put Otto into his own grave with this contract? If that were true, he would find the document missing next time he stopped by to pick it up.

Only one thing was certain: The connection between the two men was in evidence, and the contract left in the empty grave incriminated Otto in part if not completely in the murder of Frank — assuming he was still dead.

I went to the coffee pot and poured a cup. It was a mistake, perhaps. I needed sleep for tomorrow's final, but I had to finish the task of the hand-records before I could sleep soundly.

I started searching the records for a four-diamond bid before I remembered that there was no such bid. I was tired, and it took a few grains of caffeine to wake me up. After three gulps it came to me: Board 18. I found it in a hurry.

Board 18   U.S. Team Trials
East dealer
North-South vulnerable

                        North
                        ♠ K 4
                        ♡ K 5
                        ◇ 8 7 6 5
                        ♣ Q J 9 4 2
West   East
♠ 5 3   ♠ Q J 10 7
♡ 6 4   ♡ Q 8 7 2
◇ Q J 10 9 4 3   ◇ A
♣ 7 5 3   ♣ K 10 8 6
                        South
                        ♠ A 9 8 6 2
                        ♡ A J 10 9 3
                        ◇ K 2
                        ♣ A

Open Room
Barkowsky Hamman J. Mitchell Wolff
West   North   East   South
—   —   pass   1 ♣
3 ◇   double   pass   3 ♡
pass   4 ♡   (all pass)

1 ♣ = 17+
double = values

Closed Room
Rodwell Mr. Stein Meckstroth Mrs. Stein
West   North   East   South
—   —   pass   1 ♠
3 ◇   pass   pass   3 ♡
pass   4 ♠   (all pass)

244

In the Open Room, Wolff started with a big club and got jammed with three diamonds. Hamman (North) doubled to show enough values for game, and Wolff made the interesting bid of three hearts.

My first reaction to the hand was that he should have bid four diamonds, asking partner to pick a major. My second reaction, upon glancing back at the North hand, is that maybe North would take four diamonds to mean three suits and bid five clubs. My final reaction is that Wolff made a heck of a bid, bidding his stronger major rather than his higher one.

After the ◇Q lead by West, declarer was laydown. Had East returned, for example, a club, declarer could cash the ♠K and ♠A and then ruff spades and clubs back and forth for seven tricks. By then he is down to the trump A-J-10, and he can exit a spade. He trumps the next trick with the ♡10 and exits with the ◇K to score his last two tricks with the ♡A-J.

Jacqui Mitchell (East) actually won the first trick and returned a trump from her queen. Wolff, however, was able to embark on an equally successful plan. He won the ♡9, played ♠K, ♠A, spade ruff, then came back to his hand with the ♣A. He led out ♡A and the ♡J to Jacqui's queen. She had nothing to play but clubs, and whether she played the king or a low one, she would set up dummy's club suit.

In the Closed Room, the bidding took a different turn. Charlotte Stein opened one spade, and Eric Rodwell made the same tactical preempt. Those preempts sure do hurt. North had no bid over three diamonds, and South reopened with three hearts. North now guessed to play in four spades, which was not as good as four hearts.

In four spades, where the trumps were significantly worse, declarer had to lose two trump tricks, one heart and one diamond.

So what did this hand have to do with a bid of four

diamonds? And why would the killer place the 4♢ bidding-box card neatly in the mouth of a choking Frankenstein, who was North in the closed room?

I put my head down on the desk and started to ponder the question.

* * * * * * * *

The sunlight shining through the East windows slid down my face. I let out a nice yawn, then checked the clock. It was only 8 a.m. Good. I had a long day ahead of me. Sprinkling some water on my face, I looked at myself in the mirror. It wasn't a pretty picture. At the very least, I needed a shave. Maybe I could get one in Harlem.

23

I went downstairs. The financial center of the world was waking up. The salt in the cooling summer air had turned to the smell of dollars and cents. I moved quickly to the subway and took the D-Train uptown.

At 123rd Street I exited. The sun was bright now and the streets were filled with people, some going to work, some listening to radios, some just hanging out at the local shops, discussing the time of day.

At Broadway I took a right and entered an unmarked, unpretentious apartment building. I walked up three flights, hung a left and entered a door with a sign on it that read: Harlem Bridge-Whist Club. There was only one person in the room. Over at table 3, near the front desk, sat Old Leroy, drinking his morning coffee, his head bent over the afternoon's racing sheets for Saratoga. I sat down across from him and waited until he looked up. After a minute, I picked up a deck of cards and gave them a shuffle.

"I know you're here," he said, without looking up. "So cut the shuffle and fill my cup with some more coffee."

"My wife advised me not to come," I said, pouring the sugar into his cup.

"Your wife is right, boy. You a lost cause."

"What do you mean? I made it to the final, didn't I?"

"You made it by the grace of God — that's how you made it."

He took a long sip and spit it out. "Too much sugar, boy. What's wrong with you?!"

"Well, imagine if you hadn't been coaching me all this time. Then I wouldn't have even made it this far."

"You ain't been telling people I'm coaching you?" He coughed, coffee going down the wrong pipe. "You know I got my reputation to look after."

A little time went by, as he scratched off a few horses' names.

"We're playing the Italians today," I said.

"I know who you playing. You must think I don't know nothing!"

"Well, what are we going to do? I mean, what can you do? What tricks can you give me? What advice?"

"Look, sonny," he said, one eye open and one eye closed, his old wrinkles cracking between the brows, "the way your team is playing, I would skip town — that's *my* advice."

He went back to the forms and after a few more minutes I got up to leave. Pamela was right. He was an old man who had the most brilliant ideas for winning at bridge that I had ever come across, but maybe his best days were over.

I first met him 20 years ago when I was involved in the Mayfair case against Pizza McCarver. At that time, Old Leroy was head of a race-touting gang and was instrumental in discovering the line of play that the murder victim should have taken in a grand slam.

Since I moved upstate, I haven't played much bridge. On the rare occasions I travel to New York, I look up Old Leroy to obtain a few tips and bridge strategies, to compensate for my lack of constant play. He had already given me a number of ideas for the semifinal, one of which came up on the last hand: the dummy reversal. Old Leroy's real forté is imagination. Yesterday morning, he showed me a hand with a 5-2 trump fit, in which the best play was to crossruff!

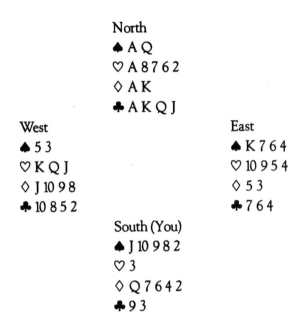

North
♠ A Q
♡ A 8 7 6 2
◊ A K
♣ A K Q J

West
♠ 5 3
♡ K Q J
◊ J 10 9 8
♣ 10 8 5 2

East
♠ K 7 6 4
♡ 10 9 5 4
◊ 5 3
♣ 7 6 4

South (You)
♠ J 10 9 8 2
♡ 3
◊ Q 7 6 4 2
♣ 9 3

In six spades, after the ♡K lead, you can't pull trumps. If you try, East can duck the second round, and if you now ruff a heart to lead a trump, East can win and tap you. However, the "dummy reversal" works splendidly. You win the ♡A, ruff a heart, cash three clubs and ruff a heart, cash two diamonds and ruff a heart. You are now in this position:

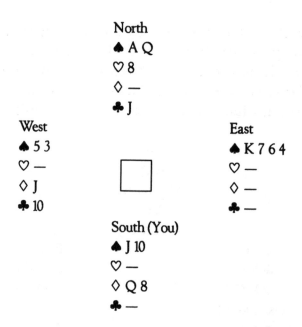

North
♠ A Q
♡ 8
◊ —
♣ J

West
♠ 5 3
♡ —
◊ J
♣ 10

East
♠ K 7 6 4
♡ —
◊ —
♣ —

South (You)
♠ J 10
♡ —
◊ Q 8
♣ —

You lead a diamond and ruff with the ace. Next comes the ♡8 or ♣J, to ruff in your hand. Finally, a diamond ruffed in dummy. East is helpless and comes to only one trick.

Yes, Leroy was filled with ideas like these and there was also the psychological factor. Just the idea that I was armed with a few new tricks up my sleeve was a confidence booster.

As I walked toward the door, a young boy with a Yankee cap on — he couldn't have been more than nine — rushed past me into the club and sat down opposite Leroy.

"Okay," I heard Leroy say. "You win. This one's got to learn a little something, anyways."

I quickly returned and pulled up a chair next to the kid.

"I'll start you off with a simple opening lead problem. Then we get our hands dirty. This is the type of thing you may run into against the Italians. They like to cuebid a lot and they get mixed up with so many cuebids."

Old Leroy scribbled this on a spare racing form:
West: ♠ 10 x ♡ Q J x x ♢ Q x x x ♣ x x x.

"Shucks, I know the hand," said the boy.

"You know the hand?!" said Leroy. "What you been doing, child — kibitzing the penny-imp game?! Wait'll I tell your mother. Well, let shamus boy answer it over here."

I guess he meant me. So I ventured to ask the auction. The kid answered:

"The contract's seven notrump."

"Don't tell him everything," said Leroy. "Here, here's the bidding:"

North	South
—	2 ♣
2 ♢ (0-2 controls)	2 ♠
3 ♣	4 ♣
4 ♢ (cuebid)	5 NT
6 ♠	6 NT
7 NT	

I thought about it deeply. There was one strange thing about the auction: North-South seemed to have fits in both spades and clubs, but ended in notrump. The heart suit was the only suit not cuebid and partner had a chance to double both two diamonds and four diamonds, if he had something there. It just seemed too easy to lead a heart.

Could an ace be missing? No, because South had bid the Grand Slam Force, asking North to bid seven with two of the top three club honors. North, it seems, had shown a partial spade fit on the way to seven clubs, but then bid seven notrump instead. Why didn't North bid seven clubs?

"Who was North?" I asked.

"Ah, so you finally ask a smart question," said Leroy. "You see," he said to the boy, "he's not as dumb as he looks."

"North is the worst imp player in the club — he plays

duplicate all the time," said the little tattler.

"Right on," said Leroy. "He can't make the transition to imps — always going for that extra notrump bonus."

Well, I thought, I guess that means I shouldn't read anything into the seven-notrump bid.

"Okay," I said, "do I have any other clues?"

"Use your racing form," said Leroy.

Racing form? I looked at it. There was the hand again.

West: ♠ 10 x ♡ Q J x x ◇ Q x x x ♣ x x x

I also noticed that Leroy had the habit of crossing off horses he didn't like. Hmm. Let's try it. Spades: declarer's suit, ridiculous lead, very dangerous. Clubs: dummy's suit, very dangerous as well. I crossed them both off on the form. Hearts: kind of safe to lead from, as long as dummy has no heart honors. Diamonds: a risky holding to lead from — for sure. Still a heart looked obvious.

"You taking too long," said Leroy. "One more clue: check out the jump-off point."

Jump-off point? Did he mean the point that South jumped toward the grand slam? Yes, I saw it now! Over three clubs, he raised to four clubs. But over four diamonds, he jumped to five notrump! He needed to hear four diamonds before he could jump to five notrump. Therefore he must be covered in hearts, but he has a hole in diamonds. And what did North have for his cuebid in diamonds? *Not the king or ace because he denied two controls with his two-diamond response and later showed two of the top three club honors (the king-queen) by accepting the grand slam.* So dummy must have cuebid a singleton diamond and partner must hold the king of diamonds!

"I lead the queen of diamonds," I said. "I must break up a potential double squeeze and if I lead a low diamond to the king and ace, I might get squeezed in hearts and diamonds — so I lead the queen."

"Almost right. Here's the hand:"

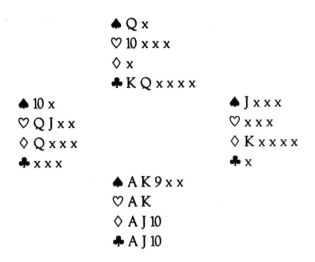

```
              ♠ Q x
              ♡ 10 x x x
              ◊ x
              ♣ K Q x x x x
♠ 10 x                          ♠ J x x x
♡ Q J x x                       ♡ x x x
◊ Q x x x                       ◊ K x x x x
♣ x x x                         ♣ x
              ♠ A K 9 x x
              ♡ A K
              ◊ A J 10
              ♣ A J 10
```

"If you lead anything but a diamond, declarer can cash ten winners and come to:

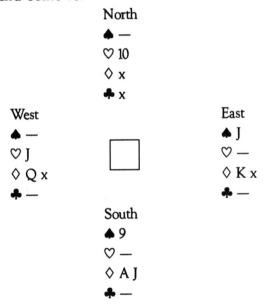

```
                    North
                    ♠ —
                    ♡ 10
                    ◊ x
                    ♣ x

West                                   East
♠ —                                    ♠ J
♡ J                  ┌─────┐           ♡ —
◊ Q x                │     │           ◊ K x
♣ —                  └─────┘           ♣ —

                    South
                    ♠ 9
                    ♡ —
                    ◊ A J
                    ♣ —
```

"On the lead of the last club, East must throw a diamond, South now throws a spade and West must throw a diamond. *Voilà* — the last two tricks are taken with the ace and jack of diamonds.

"Now if you lead a diamond to the king, you will destroy this squeeze. But if you make the fancy-shmancy lead of the queen of diamonds, you put partner in a simple squeeze and make yourself immaterial:

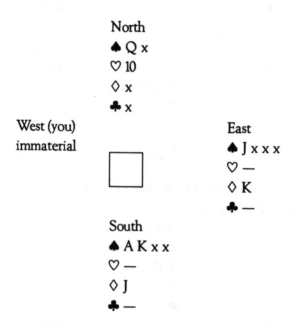

North
♠ Q x
♡ 10
◊ x
♣ x

West (you)
immaterial

East
♠ J x x x
♡ —
◊ K
♣ —

South
♠ A K x x
♡ —
◊ J
♣ —

"Here the last club is played from dummy and your partner is *kaput*.

"Lesson one, shamus baby: Eliminate the dogs on lead, look for the bid below the jump-off point and hit the weakness. But don't get too smart, boy."

"But," I protested, "why did North bid seven notrump and not seven clubs? It's ridiculous!"

"Who knows why? Maybe he did it to annoy you. Maybe he's one of your *chazrs*. It's not your problem. Your problem is to take advantage of his mistake."

He began scribbling again. "Here, here's a bidding problem — just don't get too smart."

East: ♠ K x x ♡ J x x x ◇ Q ♣ A K Q x x.

West	East
1 ◇	2 ♣
2 ◇	2 ♡
3 ♡	?

"See, I made it easy. No interference from the opponents. Just pretend you playing with your Otto guy. What's your bid over three hearts?"

Hmm. Was slam possible? My hearts were weak, but my controls were nice. I could bid four clubs, cuebid or I could sign off in four hearts. Was three notrump a possibility? Hmm. I only had the king of spades, though. Would he think my two-heart bid was not a real suit, if I bid three notrump? Wait a second — he told me my partner is Otto — keep it simple.

"I bid four hearts."

"I bid three spades," said the kid.

I was beginning not to like the kid.

"You bid three spades," said Old Leroy, patting the kid on the head and giving him a piece of candy, "but you better do it in tempo or it wouldn't be fair pool. Here were the two hands:

West	East
♠ A Q J	♠ K x x
♡ Q x x x	♡ J x x x
◊ K J 10 x x	◊ Q
♣ J	♣ A K Q x x

West	East
1 ◊	2 ♣
2 ◊	2 ♡
3 ♡	3 ♠
3 NT	pass

"You got three principles here to deal with. First, when partner doesn't jump to four hearts, it means he does not have a slam try with good trumps. You got to listen for what partner doesn't bid as well as what he does.

"Second, when you have weak cards in partner's main suits, you don't go looking for slam — you don't even think about slam — you put your head in the sand and find the best game."

"Three: All bids below three notrump are for the purpose of reaching three notrump. They are not cuebids for slam, *unless you later remove partner's three-notrump bid.* When you bid three spades, you are looking for three notrump — that's all, brothers, that's all."

"But what good is that knowledge unless your partner knows it, too? Does Otto Marx know it?" I asked politely.

"Otto Marx? Of course he knows that! You constantly underrate your partner, Shamus. He's a rubber-bridge player, ain't he? Then he understands that three notrump is the place you are searching for!"

Leroy looked at me sympathetically. "You in big trouble, boy. You be playing 'gainst Garozzo and the like. He makes all of these routine bids. You need something bad to make up for your slack. I just don't know . . . I just don't know."

"Well, how about a cardplay trick. Something new."

Suddenly the kid started jumping up and down, clapping. "The Feed'em Early Play! The Feed'em Early Play."

"Shush, boy. He's not ready for that one."

"Oh, please, Uncle Leroy."

"Okay, okay, enough with these vegetables," said Leroy. "Let's get to the mashed potatoes and gravy. Here's something for when you're desperate."

"I'm often in desperate contracts," I admitted.

North
♠ x x x
♡ K x x
♢ K J x x x x
♣ x

South
♠ Q x
♡ A x x
♢ A x x
♣ A K x x x

"Contract: Three notrump. Opening lead: queen of hearts. How do you play it?"

The kid looked up and answered first.

"You changed it. That's not fair. This one's just a diamond guess, uncle Leroy. You have to play for a 2-2 split — that's all."

I studied the hand. This was my chance — the kid obviously didn't have all the answers. But the more I looked at it, the less I saw. After a few minutes I gave up.

"It's okay, boys," said Leroy. "This is a new one. Real

desperation. You win the ace of hearts and lead a little diamond to the jack."

North
♠ x x x
♡ K x x
◊ K J x x x x
♣ x

South
♠ Q x
♡ A x x
◊ A x x
♣ A K x x x

Very strange — very, very strange. Suppose East won the doubleton queen or, worse, singleton queen and returned a spade?

"Look," said Leroy. "Garozzo won't play it that way, so here's your chance. If West has a singleton diamond, you win a lot of points. East will probably return a heart, thinking that his partner still has the ace of diamonds."

Wow, I thought. Now that's desperation. Or was it so desperate? You still break even when West has the ◊ Q, and may even gain when West has three diamonds to the queen! If East has three to the queen, you will have pulled off a psychological coup that will really upset the Italians.

"Great," I said. "Give me more, give me more."
"One more," said Leroy. "I've got to call in my daily double. You're on defense — here:

North
♠ K J x
♡ A x x x x
♢ A x x x x
♣ —

West (you)
♠ A Q x x
♡ x
♢ K Q x
♣ Q x x x x

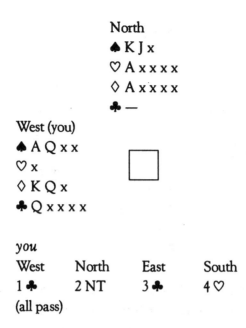

you

West	North	East	South
1 ♣	2 NT	3 ♣	4 ♡
(all pass)			

"You lead the king of diamonds and everybody plays low. What now?"

The phone started ringing. The kid picked up. "Not now, mommy, not now. Tell them I'll play ball later. . . . arr, shucks."

Good, he had to leave. Old Leroy and I gave him some low fives and the kid disappeared. I returned to the problem. Count declarer's losers. One diamond, perhaps two (if partner held specifically the jack doubleton), one spade and one or two trump tricks (if partner held something good in hearts). Hmm. Suppose partner held only the king of hearts, third. Could we manage a spade ruff? Yes, if he had a doubleton. I must lead a low spade, and he can win the trump king, and return a spade to my ace for a ruff.

"I switch to a low spade," I said. "If partner has the ♡K-third and a doubleton spade, I beat the hand."

Old Leroy scratched his head. "Well," he said, "you beat it, but for the wrong reason."

259

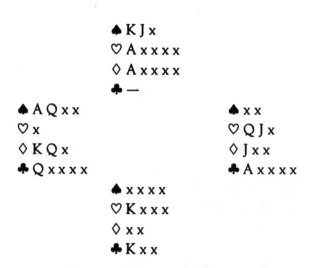

```
              ♠ K J x
              ♡ A x x x x
              ◊ A x x x x
              ♣ —
♠ A Q x x                      ♠ x x
♡ x                            ♡ Q J x
◊ K Q x                        ◊ J x x
♣ Q x x x x                    ♣ A x x x x
              ♠ x x x x
              ♡ K x x x
              ◊ x x
              ♣ K x x
```

"Declarer goes up with the ♠K, 'cause he thinks you might hold the ace four times without the queen. Now, when trumps don't split 2-2, he goes one down. Still, you beat it, so I give you half credit. Just remember the lessons, boy: Leave communication open with your partner. Imagine not only what he may hold, but what declarer thinks *you* might hold. Here you beat the hand only because declarer thinks you have the ♠A-x-x-x — assuming you don't take three hours to make the obvious shift."

"Well, I'm ready for it now, anyway. Right?"

"You ready for something, boy, I just hope it's bridge."

I got up to leave and gave Leroy the usual two C-notes for my lesson. "What about your investigation?" he said as I got to the door.

"Well, I think I have my suspect cornered — I just need one concrete piece of evidence."

"Here, boy." He went to the desk drawer and slipped me a pistol — it was the smallest gun I'd ever seen. "You're equipment is too big. This one'll fit inside the bidding box — I had it specially made. Just don't shoot the wrong man, okay?"

"Okay," I said, thanking him again.

24

It was 10:30 when I reached Victor and Jacqui's apartment on East 97th Street. The D.A. and the Gorilla were parked outside, and gave me a salute as I entered. I waved back, wondering what they were doing here.

For close to seven years of my life, I ate dinner there five nights a week. Luckily, it was in my younger and leaner years when gaining weight was not a problem. Jacqui, who in many experts' opinion is the world's number one female bridge player, is a gourmet cook — not many people know this. In between mushrooms alà russe and chocolate souffles I learned quite a bit about horse racing, baseball, gardening, dogs and bridge.

Of course those were the days when I hadn't yet joined the Jewish circuit — today I could not eat any milk product within six hours of meat, even kosher meat. So when I walked into the Mitchell's living room with the old anticipation of a pancake-with-all-the-trimmings breakfast, I was a little worried that I would have to give up on some of the trimmings (namely the bacon). It turned out Jacqui was serving cold cereals — of course with freshly made whipped cream, gourmet chocolate-coffees and freshly picked straw-berries. She just wasn't capable of serving the ordinary.

The usual crowd was there. To begin with, the dogs. There were a couple of old ones, Siberian huskies who lived under the lamps, and a few new ones, one very shaggy animal under the couch and two strays who stood their ground right under the dining room table. You've got to remember, however, that the dining room table was in the kitchen alcove — this was basically a three-room apartment for two humans and six animals.

By the way, Jimmy and Sonty were there also, as was a very red-eyed Evelyn, who had brought over the new notes of the day. The coach was visibly missing and Victor suggested that it might not be a bad idea if he disappeared altogether.

Victor, who was leaning against the wall by the TV perusing his copy of Jaws, looked tired, but no more so than usual. He told us he usually takes sleeping pills, but refused to take one last night for fear of being too groggy at the bridge table today.

I was surprised to see Jimmy, who rarely leaves his apart-ment except to go golfing, bridging or to work.

"If you saw my apartment, you'd understand why I'm here. They're reconstructing it."

"Who is?" I asked.

"The World Bridge Federation, Chew. They're working overtime. The Commissioner is putting me under house arrest at noon today, so we had to bring the VuGraph show to us."

"You should see the mess," added Sonty, looking up from some papers he was holding in his hands. "The tables and chairs, the screens, the boards, the cameras, everything scattered around the house. Patty and Pamela are helping them — or more likely protecting the walls and furniture."

"That's why I'm here, Chewy," said Jimmy. "Plus, of course,

I wouldn't miss Jacqui's breakfast for the world."

"But aren't you worried about being under arrest?" I asked.

"There's nothing to worry about, Chew. Except perhaps Belladonna. Everything will be all right . . . if we win."

Sonty was pacing back and forth during all this. His wrist had a small bandage on it, but he seemed okay. He was studying the new set of notes and kept shaking his head. I asked him what the matter was.

"These notes are impossible. How can we play these defenses without some practice? He's got us playing three-way doubles over their three-way openings and four-way overcalls after their five-way two-bids."

"Look, Sonty," said Jimmy, "it could be worse. We could be playing five-way over their four-way."

"Aha!" said Sonty. "He's lightened the load on us there."

I leaned over for a peek. It was frightening. The notes were partially handwritten, to make things worse.

"How are we going to remember this?" said Sonty.

"Maybe you should just play against Belladonna and Forquet," I suggested. "They're playing simple Blue Team, aren't they?"

"Yes," said Sonty, "but we don't have the option who we play against. Aren't the line-ups drawn out of a hat for the final? And what does it matter? Whoever plays Garozzo and Franco are going to have to deal with their new system."

During all this I occasionally glanced over at Evelyn, who was this minute in tears and the next minute in a mild sniffle. Finally, I couldn't stand it anymore and I asked her what the problem was.

"We've broken up," she cried. "Why do you think half the notes are handwritten?"

"Good grief," said Sonty. "So *that's* it. And I thought I stepped on your foot on the way in when I was trying to avoid the dogs."

"You mean," I said, "that you and the coach are no longer

a . . . a . . . whatever you were?"

"He told me to get lost last night. After I had typed 20 new pages of notes for the team!"

This had to be a put-on, I was thinking. There are men you cry over — I agree — but certainly not the coach. With the coach you cry when he *doesn't* leave.

Then again, perhaps love is indeed blind.

On the other hand, isn't little Evy here coming into quite a lot of insurance moolah? Why would the coach give her the brushoff now? I looked down at her stockings to see if she still carried her switchblade, but she wasn't wearing stockings.

"Breakfast is ready," I heard Jacqui call from the kitchen.

"Where's Belsky?" I asked, suddenly remembering that he was supposed to meet me here.

"In here," I heard from the kitchen. Yes indeedy, there was Mr. B., apron in hand, helping Jacqui with the strawberries and whipped-cream action. Some of the strawberries had disappeared, claimed Jacqui.

After breakfast, the dogs had to go out again. Victor took his copy of Jaws with him. "He reads a chapter at the park when he walks them," Jacqui informed us. "Crazy huh? It's the only book Victor's ever read."

The rest of the team returned to Jimmy's apartment, and Belsky and I went with Victor, but not before a quick question to Jacqui.

"Jacqui," I said, when we were alone. "I thought you said you'd kill the girl if she ever turned up here again."

"That was before she broke up with the coach," answered Jacqui. "I think we can do something with her now that she's acting sensibly."

Central Park is nice in the summer, but to tell you the truth, I was getting fatigued by all my running around. And it didn't help that the temperature was rising again. We caught up with Victor at the benches. I wanted to ask him what he thought of the team's chances and also what his opinion was of a certain Hungarian refugee named Otto Marx.

"Did you know, you gotta go under water if you see a shark coming at ya?" he informed us, looking up from his book.

"Victor," I said. "Tell me the truth. Do we have a chance?"

"If you burn those notes, you got a chance. When are you gonna stop with all the notes and just play bridge?"

"It's not me, it's Jimmy and his coach."

"Well, maybe. . . . I told Jimmy to get rid of him a long time ago, but he loves the practice. It's not so bad for Jimmy, anyway. The coach does a pretty good job."

I was confused, but that wasn't unusual by now. Belsky, who was holding on to one of the huskie's leashes, suggested we'd better leave soon. I think the idea of poop scooping didn't appeal to him. Besides, he had to pick up a tape down at 47th Street and it was time for me to go play.

"Should we wait for you, Victor?"

"Neh. I'll be along. You go and hobnob with the celebrities."

"But before we go, Victor, what about the murders? Do you think Otto did it, or do you think I'm just prejudiced 'cause he's been my bridge partner the last 24 hours and I've grown to despise him?"

"Now you're talking. You just go ahead and play your own game, don't let anyone bother you, that's all. You'll be all right . . . God help you. . . ."

As I walked away with Belsky, Mr. B. turned to me and said, "He doesn't give straight answers, does he, Matt?"

"Never has, Belsky. But they often contain a hidden meaning and it's up to the listener to figure them out."

"Just like the Talmud, Matt. Now I see why you love the guy."

25

Belsky dropped me at the Cayne apartment. There were some "black hats" in the building's foyer: Chasids, ultra-religious people who live in Brooklyn and wear only black suits and white shirts, topped off with perfectly round, black felt hats. I wondered where they were going as I passed them on my way to the elevator. When I walked into the Cayne apartment, I was not sure where I was going.

The Gorilla was guarding the door. He was ready to frisk anyone who entered. I slipped right by him as he let out a short and ugly scowl. Bright lights hit me smack in the face. The place had been transferred into what appeared to be a movie set. There were lights and cameras in the hallway — TV crews were setting up for interviews (one was even in progress, the midday news was talking with Edgar Kaplan *and Detective Kennedy*).

I stepped carefully over wires into what used to be the living room. Most of the furniture was gone. Chairs, lined up movie-theatre style in rows nine-deep, faced the dining room where a projector and screen had been set up. Philip Alder and Alan Truscott were testing the lights and microphones, which were positioned on what I believe used to be the dining room table in the left-hand corner of the room. This table would be for the panel of experts who would host the VuGraph show.

I stepped into the library, where video cameras were now peeping out of bookcases. A bridge table marked "Closed Room" was set up with the dreaded bidding screen hanging forebodingly above it. As long as I was there I gave it a quick feel under the screen to see if there were any sharp instruments. There was nothing but the iron curtain. Maury Braunstein, the tournament director, was fixing bidding boxes to the table. I considered putting my mini-revolver in one of them, behind the redouble cards, but I didn't know where I was going to sit in the first set.

In the hallway that led to a bedroom, where the Open Room would be, I spotted Patty with some of the Italian players, who were standing around drinking espresso and complimenting her on her apartment.

"Your wife is in my bedroom and you need a bath," said Patty. Then she returned her attention to Giorgio Belladonna, whose eyes were wide with admiration.

"Anda when you coma to Rome, you musta come to play in *my* club de bridge."

"Thank you," said Patty. "But I hope you realize that this is not a bridge club — this is my apartment."

"Ahh, your apartment!"

"Si, si."

She turned to me as Giorgio tried to explain to another Italian — I believe he was the non-playing captain of the team — how they were not in a bridge club but in Patty Cayne's apartment. (Though I think that the NPC misunderstood because he started bowing to Patty and giggling. Tannah Hirsch, who runs the Travel With Goren group and co-authors the syndicated Omar Sharif bridge columns, clarified the situation further. "The serial killer is still at lodge and by squeezing everyone into the apartment, the police have a better chance to trap him.")

As I moved down the hall, I heard about three "police" calls in heavy tones of surprise. Patty grabbed my shoulder. "This is outrageous. If Jimmy loses after all this, there'll be hell to pay. After what they've done to my house, I finally put my foot down — he's promised me that after he wins, there'll be no more tournaments for five years."

"What do you want me to do about it?" I asked.

"I want you to play your very best!! And you need a shave, too. There are reporters all over the place!"

As I passed the other bedroom, I waved to the coach, who was also helping with the set-up. He turned to me and smiled. "Can you believe Patricia forced me to help clean up her apartment all morning! I mean, after all, I have a thousand notes to go over with you. . . ."

I jolted quickly away into the rear of the apartment. In the den, Jimmy, Sonty and Otto were busy reviewing the notes. "Matthew," said Jimmy, who was back in his boxer shorts, smoking a cigar, "you want to take a look at this?"

"Victor advised me to burn the notes."

"Yes, but Chewy, these are newer notes. These are the notes that even Evelyn hasn't seen. These have things in it that will blow your mind."

"Maybe we should order a little lunch," said Sonty, who was also smoking a Havana. I tried to breathe but had a difficult time of it.

"I have to wash up," I said. "I'll be right back. How are you, Otto?"

"It's a clazy theeng, but I theenk I'm okay."

"Good," I said. "See you soon."

In the master bedroom, Pamela was taking a rest. "Are you

okay?" she asked, her head on the pillows. "*You're* the one who needs a rest."

"I'll be all right. I'm working overtime on adrenalin."

"There's a change of clothes for you over there by the bathroom door."

I quickly showered and shaved and returned to the den. Some sandwiches were on the coffee table, but frankly I was still full from breakfast. The coach was in the middle of his latest anti-artillery tactics. Evelyn was back by his side — perhaps she was only doing her job for the team.

"You'll see here on page 24 — oh, Granovetter, you've decided to join us —"

"Don't get so smart," I retorted. "I don't see Victor or Jacqui here."

"Jacqui's in the kitchen helping Patty with the Italians' antipastos," said Sonty. "I'm having one, too — you want one? I'll order it; they're really wonderful, with or without the anchovies."

"No thanks, Sonts," I said, sitting next to Evelyn, peering over her shoulder at page 24.

"I shall continue," said the coach. "As the Blue Team notrump openings are either any balanced 16-17 or 13 to 15 with precisely 3-3-3-4 or 3-3-2-5 shapes, I suggest that two clubs be a takeout of clubs — which will put us on par with the other table if the opener has the weaker variety. Now against Garozzo-Franco, who are using variable notrump openings, we stick to the variable overcall structure found back on page 19. (Shuffle of pages.) Here we bid one under for takeout of one higher if their notrump has a bottom of 14. The minute it goes to 15, however, we go to two-under, which I must concede was an earlier oversight on my part, corrected by our friend Mr. Marx (Otto smiles)."

"So let's see," says Sonty, his hands moving back and forth across his chest, referring to his opponents, his partner, and the general public. "If they open a 14-to-16-point notrump, I double to show a takeout of clubs, bid two clubs for a takeout of diamonds, bid two diamonds for a takeout of hearts, and bid two hearts for a takeout of spades. If I bid two spades, it's a takeout of two notrump and we all go home and drink up a storm. Now, if their notrump starts at 15, double means takeout of diamonds, clubs means takeout of hearts, diamonds means takeout of spades and hearts means takeout of notrump — whatever that means — and I'm not asking 'cause I don't even know how I got this far."

"Now, now, Sonty," said Jimmy, "the coach here has worked all night (sniff by Evelyn), and Evy too — all so that we can win one for the gipper."

"Who's the gipper?" asked Sonty.

"Patty's the gipper."

I couldn't help but notice a little button on Evelyn's blouse that looked exactly like the audio bug she had on the other day. I wondered it Belsky had planted it again at breakfast or whether Evelyn, in a lover's revenge, had planted it herself to get some incriminating evidence against the coach. Though what incriminating evidence there was against him I could not imagine. Every step of the way, he seemed to be on the team's side; in fact, most of his income depended on doing a good job as coach — which meant helping the team win.

"Now let's turn to page 29. (Shuffled pages.) Here we find the crux of the Garozzo-Franco system, their two-club relay response."

"Why can't we simply play that the double of two clubs shows clubs?" asked Sonty.

"Because," said the coach, "that doesn't give us enough of an edge. If they are going to make artificial bids, we have to take full advantage of them. For us to have a hand with clubs is too low a percentage. But if the double were to be two-, three- or four-way in meanings, we have something to fire back at them and wound them a little."

"I've had enough of the wounds," said Sonty.

"Sonty," said Jimmy, "the coach is trying to help. If you would listen to his advice, we could get on with this. Okay, finish it up, coach, I'm getting a migraine and I haven't even fielded one of Belladonna's opening leads."

I excused myself and left Otto there to fend for our partnership. Enough was enough. If we lost a board on one of these defenses, it was worth it not to have to sit there any longer. I couldn't help but think that the late B. J. Becker was right after all. The more conventions you play the more it will take away from your cardplay. We were about to sit down against four of the most notorious cardplayers the bridge world had ever known. Now was the time to clear our minds for thinking — not clutter them with cockamamie defenses to obscure conventions.

* * * * * * * * *

The submission of line-up cards was in, and as I passed the living room, my heart started to pound. There must have been 200 people in there, waiting to watch the VuGraph. We were matched in the Open Room, North-South against Belladonna and Forquet. System-wise we would have to contend only with a little canapé (shorter suit first) and a few simple conventions that went with the Blue Team Club. I used to play the system myself when I was a kid, so I was familiar with the style. One club was strong, and four-card majors were opened in any seat. People-wise, however, was another story. We had to contend with two bridge legends. Somehow we had to forget who these guys were and just concentrate on the game.

Otto, who I had to admit was not looking well, and who I was sure was more nervous than any bridge player I had ever come across, buttonholed me before we sat down.

"I theenk you'd better sit on Belladonna's side of the screen."

"I can't ensure that," I said. "We're locked into the positions we submitted."

Sure enough, when we sat down I was on Forquet's side. Pietro, a very handsome and comfortable looking gentleman, dressed in a bank-president's cashmere black suit, silk off-white shirt and gold tie, shook my hand. The guide card had me North, but I had been submitted as South. "Ah," said Pietro, "I am supposed to seet East."

Somebody must have moved the guide card around by accident and we corrected it. Unfortunately, this still placed Belladonna on Otto's side of the screen, and when I lifted the curtain to remind Otto that we were playing simple Landy over their notrump, I was not at all pleased by the way his hands were shaking. If only we could get started, I thought, maybe his nervousness would dissipate — mine usually did in these important matches, as soon as I got "into" the hands. But Jimmy and Sonty's table was starting first — and we would be held up for the VuGraph comparisons, said Maury Braunstein.

Belladonna, in the meantime, was examining our convention card — I could hear him on the other side of the screen giving Otto the once over, grilling him on our most simple methods. So I took the moments to ask Forquet if he still required Q-10-fourth to open in a four-card major.

"I try to have the queen and ten, but I do with what I am dealt. Giorgio, he can always have less."

While we waited for the library to finish the first two deals, I checked out the scenery. We were in the spare bedroom — the bed had been lifted and placed against the wall and the bridge table was on a small platform that used to support the mattress and springs. Two stereo units were pushed up against the closets and video cameras for the VuGraph closed-circuit were balanced on top. The Closed Room would play the boards first and we would play the boards second, our bids and plays transmitted to the VuGraph

272

audience in the living room. Sitting between me and Pietro was Evelyn, who was working the monitor and microphone. On the other side of the screen was bridge writer Philip Alder, also acting as a monitor. The coach had decided to watch the first set on VuGraph to get an overall feel for the match and our subsequent strategy.

Bidding boxes were screwed to the four corners of the table, and I took the extra time to undo the safety latch on Old Leroy's gun and place it nimbly into my bidding box. It didn't fit as snugly as Leroy had promised, so I made room by removing the redouble cards and let them drop to the floor. Playing with Otto, I would have little use for them anyway. As I looked up at Pietro, I noticed that he was observing me all the while.

"Seence we last played in the Lancia (that was 15 years ago), you have become a detective, I hear."

I nodded and he gave me a reassuring nod back. Apparently he felt secure that the gun was on his side of the screen. Even more reassured was Evelyn. She gave me a big smile when she saw the gun.

Finally Patty (the caddy!) came in with the first board. "It's a hot one," she said. We looked at her disapprovingly — she wasn't supposed to comment on the board. "Just joking, fellas," she said. "I haven't seen it, and if I did, you would be fools to listen to what I had to say about it."

♠ Q 6 4 ♡ K Q 2 ◇ 8 7 5 ♣ J 9 6 2

The auction proceeded:

Belladonna	Otto	Forquet	Matthew
West	North	East	South
—	pass	pass	pass
1 ♡	pass	2 ◇	pass
2 NT	pass	3 ◇	pass

As the auction continued, I was relieved to see that it was their hand. I have already described to you my inability to cope as declarer on the first board of a set, let alone a match as important as this one. Needless to say, I didn't expect to play the hand when I first saw my 8-point, dull-looking assortment. So I just sat back and relaxed, listening to Evelyn on my side and Alder on the other side announce the bids into the microphones.

Suddenly, however, the bidding tray came back to our side of the screen with a pass by Belladonna and a double by Otto! Alder's voice was clear and confirmed what I was looking at.

Pietro eyed the double and passed. That left it to me. What in the world was Otto doing? On the very first deal!

♠ Q 6 4 ♡ K Q 2 ◊ 8 7 5 ♣ J 9 6 2

Belladonna	Otto	Forquet	Matthew
West	North	East	South
—	pass	pass	pass
1 ♡	pass	2 ◊	pass
2 NT	pass	3 ◊	pass
pass	double	pass	?

Three diamonds was not a forcing bid in Blue Team, nor was the rebid of two notrump. But for Otto, who had passed three times, including the opening bid, to balance at the three-level was preposterous. If he were exactly three-suited, short in diamonds, I should bid four clubs — but oh, how I hated to go to the four-level with these cards! If he held a good four-card spade suit, he might have risked a one-spade overcall, so I deduced his best suit must be opener's.

I bid three hearts and everyone passed smoothly. Very nice, I thought, first board, and here I am again declaring — in Giorgio Belladonna's opening-bid suit no less!

Belladonna led the ♣K, the screen was lifted and Otto put down his cards.

North
♠ A K 2
♡ A J 8 6 5
♢ 10
♣ 10 8 7 3

South
♠ Q 6 4
♡ K Q 2
♢ 8 7 5
♣ J 9 6 2

I heard Evelyn recite the lead to the VuGraph audience as I gazed appreciatively at dummy. What a good bid Otto made! Yes, he had passed a hand that most would open — perhaps he was nervous or perhaps he's adopted a Roth-Stone approach while no one was looking — but he had the courage to reenter the fray when the auction was dying out. And I had caught the inference about his best suit. My God, were we a partnership!

The most I could imagine us getting against a diamond contract was three spades and a heart (the hearts must be at least 4-1). In clubs, we had no play for 10 tricks, but in hearts we might make nine.

Looking back now, of course, I can see my mistake on this hand was to spend so much time not only analyzing what they could make (purely a duplicate strategy) but wasting my energies patting myself on the back for my bid instead of thinking about how to play the hand. It was pride that was my downfall — instead, I should have been thinking: How do I play this contract that I have luckily stumbled into?

North
♠ A K 2
♡ A J 8 6 5
♢ 10
♣ 10 8 7 3

South
♠ Q 6 4
♡ K Q 2
♢ 8 7 5
♣ J 9 6 2

On the ♣K opening lead, I called a low club from dummy and Forquet followed with the 4. Belladonna thought a bit and switched to the ♢K, which held the trick as Forquet signalled high. Belladonna continued with the ♢J, pushing it with his huge hands out to the center of the table, as if by getting physically closer to the dummy it could tap the trump suit all the harder.

I ruffed in dummy and immediately led a club, the normal procedure in a case like this — set up the side-suit winner. If they continued diamonds, maybe there would be some interesting end position, in which I could strip the spades and perhaps put East on lead with the third round of clubs to give me a sluff-ruff.

This was the full deal:

North (Otto)
♠ A K 2
♡ A J 8 6 5
◇ 10
♣ 10 8 7 3

West (Belladonna)
♠ J 10 9 8
♡ 10 9 7 4
◇ K J
♣ A K Q

East (Forquet)
♠ 7 5 3
♡ 3
◇ A Q 9 6 4 3 2
♣ 5 4

South (Matthew)
♠ Q 6 4
♡ K Q 2
◇ 8 7 5
♣ J 9 6 2

Belladonna won the trick with his ♣Q and continued with the ♣A. Forquet sat back, and I sat forward, ready to claim at the end of this trick, so long as the trumps were 4-1 and not 5-0. Forquet, however, came to life by trumping his partner's ace and leading a third round of diamonds.

I sat back again. Dammit, I had done it again! I was forced to ruff in dummy, and with only three trumps left, I could not pull Belladonna's four.

All I had to do was draw one round of trumps — just one lousy round — before I embarked on the club suit.

I suddenly felt the sweat flow across my body, despite the excellent air-conditioning. And Otto, who had been watching my every move, had the nerve to ask *me* if I was all right!

"It's a clazy theeng," he said as the curtain came down, "but even the best players can get nervous playing against blidge legends."

"You're not supposed to be watching my dummy play!" I squawked back, though I don't know if he heard because the curtain was down and Forquet already had his pass card on the bidding tray.

I picked up my hand quickly. Now *I* was doing the shaking.

Board 1 - Closed Room
North dealer
Neither side vulnerable

North (Franco)
♠ A K 2
♡ A J 8 6 5
◊ 10
♣ 10 8 7 3

West (Cayne)
♠ J 10 9 8
♡ 10 9 7 4
◊ K J
♣ A K Q

East (Sontag)
♠ 7 5 3
♡ 3
◊ A Q 9 6 4 3 2
♣ 5 4

South (Garozzo)
♠ Q 6 4
♡ K Q 2
◊ 8 7 5
♣ J 9 6 2

Closed Room:

Cayne	Franco	Sontag	Garozzo
West	North	East	South
—	1 ♡	3 ◊	3 ♡
4 ♣	pass	4 ◊	(all pass)

Opening lead: ♡K

Trick 1: ♡K, ♡4, ♡8, ♡3
Trick 2: ♡2, ♡9, ♡A, ◊2

278

26

From a psychological viewpoint, one of the worst mistakes that you can make at imps is to underestimate your results. Pessimism makes your brain heavy and hurts your functioning on the boards that follow. Here I was all upset at having gone down in a laydown three-heart partscore, when we had actually won 2 imps on the board. At the other table Jimmy and Sonty had bid to four diamonds on the East-West cards and made four when Franco and Garozzo had a signaling error and tried to cash two rounds of hearts. Declarer was able to ruff and discard a spade on dummy's third club honor.

Meanwhile, I was bemoaning my play, while at the same time trying to tell myself it was only a partscore . . . it was only a partscore.

On the second board, Belladonna revoked (see, it happens to him, too) against a one-club contract by Otto. He made three instead of two and we gained another imp.

On the third board, Otto overcalled in the middle of their auction and put me to another guess in the bidding. They were vulnerable, we were not, and I held:

♠ J 10 5 4 ♡ 3 2 ◊ 8 7 ♣ K 10 9 8 2

Matthew	Belladonna	Otto	Forquet
South	West	North	East
pass	1 ♠	pass	2 ♣
pass	2 ♠	3 ♣	3 ♡
?			

The auction was another new one to me. What was three clubs? And why hadn't Otto overcalled one spade with two clubs? The clues were there but were they really valid?

Forquet's rebid of three hearts showed longer hearts than clubs, and a game-forcing hand — he could easily have three clubs, on rare occasions a doubleton honor. Then, again, he could have a real club suit with longer hearts.

What was Otto doing? If he really had clubs, I could damage their auction with a jump to five clubs and not get hurt. In fact, if his overcall was not a cuebid of some sort, he would, by virtue of his pass the first time, be describing a hand with clubs *and spades* — the only reason for passing over one spade.

You might ask why do you have to pass over one spade with spades and clubs when you can overcall two clubs. The answer is this. If you overcall two clubs, you can never find the spade fit, if by some chance (as on board one) you belong in the suit that the opponents have opened. This does not occur much in American bidding, where opening major suits tend to be five. But against four-card majors and, for that matter, American minor-suit openings, it can be quite a problem.

Therefore many experts play that the delayed overcall shows that suit plus the opening bidder's suit.

If this were true here, Belladonna would be void in clubs and Forquet might be void in spades! They would have a great heart fit with two black voids and it would be imperative for me to kill their auction with a five-club call.

However . . . (there always is one, isn't there?) what if Otto was not on the same wavelength? He was a rubber bridge player, after all. He didn't know these little tricks about passing with their suit and later bidding to show both suits. Or, perhaps, he had simply wanted to show diamonds and hearts (yes, he could have done this with double or two notrump) and was sitting with a void in clubs! Then what a disaster if I jumped to five clubs!!

My head started to throb. What to do? What to do?

Clues, I needed more clues. Forquet's three-heart bid certainly suggested he had short clubs, otherwise why not a double of three clubs? But we were not vulnerable and they were. Maybe he wanted to show his heart suit because he had six of them.

Belladonna's two-spade bid showed five or more spades. If he had only five and a void in clubs — in the Blue Team style he is forced to rebid a five-card major before bidding a side four-card suit — he would have to hold specifically 5-4-4 shape. The odds were against it.

If he had more than five spades, Otto's three-club bid couldn't be natural with clubs and spades because I had four spades myself. But if Belladonna had only five spades and Otto had four of them, Forquet was void. Good grief, this was impossible to figure out.

Then the thought occurred to me that Otto was making a page-73 defense to something out of the coach's notebook. In that case, I'd better pass and play it safe. Oh, what the hell, I thought — if I passed and Otto really had clubs, it might not be terrible — they might not reach the perfect contract anyway. Better to play it safe than risk a giant disaster.

I passed.

This was the deal:

North
♠ A Q 9 8
♡ —
◇ K 4 2
♣ Q J 7 6 5 4

West
♠ K 7 6 3 2
♡ Q 6 5 4
◇ A Q J 5
♣ —

East
♠ —
♡ A K J 10 9 8 7
◇ 10 9 6 3
♣ A 3

South
♠ J 10 5 4
♡ 3 2
◇ 8 7
♣ K 10 9 8 2

Matthew	Belladonna	Otto	Forquet
South	West	North	East
pass	1 ♠	pass	2 ♣
pass	2 ♠	3 ♣	3 ♡
pass	4 ◇	pass	6 ♡
(all pass)			

We went minus 1430 and I never took a bid! Not only that, but we had a fantastic little save in seven clubs. Even if East manages to score a spade ruff, the best the defense can do is take three tricks (one diamond, one club and one ruff) for 500. Not good, Matthew. Not good. But worse was my reaction at the end of the hand. I jumped all over Otto.

"What are you doing!? Why are we suddenly getting fancy with the delayed overcalls? Why couldn't you make a simple two-club call the first time?"

"Don't blame me," he said. "It's a clazy way to play, I agree, but the coach — he said the only way to handle thees canape' ees to pass first with their suit."

"I know, I know, but why now? Why have you suddenly gotten sophisticated now?!"

"When should I get sophisticated? Should I wait for the next Temple duplicate or should I get sophisticated in the final of the world championships?"

He was right, but I hated him all the more for it. I hated him and I wanted to never see him or hear him again. I slammed the curtain down and there was an explosion — no, not quite — it was ashes smoldering on the table. "Nobody touch the table," I screamed.

In a few minutes, Detective Kennedy arrived and we all got up. A new table was brought in. It was my opinion, though I was not a chemist and had only a little training at the forensic lab, that the smoldering was pure sulfuric acid. Had any of us touched it, he would still be in pain and probably minus one or more fingertips as well.

They took the table out and we waited for a new one. Patty had a spare set in the back closet, and before too long we were ready to go again, but we didn't have the screen and we didn't have the bidding boxes — and, it struck me suddenly, I didn't have my new gun — it was still in my bidding box from the ruined table.

Maury Braunstein requested that we continue verbally and we all agreed. What else could we do?

The deals went much faster without the screens and bidding boxes. Unfortunately I had to look at Otto constantly — and listen to his voice — it was getting on my nerves. He was overbidding now — on every hand he tried to compete in some newfangled way. The word pass never crossed his lips. Hand after hand he began declaring — and, thank God, they never doubled. Still, it was minus 50, minus 100, minus 200, minus 150. Yes, they could make partscores on some of them — and one hand he might have stolen a game from them — but it couldn't be good, these never-ending minuses. It reminded me of the first time I had kibitzed the Blue Team. I was only a child of 11, and deal after deal they had allowed their opponents to steal the contract — and deal after deal they had lost one imp, gained five, lost two, gained four, and so on and so forth.

We were being imped to death — I could feel it when, thankfully, the last two boards were tossed onto the table.

$$\spadesuit \, A \, K \, Q \, J \, 10 \, 5 \quad \heartsuit \, 9 \, 2 \quad \diamondsuit \, J \, 8 \quad \clubsuit \, A \, 9 \, 2$$

We were vulnerable against not and I was the dealer. I opened one spade, Belladonna passed and Otto raised to two spades. There was a slight hesitation on my right. Then Forquet said double. I said pass — it was instinctive, a tactic I have had success with my whole life. By passing, I would force a bid out of West — a bid that might help me in the play of the hand when I later reached four spades.

Belladonna bid three hearts and Otto doubled. Forquet passed and I suddenly found myself thinking. I never intended to defend when I passed the takeout double, but now maybe it was the right thing to do. This was imps — it meant that the double of three hearts was serious, not a matchpoint trigger double to collect a two-trick set. On the other hand, we had nine trumps at least between us, and we were vulnerable. Pass of the double would be a big position to take in a team game. Facing Otto, I'd better take insurance, I thought.

Wait a second. Were those beads of sweat on Belladonna's thick forehead or were they my imagination? I glanced again. That was sweat, boy. He definitely did not like the idea of declaring three hearts doubled.

On the other hand, did I really want to defend a doubled partscore with Otto against the world's number-one-ranked player in the history of the game?

284

What was I thinking this long for anyway?

I bid four spades and everybody passed. Belladonna led a somewhat hesitant ◊ 10. Nonetheless, he had a relieved look on his face.

North (Otto)

♠ 9 8 3

♡ A 7 6 5

◊ A 7 2

♣ J 5 4

(Belladonna)   (Forquet)

South (Matthew)

♠ A K Q J 10 5

♡ 9 2

◊ J 8

♣ A 9 2

When dummy hit, I saw why he was relieved. Even with only four weak trumps to the ace, my partner had them in big trouble. Instead we were now in a contract that appeared unmakeable. Nine tricks, perfect for three notrump, not so hot for four spades, stared me straight in the kisser. What would they be saying on VuGraph? How was I going to look Patty in the eye after this set of boards? *Stop it, Matthew, stop it. Just play the hand, think of a way to make it — use your imagination!*

What good was imagination? Dummy was as bare as can be. Only the ♣ J had any potential to it, and even then not much.

I ducked the diamond lead, for want of anything better, and Forquet won his queen. He thought only for a second before returning the ♡ Q. I played low and when Belladonna played low, I called low from dummy. It began to dawn on me that the fourth heart in dummy was sitting over Belladonna's four hearts, and maybe, just maybe, it would be worth something.

North (Otto)
♠ 9 8 3
♡ A 7 6 5
♢ A 7 2
♣ J 5 4

(Belladonna)   (Forquet)

South (Matthew)
♠ A K Q J 10 5
♡ 9 2
♢ J 8
♣ A 9 2

Forquet continued with the ♡J and I won in dummy with the ace. I then tried to imagine East's hand. He held the queen-jack-third of hearts and probably the king-queen of both minors. Forquet was a conservative bidder and would not venture a takeout double to the three-level *with only three cards in the missing major* on anything less than 13 highcard points. Odds were he had a singleton spade to boot.

So how did this help me? Hmm. What else did he hold? The ♢9 was probably with Belladonna, who had led the 10. What about the ♣10? What had Forquet done to indicate that card? Nothing! In fact, the absence of a club shift meant exactly that — he did not hold the king-queen-ten of clubs. A piece of information to use, perhaps . . . perhaps.

Perhaps a squeeze was in the making.

I could draw trumps and duck a club, but whoever wins may return a diamond and there'd be no squeeze against East because the heart threat was with West.

No, if there were a squeeze, it was a strange one. I ruffed a heart, all following. Belladonna still held the king. Then I drew trumps, Belladonna having started life with three, and Forquet began discarding — first a diamond, then a club. So I led my fifth trump and Forquet threw a diamond. In my mind, I could picture all four hands:

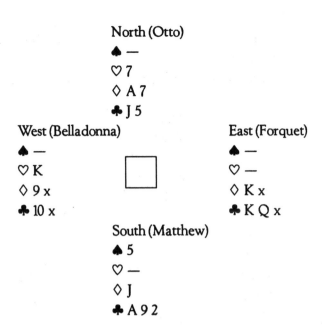

North (Otto)
♠ —
♡ 7
◇ A 7
♣ J 5

West (Belladonna)
♠ —
♡ K
◇ 9 x
♣ 10 x

East (Forquet)
♠ —
♡ —
◇ K x
♣ K Q x

South (Matthew)
♠ 5
♡ —
◇ J
♣ A 9 2

I led the ♠5. Belladonna hesitated, then threw a low diamond. I threw the ♡7 from dummy — it had served its purpose — and Forquet threw a club. It was now simply a matter of giving up a club. I won the diamond return and took the last tricks with the ace and nine of clubs.

Had Belladonna thrown a club in the end position (and Forquet a diamond), I would have taken two club tricks by leading to the ♣J, forcing out the 10 and queen — I would then be able to take the club finesse against East.

I was elated.
We passed out the final board.
When I rose to go to the VuGraph room, however, my bubble burst.

Board 15
South dealer
North-South vulnerable

Italy +39, USA +8

North
♠ 9 8 3
♡ A 7 6 5
♢ A 3 2
♣ J 5 4

West
♠ 6 4 2
♡ K 10 4 3
♢ 10 9 6
♣ 10 7 6

East
♠ 7
♡ Q J 8
♢ K Q 7 5 4
♣ K Q 8 3

South
♠ A K Q J 10 5
♡ 9 2
♢ J 8
♣ A 9 2

Garozzo	Cayne	Franco	Sontag
South	West	North	East
1 ♠	pass	2 ♠	double
3 ♣	pass	3 NT	(all pass)

Garozzo and Franco had just finished bidding three notrump. We were about to gain one imp on the board. More important, however, we had lost close to 30 imps on the set, the tally before this deal being Italy plus 39, USA plus 8.

"It's embarrassing," said Patty into my good ear.

"I'm sure the tide will turn," I retorted.

"What did you do on the final board?" she asked.

"We passed it out."

"I don't think that you turned the tide."

27

S onty and Jimmy were not smiling either. "You had your bidding shoes on, I hear," said Sonty, while giving me an encouraging slap on the back.

"It wasn't me — it was Otto. Why does everybody think it was me?"

"Well," said my wife, "you were sitting North, and North never stopped bidding. If it wasn't for that game your partner made at the end, it would have been much wors—"

"I was *South*, not North. The guide card got fouled up. Do you mean to say the VuGraph was describing me as North?"

"I knew you couldn't be that crazy."

"It doesn't matter," said Jimmy, curtly. "You're benched." He stormed off.

I don't know what I was more depressed about, the score or the fact that 200 people and the bridge press thought I was the lunatic sitting North. I walked in a fog straight into the D.A.

"The lab report came back, if you're interested, Granovetter."

"What lab report?"

"On the table screen. It was a chemical compound based on sulfuric acid — the police are checking local chemical supply agents to get a trace on their deliveries. Whoever put the stuff under the screen must have known what he was doing. The stuff burns a hole straight through metal, let alone the human hand."

"Wasn't Otto Marx a chemist before he went into the stock market?" I asked.

"Maybe, maybe, but this stuff could be purchased, too. And it would take the right connections. Yup, I would call the stuff 'cayne sugar,' if you know what I mean."

I moved into the hallway, out of the crowd. Lineups were being called for. Where the heck was Belsky? Maybe I could work on the case while I was sitting out. They had me as North, dammit. I hated Otto all the more now. People were applauding in the VuGraph room, so I went back in and took a seat in the back.

Alan Truscott had introduced Omar Sharif, who had stopped by for a brief appearance. He was going to sit in on the panel. Patty Cayne came on the microphone. "Hi, Omar, happy to have you here. Ladies and gentlemen — and I use the words loosely — please do not bring food into the living room."

"Where's the living room?" asked a few people.

"This is the living room," said Patty. "You may drink coffee in the kitchen and foyer only. And those smoking, please remember the new invention called ashtrays. Thank you. Oh, one more thing. We're in the United States, please remember that when you're rooting." (General cheers and catcalls.)

The lights went out. The VuGraph was switched on.

Alan Truscott's voice rang out. "We'll be joined here not

only by Omar but by Edgar Kaplan and Alvin Roth. Welcome, gentlemen."

"I'm here," said Roth, "against my better judgment."

Kaplan: "You mean you judge you belong someplace else?"

Roth: "No, I mean, the players belong someplace else."

Sharif: "So you don't like the way the bridge has been played so far. Frankly, I hear the score is quite low, which is usually a sign of good bridge."

Roth: "Sometimes both sides make the same mistakes."

Truscott: "Gentlemen — and ladies, excuse me — but let me tell the audience exactly where we stand. The score is 39 to 9 in favor of the Blue Team and this is the second quarter of four quarters to be played this afternoon and tonight. The Blue Team is out to recapture the Bermuda Bowl and three of the original members are with us today. In fact they have played a four-man rotation since the start of the tournament one week ago. But fatigue has not been a factor. The wisdom of age has won out. The Blue Team qualified for yesterday's semifinal by placing fourth in the round-robin. They defeated Great Britain in a nail-biting semifinal to reach today's final. The American team is here today by virtue of winning the North American Team Trials and thereby receiving a bye into the semifinal stage of this tournament. They defeated U.S.S.R. yesterday and are now 30 imps behind the Blue Team, with quite a number of boards to play. It's still anybody's match, wouldn't you say, Edgar?"

Kaplan: "Normally it would be safe to say that one of these two teams will win, if that's what you mean, Alan. However, the way things are going, who knows?"

Truscott: "Very good. Now, if the audience will look up here on the stage — in front of the china closet — you'll see a video screen, to your right, of players in the Open Room. However, we will start with boards 17 and 18 in the Closed Room, and then switch to the Open Room for a replay of 17 and 18 and onward through the 16-board set."

(Voice from the back: "Have they caught the murderer yet?")

Truscott: "No, I'm sorry to have to say they haven't caught the murderer yet. But there is no need to worry. The police have assured us that the area has been swept for bombs and everyone who has entered has been properly frisked. I repeat: There is no need for alarm."

(Another voice from audience: "What about the acid on the bidding screen?" General commotion now.)

Truscott: "There was a rumor to that affect, yes, but I believe somebody was playing a practical joke with the seltzer. In any case, we are all perfectly safe and, more important, the screen has been cleaned off and is ready for action."

A stately woman with bleached white hair piled fashionably on top of her head sat down two chairs from my left. I recognized her and nodded. It was Mrs. Kennedy.

"I didn't know you played bridge," I said.

"I don't," she answered. "I have more interesting games to play."

"You mean like bribe the Police Commissioner?"

"You are as subtle as you are clever, my dear snoop."

"Be careful how you talk to me," I warned. "I don't see your dogs around here to protect you."

"Which dog are you referring to? My old dog or my new dog?"

"Shh," said someone next to us.

Truscott: "Here in the Closed Room we have the first board of the quarter. Sitting East-West for the Italians are Benito Garozzo and Arturo Franco. For the U.S. we have the New York City partnership of Victor and Jacqui Mitchell, arguably the world's best husband-wife partnership."

Kaplan: "Interesting bid by South. Would you open four hearts, Omar?"

292

Board 17
North dealer
Neither side vulnerable

Italy +39, U.S. +9

North
♠ 4
♡ Q 7 5 4
◇ 10 8 7 4 3
♣ J 9 2

West
♠ A Q 10 3
♡ 6 2
◇ 9 6 5 2
♣ A K 8

East
♠ K J 6 5 2
♡ 8
◇ Q
♣ Q 10 7 5 4 3

South
♠ 9 8 7
♡ A K J 10 9 3
◇ A K J
♣ 6

Closed Room

Garozzo	V. Mitchell	Franco	J. Mitchell
West	North	East	South
—	pass	pass	4 ♡
(all pass)			

Sharif: "Edgar, here is a bid you don't see the experts make anymore, but it is an important principle. Shut the opponents out when you can — especially if your side is unlikely to produce a slam — the only reason for opening at the one level."

Kaplan: "What do you think, Al?"

Roth: "Standard rubber-bridge tactic — used to be made all the time. Nowadays, however, there's too much misguided science. Who made that bid? Victor?"

Kaplan: "No, it was Jacqui."

Roth: "She knows the right way. She got her training at the Mayfair."

There was little to the play, but at the end of the deal Garozzo leaned over at Franco before the screen came down and had a few words to say in Italian. Personally, I couldn't see what he wanted Franco to do. Balance with four spades? It was a great hand for our side and I was starting to feel better.

Board 18
East dealer
North-South vulnerable

Italy 39, U.S. 9

```
                     North
                     ♠ A 10 9 6
                     ♡ 9 5
                     ◊ 10 3
                     ♣ A J 10 7 4
   West                              East
   ♠ J 5 3                           ♠ K 8 7 2
   ♡ K J 6                           ♡ A 8 4 2
   ◊ 8 7 6 5                         ◊ K J 9
   ♣ K 9 2                           ♣ 5 3
                     South
                     ♠ Q 4
                     ♡ Q 10 7 3
                     ◊ A Q 4 2
                     ♣ Q 8 6
```

Closed Room

Garozzo	V. Mitchell	Franco	J. Mitchell
West	North	East	South
—	—	?	

Kaplan: "Not much to this deal."

Truscott: "Actually North-South can take quite a number of tricks with their scattered 21 points."

Sharif: "I don't think they are so scattered, Alan. The North cards are hardly the nine points that they pretend to be."

Kaplan: "Ah, yes, but then that is from our vantage point — we can see the location of the club king. From North's vantage point, he holds maybe the equivalent of a solid ten count — but then Victor was never one to accurately count his points. What say you, old Maestro of the Mayfair? Are any of these hands strong enough in your methods for an opening bid?"

Roth: "Ha, ha. You may laugh, but I know that North has the strongest hand at the table."

Kaplan: "Well, if it goes three passes to him, do you think he will open?"

Truscott: "I'm willing to wager it won't go three passes to North."

Sharif: "Did I hear somebody say wager?"

Garozzo	V. Mitchell	Franco	J. Mitchell
West	North	East	South
—	—	pass	1 ◊
pass	1 ♠	?	

Kaplan: "Well, you are right. Jacqui opened that 12-point South hand. I don't think it has two-and-a-half quick tricks, does it?"

Roth: "It has a rebid, however."

Garozzo	V. Mitchell	Franco	J. Mitchell
West	North	East	South
—	—	pass	1 ◊
pass	1 ♠	pass	1 NT
pass	?		

Kaplan: "Ah, yes, one notrump, a safe harbor, indeed."
Truscott: "You don't imagine Victor is thinking of raising to two notrump, do you? Facing a 12-to-14-point minimum?"
Roth: "I'll lay two to one he doesn't pass."

North
♠ A 10 9 6
♡ 9 5
◊ 10 3
♣ A J 10 7 4

West
♠ J 5 3
♡ K J 6
◊ 8 7 6 5
♣ K 9 2

East
♠ K 8 7 2
♡ A 8 4 2
◊ K J 9
♣ 5 3

South
♠ Q 4
♡ Q 10 7 3
◊ A Q 4 2
♣ Q 8 6

Closed Room

Garozzo	V. Mitchell	Franco	J. Mitchell
West	North	East	South
—	—	pass	1 ◊
pass	1 ♠	pass	1 NT
pass	3 NT	pass	pass
pass			

Final Contract: 3 NT (South)
Opening lead: ♠J

Kaplan: "Well, he wasn't counting his points after all!"

Sharif: "Very impressive bid by Victor Mitchell. You know, I once went to the track with Victor and after taking his advice I lost seven races in a row. I said from now on I'll take your advice on bridge and you take my advice on handicapping. And now I see I was right in my judgment."

Truscott: "Excuse me, Omar, but now moving into the picture will be the four players featured on VuGraph for the rest of the afternoon. (Applause.) Sitting North-South for the Blue Team, Pietro Forquet and Giorgio Belladonna. East-West for the U.S. are Jim Cayne and Alan Sontag."

Kaplan: "They will be playing these two boards first, won't they?"

Truscott: "Yes, let's get the previous board up on the screen."

Roth: "No one has said anything, but these are two very powerful results for the U.S. team and could put us right back in the match."

Board 17
North dealer
Neither side vulnerable

Italy +39, U.S. +9

North
♠ 4
♡ Q 7 5 4
◇ 10 8 7 4 3
♣ J 9 2

West
♠ A Q 10 3
♡ 6 2
◇ 9 6 5 2
♣ A K 8

East
♠ K J 6 5 2
♡ 8
◇ Q
♣ Q 10 7 5 4 3

South
♠ 9 8 7
♡ A K J 10 9 3
◇ A K J
♣ 6

Closed Room

Garozzo	V. Mitchell	Franco	J. Mitchell
West	North	East	South
—	pass	pass	4 ♡
(all pass)			

Open Room

Cayne	Forquet	Sontag	Belladonna
West	North	East	South
—	pass	pass	1 ♡
double	?		

Kaplan: "Ah, yes, Belladonna has opened one heart, not four, and this allowed Cayne to make a one-level takeout double."

Truscott: "It's not over yet, however. North-South can make five hearts."

Cayne	Forquet	Sontag	Belladonna
West	North	East	South
—	pass	pass	1 ♡
double	2 ♡	4 ♠	?

Sharif: "I believe Giorgio will not sell out. There is an inference he can make here with his three small spades — and that is his partner may be short in spades."

Cayne	Forquet	Sontag	Belladonna
West	North	East	South
—	pass	pass	1 ♡
double	2 ♡	4 ♠	5 ♡
pass	?		

Sharif: "There, you see, I was right. Good bid, Giorgio."
Kaplan: "Good bid, also, Jim Cayne, who passed five hearts rather than double."
Truscott: "I still don't think this auction is finished."

Cayne	Forquet	Sontag	Belladonna
West	North	East	South
—	pass	pass	1 ♡
double	2 ♡	4 ♠	5 ♡
pass	pass	5 ♠	?

(Cheers from the second and third rows — Patty, Pamela, other family members and U.S. supporters.)

North
♠ 4
♡ Q 7 5 4
♢ 10 8 7 4 3
♣ J 9 2

West
♠ A Q 10 3
♡ 6 2
♢ 9 6 5 2
♣ A K 8

East
♠ K J 6 5 2
♡ 8
♢ Q
♣ Q 10 7 5 4 3

South
♠ 9 8 7
♡ A K J 10 9 3
♢ A K J
♣ 6

Cayne	Forquet	Sontag	Belladonna
West	North	East	South
—	pass	pass	1 ♡
double	2 ♡	4 ♠	5 ♡
pass	pass	5 ♠	double
pass			

Roth: "How much you want to bet the auction is over now?" (Laughter. Forquet is on camera, thinking. Silent pause.)

Cayne	Forquet	Sontag	Belladonna
West	North	East	South
—	pass	pass	1 ♡
double	2 ♡	4 ♠	5 ♡
pass	pass	5 ♠	double
pass	pass	pass	

(Cheers again.)

Final contract: 5♠x (East)
Opening lead: ◇K
Trick two: ♡K

Kaplan: "Alan Sontag is bending over with a claim now. That's 650 points to East-West. Add that to the 450 scored at the other table North-South. What's that, Alan?"

Truscott: "Let me see here, where's my imp chart?" ("Fourteen imps!" from someone in the audience.) That's right, I believe. No, fifteen imps. Which leaves the score Italy 39 and the U.S. 24, as we go to board 18.

Board 18
East dealer
North-South vulnerable

Italy +39, U.S. 24

North
♠ A 10 9 6
♡ 9 5
◇ 10 3
♣ A J 10 7 4

West
♠ J 5 3
♡ K J 6
◇ 8 7 6 5
♣ K 9 2

East
♠ K 8 7 2
♡ A 8 4 2
◇ K J 9
♣ 5 3

South
♠ Q 4
♡ Q 10 7 3
◇ A Q 4 2
♣ Q 8 6

Kaplan: "Can we see the auction in the Closed Room, Chuck?"

301

North
♠ A 10 9 6
♡ 9 5
♢ 10 3
♣ A J 10 7 4

West
♠ J 5 3
♡ K J 6
♢ 8 7 6 5
♣ K 9 2

East
♠ K 8 7 2
♡ A 8 4 2
♢ K J 9
♣ 5 3

South
♠ Q 4
♡ Q 10 7 3
♢ A Q 4 2
♣ Q 8 6

Closed Room:

Garozzo	V. Mitchell	Franco	J. Mitchell
West	North	East	South
—	—	pass	1 ♢
pass	1 ♠	pass	1 NT
pass	3 NT	(all pass)	

Kaplan: "Thank you."

Truscott: "Yes, this was the deal that Victor Mitchell bid three notrump on only nine points over his partner's minimum rebid. Remarkable, and almost surely another pick-up for the U.S."

Cayne	Forquet	Sontag	Belladonna
West	North	East	South
—	—	1 ♢	pass
1 NT	?		

Omar: "Look at this. Sontag has begun with a one-dia-

302

mond opening on the East cards. That is a very good bid at favorable vulnerability with both majors."

Cayne	Forquet	Sontag	Belladonna
West	North	East	South
—	—	1 ◊	pass
1 NT	pass	pass	

Roth: "He stole the pot. I don't approve — it's not *my* style — but I don't entirely disapprove either — obviously because he stole the whole pot."

Truscott: "Belladonna still has a bid coming. He may double."

Cayne	Forquet	Sontag	Belladonna
West	North	East	South
—	—	1 ◊	pass
1 NT	pass	pass	pass

Final contract: 1 NT (East)
Opening lead: ♡3

Kaplan: "Ah, yes, well, I don't think one can blame Pietro and Giorgio for not entering the bidding with their cards, but this is not a good result for them."

Truscott: "Let's see, North-South should take five clubs, three spades and two diamonds — no, East will score three hearts and a spade first. Final result should be down three."

Sharif: "You see what I mean about the vulnerability."

Roth: "It's not my style — no, but it's a good gambling style. Sontag learned of lot of those tricks at the old Mayfair game. . . ."

I was glued to the screen. It was exciting and pleasing to see our team making a comeback. We gained 10 more imps on this deal.

"What does that make the score, brown eyes?"
Mrs. Kennedy was poking me with a pencil, point first.
"Italy 39, U.S. 34. We're only five behind now."
"Thanks, buster."
"Why are you keeping score?"
"What's the point without the score, huh?"

Board 19
South dealer
East-West vulnerable

VUGRAPH

Italy +39, U.S. +34

North
♠ A
♡ 9 4
♢ A 10 9 8 7
♣ A K 8 6 2

West
♠ J 6 5 4
♡ K Q 3 2
♢ Q 5
♣ Q 7 5

East
♠ K Q 10 9 8 7 3
♡ —
♢ K 6 3
♣ 10 4 3

South
♠ 2
♡ A J 10 8 7 6 5
♢ J 4 2
♣ J 9

Closed Room

Garozzo	V. Mitchell	Franco	J. Mitchell
West	North	East	South
—	—	—	3 ♡
pass	4 ♡	4 ♠	pass
pass	double	pass	pass
pass			

Final Contract: 4♠x (East)
Opening lead: ♣J
Result: Down 2. North-South +500.

Truscott: "Another good result in the Closed Room for the Mitchells. It appears that four hearts would have made, despite the 4-0 heart split."

Kaplan: "I'm sure the Americans prefer the 500-point set. Actually, it could have been less but for the excellent lead made by Jacqui Mitchell."

Cayne	Forquet	Sontag	Belladonna
West	North	East	South
—	—	—	pass
pass	1 ◊	1 ♠	2 ♡
2 ♠	3 ♣	?	

Roth: "They're all bidding a lot — on garbage."

Cayne	Forquet	Sontag	Belladonna
West	North	East	South
—	—	—	pass
pass	1 ◊	1 ♠	2 ♡
2 ♠	3 ♣	3 ♠	4 ♡
double	?		

Roth: "I don't blame Cayne — Sontag doesn't have his bids — he should have preempted the first time."

Cayne	Forquet	Sontag	Belladonna
West	North	East	South
—	—	—	pass
pass	1 ◊	1 ♠	2 ♡
2 ♠	3 ♣	3 ♠	4 ♡
double	pass	pass	pass

North
♠ A
♡ 9 4
♢ A 10 9 8 7
♣ A K 8 6 2

West
♠ J 6 5 4
♡ K Q 3 2
♢ Q 5
♣ Q 7 5

East
♠ K Q 10 9 8 7 3
♡ —
♢ K 6 3
♣ 10 4 3

South
♠ 2
♡ A J 10 8 7 6 5
♢ J 4 2
♣ J 9

Final Contract: 4♡x (South)
Opening lead: ♠5
Trick 1: ♠5, ♠A, ♠3, ♠2
Trick 2: ♡9, ♠K, ♡5, ♡Q
Trick 3: ♢Q

Kaplan: "Well, this may be 590 for the Italians. We shall see."

Sharif: "They may be able to defeat this with the queen-of-diamonds shift at some point. You see, if declarer wins in dummy, West, upon gaining the lead, can play a diamond to East's king for a diamond ruff. If declarer ducks the lead of the diamond queen, he has two diamond losers."

Truscott: "But look at the club position, Omar. Declarer might have a squeeze on East. If West leads the queen of diamonds and another diamond, and declarer guesses to play the ace on the second round, he may be able to eventually pull trumps and come down to three clubs in dummy to the ace-king-eight opposite the jack-nine of clubs and diamond

306

jack in his hand. East must hold the diamond king and therefore comes down to the doubleton ten of clubs. Now the lead of the jack of clubs forces a cover by West and the clubs come tumbling down."

Sharif: "Impressive analysis by Alan Truscott of the Times. Perhaps you would like to guest-write one of my columns."

Truscott: "If you'll ghost-write a few of mine — I need a vacation."

Kaplan: "Gentlemen, the play is the thing and we're missing it."

Roth: "Nice signal by Sontag at trick two. The king of spades was a suit-preference signal that the mayor in Hoboken couldn't miss."

Kaplan: "Ah yes, Jim Cayne did switch to the queen of diamonds. Let's see how Mr. Garozzo handles it."

Trick 3: ◇Q, ◇7, ◇3, ◇2
Trick 4: ◇5, ◇A, ◇6, ◇4

Sharif: "He's read the position. Perhaps then the mayor in Hoboken would have read it, too."

Trick 5: ♡4, ♠7, ♡J, ♡K
Trick 6: ?

Truscott: "That's the third trick for the defense, and may be its last if Garozzo finds the squeeze on East that I suggested earlier. A brilliantly played hand."

Trick 6: ♣Q, ♣K, ♣3, ♣9

Kaplan: "And a brilliantly defended hand as well."
Roth: "Did Cayne return a club and declarer win in dummy?"
Truscott: "He returned the *queen* of clubs!"

307

Roth: "Let's see. Yes, that is a good play — he's always been a very clever player—"

Kaplan: "Yes, we know, Al — he learned it all at the Mayfair."

```
                     North
                     ♠ A
                     ♡ 9 4
                     ◊ A 10 9 8 7
                     ♣ A K 8 6 2
     West                              East
     ♠ J 6 5 4                         ♠ K Q 10 9 8 7 3
     ♡ K Q 3 2                         ♡ —
     ◊ Q 5                             ◊ K 6 3
     ♣ Q 7 5                           ♣ 10 4 3
                     South
                     ♠ 2
                     ♡ A J 10 8 7 6 5
                     ◊ J 4 2
                     ♣ J 9
```

It was a great play and declarer was stuck in dummy. The only way off was in clubs and there was no escaping a diamond loser. Down one meant plus 100 in this room; add to that the 500 in the other room and we won another 12 imps!

"How do you score that one?" asked Mrs Kennedy, pencil between her lips.

"Another twelve for us. Italy 39, U.S. 44."

"Oh dear," she moaned as a firecracker went off. Which came first, the "oh dear" or the firecracker, I wasn't sure. Patty and Pamela rushed back to give me hugs and kisses.

"Now we're doing nicely, huh?"

"You just stay in your seat, sweetie — everything's going fine."

There were some loud voices in the crowd as board 20 came up on the screen. Someone let out a scream. I heard an "Oh no!"

"Ladies and gentlemen," said Alan Truscott on the mike. "Please remain seated. There is a rumor here, please wait until it is substantiated."

"Is there a doctor in the house?" asked somebody on the speaker. ("What about Dr. Zhivago?" someone blurted out. General laughter.)

"Please, quiet please, this is serious." (I recognized the voice of the D.A.) "Mr. Sontag has been shot."

28

The ambulance had come. Sonty was being carried on the stretcher to the service elevator. The bullet had grazed the left shoulder, which was covered with a towel and bloody. I tried not to look at the red stuff. He seemed to be in good spirits, considering. There was something he was holding tightly in his right hand. The medic made him open his fist and the East cards to board 20 fell to the rug. It was a nice looking 18-count, from what I could gather. A little shape, too.

Patty and Pamela went with Sonty to the hospital. "Make sure he's back by the fourth quarter, if not the third," ordered Jimmy, who started looking around his apartment — I think he was looking for a new partner.

Detective Kennedy was in the living room, examining the area surrounding the East chair for bullet remnants. I sent the Gorilla to inform him that Sonty had been playing in the other room. There was a tremendous amount of scuttlebutt concerning what the procedures were, and Edgar Kaplan, who is a walking rule book when it comes to these things, was, for the first time in his life, at a loss for words. The biggest headache at the moment seemed to be the throngs of people who were trying to get into the kitchen for refreshments. The housekeeper was having a fit and threatened to quit — and if it weren't for the Gorilla's assistance, she would have. His uncanny flair for baking English muffin pizzas surfaced at just the opportune time and may have saved the day.

No one had seen Belsky for hours. No one had seen Otto for minutes. And I decided to hide for a few seconds myself, but Jimmy found me, along with the coach, who stuck a 40-page summary of Cayne-Sontag notes in my puss. I went to the master bedroom to read them and there found Otto.

He was on his knees, hunched over the dresser. I snuck up on him, turned him around and gave him a right to the jaw. He went down like slinky, spilling across the floor. As he rolled, a gun fell out of his pocket — Leroy's gun. And when I checked the bullets, they were missing.

"Get up, you thief, you murderer, you overbidder!"

"I am not an overbidder," he said, holding his jaw. "Just because you don't understand normal bidding, do not take it out on me."

"What were you doing in Mrs. Cayne's dresser?"

"I was just looking at her pictures. She has a picture of me and my famil—"

"A likely story. And what were you doing with this revolver in your pocket?"

He rose now and sat on the bed. "It's a clazy ting, but I was just looking at the pictures when somebody stuck the gun inside my tlousers. I turned around, but he was gone and I was about to return it to the police when you came in."

He started to get up but I shoved him back down. He was a tall guy, yet easier to handle than I expected.

"Where do you think you're going? I'm taking you in. I'm

spilling the beans on you right now. I even know about the grave stealing and the lawsuit you buried, which is now in my possession."

"You're clazier than I am. You go spill some beans, but you don't know what you are saying — and I for sure don't know what you are saying. Besides, we have to fill in now that Sontag is in the hospital."

"Ha! You don't think I would sit across the table from you again! Here, look at this — they gave me the notes to study. I'm filling in with Jimmy. You are out, buddy, out for good."

"You are clazy," he said. "You want to lose the match, I don't care. But at least you must tly your best — it cannot be right to blake up the partnerships now—"

He started to get up and I grabbed him by the waist and shoved him over to the closet. "Don't resist," I said.

"I'm not resisting. I'm tlying to get you off my stomach."

We fell back into the closet, his head hitting the heel of one of Patty's shoes. He was temporarily dazed. I took the moment to tie him up. There was a whole reel of shoe-box string on the top shelf. It took a while, but I finally had him tied to the hanger post. Then I stuffed his mouth with stockings. There would be no more bids out of him for a while. I decided to leave him in the closet until the end of the half. There was too much commotion going on right now and I wanted to concentrate on the notes. I moved to the library, and when I passed the den I noticed a meeting was in progress.

The World Bridge Federation had called the emergency meeting to decide on how to proceed. The politics were heated. American supporters wanted to wait until Sonty fully recovered before continuing play. Italian supporters wanted a concession. Also, Bobby Wolff suggested a shortening of the number of boards to decrease chances of further trouble. The captain of the Italian team did not go for this because his team was behind by 5 imps. Kaplan suggested a compromise:

that we curtail the number of boards only if and when the score became tied. This was agreed to by all and the meeting was adjourned.

I was in the library bathroom, on page 17, when I heard Maury Braunstein call, "shuffle up." We were ready for action. A new Board 20 had been duplicated and was on the table. We took our places again, with me in Sonty's old seat. Kennedy's lab people were still checking for fingerprints, so we had to wait a few more minutes. This at least gave the Closed Room time to start before us, providing the refreshed VuGraph audience a chance to witness a comparison of tables. Evelyn brought me a cup of fresh, hot coffee from the kitchen and the play resumed, but not before she bent down and whispered: "Message from Belsky. He's in Brookyn and coming back soon with surprise news." I was a little taken aback that Belsky was in Brooklyn again. I was also not so pleased that one of my suspects was relaying messages from my own partner, but I nodded and sorted my cards.

$$\spadesuit \text{ J 9 8 6 5 } \heartsuit \text{ A Q 5 } \diamondsuit \text{ A K J 2 } \clubsuit \text{ 5}$$

Two passes to me and I opened one spade. Belladonna overcalled one notrump, Jimmy passed and Forquet bid three notrump. I was very relieved that I was not on declarer play for the first board.

Jimmy led the ♠2 and this is what I saw:

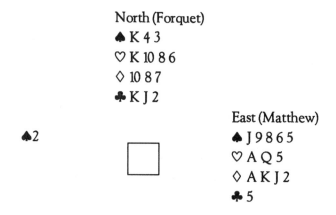

North (Forquet)
♠ K 4 3
♡ K 10 8 6
◇ 10 8 7
♣ K J 2

East (Matthew)
♠ J 9 8 6 5
♡ A Q 5
◇ A K J 2
♣ 5

♠ 2

Belladonna called low, I put up the jack, and he won the queen. Belladonna led the ♡J, low, low, queen. I was in. I started to cash the ◇K when the forensic expert behind me brushed his fingerprint blotter against my neck. When he moved his hand away, ink dripped on my fingers, and when I went to wipe off the ink, the ♠6 floated out of my hand, by accident, onto the table.

This was a nightmare! I meant to play on diamonds, for if they were 4-3-3-3 around the table and declarer had only eight tricks, I would be able to set up five for the defense.

Belladonna won the ♠A, Jimmy following, and continued with another heart, Jimmy following up the line, to the 10 and my ace.

Dammit, we now need three quick diamond tricks. Think fast, Matthew — use your imagination. Declarer has a doubleton spade and three hearts, and therefore at least three diamonds. There's no hope in bringing down the doubleton queen, but what if Jimmy has the ◇9? Declarer may think I have that card. . . .

Instead of cashing the top diamonds, I led the ◇J and waited, hoping that the deal looked like this to declarer:

North

♠ K 4 3
♡ K 10 8 6
◊ 10 8 7
♣ K J 2

West (Jimmy)

♠ 10 5 2
♡ 5 4 3
◊ K 6
♣ 10 9 7 4 3

East (Matthew)

♠ J 9 8 6 5
♡ A Q 2
◊ A J 9 2
♣ 5

South (Belladonna)

♠ A Q
♡ J 9 7
◊ Q 5 4 3
♣ A Q 8 6

If I held the ◊ A-J-9-x or ◊ K-J-9-x, Belladonna would have to duck the jack to stop the defense from cashing three tricks. Wasn't that more likely than my leading the jack from A-K-J?

The more Belladonna thought, the more I knew I had him. Yes, Jimmy must hold the ◊9 or Belladonna would have no problem covering with his queen. My only concern was that perhaps I had taken too long to make my shift. After all, if I really held the A-J-9 or K-J-9, it would be rather automatic for me to shift to the jack. It was a standard textbook card position (standard at least among experts). Is Belladonna reading into my huddle? I thought.

After a very, very long time, Belladonna played the queen. He then proceeded to claim 10 tricks. The full deal was:

North (Forquet)
♠ K 4 3
♡ K 10 8 6
◊ 10 8 7
♣ K J 2

West (Jimmy)
♠ 10 5 2
♡ 5 4 3
◊ 9 6
♣ 10 9 7 4 3

East (Matthew)
♠ J 9 8 6 5
♡ A Q 2
◊ A K J 2
♣ 5

South (Belladonna)
♠ A Q
♡ J 9 7
◊ Q 5 4 3
♣ A Q 8 6

I quickly leaned over and sorted though the South cards, relieved to see that an immediate diamond shift would not have defeated the contract either. It was not until months later, when I met Belladonna again, that he told me why he had played the queen. It wasn't my huddle but the fact that if I held the A-J-9-x or K-J-9-x, I could have shifted to the suit earlier — upon winning the ♡Q — and ensured a defeat. Therefore, he played me for the only legitimate holding, A-K-J third. Little did he realize that my failure to shift to diamonds at trick 3 was an accident.

Meanwhile, Jimmy over there in the West seat was getting irritated. "If you're going to make a deceptive play, do it in tempo," was his compliment to me.

On the next board, I had a system problem. I couldn't remember if we played transfers at the four-level or not, and the one sequence that could cause us trouble came up:

	Matthew	Jimmy
	1 NT	4 ♡

My hand: ♠ A 8 7 6 ♡ A Q 10 5 ◊ K J ♣ Q 4 2

After long thought, I decided it was natural. After all, Jimmy could have bid four spades with long spades, just to play it safe. So I passed and this was the full deal that Jimmy declared in four hearts:

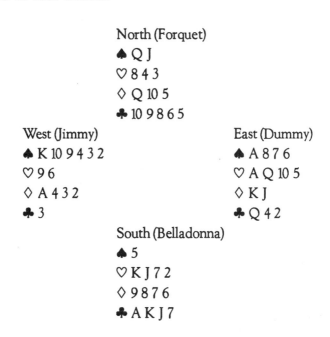

North (Forquet)
♠ Q J
♡ 8 4 3
◊ Q 10 5
♣ 10 9 8 6 5

West (Jimmy)
♠ K 10 9 4 3 2
♡ 9 6
◊ A 4 3 2
♣ 3

East (Dummy)
♠ A 8 7 6
♡ A Q 10 5
◊ K J
♣ Q 4 2

South (Belladonna)
♠ 5
♡ K J 7 2
◊ 9 8 7 6
♣ A K J 7

I had to give Jimmy credit for being a poker face. He never said a word when dummy came down, though Belladonna must have known what was going on, because he was on Jimmy's side of the screen and had been alerted by Jimmy that his four hearts was a transfer.

Forquet (North) led the ♣10 and Jimmy thanked me for my dummy. He covered with the queen and Belladonna won the king. After some thought, Belladonna returned a spade — a good play. Jimmy won the ♠A and ruffed a club in his hand.

He then finessed Forquet's ◊Q by leading to the jack. He cashed the ◊K (by this time I was wondering why trumps hadn't been pulled and was starting to nonchalantly slink under the table). Jimmy ruffed another club back to his hand and cashed the ◊A, discarding a spade. Now came the fourth round of diamonds and Forquet hesitated.

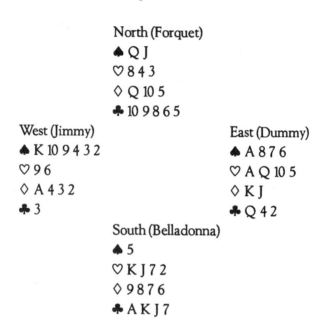

North (Forquet)
♠ Q J
♡ 8 4 3
◊ Q 10 5
♣ 10 9 8 6 5

West (Jimmy)
♠ K 10 9 4 3 2
♡ 9 6
◊ A 4 3 2
♣ 3

East (Dummy)
♠ A 8 7 6
♡ A Q 10 5
◊ K J
♣ Q 4 2

South (Belladonna)
♠ 5
♡ K J 7 2
◊ 9 8 7 6
♣ A K J 7

"Is it possible four hearts was a transfer?" he asked me.

"It's possible," I answered, wanting to die. I turned to Evelyn and asked her to play the dummy, but Jimmy heard me and ordered me to stay.

Forquet thought and thought and finally ruffed in with the ♡8, forcing the 10. Jimmy next led a spade toward his king, but Belladonna ruffed in this position:

318

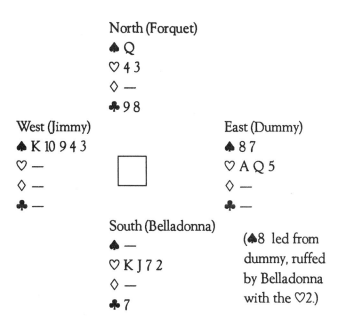

North (Forquet)
♠ Q
♡ 4 3
◇ —
♣ 9 8

West (Jimmy)
♠ K 10 9 4 3
♡ —
◇ —
♣ —

East (Dummy)
♠ 8 7
♡ A Q 5
◇ —
♣ —

South (Belladonna)
♠ —
♡ K J 7 2
◇ —
♣ 7

(♠8 led from
dummy, ruffed
by Belladonna
with the ♡2.)

The defense needed two more tricks to defeat the contract, but took only one. Belladonna was forced to return a club, ruffed in dummy. Now a spade from dummy and Belladonna ruffed with the ♡7. This held the trick and he had to lead from the ♡K-J into dummy to give Jimmy the contract.

Furious with himself for ruffing with the ♡2 instead of the ♡7 when dummy came off a spade, Belladonna raised his voice at Forquet — a very rare occurrence. Forquet, meanwhile, was gracious about the whole matter, and took the blame for wasting his ♡8 earlier. Had he held on to that card, he would have been able to overtake the ♡7 at trick 11, to lead a card through dummy at trick 12.

I was impressed with Forquet's poise, but more relieved than ever that my pass of the transfer bid did not result in disaster.

I let out a yawn, and Forquet eyed me suspiciously. I was more tired than I thought, so I drained the coffee to the bottom of the cup, then picked up my new hand.

♠ A 8 ♡ Q 10 7 6 5 3 ♢ 10 8 7 ♣ A 4

I was dealer and vulnerable, and decided to pass. My suit was too weak for a vulnerable weak two-bid and my hand was too weak for a one-bid.

Jimmy opened the bidding one spade in third seat and Forquet overcalled two diamonds. I bid two hearts. When the tray came around, Belladonna had raised to three diamonds and Jimmy passed. Forquet now passed and it was up to me. I yawned again and looked at the bidding:

Cayne	Forquet	Matthew	Belladonna
West	North	East	South
—	—	pass	pass
1 ♠	2 ♢	2 ♡	3 ♢
pass	pass	?	

My choices were poor. If I bid three hearts, Jimmy might have a singleton and we belong in spades. If I bid three spades, he might hold five spades (or worse, in third seat he might hold a four-bagger) and a doubleton heart and we belong in hearts. He might have a singleton diamond and might not. If he had as little as (yawn):

♠ K x x x x x ♡ K x ♢ x ♣ K Q J x

we were odds on to make four spades. If he had only:

♠ K x x x x ♡ A J ♢ x x ♣ K J x x

we might make four hearts. What to do, what to do?

Something rumbled in the back of my mind. Had I fallen

asleep? — how embarrassing! One way to force him to pick the right major might be to cuebid. Four diamonds must mean choose a contract. I was a passed hand facing a third-seat opener. I had already taken a nonforcing bid. Surely four diamonds could not mean a slam try.

When the tray came back, Jimmy had bid four notrump. Oh God, why had he not settled for a game?

Was this Blackwood *Keycard*? Was the trump suit inferred as hearts or as spades? I had two aces (a five-heart response), but if hearts were trumps, I was supposed to bid five spades, to show two keycards plus the queen of trumps. If spades was the trump suit, however, I had to bid five hearts, two keycards without the queen of trumps. This was ridiculous. With spades trump, I had to bid five hearts and with hearts trump I had to bid five spades. The world had gone cockeyed and I wanted to lie down and take a nap — that's *all* I wanted to do. I rubbed my eyes.

He can't have three hearts, I figured, because he would have raised my hearts with three of them. Therefore if he thinks hearts are trump, he has only two of them, and my queen can't possibly be of much use . . . unless he holds the ace and king or the ace-jack. Finally I decided I'd better show my ♡Q — hearts had to be in the picture.

"Five spades," I said aloud. Forquet pointed to the bidding box. Where was my gun? I thought. Or had that disappeared long ago?

Jimmy bid six notrump and everyone passed. I asked if I could be excused.

"After the lead," said Jimmy.

This was the full deal (I learned later):

North (Forquet)
♠ 9
♡ 9 8 4 2
◇ A 9 6 5 4 2
♣ K 2

West (Jimmy)
♠ K Q J 6 4
♡ A K
◇ K 3
♣ 8 7 6 5

East (Dummy)
♠ A 8
♡ Q 10 7 6 5 3
◇ 10 8 7
♣ A 4

South (Belladonna)
♠ 10 7 5 3 2
♡ J
◇ Q J
♣ Q J 10 9 3

Cayne	Forquet	Matthew	Belladonna
West	North	East	South
—	—	pass	pass
1 ♠	2 ◇	2 ♡	3 ◇
pass	pass	4 ◇	pass
4 NT	pass	5 ♠	pass
6 NT	(all pass)		

Forquet led a heart and Jimmy cashed the ace-king, crossed to the ♠A and played the rest of the hearts. Belladonna had to make five discards — none of them a spade. He threw four clubs and finally his last club, as Jimmy threw three clubs and a diamond from his hand. Forquet had no problem, discarding two diamonds. But on the run of three more spade tricks, Forquet had to let go of three more diamonds to arrive at this three-card end-position:

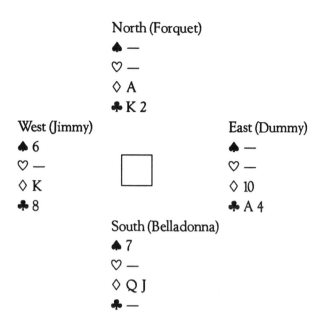

North (Forquet)
♠ —
♡ —
◊ A
♣ K 2

West (Jimmy)
♠ 6
♡ —
◊ K
♣ 8

East (Dummy)
♠ —
♡ —
◊ 10
♣ A 4

South (Belladonna)
♠ 7
♡ —
◊ Q J
♣ —

Jimmy now led the ♣8, finessing Forquet's king, followed by the ◊ K to Forquet's ace. On trick 13, Forquet played the ♣K to my ♣A in dummy.

But I was long gone. And when the next board was placed on the table, they waited three minutes before searching for me. I hear they found me in the master bedroom spread out on the bed. I was more relieved than ever to be in dreamland.

29

I dreamed of many things, most of which I can't remember.
But one subconscious scene stayed with me when I awoke.
I was back in time — to a gentler age before I was born. The
bridge game at the Caynes was called for 3 p.m. President
Hoover was to give a speech on the radio at 5. We would play
one or two rubbers and then break for tea. I found myself in
a dark suit, handkerchief handsomely propped in my jacket
pocket. My partner was my wife, my opponents were two
lovely ladies-who-lunch, one with her cards spread genteelly
like a summer fan in front of her face. The other had a
fashionable white hat and white earrings to match. Patty
Cayne had stepped near my right shoulder to watch. "Look,"
I said, "I am dummy and I have four queens." "How positively
enchanting," she said. "You must tell me how you did it."

"Wake up. Wake up, my soul, wake up."

I opened my eyes. My head was spinning. A big man with
a beard was hunched over me. I made him out to be Belsky.
Yes, it was Belsky!

"Here, try to sit up on this pillow."

I pushed my body back and my head went in three directions at once.

"Promise me you'll have some chicken soup."

"What the hell good will chicken soup do?" I said.

"It can't hurt," he answered.

I put my hand on my forehead — dry, cold sweat. So where was the soup?

"C'mon, you think you can stand, or do you want me to carry you?"

"Where's the soup?"

"Downstairs — and it's the best thing you ever tasted. It'll fix you up in no time."

Downstairs — what was he talking about? I gazed around the room. *Good God, the bridge match!*

"Belsky, what time is it? What's happening in the match?! Is it over?!"

"Slow down, slow down. It's 4:30."

"P.M. or A.M?"

"In the afternoon."

"And it's still Thursday, right?"

"You're kidding me. Of course it's Thursday."

Thank God. I must have been out for only an hour.

"I've got to get back to the table. There might be penalties. I've got to get back." I shoved his arm away and started to stand, but my head did a nosedive and I sat down again.

"Listen, don't worry. They're playing without you. They asked me to take care of you."

How are they playing? Sontag was in the hospital, I was in bed and Otto was in the closet. I jumped out of bed and ran to the closet. No Otto! I went for my pocket — no gun! "Listen," I pleaded, my head crackling, "we've got to find Otto — he's the murderer and he's loose."

"Mr. Marx? Matt, you're crazy, if he's a murderer, my mother is a murderer. Besides, he's playing bridge now with Mr. Cayne."

Worse!! Worse!! I started for the bedroom door, but Belsky stopped me.

"You can't go in there, Matt. You're in no condition. We're going to get you better. Now, just let me help you to the service elevator — here this way, through the back."

I let him lead the way, figuring I'd break away when we reached the hall. "Tell me something, Belsky, did he at least have time to read the notes?"

"Matt, I just got here a few minutes ago and I don't know what the notes are anyway."

We got to the service elevator and I tried to bolt under his arm, but the elevator was waiting for us and he had me in it before I could move. My head was still swimming, so perhaps it was for the best. There's no use fighting nature, I said to myself.

The elevator stopped two floors down, and we got out.

"Here, put this on," said Belsky, handing me a skull cap. He had his *yarmulke* on and suddenly we were in a room with a huge screen in the middle — about a hundred black-suited, black-hatted men on one side, and the other side filled with well-dressed women. Incredibly delicious aromas of food were coming from the dining room.

"Where have you taken me, Belsky?"

"The guy at the electronics store — you remember — over on 47th Street? He wasn't in today, so I tried to track him down in Brooklyn, and, well, to make a long story short, his mother-in-law reminded me that he was the *Mohel* today, and when she gave me the address, boy, was I surprised.

"I'm hoping he brought the tape with him. Besides, it's a great *mitzvah* to attend a *bris*. I know it's a little unorthodox to meet him here, but it must be in the cards, Matt, 'cause what's the chance that the *bris* would be in the very same building as your bridge championship, huh? Now, just sit tight for another minute or so and I'll see if I recognize him. He's probably the one with the knife."

326

I followed Belsky to the far corner of the room. People were standing now, prayer books in hand. Suddenly I noticed to my right a bundle of some kind. It began to cry. *There's a baby over there, for crying out loud.* A man with a doctor's satchel was bent over him. Then I saw a sharp silvery scissors sparkle in the light and then someone said, "Hold him, tight," and then there was red stuff oozing out, white bandages, crying, sniffling, sudden chanting in Hebrew, *mazel-tovs,* jumping, dancing, all the men holding on to one another by the shoulders—

"Belsky," I said, grabbing his arm, I'm feeling like I'm going to faint."

"Don't worry, Matt. The kid's old man fainted a minute ago."

I was suddenly on the floor, my head floating again into dreamland. I shouldn't have looked at the blood, dammit. Dreams went by quickly. Now I was forward in time — now I was back in time — now I was forward in time. Now I was sitting at the table again facing the bidding screen. I pushed a button, my cards popped up:

♠ 9 6 5 2 ♡ J 3 2 ◇ A J 3 ♣ Q 5 3.

The contract flashes on a mini VuGraph set smack in the middle of the bidding screen:

3NT (South).
West to lead. . . Waiting. Granovetter, you are West, waiting. . .

Suddenly I see buttons under my electric cards. I push the ♠6 button.

North
♠ Q 10 8 3
♡ A K 7
◇ 10 5 2
♣ 10 7 6

West (you)
♠ 9 6 5 2
♡ J 3 2
◇ A J 3
♣ Q 5 3

The cards to the first three tricks seem to be playing by themselves:

Tricks
1) ♠ 6 . . . ♠ 8 . . . ♠ J . . . ♠ A.
2) ♡ 5 . . . ♡ 2 . . . ♡ A . . . ♡ 4.
3) ♣ 6 . . . ♣ 4 . . . ♣ J . . . ♣ Q
4) ?
Your play, your play, waiting, your play. . .

I push the ♠2 button.

4) ♠ 2 . . . ♠ 10 . . . ♠ K . . . ♠ 4.
5) ◇ Q . . . ◇ K . . . ◇ A . . . ◇ 2.
6) ?
Your play, your play, waiting, your play. . .

I push the ◇J button. An alarm goes off.

Suddenly the huge screen flies up two feet in the air and facing me is Frankenstein! He is partially withered away, half man, half skeleton.

"AAAAAAIIIIII," he screams. "Can't you underlead the diamond?!!"

The screen flashes the full deal:

North
♠ Q 10 8 3
♡ A K 7
◇ 10 5 2
♣ 10 7 6

West
♠ 9 6 5 2
♡ J 3 2
◇ A J 3
♣ Q 5 3

East
♠ K J 7
♡ 9 6 4
◇ Q 9 7 4
♣ 9 8 4

South
♠ A 4
♡ Q 10 8 5
◇ K 8 6
♣ A K J 2

Yes, I should underlead the diamond. Declarer may play me for the nine and East for the queen-jack, but all I can think about is getting that screen down. I can't bear to face him anymore. I keep pushing buttons on the screen, but nothing happens — the darn screen won't drop.

My head is spinning and my eyes open. Belsky is there again. And another man, red beard this time, is looking down at me.

"Don't move. Just keep your head back."

"I told him that you were sick," said Belsky.

"I'm not sick," I said.

"Just relax — I'm Doctor O'Brien."

"O'Brien?"

"My father was Irish. Want to make something of it?"

I shook my head, which wasn't easy from the floor.

"We're going to get some chicken soup for you," continued the doctor.

"He promised me the soup an hour ago."

"Do you have a history of this, Mr. Granetter?"

"Granovetter, and no. It was the blood. I can't stand the sight of it. Now help me up."

"Hold on, hold on. You were mumbling all sorts of crazy things."

"I was dreaming."

"Nice dreams? You want to tell me about them?"

"What are you, a shrink?"

"Ha, ha. No, I'm an internist, that's all. But I specialize in fainting chess players."

"Bridge, not chess."

I was up now and they helped me over to a table. Other men were eating and I was handed a piece of bread and a bowl of soup.

"Eat slowly," the doctor said. It was hard to do — the food was scrumptious.

After my second portion, other foods were brought to me: puddings, noodles, vegetables, salads, and Dr. Brown's cream soda (!) to wash it all down. My head was feeling much, much better.

"What is your name?" a man sitting across from us asked.

"Matthew Granovetter."

"Ah, Matisyahu — the same name as the baby! L'chaim!"

He drank a shot of vodka and dabbed his lips with a napkin.

"How're we doing?" asked Belsky.

"I'm feeling much better," I said. "How's the baby doing?"

"The baby didn't know what hit him."

"These circumcisions are big affairs," I said. "But why all the black hats?"

The doctor answered. "The parents are *baal tshuvah* — returnees to Judaism. They have a child who attends our Lubavitch school. Rather than bring the baby to Brooklyn, Brooklyn came to Manhattan.

"You live here, Matisyahu?"

"No, no, my friends are two flights up — the Caynes."

"Ah, your friends live upstairs. So it's *beshairt* that we meet."

"Bewho?"

"*Beshairt*. In the cards."

"He knows that expression," said Belsky. "We're from Saratoga," said Belsky, "upstate New York."

"I know Saratoga," said the doctor. "The spas are there — some Chasids go up for the summer — very lovely. So what are you doing here in the hot city when you could be in Saratoga?"

"Matt and I are detectives," said Belsky. "There's a murder case we're on at the moment, and Matt's in the middle of a world bridge championship as well."

"All those things at once? Quite busy — maybe too busy. You are so busy, maybe you don't have time for studying the Torah."

"Oh, I say my prayers three times a day, Doc, but Matt here is just getting used to the idea."

"Who am I to say what you should do?" said the doctor. "There is a reason for everything, and there must be a reason for even you."

"Thank you," said Belsky.

"Listen to me, Belsky," I said, "It's time to leave. They might be starting the third quarter."

"Not yet, Matt. Let's wait for the *shiur*."

"What's the *shiur*?"

"The Rebbe is going to give a little lesson, a little talk — it's traditional at every meal, especially a festive one. It would be rude to leave."

"Just find the guy with the tape, Belsk. That's the reason we came."

"You're right, Matt. Though now it seems it's not the only reason. Let me have a look around."

As Belsky got up, another man sat down. He was in blue jeans and t-shirt. "Hi," he said. "Allow me to intloduce myself.

I am Borskanov — a chess champion. I am recent emigré from Russia. I hear you are also chess champion."

"Bridge," I said. "You know — the card game."

"Ah, breedge. Yes, I play a little, but not serious."

He turned away and a young lady came over to ask if I would like some coffee. I nodded thank you, then I remembered the last coffee I had. I'd been drugged! "Belsky, I was drugged."

Where was Belsky?

The chess player shushed me. "The Rebbe is about to speak."

"Absolutely," I said, to no one in particular. "Evelyn served me the coffee, but I can't believe she would do it. Even if she were in on the murders, she loves bridge too much to sabotage the world championships. No, Otto must have given it to her."

"Shhh," came from down the table's end. "Nu? Nu?"

The Rebbe, a handsome man with long beard and eye-glasses, seemed to be looking at *me*.

"First of all, I would like to say *mazel-tov* to the grandparents."

Everyone lifted a cup: "Mazel-tov!"

"Now I would like to welcome the guests from upstairs, our friend Mr. Belsky from Saratoga and his associate, who has the same Hebrew name as the baby, Matisyahu (oohs and nods) Granovetter."

I nodded.

"He is a famous chess champion—"

"Bridge," I said.

"Yes, and he is currently playing in a world championship! (More oohs and nods). We wish you the best, Matisyahu. And if you don't mind, I would like to say something concerning chess, or bridge — whatever — that is relevant to this week's reading, Va-etchanan, from Deuteronomy.

"Moses speaks to the Hebrew people. He recounts the

revelation of God on Mount Sinai to the 600,000 families.

"Verse five, Moses says '*Anochiomed bain Hashem uvenechem,* I stand between the Lord and you.'

"Besides the literal meaning, the Sages interpret the word 'I' to mean the I, or ego, in all of us. That is to say: Our own ego stands between ourselves and God.

"The Rebbe Shlita once spoke on what the game of chess teaches. Most of us know this rule: If you get the pawn to the end of the board, you can exchange it for a queen. Only the lowly pawn becomes a queen, while pieces of higher rank, like the castle and the knight, cannot. The lesson is that you can only become a queen — become successful — if you take one step at a time.

"There is another lesson as well. The pawn is the most humble piece on the board.

"Our guest, Matisyahu Granovetter, is trying to win a bridge championship. Our new baby, may he grow strong and wise, through the study of Torah, will have his own tests and choices, great and small. Whatever your endeavors, remember: There is a much greater being above you. Let's not forget our humble beginnings and our humble ends; remember, too, when we empty ourselves of ego, we make room for God. Then wisdom can flow through the gates of our minds. L'Chaim!"

"L'Chaim!"

30

I found Belsky at the dessert table. The tape of the coach and Evelyn's ferry ride to Staten Island had not been brought to the affair. I wasn't surprised. I instructed Belsky to retrieve it, listen to it, put together the rest of the clues and decide whether Otto was really our man. Then I took the elevator back up to the Caynes.

I was ashamed to admit that I might have been wrong about the mad Hungarian. Was it my pride that had produced my prejudice? I didn't like the way he played bridge, so I made him my number one suspect. Still, there were questions that he had to answer better; and then, if he wasn't the killer, who was?

"Where have you been!?" asked Patty in not her softest tone.

"I've been learning Torah," I said.

"God help you now — do you know what's happened?"

I shook my head.

"The third quarter started without you. Otto Marx drove Jimmy completely crazy in the last half of the second quarter and the match was an exact tie at the half."

"Well, that's good. We picked up 30 imps."

"It should have been 60. The coach wanted Jimmy and Otto to continue the third quarter together but luckily I got home in time and put my foot down. Victor is playing with Otto and Jacqui is playing with Jimmy. But they've reduced the number of boards to sixteen and I don't know if that's good or bad for Jimmy."

"You mean sixteen for the entire second half?"

"No, I mean sixteen for the Jersey City duplicate. Yes, sixteen, eight boards each quarter. They're on the last board of the third quarter right now."

We were standing in the hallway and no one was in sight. "Listen," I said in confidence. "Has anything happened? I mean, has the killer made any new attempts?"

"They found rat poison in Jimmy's favorite diet soda, that's all. Now the police are here and checking everything, so I want you to concentrate only on bridge."

"Where's Sonty? Is he still in the hospital."

"I was just going to phone. Pamela is still with him. And we need him desperately for the fourth quarter. Otherwise you'll have to play with Otto — which is ridiculous at this point."

"Tell me something, Patty. If Otto is such a bad player, why was he added to the team in the first place? Jimmy certainly had better players to choose from."

"Don't you know?" she said. "Jimmy always gives Otto a spot on his local teams when he can. Otto is the sweetest person in the whole world — ever since his business on Wall Street became self-sufficient, he's devoted himself to charity work. He works twelve hours a day for the Yeshiva, the Children's Hospital and the homeless."

"He's never said one word about it. All he's ever mentioned about his personal life is his family."

"Tragic."

"Tragic?"

"Yes. They died in a car crash five years ago. Why do you think we feel so sorry for him? I even have some photos of them that I put out for show when he comes for dinner."

"Do you keep them on the dresser in your bedroom?" I asked.

"Yes, how did you know?"

"I, uh . . . I came across them one time. . . ."

I walked into the VuGraph room in a state of shock. Poor Otto. How could I have misjudged him so? But there was still the buried lawsuit in Frankenstein's grave. Could it be that somebody else buried that contract? But why?

The room was dark — I was thinking too much about the investigation — I had to switch back to bridge and stick with it. I couldn't make out the score on the VuGraph screen — too much smoke was in my line of vision. I moved to the back of the room and found a seat. Mrs. Kennedy was in front of me and I tapped her shoulder.

"Oh, you. Did you solve your little mystery or are you still annoying the spectators?"

"The police have taken over."

"They're so good at it, too."

"Would you mind telling me the score?" I asked.

"My, my, and you the big shot. Do you want all my figures?"

"Just the vital ones."

"Here," she said, handing me a convention card. Inside was written: Italy 96, U.S. 86. (The Finesse: 516-822-4443).

"What's this, your boat phone?"

"So you remember my boat. I hope boats don't make you seasick."

"You guessed it."

"I have something for that."

"I'm sure you do. You know something," I said, tapping the scorecard against my forehead. "I still can't figure out why you're here."

"My husband is in charge of the case, isn't he?"

"Yeah, but you don't play bridge and you don't seem to care who wins and who loses. Yet you're sitting here glued to the chair keeping score. Are you working for him — as part of a stakeout?"

"You are partly right, you clever shamus you. When you get it all, give me a call."

Here I was busy with the case, and I had missed the seventh deal of the third quarter. Now the last deal was up on the screen.

Tannah Hirsch: "No swing, so the score remains Italy 95, USA 85. And here's the last board of the third set, board 40:"

Board 40
West dealer
Neither side vulnerable

North
♠ 7 2
♡ J 9 7 2
◇ 8 7 4
♣ 8 6 5 3

West
♠ 4
♡ K Q 10 8 6
◇ A J 5
♣ Q 10 9 4

East
♠ A J 6 5
♡ A 4 3
◇ K 10 9 6
♣ J 7

South
♠ K Q 10 9 8 3
♡ 5
◇ Q 3 2
♣ A K 2

Closed Room

Belladonna	J. Mitchell	Forquet	Cayne
West	North	East	South
1 ♡	pass	1 ♠	2 ♠
pass	pass	3 ♠	pass
4 ♡	pass	pass	pass

Final contract: 4♡ (West)
Opening lead: ♠7
Result: Making 10 tricks. East-West +420.

Wolff: "Here we see in the Closed Room the Blue Team auction. That's not a cuebid by Cayne — most experts play the direct overcall of responder's suit as natural. We have the

338

play record here, and Belladonna was perfect in his tech-nique. He drew two rounds of trumps, saw the bad break, and switched to clubs. Cayne, South, won the club and led a high spade, ruffed by Belladonna. Declarer continued clubs and Cayne won and returned a club. Belladonna now cashed his clubs, drew a third round of trumps and led a diamond to the king. He then led a spade out of the East hand and ruffed with his last trump. North overruffed, but, down to only diamonds, was forced to break the suit, eliminating declarer's need to guess."

Kaplan: "Yes, indeed, a well-played hand. I think, how-ever, most lines of play will make four hearts — that is, except a diamond finesse through North. Here's the Open Room auction starting:"

Open Room			
Marx	*Franco*	*V. Mitchell*	*Garozzo*
West	North	East	South
1 ♡	?		

Hirsch: "The auction may go the same way, let's see."

Marx	*Franco*	*V. Mitchell*	*Garozzo*
West	North	East	South
1 ♡	pass	4 ♡	?

Hirsch: "Well now, there's a bid I didn't think of."

There's the kind of bid I should have been making with Otto, I thought. Instead of beating around the bush, Victor is making life simple for his partner. Yes, four hearts is supposed to show a different type of hand, a weak hand with five trumps. Still, facing a player like Otto, it's better to keep it simple and not worry about the fine points of bidding.

North
♠ 7 2
♡ J 9 7 2
◇ 8 7 4
♣ 8 6 5 3

West
♠ 4
♡ K Q 10 8 6
◇ A J 5
♣ Q 10 9 4

East
♠ A J 6 5
♡ A 4 3
◇ K 10 9 6
♣ J 7

South
♠ K Q 10 9 8 3
♡ 5
◇ Q 3 2
♣ A K 2

Marx	Franco	V. Mitchell	Garozzo
West	North	East	South
1 ♡	pass	4 ♡	4 ♠
pass	?		

Kaplan: "Ah, yes, a typical Vic Mitchell bid and Garozzo could hardly resist entering the picture."

Marx	Franco	V. Mitchell	Garozzo
West	North	East	South
1 ♡	pass	4 ♡	4 ♠
pass	pass	double	?

Wolff: "Nice, calculating bid by Vic."
Roth: "Not my style, but a good gamble by Mitchell. At least he knew his partner had a five-card major."

Open Room

Marx	Franco	V. Mitchell	Garozzo
West	North	East	South
1 ♡	pass	4 ♡	4 ♠
pass	pass	double	pass
pass	pass		

Final Contract: 4♠x (South)
Opening lead: ♡K

Kaplan: "What will this go for? Let's see. Declarer has to lose two spades, one heart, three diamonds and one club: down four, minus 800. That should be a swing of 380 points or 9 imps."

Hirsch: "That will make the match very close, only a single-imp lead for the Italians, with one more session to play."

Wolff: "Under the amendment of boards to be played, it means we may have the most exciting eight boards in the history of the Bermuda Bowl coming up here."

Kaplan: "What time will the final session begin?"

Roth: "Good question, I'm hungry. I thought I was going to have a break for dinner."

Wolff: "We're starting almost immediately, Al. Supper will have to wait. We would appreciate it if the VuGraph audience would remain seated — Patty Cayne has a short announcement."

P. Cayne: "Thank you, Bobby. Listen to me — This is the last time I'm going to warn you. I want no more drinking or eating in this room. You can get coffee or soda in the foyer — at your own risk. And let's hear a little more cheering for the home team, guys, okay?" (Applause.)

"Oh, Matthew — Are you out there? There you are — team meeting in the den in three minutes. Thank you."

31

When I got to the den, only Patty was there. "The meeting's in the kitchen. The den is a decoy."

"Thanks, Patty."

Before I reached the kitchen, I ran into Sonty and Pamela. Sonty was looking great, that is for somebody who'd been knifed the day before and shot earlier that afternoon. In fact the only sign of anything out of the ordinary was that his arm dangled a little in the sling.

"As long as I don't have any new notes to study, I think I'll be all right," he said. "I even have a special card rack to hold the cards. Where's the meeting?"

"In the kitchen," said Pamela. Then she took me aside. "I hear you've been chatting up the coach's new girlfriend."

"What are you talking about? I don't chat up strange women."

"Good, because she's poison and I would appreciate it if you didn't talk to her in public."

"Fine," I said. "I won't. Only one thing: Who are you talking about?"

"The one with the dyed white hair. Patty told me she's been here a number of times."

"Yeah, she's staked-out at the VuGraph."

"I'm talking about before. With the coach. She's been seeing the coach for more than a month. And she's poison with a capital P. So you stay away!"

We both smiled quickly as Jacqui and Victor walked past us to the kitchen. Then we followed them in. Jimmy, Otto and the coach were there, too. And to tell you the truth, it was a tight squeeze, with a lot of the living room furniture piled up on the side and kitchens not being the roomiest spots in New York City apartments to begin with.

The score was confirmed as a one-imp deficit. Jacqui said she thought it best that I play with Victor the last session, along with Jimmy and Sonty. The coach shook his head and said with all due respect to Victor, the only way to go was with regular partnerships — Otto had to play with me. Otto said he was happy to play or not play with the proviso that I would not smack him around anymore. I said I would never smack him again and begged his forgiveness. Patty said it's two minutes to game time, so we'd better make up our minds before we get a penalty. Victor said in all his years in international play, he had only once before heard such a discussion and that was when he was at Belmont racetrack when four handicappers owned a winning daily-double ticket that had been tossed in the sewer by accident.

Pamela suggested that Jimmy have final say on the lineup and Jimmy said he would. And he did. We would do what Jacqui suggested. He and Sonty would play in the Open Room while Victor and I played in the Closed Room. The coach was upset but I reminded him that Victor and I had played many sessions together on Sam Stayman teams, including three world olympiads.

"Listen to me," he said, taking me aside. "I know Victor

was once a great player — but bridge has changed. He's still blasting into games and slams. He would not have any idea what you were doing if you made that excellent choice-of-games cuebid that you made with Jimmy." Suddenly his face turned red, matching his colorful ascot. "Victor still thinks a cuebid shows the ace!"

It was strange to see him so upset. I put it down to nerves. The poor guy was desperate to win. I imagined there would be a juicy bonus in it for him. Patty was waving for me to come take my place in the Closed Room. I gave the coach a handshake; he first stuck out his left hand, then stopped himself and shook with the right. I told him not to worry — that I had never been in a better frame of mind, and was ready to trounce my opponents. Victor, I said, was a partner I could count on — unlike Otto — which is half the battle. If he can make me play my best, I'm happy to pass up on the obscure choice-of-games cuebid.

As I walked into the VuGraph room, something was nagging at me — something about the coach's fetish with choice-of-games cuebids, something about the four-diamond bid that was found inside the mouth of Frank Stein, something about Frank Stein's failure to make that bid on Board 18 of the Team Trials. I tried to put it all in the back of my mind, but it wouldn't go away. So I decided to concentrate all my energies on the upcoming battle. For some reason, however, humility came to mind. Consider this, Matthew (I said to myself) you haven't exactly shone this tournament, yet you still have a chance to win. The way to win is this: Respect your opponents, remember their strengths, and play the game to the best of your God-given ability. That's all you can do.

The VuGraph audience had grown, despite the dangers of poisoned food and stray bullets. Al Roth came up to me to wish me luck and warned me about opening too light. "You gotta watch yourself like a hawk on those twelve-point hands."

I couldn't see Mrs. Kennedy, but I noticed the two Stein kids were there, brother and sister, sitting together in the third row. I wondered why they had come to watch. And she hated bridge! The shadow of a tall man seemed to pass as Otto put his arm around my shoulder.

"It's a clazy ting but I theenk we have a chance."

"Are you gonna watch?" I asked.

"I'll kibitz some, but I'm vely nervous for you. Can you imagine what my wife will theenk if we win?"

"Your wife?" I said. "But Otto, your wife—" I held my tongue. The poor guy was deluded as ever. I shook his hand and he took a seat in the third row.

Pamela and Patty approached to ask what I was doing there. They was right. I was supposed to be in the library. "One thing," I said. "Why hasn't Otto ever remarried?"

"Who would marry Otto?" said Patty. "He hasn't gotten over his first wife. Besides, he's too busy helping others to help himself. Now don't worry about Otto. As the good book says, first take care of your own — and in this case I mean your own cards."

I walked briskly to the Closed Room headquarters and took a seat at the table.

I was South. On my side of the screen to my right sat Benito Garozzo. We shook hands. I knew Benito from previous battles. He was one of the nicest people I had ever met in the bridge world. He had once played bridge with me as a birthday present when I was 21 years old. At the table, he was not so nice, however. He was hard on his partners and merciless on his opponents. He always played his best when the battle was close. It would not be easy to defeat him. I noticed Lea duPont behind him. The two of them have been together for many years. She smiled a hello to me, but I knew in my heart what was in hers: that every finesse I take should be offside and every trump suit should split 5-0.

On my left, behind the screen, was Arturo Franco. I leaned over and shook hands with him. I also had played against Arturo before. He was a tough rubber bridge player, just barely tough enough to face Benito as a partner for an entire world championship. He looked tired. I wondered if I could count on an error or two, but then shrugged off the idea. Adrenalin was flowing through all our veins. Errors would be hard to come by. Perhaps a revoke, I thought. I couldn't help but notice that his bidding box was missing. He called the director and Maury said he had no idea what happened to it, but would try to find another. A few minutes later Evelyn walked in with the spare and attached it to the table.

As I watched her hook it up, I couldn't help but notice that my partner was missing as well.

Of course, it was not unusual for Victor to be missing. He was often busy, walking his dogs, placing a bet at OTB, or simply having a quick drag in the hallway. There were legendary occasions where Victor did not show at all. Once, a partner of Victor's was shuffling the boards with him at the table, and when he looked up, after dealing the cards, a new player was in Victor's seat. This can happen because Victor hates to say no to people who ask him to play, which inevitably results in Victor having two or more partners for the same event. One of Victor's greatest coups as a professional bridge player was to have both his clients play together and get paid by each of them! Another time, Victor was on two teams in the same event, but he managed always to appear for comparisons of scores. So you see why I wasn't surprised when I sat back down, peeked under the screen and spotted Jacqui doing her needlepoint, a Kellerman paperback wedged inside her bidding box.

"Where's Victor?" I asked.

"Good question," said Jacqui, looking up. "I saw him leave with the coach. My guess is that the coach was about to kibitz at Jimmy's table, and Victor thought it was not a good idea, so he took him for a walk."

"But we've never played before," I said, not a little nervous.

"Just have all your bids and don't get clever," said Jacqui.

"But what do we play?" I asked, starting to panic.

"You've eaten dinner at my house for five days a week for five years. If you don't know what I play by now, you'll never know."

"Yes, m'am. But, err, can I have your convention card with Victor, so I can alert Benito."

"Here," she said, slipping it under the screen. I quickly opened it up and reviewed it. There wasn't much to review. No transfers, no limit raises; check-back Stayman, weak two-bids and negative doubles. Then there were some old Stayman-Mitchell conventions, like Namyats, for one, which now came back to me. I noticed also that we were playing Rusinow leads — I'm not used to leading the lower of touching honors, so I was a bit shaken. The first board had been placed on the table and Maury asked us to start. I said a silent prayer that I would not have to declare the first hand, then peered at my cards.

♠ K Q J 10 9 8 7 2 ♡ K ◇ A ♣ J 5 3

The bidding tray was passed quickly to our side. Jacqui had passed. I watched Benito, who was in deep concentration. He put the green pass card out. I saw a chance not to play the hand.

I opened four diamonds, Namyats. This showed a solid spade suit and a slammish hand. My hand was not so slammish, but I still bid it. It was worth the gamble.

When the tray came back I saw double by Arturo and pass by Jacqui. Benito also passed and I redoubled. Jacqui would get the message and grab the contract . . . I hoped.

The tray came back. Arturo had passed and Jacqui bid four hearts. Pass by Benito. I was endplayed in the bidding and had to bid four spades. This ended the auction as everybody passed. Arturo led the ◊K.

Jacqui
♠ —
♡ A J 4 3 2
◊ 9 7 6 5 3
♣ K 4 2

Arturo   Benito

Matthew
♠ K Q J 10 9 8 4 2
♡ K
◊ A
♣ J 5 3

Benito followed with the ◊4 and I won the ace. I counted seven spade tricks, one heart and one diamond for sure. The tenth trick could come from the club suit, with the ace on my left or the queen on my right. At matchpoints I would cash the ♡K and play on trumps, hoping eventually to score 11 tricks, if the ♣A were on my left. At imps, however, I had a safer line of play.

I could lead a club to the king. If it won, I had 10 tricks. If it lost, I could overtake my ♡K later and lead a club toward my jack. This was a 75% chance. On the other hand, I hated to play clubs immediately. Better examine this a little more carefully, I thought.

West had doubled four diamonds, and led the ◊K, probably from a five- or six-card suit. If East has the ♣A, he needs specifically the ♣Q as well for an immediate club play to be necessary. Also, there was the danger of a ruff. No, I thought.

I prefer to see who has the ♠A before commiting myself in clubs. It dawned on me that if I drew trumps first and East had no more diamonds, I could cash the ♡K and lead the ♣J to East hypothetical ace-queen. Then he would have to return a club or a heart.

This was getting complicated. But the idea of endplaying Benito was exciting, so I decided to play on trumps, by leading the ♠8. First, however, I cashed the ♡K to get it out of the way. If Arturo won the ♠A, I wanted to force a diamond return, in case Benito started with two of them. That way Benito would have no more diamonds when I tried to endplay him later.

I cashed the ♡K, and led the ♠8. Arturo won the ace on the first round. Hmm, it looked like a singleton ace. He led back the ◊Q, Benito playing the ◊2. Good. I ruffed and started pulling trumps. Arturo showed out on the second round. I pulled a third round, but before I got to the fourth round, I stopped cold in my tracks. Why not endplay Benito immediately? I led my lowest spade — the 4.

Benito would have to win and lead a club to dummy or a heart into the A-J. Either way, I sacrifice one trick but get back two!

Unfortunately, my ♠4 held the trick, as Benito followed with the ♠3.

Desperate, I tried the lead of the ♣J, in case Benito had both the ace and queen. But Arturo covered with the queen and dummy's king was scooped up by Benito's ace. The defense cashed two more club tricks, for down one. This was the full deal, as seen in the VuGraph room.

Board 41
North dealer
East-West vulnerable

Italy +95, U.S. +94

North
♠ —
♡ A J 4 3 2
♢ 9 7 6 5 3
♣ K 4 2

West
♠ A
♡ 10 9 6
♢ K Q J 10 8
♣ Q 10 9 6

East
♠ 7 6 5 3
♡ Q 8 7 5
♢ 4 2
♣ A 8 7

South
♠ K Q J 10 9 8 4 2
♡ K
♢ A
♣ J 5 3

Franco	J. Mitchell	Garozzo	Granovetter
West	North	East	South
—	pass	pass	4 ◊
double	pass	pass	redouble
pass	4 ♡	pass	4 ♠
pass	pass	pass	

Benito had thrown the ♠5, 6 and 7 on the first three rounds of trumps. Had I not ruffed the second diamond lead with the ♠2, I would still have been able to endplay him. I looked at the ♠2 and wanted to cry. The deuce . . . the lowest trump in the deck, the most humble of cards.

Good God, the Rebbe was right!

How could I have been so stupid as to waste it?!

Think HUMBLE, Matthew. Just think HUMBLE!

Board 42 was on the table. I sorted my cards.

♠ 10 9 8 7　♡ K 9 2　◇ J 4　♣ J 10 8 7

Well, I thought, serves me right for thinking humble. Why, oh why, couldn't this have been my hand on the first board?

Benito opened one club, strong and forcing, in front of me. I passed. When the tray came back, we saw two hearts by Franco and four diamonds by Jacqui. Benito tapped the alert card that was attached to the bidding box. I pointed to the pad and pencil. He wrote, "2H = two-suited hand, spades and minor 8+ points."

Benito bid four spades. I passed. The tray went over. We waited. It came back. Arturo bid five clubs. Benito tapped the alert card. I tapped the pad. He wrote, "cuebid in clubs, no heart control." Benito went to his bidding box and pulled out the five-diamond card. I passed. The tray went over. We waited. Back it came. Arturo bid six spades. Benito tapped. I tapped. He wrote, "No further control. Enough for slam."

We all passed. And I had to find a lead. Nothing fancy, I thought. The trumps are not breaking. I led the jack of diamonds, my partner's suit, and saw:

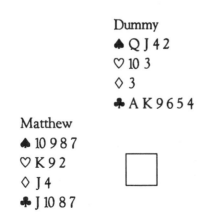

Dummy
♠ Q J 4 2
♡ 10 3
◇ 3
♣ A K 9 6 5 4

Matthew
♠ 10 9 8 7
♡ K 9 2
◇ J 4
♣ J 10 8 7

Benito won the ◇A in hand, cashed the ♠A-K, Jacqui

showing out on the second round, and led the ♣Q. Next he led a club to the ace, Jacqui again discarding, and continued ♣K, club, ruffed in hand. He then led his last trump to the dummy and drew my last trump. He still had the ♡A, so he made six. The full deal was:

Dummy
♠ Q J 4 2
♡ 10 3
◊ 3
♣ A K 9 6 5 4

Matthew
♠ 10 9 8 7
♡ K 9 2
◊ J 4
♣ J 10 8 7

Jacqui
♠ 3
♡ Q 8 7
◊ K Q 10 9 8 7 6 2
♣ 3

Benito
♠ A K 6 5
♡ A J 6 5 4
◊ A 5
♣ Q 2

Arturo	Jacqui	Benito	Matthew
—	—	1 ♣	pass
2 ♡	4 ◊	4 ♠	pass
5 ♣	pass	5 ◊	pass
6 ♠	pass	pass	pass

Before the bidding screen went down, Benito said to Arturo, "Why you don't bid six clubs, cuebid?" Arturo responded, "I have queen-jack of spades and do not want to play six clubs." A little further squabbling developed, mainly in Italian. And I wondered what would have happened had they had a bad result. As it was, my opponents could not have done much better on the first two boards, and I wondered what the score was. Had we lost on either hand? Probably. But there was no use worrying about it. The players are not allowed to compare scores until all eight boards are played. On the other hand, there was a clue as to how we were doing. The living room was not far off and the audience might let out a cheer if we did well. I asked Jacqui what she thought. She told me to pick up the next hand and forget the previous ones. She was all-pro.

Board 43. I was dealer and held:

♠ A K J 3 ♡ A 7 4 ◇ 5 3 ♣ A J 10 7

I know Jacqui plays 15-17 notrump openings. And I know she's very strict about the range. But wasn't my hand too good for one notrump? I could open one club and rebid spades with no problem. On the other hand, if I didn't open one notrump and it didn't work out, Jacqui would not be happy — and who was I to overrule her system? So I went simple and opened one notrump. But, ugh, I hated it.

The tray came back, and Jacqui had bid two clubs, Stayman. I bid two spades. I was getting to show my hand after all. On the next round she bid three diamonds, which showed long diamonds and a slam try. I didn't have anything in diamonds, but I did have a great hand in controls and points, so I bid three hearts, to hear what she would do.

She bid four notrump, a bid I did not feel good about. She obviously thought my three-heart bid was natural and was asking for aces. I had three aces — that was the good news. The bad news was that I had only three hearts. Oh well, I thought, I better show my aces. I bid five spades and when the tray returned, I saw five notrump on it. She was asking for kings, trying for a grand slam. Now, on the one hand, I had a king, and it was my duty to show it. On the other hand, a little lie in the interest of the team may be appropriate here.

♠ A K J 3　♡ A 7 4　◇ 5 3　♣ A J 10 7

I didn't like the idea of playing a slam in hearts on a 4-3 fit, let alone a grand slam. So I did the unpardonable: I bid six clubs — no kings.

Six hearts came back at me and I paused. Perhaps I should convert to six notrump, where trumps would not be a consideration. I hated the idea of playing the 4-3, but on the other hand, I might be able to ruff a diamond in my hand in six hearts, setting up the diamond suit. On the other hand, if I played six hearts, Jacqui would surely count the trumps as they were drawn and see that I only had a three-card suit — I could hide the length of my hearts so much better in notrump, where I might pitch them on her diamonds. Hmm. What to do? What to do? Wait a second. In six notrump I'll never be able to hide the ♠K, and when she sees that card, she'll flip. I better play in hearts where just possibly the ♠K won't be relevant. Wait a second. This is all vanity. Why am I worrying what Jacqui will think of me? I should be worrying about the best contract. Hmm. What to do? What to do?

Finally I bid six notrump and everyone passed.

There is talk behind the screen now. I hear Jacqui answer Arturo's questions about my bidding. She says, "We bid spades first over Stayman, but he probably forgot, and from the way he's hesitating over there, I wouldn't be surprised if he has only three hearts, and lied about a king or two, to boot."

The opening lead was the ♠6 and this was what I saw:

North (Jacqui)
♠ Q 2
♡ K Q J 2
◇ A K J 9 6 2
♣ 2

♠6

South (Matthew)
♠ A K J 3
♡ A 7 4
◇ 5 3
♣ A J 10 7

I said "Thank you," when dummy hit. It was a great dummy, and the jack of hearts made it even better. The only problem was if diamonds were 4-1.

If East had the singleton, I had to finesse on the second round of diamonds.

If West had the singleton, I was in trouble, unless it was the 10 or queen. Was there anything to taking a first-round finesse in diamonds? Suppose, for example, that East held ◇ Q-10-x-x and the ♣K-Q. Then by taking an early finesse in diamonds, I retain one in my hand for a squeeze on East. He wins the first-round finesse and returns the ♣K. I win, run the hearts and the spades, ending in my hand with one diamond and the ♣J-10 opposite the ◇A-K-9. He cannot keep three diamonds and the ♣Q. Yet, what are the odds that East holds all those cards?

As I gazed at my hand and back at dummy, I couldn't help but notice there were a lot of humble cards in dummy, the humblest being the two of clubs. Could it be of any value? Could it be traded for a queen? One step at a time, I thought.

I counted my tricks — something I should have done in the first place. I had four spades, four hearts, two diamonds and one club: 11. Suddenly the answer came to me. It was so simple, too.

I won the ♠Q and cashed the ◊A, all following low. I came to my hand with the ♡A and led a diamond. If West followed, I would stick in the ◊J and claim no matter what happened. But Arturo discarded a heart, so *I went up with the ◊K*. I was still okay if the major suits behaved. I cashed the spades first. They split 4-3, then I cashed the hearts and they divided 4-2. I was down to:

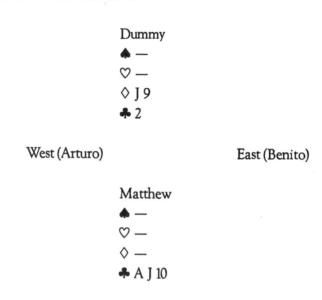

Dummy
♠ —
♡ —
◊ J 9
♣ 2

West (Arturo)   East (Benito)

Matthew
♠ —
♡ —
◊ —
♣ A J 10

I simply led the ♣2 toward my hand. If Benito had both the king and queen of clubs on my right, I'd be down, but the odds were against it. Actually the honors were split and when Benito played second-hand low in clubs, I put in the 10 and showed my cards. Making six notrump. Phew! This was the deal:

North (Jacqui)
♠ Q 2
♡ K Q J 2
◇ A K J 9 6 2
♣ 2

West (Arturo)
♠ 9 6 5 4
♡ 10 9 6 5
◇ 4
♣ Q 8 5 3

East (Benito)
♠ 10 8 7
♡ 8 3
◇ Q 10 8 7
♣ K 9 6 4

South (Matthew)
♠ A K J 3
♡ A 7 4
◇ 5 3
♣ A J 10 7

Jacqui, I was pleased to note, did not say an unkind word to me. Of course that could have meant she wasn't speaking to me or it could have meant she was too engrossed in her mystery novel, which she had been reading while dummy One night about seven years ago I didn't walk my dog on time, and the dog made on Jacqui's living room rug. Jacqui didn't speak to me for three months. How much greater were the sins of bidding a three-card suit and misreporting my kings in a Blackwood auction? Still, down deep, I knew she had to be happy about the hand — winning a world champi onship would go a long way to relaxing her principles on partnership trust.

"Why they not play in diamonds?" I heard Benito mumble.

Board 44.
♠ 8 7 6 ♡ 3 ◇ K 10 6 5 ♣ J 10 9 4 3

The bidding tray was on the other side and I was feeling at ease. This could be the turn-around we needed. When the tray came over, it read pass by Arturo, one notrump by Jacqui. Benito bid two hearts. I wanted to compete, but I wasn't sure how to do it. I tried to remember if Jacqui played three clubs as forcing or competitive. Finally I remembered that we play two notrump as *lebensohl*, which usually shows a weak hand with a minor. But then I stopped myself. Why am I bidding with four points? Why stir-up trouble? Besides, did I have any defense to any contract in their direction? I passed.

When the tray came back, Arturo had bid two notrump and Jacqui passed. Benito alerted and wrote that two notrump asked for shortness. He bid three diamonds, alerted as a singleton or a doubleton with extra strength. I passed, sorry I had given them all this bidding room. I was soon sorrier when Arturo jumped to four hearts and Benito made a great play to make it.

I led the ♣J. This was the full deal:

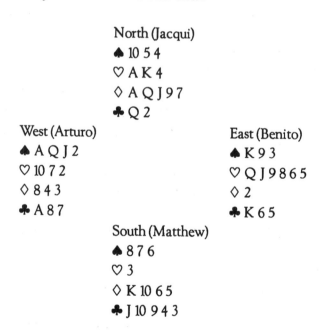

North (Jacqui)
♠ 10 5 4
♡ A K 4
♢ A Q J 9 7
♣ Q 2

West (Arturo)
♠ A Q J 2
♡ 10 7 2
♢ 8 4 3
♣ A 8 7

East (Benito)
♠ K 9 3
♡ Q J 9 8 6 5
♢ 2
♣ K 6 5

South (Matthew)
♠ 8 7 6
♡ 3
♢ K 10 6 5
♣ J 10 9 4 3

My ♣J lead was won by Benito in his hand with the king.

He studied the deal for about 30 seconds and then made a very strange-looking play. He led the ◇2. It didn't matter what we did after that — he made his contract. Notice that we could never score a club trick — all we got were two trumps and a diamond. Benito had effectively cut the defense's lines of communication.

It was depressing. And I told Jacqui so, as we broke for a minute to let Arturo wash his face. He was very tired and we all took drinks of water.

Jacqui told me not to worry, if I had bid two notrump, Arturo would have doubled and Benito would have made the same short-suit game try. "Besides," she said, "we have good teammates and they'll make the same equally fine bids and plays."

"Perhaps," I said, "but Benito is up to his old tricks again — you know, like playing flawlessly and bidding perfectly. We can't expect to win if he's going to be double-dummy on every hand."

"Matthew, you can only do your best. Try playing *your* best and we'll do fine."

We sat down for board 45. There were only four boards to go. I picked up:

♠ K 10 5 ♡ A K Q J 10 ◇ K 6 ♣ J 7 4

Jacqui dealt and passed. Benito passed. I had to decide between one notrump and one heart. One notrump would solve my rebid headaches, but might miss the 5-3 heart fit. Besides, my rubber bridge instincts were to make hearts trumps and I duly opened one heart.

When the bidding tray came back, Arturo had doubled and Jacqui bid two hearts. Benito passed. What now?

The takeout double meant my kings were less valuable. On the other hand, Benito was sounding like a man with very little, and when you have all the defensive strength stacked in one hand, you often can make contracts you might otherwise not be able to. I didn't want to invite with such good trumps, because Jacqui, who must be staring at little ones, would have a difficult time bidding game on a marginal hand. So I leaped to four hearts, hoping for the right dummy. Everyone passed and Arturo led the ♡9.

North (Jacqui)
♠ 4 3
♡ 7 6 2
♢ Q J 7 5 2
♣ K 10 2

West (Arturo)   East (Benito)

South (Matthew)
♠ K 10 5
♡ A K Q J 10
♢ K 6
♣ J 7 4

It wasn't exactly the best dummy I had seen in a while. In fact, without too much imagination, I could see myself losing five or six tricks. I tried to concentrate. The only hope lay in the diamond suit. If West held all three aces and the ♣Q, I could use the diamond suit for spade discards. I couldn't draw trumps before attacking diamonds, or West could shift to spades and set up a second trick there, while the ♣A was still in his hand. So I banged down the ♢K and watched.

Arturo won the ace and went into a long study. He finally came out with the surprise card of the ♣Q. This was too easy, I thought. I won the king in dummy, drew three rounds of trumps (Arturo followed to all of them and Benito discarded a small spade), then played on diamonds. Everyone followed to the ◊ Q, but on the jack, Arturo discarded a spade after I did. So I ruffed out the fourth diamond (Arturo throwing a second spade) and then I broke out in a sweat. The position was:

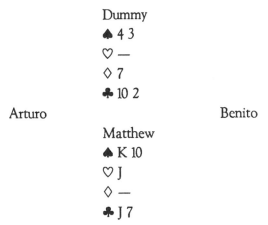

Dummy
♠ 4 3
♡ —
◊ 7
♣ 10 2

Arturo   Benito

Matthew
♠ K 10
♡ J
◊ —
♣ J 7

How was I to get back to my winning diamond? If I lead the ♣J, Arturo will duck. If I lead the ♣7, Arturo will go up with his ace and lead one back!

Yet all I had to do to make this hand was to unblock the ♣J when Arturo had returned the queen! Darn it! A vulnerable game thrown away! Benito would have seen the unblock in a split second. Why hadn't I?

I stewed for a while in my depression. A thought struck me: If I never played a card, I could never go down. I closed my eyes and imagined Arturo's hand. He held the ♠A-Q and the ♣A-x-x. I reviewed the scenario again. If I led a low club, he would rise ace and lead one back — that was hopeless. If I led the ♣J, he was forced to duck it. Hmm. Was it possible that he had started the hand with only three clubs? Was he down to the ♠A-Q-x and the ♣A-x. If so . . .

I led the ♣J and he ducked. Then I led my last club. He folded his cards and put them in the board. I did the same. The whole deal had been:

North (Jacqui)
♠ 4 3
♡ 7 6 2
◇ Q J 7 5 2
♣ K 10 2

West (Arturo)
♠ A Q J 6 2
♡ 9 8 3
◇ A 3
♣ A Q 8

East (Benito)
♠ 9 8 7
♡ 5 4
◇ 10 9 8 4
♣ 9 6 5 3

South (Matthew)
♠ K 10 5
♡ A K Q J 10
◇ K 6
♣ J 7 4

"Nicely done, Matthew," said Jacqui, not even looking up from her needlepoint.

"Why you play the queen of clubs?" complained Benito.

"What do you want me to do!" yelled Arturo.

Benito leaned over and examined the cards.

"Ah, I see. Amazing. Why is he so lucky tonight?"

Board 46. Third from the end. I held:

♠ A Q ♡ Q 4 3 2 ◇ K Q J 10 6 ♣ A K

Benito was dealer and opened one spade. I doubled. The tray went over. When it came back, Arturo had bid two spades and Jacqui three clubs. Benito passed and I bid three notrump.

This ended the auction. Arturo led the ♠8 and this is what I saw:

North (Jacqui)
♠ 4 3
♡ K 10
◊ 4 3 2
♣ Q J 10 9 6 5

West (Arturo)   East (Benito)

South (Matthew)
♠ A Q
♡ Q 4 3 2
◊ K Q J 10 6
♣ A K

Benito put up the ♠K and I won the ace. If I attacked diamonds, Benito would drive out my other spade and all I could take would be two spades, four diamonds and two clubs — one trick short.

If, on the other hand, I could score six club tricks, I would need only two spade tricks (which I had) and one red-suit trick. There was a problem in communications, however. The only way I could reach dummy to score those club tricks was by leading a heart to the king (if West had the ace) or a heart to the 10 (if West had the jack). Hmm. Not many points out there — 13 to be exact. What in the world were they bidding on? My guess was that Benito opened on 11 and Arturo had both major-suit jacks.

I cashed the ♣A-K. Then I was about to lead a heart to the 10 when something in the back of my mind came to me.

It was that Feldesman play that Roth had told me about the other day at the Mayfair. You know, where you bang down an honor and nobody dares win it for fear of your creating an entry to dummy. It was a way of stealing an extra trick. Only this time, the play was legitimate.

I led the ♡Q out of my hand. If Benito won it, I could reach dummy, so he was forced to duck. I then played on diamonds. The best Benito could do was win and cash three heart tricks (they were divided 4-3). I made my nine tricks. The whole deal was:

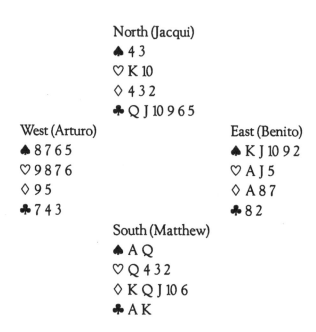

North (Jacqui)
♠ 4 3
♡ K 10
◊ 4 3 2
♣ Q J 10 9 6 5

West (Arturo)
♠ 8 7 6 5
♡ 9 8 7 6
◊ 9 5
♣ 7 4 3

East (Benito)
♠ K J 10 9 2
♡ A J 5
◊ A 8 7
♣ 8 2

South (Matthew)
♠ A Q
♡ Q 4 3 2
◊ K Q J 10 6
♣ A K

"Nicely played," said Jacqui. And this time she actually looked up!

I was beginning to enjoy myself. Back-to-back successes — a roll. I listened closely for the sound of any applause that might come from the living room. If I heard a loud thunder of noise, I would know that we were making a comeback. Anxious to get to the next board, I bent down to the floor to retrieve it. Lucky for me I did. Because there was an explosion, but it didn't come from the VuGraph room. When I next got up off the floor the library was in smithereens.

32

As I gazed up from the floor, there was Belsky. I knew him by the beard. He was always there in these memorable moments and if it hadn't been for the fact I trusted the guy like my brother, I would have suspected him as well.

Suddenly I thought of the match. I had been on a roll — why now of all times did the bomb have to go off? Couldn't it have waited two more deals? Then it occured to me that the timing was no accident. Or maybe I was deluding myself — maybe everything *was* an accident, as some scientists like to tell it. Maybe it doesn't matter what we do, say, or how we live our lives, 'cause we're all headed for a one-way street called Graveyard Avenue. And nothing we ever did counts for anything.

I shook my head. My eyes were coming back into focus. No, it couldn't be. The pundits had to be wrong. Otherwise there would be no difference between me and the guy who planted the bomb — the guy who had murdered three people.

The joint was a mess. I knew Patty was looking forward to redecorating, but not from scratch.

"Anybody hurt bad?" I asked.

"No," said Belsky. "It was a miracle. They say the screen across the table took the brunt of the flying scraps."

I looked at it. It had a hole in the middle the size of a duplicate board. Maury Braunstein was bandaging it up this very moment. The players were sitting around the floor, checking their bodily equipment. Benito was going over the scores with Lea. Evelyn had had the worst fall. Her blouse had torn at the top and Arturo was gracious enough to help her patch it up. Jacqui was reading a book that had fallen from the library shelf. I think it was an Edgar Allen Poe anthology. The big commotion was outside in the hall. The WBF emergency committee had placed Bob Hamman to stand guard so that no one who knew the score of the match could enter the library. With only two boards remaining, they didn't dare risk a leak. That meant my wife couldn't get in to see how I was. I screamed out that I was fine, but I don't know if she heard me.

It was amazing how few of the spectators were leaving. It was a clue that victory was within our grasp. Only two boards to go — I wished we could get started again. Detective Kennedy was taking prints of the bidding box that exploded — I should say: what was left of the box. Evelyn was on her feet now, helping Maury attach the new boxes. I remembered that it was Evelyn who brought the new bidding box into the room and I wanted to ask her where she got it when Belsky pulled me over to the corner for a private *tête-à-tête*.

"I have the tape, Matt. And I listened to it. And I think we got our man."

"I'm all ears, Belsky. To tell the truth, I'm not much else."

"Good, here's the tape player — you can hear it from the horse's mouth."

Belsky was getting good with the lingo. We moved into the bathroom and he turned on the machine.

(Static) . . . the coach's voice: "It proves that I am the

366

greatest theoretician in the history of the game. But, you see, the world does not yet recognize the fact. If only I had the time, I could show the world."

Evelyn's voice: "You think you can show the world by coaching the Cayne team? You think this is going to go on forever?"

The coach: "And why shouldn't it? Ha! He's not quitting until he wins a world championship — what are the odds on that one?! By the time I'm through I'll have over a million hands to prove my theories."

Evelyn: "I hope you don't expect me to type them all."

The coach: "You'll do whatever I say, when I say."

Evelyn: "You must be joking. If I don't get a place on this team, I'm calling it quits, buster. And maybe worse, maybe I'll throw you to the cops."

The coach: "Listen to me. It was your suggestion to get rid of the Steins and you'll pay for it if I'm caught. So watch your big mouth."

Evelyn: "All I know is someone else has to go if they're planning on playing four."

The coach: "You don't murder your own father just to get on a bridge team."

Evelyn: "No one said anything about my father. Go after Sontag if you must."

The coach: "I told you I've had enough. I've got to concentrate on my conventions. You want to play so badly, you do it. Actually it would be helpful if you were on the team. Then I wouldn't have to worry about the team winning."

(Sound of a loud slap!)

The coach: "What are you, crazy? I'll teach you to strike me."

Evelyn: "What are you doing? Why are you looking at me like that? Why are taking off your ascot? Get that filthy thing away from me. Look, somebody's coming."

The coach: "Don't worry, little bird. You'll get yours one way or another."

(static)

Click. Belsky pushed the rewound button.

"The tape is done, Matt. That's all we got. I think it's more than enough."

I was lost in the diabolical scheme of it all. The coach's motive was also his alibi. He wanted to sabotage the team to save his job, and who in the world would suspect that he, of all people, would want the team to lose? But was this tape enough to get a conviction?

"We might need Evelyn's testimony to corroborate this, Belsky. Trouble is she's definitely in this with him."

"I don't know about that," said my partner. "She was scared on that tape. He went after her with the ascot. Maybe she planted a seed or two, but that's a long way from conspiring."

True, I thought. She brought the bidding box that had the bomb in it, but she didn't run away. I think she didn't know about the bomb. I know she's a loyal kibitzer, but not that loyal. Maybe she *was* okay. "But this may be bad news for Jimmy. The cops will say that the coach was working for him."

"Mr. Cayne wouldn't sabotage his own team, Matt."

"No, but that's the D.A.'s line. That the coach worked first for Jimmy and later against him. First he knocked off the worst elements of the team and later had to sabotage the team to stop Jimmy from quitting bridge. We need more evidence that points only to the coach."

"What makes you think that the coach is going to claim Jimmy hired him to murder the team? That doesn't make sense, Matt. Unless somebody's already planted the idea in the guy's head."

"That somebody is Mrs. Kennedy," I said. "I'm afraid the idea came from her in the first place. She gave it to her husband, he gave it to the Commissioner, and he gave it to the D.A. If the coach is going down for the count, he's planning on taking Jimmy with him, or maybe it's just an ace in the hole to save his neck if things get really tight."

"Game time!" It was Maury's voice. Good God, this was a fine time to be playing the last two boards of a world championship!

The whole thing explained the mystery of Otto as well, I thought. He was nothing more than a pawn. Yes, Otto was a nice guy, and Jimmy had a lot of sympathy for his fellow man. But since when does a team captain put players on his team out of sympathy? It made more sense that it was the coach who recommended Otto. The coach had said Otto's game had vastly improved and his rubber bridge experience would help enormously. The coach had added Otto to the team for the sole purpose of sabotage.

I sat down in the tattered South seat and put my head in my hands, resting it on the table for a moment. Cameramen were still setting up. New bulbs had to be brought in. Yes, the coach was our man, all right. But we still didn't have the goods on him. Oh, the tape was incriminating all right, but I wasn't sure it was admissable in court. And even if it was legal, was it enough? We needed something more.

I heard a duplicate board drop on the table. I lifted my head. Suddenly the screen flew up in the air and sitting across from me was Frankenstein! I let out a scream. My God, this was no dream — there he was in the flesh!

"Mr. Granovetter," said Frankenstein, "My name is Jordan. I'm Detective Kennedy's junior partner."

I noticed now that he was much younger than Frankenstein, but the resemblance was frightening. This is the guy that Jinks must have run into on Wall Street — the ghost he had told me about during our subway ride to the Mayfair.

"I think we have the case sown up now," he continued.

"Detective Kennedy asked me to hold up the game for a few minutes until he apprehended the killers. I hope nobody objects to the wait."

I looked at Benito and Arturo. They seemed to be in a state of shock over the whole affair. And Jacqui was still reading her book in the corner.

"Well, I guess not," I said, wondering whom he meant by "the killers."

Maury Braunstein rapidly took the initiative of switching the VuGraph order. We would play the boards second while the Open Room would play them first. We all gave Maury a nod. Good idea, Maury. Then we turned to the entrance, where Detective Kennedy was motioning for the Gorilla to bring in the prisoners.

The Gorilla was prodding the two Stein kids, who were both in handcuffs. "I picked 'em up two blocks from here," said the Gorilla. "It was like stealing candy from a baby."

I started to object. They were not the killers — the coach was. My eyes met Belsky's and we both shook our heads. Then Evelyn gave me a similar look. Still, I held my tongue until they played out their hand.

"We're not saying one word," said the Stein boy. "Not until we speak with our lawyer."

"Quiet," said his sister. She obviously wasn't singing either — and as far as I was concerned it was a good thing.

Detective Kennedy moved toward his prisoners. "A few of the fingerprints on this time bomb (holds remnant of bidding box in hand) are yours, son. And, I might add, the box is missing any remains of a four-diamond bid, the bid that was found in Frank Stein's throat one week ago today. I have been watching VuGraph and not one four-diamond bid has been made by Mr. Franco with this box!"

"I was just helping Evelyn with the box," said the boy. "I was on my way from the kitchen after getting a drink when she walked by with this bidding box. I asked if I could see it for a minute and she let me. Maybe the four-diamond bid slipped out while I was playing with them. I wanted to imagine what it would be like to be in a world championship — which I'm gonna do one day, just like my mom."

"You'll play prison duplicate from now on — that's what you'll play."

The boy was wacko and Kennedy was miffed. He collected his thoughts and took out a handkerchief to wipe his brow. It was getting warm in the place because the air-conditioner had broken down when the plastic explosive went off. Suddenly I noticed it was no handkerchief, it was one of the coach's ascots! He started speaking again: "We also have evidence that you (pointing to Bobby) dug up your father-in-law's grave and stole his body! My own partner (points to Jordan) trailed you to the cemetery and was an eyewitness!"

"Okay, so I stole his body. That doesn't make me a murderer. The thought of that horrible man next to my mother for eternity was too much to bear."

"How could you!" said the girl, turning on her brother. "Why, you know that it was your mom who drove my father crazy at the bridge table. Why, you're as bad as the rest of them! Where is my father?"

"In the Hudson River."

"Oh, how could you—" She broke down in tears. It was a sad sight. Meanwhile nobody mentioned anything about Frankenstein's lawsuit, which was lying in the coffin when we came upon it and was currently residing in my inside jacket pocket. For my money, the kid never bothered with it. He would have been too busy and nervous removing the body. No, the lawsuit had been planted earlier by the coach, another ace in the hole. If he were accused of the murders, he would suggest we dig up Frank's body and there would be incriminating evidence against Otto Marx. I had to find out if that letter was really written by Frankenstein, or if it was a forgery. If I could prove that the letter was written by the coach, I would have the second piece of evidence I needed. I slipped the letter out of my jacket and opened it. Then I bent down to the floor, where a few pages from the most recent set of bridge notes had settled.

The coach shouldn't have ended his relationship with his typist, because in doing so he had provided me with a copy of his handwriting and, as far as I could tell, it matched very closely with the writing on the lawsuit. Now if I could get Evy to agree to testify, it was all over.

Meanwhile, Detective Kennedy was holding court. The D.A. was there, too, and he was rubbing his chin in dismay. I think he saw the weaknesses in the Detective's evidence.

"As to the mental state of the boy here, I believe socially he was deprived — he was raised a bridge orphan. His parents spent all their time playing bridge and had very little time for him.

"There's no doubt about it. The boy here murdered Frank Stein not only out of revenge for taking his mother away from him, but because he had learned the game of bridge and believed his side of the family was the better half. She was the better player, he thought. And *Frank* was getting all the good press. And he stuffed the four-diamond bid in his stepfather's throat, to teach him a lesson."

The detective now turned on the girl.

"Then this one murdered her stepmother, because she believed that her stepmother had murdered her father. She attached the eight-of-diamonds card to her blouse because she knew this would make the murder seem as if it had been committed by a bridge player and not her!"

The two kids looked at each other. Hatred flared up in both of them, and then subsided just as quickly. The Gorilla decided to separate them, anyway.

"Who is this guy?" screamed the boy. "He's wrong, he's

wrong."

"Wait a second," I said, finally objecting. "That ascot you've got in your hand. I believe, sir, that that is the murder weapon."

Kennedy waved it in my face. "These ascots were picked up from the coach's dresser and tested in the lab, Mr. Granovetter. You think we're inept, do you? You see, they could not be the murder weapon because they give off lint of various colors. No such threads were found on any of the victims."

"And what about my father?" cried Evelyn suddenly.

"Your father left the Mayfair club and entered the subway at six p.m," said the junior detective. "I was staked out near the Mayfair, waiting for the Stein boy to leave. Meanwhile, your poor father was left unguarded. My fault, I take some of the blame. But I can't be everywhere at once. This girl murdered your father, Miss Barkowsky, because, having strangled her stepmother, she was now aiming to destroy the bridge team completely. Remember, you yourself, Mr. Granovetter, had riled her that very afternoon during your meeting with her downtown."

"Wait a second," I protested. "You can't blame me for the girl strangling Barkowsky. Besides, you fools, she didn't do it."

"Now, now," said Kennedy, "we can't all play detective. The subsequent attacks were all her doing. After her second murder, she was let loose. The idea that the team would continue was an affront to her. She hates bridge, Mr. Granovetter, and she hates bridge players more."

The girl was standing there, perfectly still. She never opened her mouth. Junior spoke up again:

"The final incriminating evidence comes from England, Mr. Granovetter. There was an unsolved strangulation there nine years ago — I checked it out on the computer — it was the very same week that both Stein children were in London, their parents playing bridge in the Sunday Times Pairs."

"Nine years ago?" I asked. That was exactly when the coach came to this country. It all made sense, but they had it all wrong. I looked at the Stein girl again and rubbed the back of my neck. "Why were you here tonight if you hate bridge?" I asked suddenly.

"I came with him. I'm his sister, see. He wanted to come watch, and I was against it. But he insisted, so I came with him. But after a short time, he broke down and started to cry. So I took him down the block, when this baboon of yours (pointing to the Gorilla) attacks us and brings us back in these (shows the handcuffs). I admit I was wrong about you people — these detectives have shown me the light. You guys aren't evil — you're out of your minds!"

"Excuse me," said Maury Braunstein, wiping his brow. "it doesn't bother me and I could stay here all night, but the air-conditioner is broken, so I suggest we get on with it."

"Well, at least this clears Mr. Cayne," I said to the D.A., as Detective Jordan, the Steins and the Gorilla went to the elevator. (Detective Kennedy stuck around to kibitz the last two hands.)

"It clears him," admitted the D.A. "But I don't know if any of this is enough for a conviction."

"Hang on till the match is over," I confided, "and I'll give you some evidence that is."

I motioned Belsky to the bathroom and grabbed Evelyn's sleeve on the way. "Put the recorder on," I told Belsky. He nodded.

"Okay, Evy," I said. "It's time to play ball or you're going up river with the coach. Belsky and I know the truth — we have it here on a little tape recorder. And we have a little piece of forgery to go with it. Now talk quick. What do you know about the bidding box?"

"Hey, I'm happy he's caught. How would you like to type

hundreds of pages of bridge notes night after night? Let's face it, he's slightly off his rocker. Yes, he gave me the bidding box, but I didn't know it was loaded."

"And my afternoon coffee?"

"The coach, the coach. He handed me the cup and said it would help keep you alert."

"The clues he left on the bodies?"

"Well, you know how he hates imperfections. And he's got a point. Charlotte should have played back the eight when she held queen-eight-seven fourth. I don't say she should have died for it, but it was a bad play. And you know how the coach loves the choice-of-games cuebid. But Frankenstein simply refused to play it and we lost a big swing in the Trials because of his old-fashioned stubbornness. I wasn't sorry in the least when he did Frank in."

At least she was honest. "And your father?"

"I don't know. Probably he murdered him, too. The coach wouldn't admit it, because I wasn't happy about it. I'm not that bad, you know."

"What about Mrs. Kennedy?" I added.

"That two-timer has been working with him. She's probably keeping score out there right now — if I know him, he told her to keep a tally and whenever the team took the lead, to let him know and he would do something about it."

Suddenly I heard static. It came from the microphone around her neck. It was switched on. Everything we were saying was being broadcast into the VuGraph room. I wondered if Mrs. Kennedy heard. For that matter, where was the coach? We bolted out of the bathroom.

"Has anyone any idea where the coach is?" I called out.

"He went off with Victor hours ago," said Jacqui, who was sitting at the table now. She looked a bit peeved that we were still discussing the case.

"Good God," I said, "we better get up to the apartment."

Jacqui suggested I sit down and pick up my cards.

"Even if Victor is in danger," said Jacqui, "his priority would be the championship. Let's play the last two boards and then we'll go look for Victor."

"Well, then Belsky can go," I suggested.

"Let Mr. Belsky sit for a while," she answered. "Victor will be all right, trust me."

We all nodded; after all, he had the dogs to protect him.

Maury placed board 47 on the table. Then I picked up my hand:

♠ 9 4 2 ♡ A 3 ◇ A Q 5 2 ♣ Q 8 7 5

I was dealer and passed. I was bidding on instincts now. There wasn't much left — I had to hope they were good instincts.

Roth had warned me off opening a 12-point hand. This 12 was not a good 12 either. The tray, or what was left of it, was pushed gently to the other side. When it came back, Arturo had opened with one heart and Jacqui passed. Benito bid two diamonds and alerted. I asked and he whispered (the pad had been destroyed), "eenvitational, any suit."

I thought of doubling, and perhaps I should have, but I was still not functioning smoothly. I passed, and then realized I was worth a lead-directing double. The coach's words, "You've got to take advantage of their artificial bids," came back to me.

The tray returned with two spades by Arturo, pass by Jacqui. Now Benito bid two notrump (alerted as a relay: Tell me more). Arturo told him three notrump (alerted as a good 4-5-2-2 shape). Benito bid four hearts. Now I was really sorry I hadn't doubled two diamonds or opened one diamond. But it was too late now and everyone passed. C'mon, Matthew, I said to myself, get into this — think deeply.

Jacqui led the ♣4 and this is what I saw:

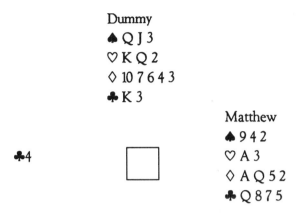

Dummy
♠ Q J 3
♡ K Q 2
◇ 10 7 6 4 3
♣ K 3

Matthew
♠ 9 4 2
♡ A 3
◇ A Q 5 2
♣ Q 8 7 5

♣ 4

I quickly counted the outstanding points. Ace-king of spades — 7. Jack of hearts — 8. King-jack of diamonds — 12. Ace-jack of clubs — 17. Jacqui could have at most three or four points in her hand.

Arturo played low from dummy, I played the ♣Q and he won in his hand with the ♣A. He then led a heart to the king. I won the ace. Maybe I should have ducked, I thought. C'mon, count your tricks. Unless Jacqui has the ♡J-9-x, we are not getting more than one heart trick. If she has a spade honor, we will score it — there's no rush. What about diamonds? Unless Jacqui has that miracle trump holding, we'll need two diamond tricks. I wish Jacqui held the ace instead of me. FLASH!

Yes, what if she did! And what if I held the queen-jack? — I had hesitated too long, perhaps, but the ◇Q now came out of my hand and hit the table with a gentle thud.

This was the full deal:

Benito
♠ Q J 3
♡ K Q 2
◇ 10 7 6 4 3
♣ K 3

Jacqui
♠ 8 7 5
♡ 10 8 7
◇ J 8
♣ J 9 6 4 2

Matthew
♠ 9 4 2
♡ A 3
◇ A Q 5 2
♣ Q 8 7 5

Arturo
♠ A K 10 6
♡ J 9 6 5 4
◇ K 9
♣ A 10

Arturo went into a long thought. If I held a similar hand with the ◇Q-J and Jacqui held the ◇A doubleton, the deal would look like this:

Benito
♠ Q J 3
♡ K Q 2
◇ 10 7 6 4 3
♣ K 3

Jacqui
♠ 8 7 5
♡ 10 8 7
◇ A 8
♣ J 9 6 4 2

Matthew
♠ 9 4 2
♡ A 3
◇ Q J 5 2
♣ Q 8 7 5

Arturo
♠ A K 10 6
♡ J 9 6 5 4
◇ K 9
♣ A 10

As long as Jacqui did not hold four trumps to the 10, declarer could afford to lose two diamond tricks, but could not afford a third-round overruff. If he covered my queen with his king, Jacqui would win her ace, return a diamond to my jack and I could lead a third round of the suit, promoting Jacqui's ♡10.

Of course, Arturo had seen that I was capable of making some good plays, which made him wary. Still, he had to consider the two dangerous diamond holdings. Though it was 2-to-1 that I held the A-Q-x-x rather than the Q-J-x-x, because I might have returned the ◊J from the latter holding, the bidding clearly indicated that I was unlikely to hold the A-Q-x-x. With that holding, I probably would have doubled the artificial two-diamond response or opened the bidding with my 12-point hand. Here, again, was the inference taken from what someone did *not* do.

Arturo played low on my queen. I cashed the ◊A, my hands shaking in excitement, and continued with a third diamond, ruffed with the ♡9 and overruffed with the ♡10.

The applause from the VuGraph room was clearly audible and the Italians looked at each other in dismay. I silently thanked Old Leroy for planting the notion in my head and gave a little thank you to the Lord as well.

The final board was placed on the table: Board 48. I held:

♠ Q 9 2 ♡ A K J 7 3 ◊ 4 3 2 ♣ A 8

They were vulnerable, we were not. Arturo was the dealer. As I waited for the tray to appear, I smelled smoke. At first I thought it was my imagination. When I looked toward the hall, there were flames. Suddenly I heard sirens. A fireman was tapping at the window. I told Benito to hold his hand back, and got up to let him in. They were spraying water in the hallway now. Meanwhile, Arturo had passed and Jacqui had opened one spade. Benito passed and I bid two hearts.

♠ Q 9 2 ♡ A K J 7 3 ◊ 4 3 2 ♣ A 8

Maybe I should have bid three spades, which Jacqui plays as forcing. There were two reasons for the direct three-spade bid: 1) Jacqui prefers showing support immediately — it gives away no information to the opponents; and 2) if this were a slam deal, it would be best to make it as short an auction as possible, considering the fire in the hallway.

Anyway, I had bid two hearts, and I had to live (or die) with it. Another fireman, axe in hand, climbed though the window as the tray came back. Arturo passed and Jacqui bid three diamonds. Benito passed. I couldn't afford to think too long, so I just went with instincts and bid four clubs. This was an advanced cuebid in support of spades, and, if the firemen were competent, I'd get a shot at showing the spade support on the next round. The tray came through and Jacqui had bid five spades. Nice call, Jacqui. Should speed things up. I bid six spades before Benito even passed and sent the tray flying back under the screen. I heard an Italian exclamation as Arturo's drink went flying to the wall. The tray returned with a wet double by Arturo and a pass by Jacqui. Benito also passed and I considered briefly the idea of running to six notrump but decided against it. There just wasn't enough time for another round of auction.

Maybe if I had another minute to think I would have removed, and maybe I had been maneuvered into passing by forces far greater than I. All I knew was breathing was getting near impossible.

The smoke was getting thicker, and I hoped Jacqui would be able to see the dummy. I had to give credit to Evelyn, who never left the VuGraph microphone for a second. Apparently she had passed out, because she was being carried away in a stretcher. As far as the Italians were concerned, I don't think they noticed. Their concentration was impeccable. Meanwhile, it didn't look good for the home team. I was short a few highcards for my raise to six, and if Arturo was ruffing the opening heart lead, we'd have one less trick besides.

The opening lead was the ♡5. The screen came up midway and I put my dummy down, waiting desperately to hear Jacqui say thank you. She actually said, "Okay, Matthew. You're not needed anymore; you may go find Victor and see that he's all right. Oh, and by the way, we bid three spades directly with those hands."

I nodded, motioned to Belsky and headed out of the room.

When I reached the hallway, I turned back. Jacqui had not called a card. On our way out I peered into the dining room, my curiosity killing me. This is what I saw on the screen:

Board 48
West dealer
East-West vulnerable

Italy +141, USA +142

North
♠ A K J 10 8
♡ 9 4
♢ A K Q
♣ 4 3 2

West
♠ 5 4 3
♡ Q 10 8 6 2
♢ 9 8 7
♣ K 7

East
♠ 7 6
♡ 5
♢ J 10 6 5
♣ Q J 10 9 6 5

South
♠ Q 9 2
♡ A K J 7 3
♢ 4 3 2
♣ A 8

Open Room

Cayne	Forquet	Sontag	Belladonna
West	North	East	South
pass	1 ♣	pass	2 ♢ (5 controls)
pass	2 ♠	pass	3 ♠
pass	4 ♢	pass	4 ♡
pass	4 ♠	pass	6 ♠
pass	pass	pass	

Final contract: 6♠ (North)
Opening lead: ♡5

Trick one: ♡5, ♡A, ♡2, ♡4
Trick two: ♣A, ♣7, ♣2, ♣6
Trick three: ♣8, ♣K, ♣3, ♣Q
Trick four: ♡6, ♡9, ♠6, ♡3

Result: down one, East-West +50

Closed Room

Franco	J. Mitchell	Garozzo	Granovetter
West	North	East	South
pass	1 ♠	pass	2 ♡
pass	3 ◇	pass	4 ♣
pass	5 ♠	pass	6 ♠
double	pass	pass	pass

Final contract: 6♠x (North)
Opening lead: ♡5

Trick one: ♡5, ?

I jotted down the hand quickly, noting that Jacqui had still not called a card from dummy. I wanted to stay until she played, but then there was Belsky reminding me that duty called. Reluctantly, I made my way to the back staircase.

We were one imp ahead going into the board, but now Jacqui had to make the slam or lose the match. The difference was Arturo's penalty double. Down one would mean minus 100 versus the plus 50 we scored in the other room. Two imps. Two of the biggest imps in town. Two of the biggest imps in the history of my life. But what if Victor was in danger? I just couldn't risk kibitzing.

Downstairs, I overheard the doorman say that the fire was under control.

33

As Belsky hot-rodded it uptown, I rewrote Board 48 with declarer as South, so it would be easier to follow.

Dummy
♠ Q 9 2
♡ A K J 7 3
◊ 4 3 2
♣ A 8

Sonty
♠ 7 6
♡ 5
◊ J 10 6 5
♣ Q J 10 9 6 5

Jimmy
♠ 5 4 3
♡ Q 10 8 6 2
◊ 9 8 7
♣ K 7

Pietro
♠ A K J 10 8
♡ 9 4
◊ A K Q
♣ 4 3 2

Forquet had gone down in six spades after taking a technically sound line. He won the heart lead with the ace and led the ♣A and another club. Of course, it was over for him. Jimmy won with the ♣K and gave Sonty a heart ruff. Forquet had no idea about the bad heart split, and his line — to ruff a club in dummy — was certainly sound. Little did he realize that he could have made his contract by not playing a second round of clubs.

If he won the opening heart lead with the ace, cashed the ♣A and drew three rounds of trumps followed by three rounds of diamonds, he could then lead a club to Jimmy's ♣K, forcing a heart play into dummy's ♡K-J.

Of course this line is double-dummy. Without knowing the whole deal it is totally ridiculous. It was interesting to note that Jimmy could not afford to unblock his ♣K under the ace (not that he wanted to, because he knew another club was about to be led). If he did throw the ♣K away, the ♣8 would next be led to Sonty, and the contract would be made by declarer ruffing a club.

The sad thing about the hand from my viewpoint was that Jacqui had to go down one — personally, I thought she would go down one at trick one by ducking the heart lead, because the Lightner double sure sounded as if Arturo was void. It was entirely reasonable for Jacqui to assume the deal looked something like this:

                    Dummy
                    ♠ Q 9 2
                    ♡ A K J 7 3
                    ◇ 4 3 2
                    ♣ A 8

Benito   Arturo
♠ 7   ♠ 6 5 4 3
♡ Q 10 8 6 5 2   ♡ —
◇ J 10 6   ◇ 9 8 7 5
♣ Q J 10   ♣ K 9 7 6 5

                    Jacqui
                    ♠ A K J 10 8
                    ♡ 9 4
                    ◇ A K Q
                    ♣ 4 3 2

If Arturo held a heart void, ducking the ♡5 lead would permit a later finesse of the ♡J and two discards on the ♡A-K for her two losing clubs.

Big deal, I thought. That's not the way the cards were, so what was I dreaming about? Reality set in — a one imp loss in the world championship — I might never get another chance. Belsky, bless him, interrupted my morbid thoughts.

"Matt, better get the guns."

We were at 89th and Madison, eight blocks away. I felt under the dashboard and unclipped two automatics, tossing one into Belsky's lap. I wondered where Old Leroy's pistol was.

When we get to Victor's building, we rushed past the doorman and took the elevator to the 10th floor. The door of the apartment was slightly ajar. I flung the door open, my gun ready for firing.

Four Siberian huskies looked up at me, then went back to their bones; one mutt sauntered over to be petted. Victor was sitting in his easy chair, reading Jaws. He looked up at us.

Then he went back to his book.

"Where's the coach?" I cried.

"Probably on the Staten Island Ferry," said Victor, without looking up.

"What?! Wh-Wh-What the heck is he doing there?"

"That's where I would be if I wanted to meet a boat off the three-mile limit."

"We better go, Matt," said Belsky, looking at his watch. "Maybe we can still catch him."

"You got plenty of time," said Victor.

"Why's that?" asked Belsky.

"Cause he stopped off at the Caynes' to set fire to the joint. I think he was planning to pick up the Barkowsky girl as well."

"How do you know all this? What happened?" I asked.

"What do you think happened? Nuttin happened."

"But Victor, you didn't show up to play. Where did you go?"

"Oh, that. Well, I figured I better let Jacqui play — she was as sharp as they come and I was a little tired. So I told the coach I wanted to talk to him about the future, about possibly playing with me on some of my teams. I think it was the first time I ever spoke to him directly. He was very excited. But when we got back here, the dogs took an immediate dislike to him. ('Bark' from under the coffee table.) Little Imp over there started growling ferociously. And Bambi was impossible to control. I think he got scared. I told him not to worry, where he was going the guard dogs were much worse. This didn't sit too kindly with him. He asked to borrow my matches — and I stupidly gave them to him, forgetting that he didn't smoke. Then he grabbed Bambi's new leash and took off, saying something about a date with Evelyn."

"Bambi has a new leash?" I asked, subconsciously realizing the implication.

"Yeah, we lost the other one two weeks ago."

Oh my God. I grabbed Belsky, or he grabbed me — I don't know which — and sped out the door.

"Wait a second, Matt," called Victor. "How did we do? Did we win?"

I ran back and tossed him Board 48. "Don't know. Jacqui's still playing it."

As I exited, I heard Victor make a soft whistle. "Possible," was his last word . . . "possible."

We spun over to the FDR drive. Belsky proved himself the best wheelman in town. In three minutes we were speeding past the U.N. In one more minute we were flying by the Empire State. In another half a minute the World Trade Center came into view as we turned the bend, the night sparkles of the East River flooding into the Hudson. I grabbed the flashlight from the back. As we stepped out of the car and ran into the Ferry station, the Statue of Liberty, which was dead ahead, seemed to be staring directly at us.

The 11:30 boat was just getting ready to depart. We boarded the Ferry but spotted no coach and no Evelyn either. After a few minutes, we went to the pilot's deck, showed our special I.D.s and asked if he had seen a tall man with a dog leash and a blond woman? He was a young pilot and seemed excited about the idea of helping out with a manhunt. But he had no information. The previous ferry was at 11, and there was a large crowd of people. It was impossible to remember who was on it. We asked him to speed up the boat and he cooperated. The passengers must have been surprised.

As we passed the Statue, I got shivers. It was spooky, let me tell you. There in the dark was this giant woman holding a torch, the full moon right behind her crown. And in the background, the tip of Manhattan was being transformed into a toy city of skyscrapers. Belsky, who had been searching the deck, came up to me, evidence in hand.

"Looks like we got a Gretel on our hands."

"What are you talking about?" I asked.

"Hansel and Gretel. Here, look."

He handed me two torn pieces of a convention card. I recognized them immediately — the scores to Boards 41 and 42 were on one side of each slip. Good for Evelyn! We were on her trail. Only thing was, who was going to verify the Closed-Room score back at the tournament? I put the slips in my pocket. Maybe I could scotch-tape them together later. That is, if we found them all.

The pilot made darn good time. We jumped off onto the dock before the plank came down. Then we walked carefully through the boathouse, picking up the score to Board 43 on the way.

Belsky was familiar with Staten Island and pointed to the right as we left the station. The cab sign was there, but only one cab was waiting.

"Been here long?" we asked.

"What are you, cops?" asked the man, who'd been reading a newspaper.

"Private," I said. "We're looking for a tall guy with a dog leash and a blond girl."

"Never seen 'em," he said. "I'll radio and see about the others." He talked into his two-way. "Anybody see a tall guy with a leash and a blond dame?"

"I took a couple over to Tony's," said a husky voice, over the static, "but I didn't notice her hair."

"Ask him if there are any slips of paper in the back seat," I said.

"Any, uh, slips of paper left behind?"

"Wait a second. . . . Yeah, I see one. It says 'four hundred and twenty' and, next to it, if I can make this out — hold on — 'Chicken pass by Matthew' — whatever that means."

"Board 44," I said. Nice of her to be criticizing me on the

official scorecard, I thought.

We took the cab to Tony's Dock, only a mile down the road. We were too late, though. The full moon allowed us to see the two of them on a motorboat, heading out to sea.

"I didn't know there was anything wrong," said Tony. "I thought they were lovers out for a ride. But where are they heading? They can't go more than a few miles in that thing."

"What else you got?" asked Belsky.

"I got my own cruiser. It's faster than their's. You want to rent it, you can. If you hurry, you might catch them at the second buoy. But there's an undertow tonight — the barometer is rising and . . ."

Belsky and I looked at each other. It was nice to be on the same wavelength. We both put our hands on Tony and informed him that he was elected captain. "That's extra," he said.

We climbed aboard and were soon underway. The coach and Evelyn were a small dot at first, but slowly they grew. I asked Tony if he had a megaphone, but he didn't. "I could put the siren on, if you like."

"Absolutely not," I said.

The water was getting choppy and some fog rolled in, but we were soon within a couple hundred feet of them. "I might as well put the siren on," Tony said. "They can hear my engine, so what's the difference."

"He's right," said Belsky. "Maybe it will give Evelyn some breathing room."

"All right," I said.

"And maybe we should radio the Coast Guard, too," said Tony.

I turned to Belsky and slapped my forehead. Why hadn't we done that already?!

The siren turned on and we could make out the two

figures on the boat ahead of us. "Slow down," I said, "or we'll run 'em over."

"Look," said Belsky. There was a boat another mile out coming toward us. It was a nice size, too.

"Great!" I called. "The coast guard."

"I don't think so," said Tony, who was slowing the engine.

"I can't hear you — turn off the damn siren."

He switched it off.

"I said, it's not the Coast Guard. I know their boats. That's a private sail."

"Help!"

A cry came across the wet wind, water now spewing in my face. It was Evelyn. Or was it the coach? They were in some sort of struggle. We were only 20 feet or so from them and the captain was doing a good job keeping us close.

"Do you swim, Belsky?" I asked hopefully.

"I should," he said.

"But you don't," I added. He nodded.

I told Tony to speed up and cut in front of them. The coach had his hands full with Evelyn, so we had a chance to overtake now.

"This is the three-mile limit," said Tony. "I'm not licensed to go across."

"Just do it!" I called out, grabbing a life jacket. I strapped it on, stuck my gun in the left strap and jumped. "Hey, this is shark season," yelled Tony, a few seconds later than I would have preferred.

The water was cold for August. I came up quickly and got my bearings. Over my shoulder I heard cries for help. The life jacket was restricting me, so I unbuckled it, turned and dove down again, coming up two feet from Evelyn. Unfortunately, I'd left the gun in the jacket.

The coach saw me and let go of her. That wasn't good for me. He tried to steer the boat away — then suddenly backed the thing up. I swam hastily away, before the propeller made mincemeat of me. The new boat was now coming around the bend. Three boats and one human — this wasn't easy. Then I got an idea. Unfortunately so did the big fish with the full set of white choppers swimming toward me. I took a gulp of air and dove deep — that's what Victor said to do when sharks were around — pretend that I was the bigger fish. After a half-minute, my hands felt a boat. I came up and the coach was facing the other way. I held onto the side and catapulted over the gunwale, knocking him to the bottom.

He was down but not out. As he lunged forward, I noticed a small pistol, small enough to fit inside a bidding box. He pointed it straight at my heart. I backed off rapidly. Evelyn was coughing. He hesitated. Suddenly a dog leash was around his neck. I grabbed the gun and told her to stop choking him. She argued.

"No, no mercy on him — he's a madman."

"He's evil, not mad," I retorted, trying to pull her away.

"He wants Jimmy and Sonty to switch to a big-club system, at favorable in second and third positions only. Now you're gonna tell me that's not mad?"

She let go of the leash, grabbed my arm and pointed the gun at his head — I couldn't stop her in time. She pulled the trigger, but we heard only a click.

"The gun's a dud."

"Ha," laughed the coach, rubbing his neck. "You're not loaded! There was only one bullet and that one was for Sontag."

He jumped on me, all six-feet-seven of him. I rolled around the wet seaweed at the bottom of the boat, the coach pounding his fists into my ribs. If he hit me one more time, I was going to pass out. Suddenly I heard a cry. The coach stood up, backed away and fell overboard. Evelyn, her switchblade in hand, had cut his ear.

I leaned over the boat and stuck out my arm to help him

back, but he was swimming in the other direction. "C'mon," I said, "there's sharks out there and you're bleeding."

"There's something better than sharks," he called back.

Yes, there up ahead was the "Finesse," Mrs. Kennedy's houseboat. I looked up. She was standing on deck, waving to the coach. I cupped my hands. "Back off! If you pick him up, we'll have you for aiding and abetting!"

She lifted a megaphone and said, "I came to get you, brown eyes — not him!"

I looked out at the water. A pretty group of black points were headed the coach's direction.

"Hey," I yelled back, "he's in trouble! Pick him up and hold 'im for me!"

The coach was frantic. He started splashing wildly — the worst thing you could do.

Mrs. Kennedy chuckled. "Let him be," she said. "He'll just be in the way."

"You're crazy!" I screamed. "Throw him a rope!"

"I'm not crazy," she called out. "I'm bad."

Evelyn let out a stifled cry and turned her face away. I glanced briefly into the water. It was a good thing it was night or I would have fainted. The last thing I saw was his pink and white ascot floating softly along the waves.

34

"The Talmud says that the world depends on three things: Torah, prayer and loving kindness." Belsky took a sip of champagne and continue, "But it also says those who show kindness to the evil will be cruel to the good. L'chaim." He finished his cup.

We were in the Mitchell's living room, celebrating. It was almost dawn and most of New York City was still asleep.

Alan Truscott, of the Times, asked what happened to Mrs. Kennedy and her boat, "The Finesse."

"First of all, I didn't get on board.

"If he did," said Pamela, "I would have given the papers a better story to write."

"This guy, Tony, had steered his cruiser back across the three-mile limit, but then Belsky forced the issue with one of his automatics and they picked up Evelyn and me pretty quickly. As far as I know Mrs. Kennedy will be brought up for corruption charges. They don't have anything else on her."

Truscott took me aside. "But," he whispered, pad and pencil in hand, "what about the girl over there (pointing to

Evelyn). How is it that she got off? Wasn't she conspiring with the coach?"

I shrugged. "I think she's really innocent — the police are satisfied, anyway."

Of course, she was not innocent. Oh, did she give me a story on the Ferry ride back, and there was no coach to refute it. Frankly, I was sick of her, and I told her she was going to be the fall guy. She pleaded with me, said that she didn't mean anything by the criticism on Board 44. It's always good to be made aware of your errors. How else were you going to improve? Don't hold it against her, she said.

I told her that when you suggest to an evil guy like the coach that he start knocking off people just so you can join a bridge team, you don't get off scot free.

"I'd do anything to avoid jail," she told me. "Anything."

The door opened and Jimmy, Patty and Otto entered. "It's so nice to be in a room without smoke," said Patty. "Win a world championship, lose an apartment — all in a day's work, eh?"

Victor asked Jimmy if he was all set to quit bridge now that he had won, and Jimmy laughed. "Of course not," he said. "I love imps — in fact, I just signed-up Otto for next year's Grand Nationals."

Otto was looking lonely, but not for long. The first one to greet him was Evelyn. She gave Otto a big hug and kiss — boy, was he surprised. His face lit up and my wife wiped away a sentimental tear from her eyes.

Back on the Ferry I had told Evelyn there was one alternative. I knew a guy who was in need of a good wife. He wasn't a great charmer but he did play bridge and had a world championship first or second under his belt. Evelyn asked who it was. When I told her it was Otto, she hesitated.

"Oh well," she said, "I think I could make him happy. I'll do it on one condition." "What's that?" I asked. "He and I never play together." "You're in no position to make conditions," I answered. When she saw the police at the dock, she succumbed. So I pinned the whole thing on the coach and called it a night.

"Tell us how you made it," said Sonty. "They took the VuGraph down before we had a chance to see."

"Yeah, Jacqui," said Jimmy, "how in the world did you figure out the doubleton king?"

"Well," said Jacqui, who had just brought out a little strawberry shortcake and placed it on the coffee table, "it certainly wasn't by playing for the king of clubs doubleton."

Truscott whipped out his pad and pencil again.

```
                    Dummy
                    ♠ Q 9 2
                    ♡ A K J 7 3
                    ◇ 4 3 2
                    ♣ A 8
Benito                              Arturo
♠ 7 6                               ♠ 5 4 3
♡ 5                                 ♡ Q 10 8 6 2
◇ J 10 6 5                          ◇ 9 8 7
♣ Q J 10 9 6 5                      ♣ K 7
                    Jacqui
                    ♠ A K J 10 8
                    ♡ 9 4
                    ◇ A K Q
                    ♣ 4 3 2
```

"First of all," said Jacqui, "I considered ducking the heart lead. But then if Arturo had doubled with a heart void, why hadn't Benito led the ten or the queen? Either lead would force a high card from dummy, where the honors rated to be, and I could never make the hand.

"Besides, I'll tell you something. I don't think Arturo would double with a heart void. He would still need another trick to beat me, and I don't think he would risk us running to six notrump. No, I was pretty sure he held the length in hearts and a club honor or two. We hadn't exactly bid the slam with confidence, you know."

"You're telling me," said Patty.

"Anyway," continued Jacqui, "I went up with the ace of hearts and pulled trumps. What else could I do? I couldn't afford to play on clubs or Benito would get a heart ruff. When Arturo followed to three rounds of trumps, I started thinking that maybe this was one of those hands you don't see very often — you know the kind — where one opponent has all the cards behind you, but you squeeze him anyway. Basically, I just counted his hand out, that's all. I took three diamond tricks and it looked as if he started with three-five-three-two distribution — nothing unusual. So I led a fourth trump and discarded a heart. And Arturo also discarded a heart. Poor thing. When I played my last trump, throwing a club from dummy, he also had to throw a club. By now I was down to one heart and three clubs in my hand and three hearts and one club in dummy." Truscott jotted down the position:

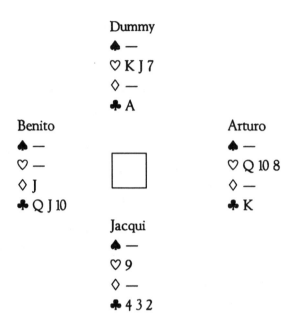

Dummy
♠ —
♡ K J 7
◇ —
♣ A

Benito
♠ —
♡ —
◇ J
♣ Q J 10

Arturo
♠ —
♡ Q 10 8
◇ —
♣ K

Jacqui
♠ —
♡ 9
◇ —
♣ 4 3 2

"You see," continued Jacqui, "if Arturo threw a heart and kept two clubs, I could just give him a heart trick, setting up the dummy. It was a little strange that he had to hold exactly what I held, but nevertheless that was the case. There was nothing more to the hand. I led a club over to dummy to get rid of his club and led a low heart. Arturo had to win and give me the last two tricks."

"Wait a second, Jacqui," said Truscott. "Why couldn't Arturo have put the 8 of hearts on your 7 and let you win the 9 in your hand? Then you would lose the last two club tricks."

"No, no, no," said Jacqui, "I had the 4 of hearts, not the 9. I threw the 9 a long time ago — on the first trick."

With that Jacqui went to cut the cake, but Belsky had beaten her to the punch.

After coffee, the doorbell rang and the dogs started barking. It was the D.A. He wanted to tie up loose ends. He needed a statement from the girl. Evelyn sat down with him at the kitchen table. She told him that the coach loved bridge, perhaps too much — more than he loved life. He had gotten so riled with Frankenstein's old-fashioned bidding that he murdered him, and then the idea of doing away with other members began to catch his fancy.

"His conventional bids may have been superior," she said of the coach, "but the trouble was that he had too *many* superior bids and not enough precise ones." The D.A. wrote it all down, but I don't think he fully understood.

As everyone was getting ready to leave, Otto buttonholed me. "I theenk," he said, "now that I have mastered imps, I take up this matchpoint game."

"What gave you that idea, Otto?"

"Eet was when I was in Patee's closet. She had a copy of your book, 'Murder at the Bridge Table.' Vely intlesting matchpoint ideas you have. I told Evy just a few minutes ago, and she suggested we play in the Blue Ribbon Pairs, you know, maybe we start there and work our way up. What do you tink?"

"I tink, I mean I think it's great. You and Evelyn will make a crackerjack pair."

"No, no, you misunderstand. Evy is going to take the coach's place, so she'll be too busy. It's me and *you*. How 'bout it, eh? The matchpoint pair of the century!" His eyes were ablaze and I was sorry now for having let the girl off the hook.

With that I grabbed Belsky and Pamela and bid the rest adieu. Belsky was smiling broadly — even through his beard I could see it. "The coach was due a bonus for winning," he said in the car.

"So?" we asked.

"So Mr. Cayne gave it to me instead."

THE END